KU-676-643

COLD GRAVE

CRAIG ROBERTSON

Northumberland County Council	
3 0132 02118935 7	
Askews & Holts	Jul-2012
AF	£12.99

**SIMON &
SCHUSTER**

London · New York · Sydney · Toronto · New Delhi

A CBS COMPANY

First published in Great Britain by Simon & Schuster UK Ltd, 2012
A CBS COMPANY

Copyright © Craig Robertson, 2012

This book is copyright under the Berne Convention.
No reproduction without permission.
® and © 1997 Simon & Schuster Inc. All rights reserved.

The right of Craig Robertson to be identified as author of this
work has been asserted in accordance with sections 77 and
78 of the Copyright, Designs and Patents Act, 1988.

1 3 5 7 9 10 8 6 4 2

Simon & Schuster UK Ltd
1st Floor
222 Gray's Inn Road
London WC1X 8HB

www.simonandschuster.co.uk

Simon & Schuster Australia
Sydney

A CIP catalogue record for this book is available from the British Library

Trade Paperback ISBN 978-0-85720-416-5
Ebook ISBN 978-0-85720-418-9

This book is a work of fiction. Names, characters, places and
incidents are either a product of the author's imagination or are
used fictitiously. Any resemblance to actual people living
or dead, events or locales is entirely coincidental.

Typeset by Hewer Text UK Ltd, Edinburgh
Printed and bound in Great Britain by
CPI Group (UK) Ltd, Croydon, CR0 4YY

To Debbie, Harvey, Jade, Karen, Lewis and Victoria

November 1993

Everything was bathed in blue. That's what he remembered most: a cold, rich Persian blue that washed over land and sky and lake, and made it all shiver. It made it almost magical, like a neverland that was never quite dark and never quite light – and would never be quite the same again.

It shimmered, this strange new world, where you could walk on water and all sorts of astonishing possibilities lay ahead. Some of what might happen scared him but he was excited more than afraid. There was no uncertainty about what he was going to do; he'd already made his mind up about that, and could feel the exhilaration and anticipation building in him.

The ice kingdom had winked at them on their arrival: a teasing glimpse framed between the old church on one side and the arthritic arms of a barren chestnut tree on the other. As they inched closer, almost fearful of its wonder, it unfolded before their eyes and they were assaulted by its sights and sounds. From the shore it looked like a Lowry painting, thick with matchstick people, graphite grey and black against the icy canvas, with only vague flashes of colour breaking up the monotone sketch. The collective breath of those gathered on

1

the frozen lake fogged the air above them and offered an enchanted border to the blue.

The noise was terrific. The sum of its parts was raw excitement, its constituents the roar of curling stones across the ice; the screams of children's laughter; and cheers from all corners. There were people everywhere, clad in ski gear, climbing outfits, jeans and kilts, every head covered in a hat.

Getting closer, they could see the ice world contained colours after all. A little girl in a scarlet jumpsuit sat giggling on a sled pulled by a panting Springer Spaniel; a green-kilted warrior whooped as he followed his curling stone down the hastily formed rink; two men with bright yellow hats and beaming red noses shared the national drink from a metal hipflask. Blues and browns and purples and oranges all whirled and birled and skirled in a cacophony of sound and fury.

The skaters, the curlers, the sliders and the walkers extended all the way to Inchmahome Island, a ghostly shape far across the ice. A carnival of people were taking advantage of something that hadn't happened for fifteen years and might never happen again. They'd been walking to Inchmahome, half a mile away across the lake, ever since word spread that the ice had frozen solid, possibly a once-in-a-lifetime chance both to defy and take advantage of nature.

By all accounts, the two days before had seen even more people on the lake – as many as 10,000, it was said. There were fewer now: some of them had gone back to work; others were scared off by temperatures that had crept back up towards zero. More were leaving with the approach of the day's end.

He was relieved that she had been easily talked into staying near the shore for a while to enjoy the last of the people-watching before they took their own turn to venture across to the island. It was nearly dusk and the fading light was accompanied by surface water dancing and glistening on the ice, signalling that the frozen bridge to the island might soon disappear. The sensible thing would have been to go immediately and not run the risk of waiting any longer but a smile and wink were enough to persuade her of the benefits of waiting for it to be dark and quiet over there.

Only the brave and the reckless were still attempting the walk to Inchmahome. She was one of those and he was the other. God, she was only a few years younger but she had an innate wonder about her that he envied. Life was still an adventure to her, a world to be explored. For him, it was already beginning to be a chore but he was compensated by the knowledge that he wouldn't need to be jealous of her innocence much longer.

Finally, as the numbers crossing the lake dwindled, he gripped her hand, feeling the threads of her pink gloves lightly tickle his bare skin, and they both took a deep breath before making their first stride. Suddenly it seemed so much further away, the expanding dusk adding distance and doubt.

'Ready?' he asked her.

'Ready,' she laughed.

Every step took them further from the shore, the lake deepening beneath them and making them both acutely aware that all that was holding them up, keeping them alive, was a quirk of science. Still they pushed on, through the diminishing crowds, deeper and darker into the lake.

A couple of hundred yards from shore, a noise stolen on the breeze made them turn to see a slim skater clad in black, a spinning silhouette against the falling gloom of blue. The girl whirled as another shadow stood twenty yards from her, filming the scene. She was mesmerising to watch: a vision that spun on one axle, arms high and locked together, then turned out gracefully in a wide arc before returning to her mark to spin once more, finally sliding to the ice like a dying swan.

There were dogs out there too, chasing wildfowl and their own tails as they slid and slipped across the surface, the darkness beginning to envelop them, scooping them up. She laughed to see them careering over the ice, giggling as they spun on their backsides, their paws unable to keep up with the haste of their minds. He tried to laugh along with her but he was tenser than she was, more nervous.

They picked their way round the bore holes that were dotted over the lake, peering down into the depths through the cracked circles left where the ice had been tested to make sure it was thick enough for the grand match, the great curling bonspiel that had been promised but had not taken place. Twenty thousand people had been set to descend on the lake for the once-in-a-lifetime match between the north and the south of Scotland but it had fallen an inch short of being held – six inches of ice were measured rather than the required seven.

Almost all the people they were passing now were on the return journey to the shore and the warm promise of the hotel bar. She gripped his hand tighter, the first sign of anxiety at their adventure accompanied by nervous laughter. He squeezed her hand in return, his own nerves having been replaced by adrenalin and a pounding in his heart in anticipation of what was going to happen.

The island's shoreline was just yards away now and they could see the tiny wooden jetty where the ferry tied up in the summer months. A few more steps and they'd be there. With a final, exultant leap they left the ice behind and landed with a crunch on the snowy shore of Inchmahome, celebrating with a hug and a look around to see who was still there. They were both thrilled to see there was no one in sight.

Just twenty minutes later, he was walking back across the ice on his own, every step washing away behind him, every footprint slipping softly into the lake. The crunch of foot on snow and the glide of boot on the icy bridge to neverland disappeared without trace. All he and she had ever been were ghosts and every sign of them had become lost in the blue.

Almost all of the ice revellers had left the lake – just a noisy rump of curlers remained near the shore and a straggle of kids sliding recklessly on the wet ice by the edge. None of them paid any attention to the last shadow that walked back towards the hotel, the lone spectre that slipped into the night.

CHAPTER 1

Nineteen years later.
Saturday 17 November 2012. Glasgow.

'So tell me again why we're going away for the weekend?'

Rachel Narey didn't take her eyes off the road to answer him but instead exhaled testily, then shook her head.

'What's so hard to understand, Tony? We're just going away for a day or two, just like any normal couple.'

Tony Winter let loose a snort of derision.

'But we're not a normal couple,' he retorted. 'Sometimes I'm not even sure that we *are* a couple. Not a public one at any rate.'

A patently false smile stretched across Rachel's face as Winter watched her drum her fingers against the steering wheel. She was not only containing her anger but making a show of doing so – a tactic both designed and guaranteed to annoy him.

'Well, we are this weekend,' she finally and tersely replied, her brown eyes pointedly fixed on the road ahead. 'You're always moaning we never go out together, and now that we are, you can't just be happy.'

'Rachel, you haven't even told me where we're going.'

She blew a thin burst of exaggerated exasperation between pursed lips and shook her head. It had become a familiar pose of late and Winter wasn't sure whether that said more about him or about her – or about them. All he was sure of was that it was becoming a pain in the ass. Where were they going? Maybe that was too big a question to answer.

'Oh, for Christ's sake. Shut up,' she told him. 'There's a bar and a big bed. What more do you want?'

It was unarguably a winning combination and he laughed despite himself. Time for the voice of compromise and geniality.

'Fair enough, you win. Right, driver, let the mystery tour continue. How long until we get to wherever it is?'

Rachel smiled.

'Not long. Another forty-five minutes or so.'

It had been a little over ten minutes since they'd left Rachel's flat on Highburgh Road in Glasgow's west end and they were now heading out of town on Great Western Road. Narey's black Renault Megane held three bags in the boot, two of hers and one for Tony, plus his camera bag. Pack casual things for during the day but something smart for dinner was all the information she'd offered him. With a bemused shake of his head, he'd thrown jeans, trousers and shirts into the bag and given in.

Winter actually wasn't sure when they had become a couple, even if not in a conventional sense. Their relationship was a secret from just about everyone around them, much to his irritation. She was a detective sergeant in Strathclyde Police and he was a police photographer, a civilian. Fraternising with the lower species of the crime scene community wasn't exactly encouraged and, as far as Rachel was concerned, it was easier all round if no one else knew. He'd appreciated that – at first.

Something had changed somewhere along the way, from the secret first-night kiss to his semi-residential status in her Highburgh Road pad. It was one of those slow-moving rivers of a relationship and he couldn't pinpoint the place in the bend where his Facebook status changed from 'Single' to 'It's Complicated'. Hers remained resolutely 'Fuck off; it's none of your business.'

He glanced over at her, seeing her shoulder-length brown hair shine in the glow of the midwinter sun as she drove, and reflected, not for the first time, that whatever their status was, he had done all right for himself. It wasn't just that she was beautiful, although she certainly was. She had 'been there for him' too. Maybe he didn't really know what that meant, given that it was the sort of emotional claptrap that constantly eluded him, but he knew she had. When his demons came to visit, Rachel was always the one who chased them away.

She sensed him looking and turned to stare questioningly at him.

'What is it?' she demanded.

'Nothing. Just thinking. So, an hour or so from Glasgow, heading west. Can we get to Teuchterland in that time?'

'Of course,' she answered playfully, 'given that anywhere north of Glasgow is for teuchters.'

'But not your proper Highlands, which would take much longer. Hm. Maybe Inverary or Crianlarich. You could just about do either of those in that time.'

She laughed.

'Keep guessing. And while you're at it, turn the heating up a bit, will you? It's freezing in here.'

She was wrapped up in a white woollen coat, buttoned almost to the neck, while he sat comfortably in an open-necked shirt. He'd long stopped trying to argue about their differing resistances to cold temperatures and determined he would sneak the dial back down when she wasn't looking.

A moment later, Rachel glanced in the rear-view mirror before signalling right at Anniesland Cross and taking the Bearsden road, almost immediately having to bat away further guesses from Tony about their destination. Arrochar? No. Stirling? No? Callander? No.

They slipped through Bearsden and onto the Drymen road, Tony continuing to be amazed at how you could be deep in the countryside just a few minutes after getting out of the city centre. In no time at all, it was all rolling hills, sheep, cattle and a twisting road to somewhere. Finally, Rachel pulled off the A81 and into the car park of the Lake of Menteith Hotel and he still hadn't worked out where they were going even though they'd arrived.

'This is it?' he asked her.

'Uh huh.'

'But we're nowhere. The middle of nowhere, in fact.'

'Shut up and get out. We are in what is known as "the country". You'll get to like it.'

Tony got out of the car in exaggerated wonder, sniffing the air and looking around, seeing only big sky, trees and the church that loomed above them. They'd come no distance at all yet they were a world away from the hustle and bustle of the city. He wasn't entirely sure that he liked it.

'Hear that?' he asked her.

'What?' Rachel looked around, puzzled. 'I don't hear anything.'

'Exactly. It's as quiet as the bloody grave.'

'Great, isn't it?' she grinned. 'Come on; stop moaning. I hear the sound of a pint being poured with your name on it.'

'Ah, you always say the right thing. Okay, let's go.'

The whitewashed walls of the hotel lay before them and Winter picked up his bag and one of Rachel's, leaving his camera bag in the car's boot. He'd return for it almost immediately; he never liked it out of his sight for too long. To his right, in the gap between the church and the hotel, he could see a dark, foreboding glimpse of the lake. It looked bloody freezing.

'Tell me we aren't going swimming?'

She grinned again.

'You wouldn't be tempted by a bit of skinny dipping?'

Winter shook his head.

'Nope. Not even with you. It's bound to be almost freezing over out there.'

'Funny you should say that,' she murmured. They skated along the icy paving stones, laughing, to the front door, where a solid white porch supported on black pillars reached out to meet them. Winter dropped one of the bags and opened the door for Rachel, ushering her in with an exaggerated sweep of his arm.

They tumbled into the hotel, immediately hit by a wave of heat that contrasted with the bitter cold outside. An open fire crackled to their left, with tables near the raised hearth that struck Winter as being the perfect place to sit and sample the range of malts he had already spied in the well-stocked bar to their right.

'I could get used to this sudden impulse for weekends away,' he told her.

All Rachel offered in return was a shake of her head as she led them to reception to sign in.

'Hi, we've got a lake-view room booked in the name of Narey for two nights,' she told the bespectacled blonde woman behind the desk.

'Ah yes, that's right. We spoke on the phone. How was your journey?'

'Fine,' Rachel told the woman. 'We've only come from Glasgow so it took no time at all.'

'Good, good,' the receptionist replied brightly. 'Now, let me get your key. You're in Osprey.'

'All the rooms are named after the area and the wildlife,' Rachel whispered to Tony, seeing the look of confusion on his face.

'How come you know so much about this place?'

'I'm a detective,' she answered. 'It's my job to know things.'

The receptionist returned before Winter could question Rachel further and they took possession of the large wooden fish, with a key attached, that was offered to them. 'It's a great place you've got here,' Rachel was saying enthusiastically, looking around her. 'I've always meant to come. Have you worked here long?'

'Oh, it will be nine years now,' the woman replied. 'It's a smashing place to work, I must admit.'

Rachel smiled again, thanked the receptionist and they made for their room.

'*Very* nice,' Winter hummed appreciatively as they got inside, the bottle of Prosecco on the table and the large double bed immediately catching his eye. But even they were quickly overtaken by the view across the lake from the floor to ceiling window.

'Wow,' he admitted. 'Quite a view. I'm glad I brought my camera. You did well choosing this place.'

Rachel didn't answer. Instead she walked over to the window and gazed out at the expanse of lake and the island on the horizon. The lake circled in front of them, almost but not quite coming together in the distance, the island neatly in the middle between either shore, before the lake widened again beyond it.

She watched a pair of ducks scudding low across the glassy surface of the lake, the waters rippled only by a trio of snow-white swans that were gliding gracefully at speed with fifty yards of wake behind them. It was a stunning scene but the beauty was lost on her. All the time, her eyes kept being drawn to the tree-topped skyline of Inchmahome as it blinked at her above the mist.

She stared at the island, lured by its darkness and mesmerised by its secrets. A shiver ran through her that she tried and failed to suppress. She was well aware that Tony, obsessively fascinated as he was with capturing Glasgow's darkest moments through his camera, would have a very different view of Inchmahome from hers. If only he knew what she knew.

He had always had this thing about seeing beauty in death as he photographed it but Rachel had never been able to understand his thinking. For her, working on the streets of the no mean city meant death was anything but beautiful. It was ugly, and the more brutal the death, the uglier it was. She looked across the lake, beyond the serenity and splendour of the slowly swelling surface and saw only something hideous. She suddenly regretted their trip there, wondering whether they'd be better tucked up together in Highburgh Road instead. She was starting something and she had no idea where it would end – or even if there would be an end.

Lost in her worries, she didn't hear Tony sneaking back across the room until he was behind her and his arms slipped through hers. She was still shivering.

'You cold? Want me to turn the heating up a bit?'

'Hm? Yes, please. Full blast.'

'Paradise, isn't it?' he asked as he muzzled into her neck.

'Yeah. Paradise.'

CHAPTER 2

'I just can't sleep.'

'Laurence, have you been taking your medication?'

There was silence on the other end of the phone.

'Have you, Laurence?'

'Sometimes.'

'Why only sometimes?'

'Oh, for God's sake. Sometimes I just don't want to sleep.'

'The dreams again?'

'Yes.'

'We've been through this, Laurence.'

'I know but it's the lake. I keep dreaming about the lake. I just can't . . . just can't stop myself. It's the time of year. It gets to me.'

'Laurence, we are going to have to schedule something. I thought we were making progress with this but sense a relapse that could be quite damaging.'

'You always want to schedule something. It's not doing me any good. I can't sleep and when I do sleep it's worse. She's there all the time. I can't stop thinking about her.'

'Calm down.'

'Don't tell me to calm down. You don't understand. No one can understand.'

'Laurence . . .'
'No. Don't talk to me. Enough.'

CHAPTER 3

Glasgow

'Christ, it's freezin, man. It's colder than a witch's tit oot here.'

'Tell me aboot it. My bollocks are like ice cubes, Pedro. How much longer are we gonnae stand on this fuckin corner?'

'Telt ye already. Till we shift all this gear.'

'Fucksake.'

Pedro cupped his hands together, blowing on them hard in a vain attempt at heat, and glared out at Marky from under his hoodie.

'Stop moanin, man, will ye? We're makin good money so shut your hole.'

'Am just saying.'

'Aye, well gonnae no, Marky, eh? These student bastards are pure minted and they're taking this stuff like it's sweeties. We'll be oot of here in nae time.'

Marky smiled at that, a manic nodding driven by the cold and the thought of cold cash. His fake Lacoste trainers did a little Ali shuffle on the frosted pavement, a wee dance at the thought of soon being able to buy a real pair. The fact that they were making the dosh from the university poofters just made it all the sweeter.

'Cool, Pedro, cool, man. I'm seeing a wee burd later and am gonnae need my dick in good working order. No gonnae be any use if it freezes and draps aff.'

Pedro swore under his breath. Sometimes Marky did his head in.

'Gonnae shut your moanin gub, Marky? Am wantin out of here as quick as possible anaw, man. But it's no 'cos I'm worried about you getting your Nat King. We're wantin to be oot o' here afore someone sees us, know ah mean?'

A muscle on Marky's cheek twitched the way it always did when he was nervous.

'Gilmartin's boys?'

'Naw, the Salvation Fuckin Army. Course Gilmartin's boys. No exactly gonnae be chuffed if he hears we're under-cutting his troops, is he?'

Marky did another Ali shuffle but this time it wasn't one of excitement.

'He'd go mental, Pedro. Absolutely radio rental. Just as well he disnae know, eh?'

'Too right, Marky boy. Who's this wee burd you're seeing anyway?'

Marky pulled himself deeper inside his dark grey hoodie, turning his head slightly away from Pedro's flinty gaze.

'Och, ye dinnae know her,' he muttered, his feet dancing a slower beat.

'Whit's her name?' Pedro persisted.

'Disnae matter.'

'Whit's her name, ya wee nobber?'

'Clarice.'

Pedro snorted in disbelief, a malicious grin appearing on his unshaven face.

'Clarice? That wee skanky blonde thing fae the Springburn that's always got love bites aw o'er her neck?'

Marky reddened, his cheeks marked by a furious blush that defied the cold.

'Naw,' he protested. 'It's no her.'

'It fuckin is, innit? Ya dirty wee bastard. She's hinging, man.'

'She's awrite. She puts oot; that's good enough for me.'

'Fucksake, man, she puts oot for half of Glasgow. Just as well we're making top dollar oot here 'cos you'll be needin it for clap cream.'

'Piss off.'

Pedro could barely contain himself, a huge smirk stretching across his lean features as he wallowed in Marky's discomfort.

'Tellin you, Marky man,' he laughed, 'You keep shaggin her and ye'll no need to worry about the cold damagin your tadger. Anyway, shut it. Someone's coming.'

'Sweet,' Marky muttered, glad of the diversion.

The dark figure coming towards them was on the side of the street sheltered from the streetlamp's neon glow, seemingly taking advantage of its gloomy shadow. It was a young guy, fairly tall and broad, casting regular glances over his shoulder to make sure no one was following him. Marky let out a little nervous laugh, glad to see the predictable nervousness on the part of the prospective buyer.

'Sweet,' he repeated softly, his hands rammed into the pouch pockets of his sweatshirt.

'Awrite?' the stranger asked, nodding his head at them by way of greeting.

'Awrite,' Pedro replied, taking a half-step back into the shadow of the corner and letting the stranger follow.

'You're the guys, aye?'

Pedro and Marky exchanged quick self-satisfied glances. Aye, they were the men. Marky could almost smell the leather of his new Lacostes, and Pedro was happy they'd soon be done for the night, cash in pocket.

Neither of them saw anything more than a flash of silver in the moonlight, a fleeting, gleaming glimpse that passed from the guy in the long leather coat to the pair of them. The man paid Pedro off first and then did the same to Marky before either could move. It was the first time that night that Pedro had felt any warmth and for a few dizzying seconds he liked the hot feeling that flared and tickled inside him. Marky was different: he'd felt the blade once before, remembered its sting and hated it instantly.

The guy had turned and begun to walk away before it dawned on Pedro and Marky that he had left without buying anything. By the time they realised he'd taken the money and the gear from their pockets, it was far too late for them to do anything about it.

Pedro clutched the hole in his stomach, the blood seeping between his fingers, and Marky giggled nervously, wondering how he was going to explain to Caprice that he probably wasn't going to be able to see her that night.

Neither of them were badly hurt; flesh wounds that stung and ran red but that had missed all the vital bits inside. If the stranger with the flashing blade had wanted it, they'd both be fighting for their lives. Instead, they had been given a painful warning and they knew they were out of the dealing business for good. At least it would be warm in the hospital.

CHAPTER 4

Twenty minutes after unpacking and Rachel successfully swatting away Tony's attempts to christen the bed there and then, they were sitting in the Lake of Menteith Hotel's Port Bar. Winter was happily sipping a large Balvenie DoubleWood and throwing occasional glares in the direction of the young couple who had possession of the seats nearest to the fire. His attempt at mind control failed to budge them.

Rachel had a glass of Petit Chablis and was looking round at the goose-grey panelled walls and wooden floors, the framed photographs and sketches of yesteryear and the curling stone that was warming on the hearth. Her eyes kept wandering through the large windows to the lake and the island beyond.

They'd sat there for twenty easy minutes, saying little but savouring the rare opportunity to relax, when Rachel looked up to see an older man passing the window, wearing a heavy jumper underneath a dark bodywarmer, a bobble hat snug on his head. He was carrying gardening tools and his breath froze before him. He seemed to be heading purposefully, if slowly, along the shoreline.

'Right,' Rachel suddenly announced. 'Let's go for a walk.'

'A what?' Winter asked unbelievingly.

'A walk.'

'You *never* walk. Anywhere. You don't do walks.'

'Well I do now. Come on, shift your lazy arse and get a jacket on.'

'You're kidding me, right?'

'No. Move.'

Winter shook his head incredulously and threw the last of the Balvenie down his throat, feeling it sting and soothe in one go.

'Okay, whatever. But I'm beginning to think the real you has been abducted by aliens.'

Their feet were soon crunching along the pebbled path that dissected the lawn in front of the lake, Rachel setting a fierce pace in the direction the old man had taken. As they swung anti-clockwise by the end of the hotel, the lake on their left, Rachel saw a bobble-hatted head nodding up and down by a bush some forty yards away.

'Oh, hello,' Rachel said casually as they reached the place where the gardener crouched. 'Didn't see you there. Nice day, isn't it?'

The man stood up, failing to conceal a groan of old age as he did so.

'Yes, beautiful,' he replied cheerily. 'Bit cold for some, I suppose, but I like it. Not many people venture along here in this weather though. They tend not to wander too far from the bar.'

Smart people, Winter thought irritably.

'Oh no, it's lovely out at this time of the year,' he heard Rachel replying, not believing his ears. 'We like to work up an appetite for dinner. I'm Rachel, by the way, and this is Tony.'

'Dick Johnson,' the old man replied, shaking off a glove and offering each of them his hand in turn. 'Nice to meet you.'

The man was in his mid-sixties and had a whiskery white moustache that reminded Winter of Tom Weir, the television presenter who used to do programmes about Scottish towns and the countryside – shows that always seemed to be repeated at two in the morning. Dick Johnson had a red whisky nose like old Tom as well.

'How long have you worked here?' Rachel was asking him.

Johnson puffed out his cheeks, raising his eyes to the heavens as if counting, even though Winter was sure he knew to the day just how long.

'Twenty-four years,' he answered finally.

'Twenty-four years,' Rachel echoed with a sweet smile. 'You must love it to have stayed here this long.'

'Well,' he looked almost bashful, 'I do but don't tell them up at the hotel or else they'll be wanting me to do it for nothing.'

The gardener smiled at Rachel and Winter could see that the old rogue was smitten – not that Winter could blame him.

'Oh, I won't,' she laughed. 'Although . . .' she deliberated as if trying to work something out, 'if you've worked here that long you must have seen all sorts of things, I'll bet.'

Something in the way she phrased it jarred with Winter. What the hell was she getting at? A look of wariness passed over the old man's face as well and his eyebrows knotted in a measure of confusion.

23

'Aye, I suppose I have,' he said slowly. 'Nothing too excit-ing though, mainly weeds and wildfowl. That's how I always describe my job: weeds, wildfowl and water. Not that people stop to ask too often.'

'All the Ws,' Rachel laughed. 'What about whisky?'

A smile spread across his weather-beaten face.

'Well, that's the way I like my water best. A splash of it in a good malt.'

'Tony likes a malt, too. Don't you?' she asked him rhetori-cally. 'What was that you had earlier?'

A rushed waste of a twelve year old, Winter thought moodily.

'A Balvenie DoubleWood,' he told the old man.

Johnson nodded thoughtfully, as if to leave no doubt that whisky was due proper consideration.

'Aye, a nice enough drop. Maybe a touch sweet for my taste but good and spicy too.'

'Sounds like you know your stuff, Dick. Well, listen, we're nearly done with our walk and I know Tony is going to fancy another whisky in the bar. Maybe you could join us for a wee half once you're done?'

The man smiled brightly at the thought and Winter could see that the prospect of a warm fire, a whisky and a pretty young woman was an easy choice to make after pottering about on the frozen shore all day.

'Well,' he hesitated, 'Ella, my wife, will have my dinner ready. But . . . sometimes I take the long way home, if you know what I mean.'

Winter sighed inside. He was never shy of sharing a drink with someone but he'd just rather not be sharing Rachel with this old geezer and his war stories. Rachel, however, in a sudden burst of unfamiliar sociability, had other ideas.

'Great,' she breezed. 'Well, we're going back now and Tony can set them up. What would you like?'

Johnson thought about it for a moment before shaking his head wistfully.

'Ah well, you can't always get what you want. But I'd happily settle for a Glen Garioch. It's a nice wee cheap half.'

'Ach, sometimes you *can* get what you want,' Rachel mock-scolded him. 'What's your favourite? I know it's not the Glen Garioch.'

'Well . . .' Johnson deliberated. 'They do have a 1975 St Magdalene that really hits the spot. It's a whisky for high days and holidays though. I really couldn't . . .'

No, of course you couldn't, Tony thought. Sly old bugger. He'd seen the St Magdalene on the malt vault list and knew it came in at £12 a measure.

'Okay, what's going on?' he asked Rachel as they walked back towards the hotel, the whisky choice having been settled.

'Going on? What are you talking about?'

'Why are we talking old Tom Weir in for a drink?'

'His name's Dick and he's a nice old man. Stop being such a grouch and show some respect.'

'Rach . . .'

'Oh, come on,' she cut off any further argument. 'Do you fancy one of those St Magdalenes yourself?'

'Well . . . I suppose I could be persuaded.'

'You usually can,' she smiled. 'What are you looking so miserable about anyway?'

Winter didn't have a face that naturally inclined towards a

smile. A grimace was his default setting. It wasn't so much that he was never happy; it was more that his brain had never got around to letting his face know.

They had only been settled back in the bar a matter of minutes when the sound of shoes scraping on the doormat signalled Dick Johnson's arrival. He pulled off his hat and nodded to the barman, a tall, angular and balding man in his late fifties, who didn't seem at all surprised to see him, before pulling up a chair beside Rachel and Tony. The malt was already on the table and Dick surveyed it for an age before he even picked it up. He then embarked on a seemingly well-practised routine of holding the glass to the light and drawing in a deep breath of the cratur, smiling at the smell of it.

It reminded Winter of his favourite Gaelic word, *sgriob*, the tingle of anticipation on the lips before tasting whisky. Winter had his own form of *sgriob* but it was for something different entirely. His mind drifted briefly back to the streets of the city he'd left behind that morning and the dark possibilities it offered for fulfilling his particular itch: stabbings, beatings, high flat jumpers, drug overdoses, murders, all waiting to be photographed. Hell mend him but he missed it.

Rachel's words snapped him out of his obsessive wonderings and brought him racing back into the hotel bar.

'Tony, could you go and get my jumper from the room? The green one. I'm still chilly from being outside.'

Winter sighed, wondering how she could still be cold given the heat from the fire but glad enough not to have to sit out the agonising wait to see if Johnson was ever going to get round to drinking his expensive whisky.

'Sure.'

'Ta. It's in my white bag.'

Tony left Rachel with the gardener, a raise of his eyebrows receiving an ironically sweet smile from her in return. However, the jumper wasn't in the white bag, nor was it in the black one. It still wasn't in the white one when he looked a second time and it was a good five minutes before he found it put away in a drawer. Rachel had a mind like a vice and it was very unlike her to have forgotten where she had put something such a short time before. He was more inclined to believe she hadn't forgotten at all. Back in the corridor that ran the length of the restaurant and passed the bar, he could see Rachel and the old boy were still deep in conversation. As he got nearer, he saw Johnson get to his feet.

'My dad worked here at that time,' he heard Rachel saying. 'He told me about her. Long time ago now though. Won't you stay a bit longer?'

'No, sorry, it's time I was going,' Johnson sounded irritated. 'Ella doesn't mind me taking the long way home but she gets annoyed if I go round the lake twice, if you know what I mean.'

The old man put his hat back onto his head and began pulling his coat around him.

'Thanks for the drink. I don't mean to be rude but . . . but I really do need to go.'

Johnson waved a curt goodbye to the balding barman, who seemed to be listening in on their conversation, and opened the door to leave, pausing reluctantly on the mat.

'What was your dad's name? I might remember him.'

Rachel hesitated.

'Narey. Alan Narey.'

Johnson looked hard at her before exchanging a curious glance with the man behind the bar. 'No. I guess my memory's not what it was. Thanks again.'

Winter waited until the door had closed behind Johnson, a blast of cold air sweeping across the table, before he began his own interrogation.

'Right, answers. First, your dad used to work here?'

'No, just around here. For a while.'

'What did . . .'

'I've got an idea,' she said interrupting him. 'We've got an hour before dinner, why don't we head back to the room until then?'

'What did you mean by . . .'

'Tony, maybe you didn't understand me. I meant *back to the room.*'

The penny dropped.

'Ah. *Back to the room.* Why didn't you say so?'

Tony led the way back to Osprey and its large, comfortable bed, not seeing the pensive look on Rachel's face as she glanced back at the door through which the old man had departed.

CHAPTER 5

'Have you seen it?'

'Of course I've seen it.'

'That's all you have to say about it?'

'What do you expect me to say? You think I'm going to fall to pieces, don't you? Think I'm not going to be able to handle it.'

'Are you?'

'I don't know. I don't bloody know. Who is doing this?'

'Who do you think it is?'

'Christ, I don't know. How the hell am I expected to know? It could be anyone. But why now? Who would do something like that now?'

'Are you going to be okay?'

'No. Probably not. I've not been doing too well as it is. And now this.'

'You have to stay calm.'

'That's easy for you to say. I couldn't believe it when I saw it. My nerves . . . they're not good. I don't know what to do.'

'Do nothing.'

'I can't.'

'You must.'

'I'm sorry. I don't think I can do that.'

CHAPTER 6

Sunday morning broke cold but bright, the sun streaming through the windows as soon as Rachel pulled back the curtains. She stood and stared across the calm, glassy surface of Scotland's only lake – though even if it was a lake by name, it was as much a loch as any other – at the island that now stood clear and green in the middle distance. The mist that had formerly framed it had disappeared but the place was no less foreboding, to her at least. It seemed bigger than before, almost as if it were nearer. The island had certainly come to her in the darkness of her dreams and now it looked as if it had sneaked closer while the curtains were drawn.

'You'll see it better with these' came Tony's voice from behind her. She turned to see him standing a couple of feet away with a pair of binoculars in his hand.

'Where did you get those?' she asked him, aware of the note of envy in her voice. 'You didn't bring them with you, did you?'

'No. I got them from reception.'

'Oh. Can I have a go with them?'

'Sure, in a minute. I want to . . .'

He got no further, as Rachel took the binoculars from him

30

and turned back to the window, fiddling with the focus until the island was clearly in view.

'Yeah, go ahead. Help yourself,' she heard him saying. 'Don't mind me.'

At length, she grudgingly lowered the binoculars and handed them over, ignoring the look of consternation on his face.

'It's time to go for breakfast anyway,' she said.

'Hold your horses,' he told her. 'Breakfast's going nowhere and I want a look as well. You can just make out the abbey on the island. Pretty amazing, isn't it?'

'Priory,' she corrected him. 'It's a priory not an abbey.'

'Whatever. I'm going to try to get some photos of that later. How do you get across to it?'

'You can't, not in the winter,' she told him. 'There's a ferry that takes you across during the summer season but the only way to get across in winter is if the lake freezes and you can walk there. But that's happened only three or four times in the last seventy years.'

'You wouldn't catch me walking over there on the ice. No chance. How come you know so much about this?'

'Listen, I'm starving. And I can smell bacon.'

Winter could feel an impatience growing in him at her evasiveness and wondered what the hell she was up to. He decided that, for one last time, he would let it go.

'Rach, you are avoiding far too many questions for my liking but okay. I'm hungry too.'

After filling themselves with sausage, bacon, black pudding, eggs and toast washed down with mugs of tea, they returned exhausted to the bedroom and collapsed on the sofa overlooking the bay window and the lake beyond.

Rachel got her Martina Cole novel from the bag and sat with her knees pulled up to her chin, her eyes occasionally stealing fleeting glances above the pages to the view through the window. Tony opened the Sunday newspapers and they both fell into a silence that was contented on his part, uneasy on hers.

They sat like that for half an hour without a word passing between them, their pact of relaxation being broken only when Winter lowered his paper and looked at her. Rachel ignored him and Tony raised the pages of the newspaper again. A couple of minutes later, however, he placed it down open on the table in front of them.

'Tell me what this is all about.'

'What are you talking about?'

'Enough. Don't take me for an idiot, Rachel. This—'

He turned the pages of the newspaper towards her until she saw a large advert headed in block capitals 'INCHMAHOME MURDER'.

'What's going on?' he persisted. 'According to this ad, someone is seeking information about a girl found murdered on that island out there. They think she was murdered nineteen years ago this weekend.'

'And your point is?'

'And my point is that you are a fucking detective and you've been acting strangely from the minute we left Glasgow.'

Rachel gave a resigned shake of the head. She put her book down on top of Tony's paper and, taking his hand in hers, led him to the bay window.

'The media called her Lily,' she explained, looking out

towards the island, 'as in Lily of the Lake, a typically glib sound bite. Her body was found in late March 1994, four months after the probable date when she was murdered on that island out there. It had been the worst winter in thirty years and the police were sure she was killed on the last of the days when the lake was frozen. If it had been any earlier, her body would have been found because there were so many people walking across to the island. Some bastard caved her head in.'

'Okay. I vaguely remember the case,' he admitted. 'I was at secondary school and staying with my Uncle Danny and Auntie Janette. I remember Danny being really angry about it and Janette was upset. Who was she?'

'She was never identified,' Rachel replied. 'Various families came forward thinking she might be their missing daughter but it wasn't any of them. Her body was so badly decomposed and eaten away that dental records were all they had to go on but they proved nothing. The four months in between the murder and the body being discovered meant no one locally remembered a girl who could barely be described.'

Winter shook his head, recognising anger building that she had conned him into being there. He should have known her sudden urge for them to be away as a couple was too good to be true.

'So that's why we're here? That's the reason for this sudden urge for a weekend away? Nothing to do with you and me?'

'Partly,' she admitted.

'Great. Rachel, I don't remember much about this case because I'd have only been about 16, in which case you'd have been 17. How come you remember this so well?'

'It's personal.'

'What do you mean?'

'The man in charge of the investigation was my dad. Police Inspector Alan Narey. This was his last case and he couldn't even find out who the girl was, never mind who'd killed her. It's haunted him ever since.'

Tony bit on his lower lip and thought about what she was saying.

'Unfinished family business?' he asked her.

'Yes.'

'And this ad in the paper – what's that all about? Who put it there?'

'I did. And I placed one in every other Sunday paper in Scotland as well. I wanted to make sure that it was seen by as many people as possible.'

He sighed, pissed off that she had dragged him along on false pretences but more because she had chosen to shut him out of whatever it was she was up to. Yet his dark itch was also working overtime at the prospect of learning more about what had happened on the island so tantalisingly close across the water.

'Tell me everything.'

So she did.

CHAPTER 7

The body had been found half-hidden in undergrowth in the grounds of Inchmahome Priory by two men who had gone over to the island to do maintenance work in time for the spring opening. The little that was left of her had been half-eaten by animals and insects, a bag of bones wrapped up in a red anorak. Her head had been repeatedly struck with a blunt object until the skull shattered, then her face had been smashed until it was unrecognisable. Decay, the freezing winter and the local wildlife did the rest.

It was thought that the girl was in her late teens. No one local had gone missing; no one local had any idea who she was. Rachel's father had cops knock on every door in the area but all to no avail. He'd dispatched them wider afield, setting up incident centres everywhere from Callander to Aberfoyle, from Lochearnhead to Stronachlachar. Nothing.

Vague sketches went nationwide and they'd even bagged a spot on *Crimewatch* but, other than scaring up the usual nest of nutters, it had earned them nothing. Distinguishing the genuine sightings from the wild-goose chases was a thankless task. Identifying her proved impossible.

'The real problem was the damage to the girl's skull.

According to my dad, it was horrendous: the worst he'd ever seen, and he'd seen plenty in his thirty years. It was smashed to bits. Most of the blows were to the back and side of the head and that was the principal area of attack. But there were also blows to the face, breaking the nose and teeth. In all, they estimated that she was hit twenty-two times in the head and face.'

'Jesus Christ. Twenty-two?'

'That many blows isn't a lashing-out. It isn't a flash of anger. It's deep-seated rage. It's sadistic. She would have been dead after less than a dozen hits. The rest was either to make recognition even harder or else it was borne out of pure evil.'

'I thought you didn't believe in evil?' he asked her, immediately aware it wasn't the wisest thing to do.

It was an argument they'd had many times before and one they'd never resolved. Winter was sure true evil existed and he had the photographs to prove it: fatal stabbings, shootings, torture and mutilation. Rachel, however, believed only in the evil that men – and women – did. Her job was to catch them, not psychoanalyse them.

'I don't,' she fired back at him. 'But whatever it is that resides in people that can make them carry out evil things, this was pretty damn near to it. It was a real jigsaw job for the pathologist – fragments all over the scene.'

'So what were they able to establish, evidence-wise?'

'Not much. There was no sign of a murder weapon. There were various tree branches and bits of brick that could have done the job but none with any remnants of her on it. Even after a few months of Scottish winter, they'd still have carried traces. The best guess was he'd thrown it across the ice on the far side of the island, knowing it would soon melt into the lake.'

'You said "he". Definitely a man then?'

'Not definitely. It was always assumed it was a man from the sheer ferocity of the attack but nothing was ruled in or out.'

'What else?'

'The snow had conserved some lividity, enough to suggest she'd died where she was found. That made sense anyway; it was stretching things to suggest she'd been carried over the ice to the island after she was killed. She'd walked there.'

'So she knew him?'

'Probably. Or else she didn't walk there with him but walked on her own and he met her there.'

'You buy that?' he asked doubtfully.

'No. The extent of the violence, the number of blows – that wasn't an attack on a stranger. I'm sure they walked there together and he murdered her, left her there to rot, then walked back across the ice on his own, knowing full well that any trace of him would soon melt away.'

The investigation had gone on for months but it petered out in the end. Like all unsolved murders, the case was never officially closed but practicalities took over and people got moved on to something that became more pressing. They pulled out the stops again a year after the murder, got TV and newspapers down to the lake and tried to push every button they could but nothing. Well, almost.

'My dad's main suspect – in fact, his only suspect – was a guy called Laurence Paton. He was twenty-three, a student teacher at Jordanhill in Glasgow. There was no evidence against him, nothing concrete to go on, just my dad's well-practised copper's nose.'

'Why this guy?'

'He was at the lake for the reconstruction on the anniversary. My dad spotted him and something set off his spider sense. He says there was something overly nervous about the guy. Paton said he was just there out of curiosity because he'd read about the killing and thought it was terrible. Plenty of other people were there on the same basis, right enough.'

'But your old man didn't believe him?'

'He's not an old man,' Rachel snapped. 'But no, he didn't. He hauled Paton in for a chat but got nowhere. Paton said he'd been in Glasgow the weekend of the murder and had been in various pubs. No way anyone was going to be able to confirm or deny that after so long though. My dad couldn't budge him but was sure Paton was hiding something. He could smell it.'

Winter looked out of the window, Inchmahome popping in and out of the mist like a ghost winking at him, and now realised why she had stared so fixedly at the view, why she had been so desperate to grab the binoculars and study it.

'What did the other cops think?'

Rachel shook her head.

'They didn't make Paton for it. Said they had absolutely nothing tying him to the girl and they should look elsewhere. My dad was sure though. He never stopped thinking of Paton as his number one guy. He never stopped thinking of the case full stop . . .'

Rachel let her voice trail off.

'And he still hasn't?' Winter guessed.

She shook her head sadly.

'It was his last case – the last one of any significance anyway. He had done his thirty years and was due to retire. It wasn't the way he wanted to go out though. He felt he'd let the girl down. He couldn't even find out who she was. He had . . .'

Rachel lost her words again and Tony slipped his arms round her, sensing her mounting distress.

'Go on, if you're ready to.'

'I'm fine. It's okay. He had always kept an eye out for the case and for Laurence Paton. For years, it seemed not to bother him as much. Or at least I thought so. But in the last year . . . he hasn't been well, not himself at all, and he keeps talking about the Lake of Menteith and the girl. He's really not well, Tony. I've been kidding myself that he's getting better, that he'll be okay, but he's not.'

'What exactly is wrong with him?'

She breathed deep, composing herself before answering but still choking on her words.

'Alzheimer's. They say it's at a relatively early stage, certainly of its detection, but the symptoms seem to be progressing quickly. He's moved out of the house and into a home. He's always looked after himself with no problem since my mum died but . . . well, it's his decision.'

'And you've known about this for how long?'

'Christ, Tony, don't give me a hard time over it, please. I've known for over a month but I've been in denial, I suppose. I'm sorry I didn't tell you but, if you remember rightly, you weren't exactly forthcoming with details about your own parents either, were you?'

It was a low blow but she was right. Winter's mother had died when she was hit trying to save him from a speeding car. He was only five and had been playing in the street when he shouldn't have. He knew it was his fault, no matter what anyone said. His father followed suit less than four years later, dead from chronic liver failure and a broken heart. When they'd first met, Winter had let Rachel believe that his parents had both died in a car accident. He'd always reasoned that was preferable to telling her the truth – his unwavering belief that he had killed them both – and admitting it was the source of his unhealthy interest in death.

'Yes, okay,' he muttered. 'I've apologised for that enough, don't you think?'

'I just thought you might understand why sometimes it's difficult to tell other people about your parents.'

'I do,' Winter conceded, pulling her closer in. 'So how bad is he?'

'Bad enough. He doesn't want to be a burden to anyone else but this Inchmahome case is eating away at him. It could even be the trigger for his condition.'

'Trigger?'

Rachel rubbed at her eyes and let a sigh slip wearily from her lips.

'No one knows what causes Alzheimer's. Beyond the fact that the principal factor is old age, no one knows why some people get it and others don't. They *think* that smoking increases the chance of developing it. They *think* that high-blood pressure and high cholesterol levels are risk factors. They *think* that stress can cause it. They think but they don't bloody *know*.'

She was getting louder and losing the fight to control the anger that was rising inside. She exhaled noisily and continued.

'There's two proteins that they suspect gather in clumps in the brain and cause the problem. One is beta-amyloid and they've been talking about that for years. The other is tau protein and the research on it is relatively new. Either way, they *think* that stress can cause neuropathological changes that lead to the formation of the proteins. Prolonged stress over something like this bloody case could be enough to trigger it.'

'It isn't genetic then?' Tony asked.

Rachel fired him a glare that fizzled and faded almost as soon as it had flared.

'Probably not. Well they don't know but it doesn't look like it. Less than ten per cent of cases are genetic. The problem is that they don't know what causes the other ninety per cent.'

'You've been doing your homework then?'

She offered a sad smile.

'Yeah, just a bit.'

Rachel turned her eyes away from him and stared out of the window, gathering herself.

'Either way, I have to give him some kind of peace and . . . And I don't know how long I've got left while I might still be able to do that. The rate of deterioration seems to be rapid and he might not be able to take in what I tell him.'

A silence settled on them again. They both stared out of the window, watching the mist that was forming round the rim of the lake, seeing it rise and close in on the island. Neither of them could take their eyes off it.

'So,' Winter finally said quietly. 'This Laurence Paton, your dad's main suspect, where does he live now?'

An oddly cold look passed over Rachel's face.

'He lives in Stirling and teaches English at the High School. He and his wife stay in a mid-terrace house just walking distance from the city centre.'

Winter looked at her thoughtfully, taking in her words.

'Okay. I understand how you would know where he lives and works. But how do you know what kind of house it is?'

Rachel hesitated, seemingly deliberating. In the end she held his stare, admitting no need to feel any guilt.

'I know because I've been to his house. And I'll be going back.'

CHAPTER 8

In the summer, Callander bustled with tourists and its main street was thick with cars inching along in the vain hope of finding a place to park. It was no more than forty minutes or so north of central civilisation yet it qualified as a Highland town, drawing hordes of visitors who were either too lazy or too short of time to go to the Highlands proper.

The winter months were different though and the lesser spotted elderly tourist was more likely to be dodging sleet or snow showers as they investigated the woollens, the tartans, the fudge, the bric-a-brac and the tat. The town returned to the keep of the locals, who were grudgingly glad to have it back to themselves.

It took just one visit to the Crown Hotel for Tony and Rachel to learn what they needed to know. They left the car where it was and walked briskly towards The Waverley further along the road, glad of the heat the extra movement was bringing to their bones. The snow-covered Ben Ledi towered over the town and it didn't need much imagination to see that soon some of the snow would be falling at ground level too.

The Waverley was busy with a Sunday lunchtime crowd and a room off the bar was packed with football fans watching the live game on a big screen. The noise and the heat inside the pub were such a contrast to the street they'd just come from that Tony and Rachel just stood there for a moment letting both wash over them. The spell was broken only when Rachel nodded towards the end of the bar where a man stood polishing glasses. He had a shock of white hair that made him look older than the fifty-odd years she knew him to be. Wearing a navy blue V-neck jumper with a white shirt underneath, he was chatting to customers and nodding at whatever was being said.

'Go on then,' Rachel said, sensing Tony's conflicting interest in the football match and making his mind up for him. 'It's probably better if I talk to him on my own anyway.'

'You sure? Just shout if there's a problem,' he told her.

'My hero. Get us both a drink, then go.'

Winter shouted up a pint for himself and an orange juice for Rachel, handed it over and started to move towards the shouts of the football fans.

'Hang on,' she stopped him. 'Who's playing?

'Rangers against St Mirren,' he grinned.

'Great,' she murmured ironically. 'Will you manage to behave yourself?'

He smiled again. 'I'll do my best but no promises.'

Winter was a die-hard Celtic supporter and had been known to let his mouth run away with him while watching football in a room full of Rangers fans. And the chance of there being many St Mirren supporters in a pub in Callander was miniscule.

Rachel shook her head at him ruefully and turned back towards the bar. The white-haired man was now serving customers and she manoeuvred her way through the crowd till she was standing at the bar near him. A couple of the locals eased aside to let her in, accompanying their hospitable gesture with a barely disguised leer.

'Thanks,' she told them. 'Brrr, it's freezing out there.'

'Nice and warm in here with us,' one of the men said with a laugh, the whiff of lunchtime beer evident on his breath. 'You on your own?'

'Nah. I'm a football widow,' she told them with a bob of her head towards the lounge area. 'He's over there.'

'More fool him,' the other one laughed. 'I saw a bit of it earlier. Terrible game.'

'I'm just glad to be inside for the heat,' she replied. 'We're staying out at the Lake of Menteith and it's baltic out there. They reckon the lake could freeze over again if this weather gets worse.'

Subtle it wasn't but then understated wasn't in her game-plan. There wasn't time for that.

'Aye, it's brass monkey weather, right enough,' said the taller of the two, a brawny farmer-type with a ruddy complexion that didn't come just from working outdoors.

'Ach, it's no that cold, Dazza,' the guy to her left chipped in; he was slightly shorter but broad and with equally florid cheeks. 'I barely bothered with a coat this morning.'

'Yer arse, Kenny,' Dazza responded. 'It's freezing and they say it's going to get a lot worse, eh? I read that there's some big cold front coming over from Russia.'

'Brilliant,' Narey shivered. 'So how cold does it have to get before the lake freezes? I've always fancied going over to Inchmahome if it does.'

'Och, it needs to be like minus ten for a few weeks,' Kenny told her. 'It's nowhere near that. Mind you, if it does freeze, then you should be careful about walking over to the island.'

The man seemed to have timed his remark just as the barman walked by them to serve someone at the end of the bar nearest to the door. He threw a dirty look in Kenny's direction, clearly having picked up on what he said.

'Why should I be careful?' Narey asked the two men. 'What am I missing?'

Kenny and Dazza exchanged supposedly cryptic smiles over her head.

'Steady, Kenny,' Dazza warned him in mock seriousness, raising his voice slightly. 'You're stepping on thin ice now.'

Kenny sniggered, seemingly enjoying his pal's joke. The barman didn't seem quite so amused though, looking back at them suspiciously from the till.

'Come on,' Narey persisted. 'What's the joke?'

'Oh, it's no joke,' Dazza said solemnly. 'No joke at all. There was a deid body found on that island.'

'What? When?'

'Och, it was nearly twenty years ago now. You probably won't remember it, young thing like you.'

Narey swallowed down the answer she'd rather have given and instead smiled at the man, fluttering her eyelashes at the compliment.

'So tell me then, what happened?'

The two men glanced conspiratorially at each other, looking around as if making a show of checking no one else was listening – no one except the white-haired barman. They moved in closer on either side of Narey on the pretence of sharing a secret.

'Well . . . it was the winter of '93–'94,' Dazza began, slightly louder than was necessary for any would-be conspirator. 'A wee lassie, not all that much younger than you, was found battered to death on Inchmahome. Her heid was caved in. Terrible sight, so they say.'

'She'd walked over the frozen lake, you see,' Kenny took up the story. 'Never made it back. Poor wee thing. Murdered in the old priory. Blood and broken bones everywhere.'

Narey let a shudder visibly ripple through her, her shoulders shaking in a girlie manner sure to encourage them to continue their tale of gore.

'So who was she?' she asked, lowering her voice as if joining in on their intrigue.

'No one knows,' Kenny told her. 'Never identified. Her face was bashed in so no one really knew what she looked like.'

'Never found out who killed her either,' Dazza added with a barely concealed grin. 'He's still out there somewhere.'

Narey dutifully squirmed. She wasn't the only one: the barman had his back half-turned to them but she saw him wringing the life out of a pint glass, rubbing at it with a towel as if trying to wipe the logo from it.

'You hear all sorts,' Kenny confided, leaning in towards Narey, clearly revelling in the story. 'I was told it was one of them paedophile rings. Tried to kidnap her but it went wrong and they had to murder her.'

'Nah,' Dazza disagreed. 'She was too old for that. I heard talk of her being a gypsy girl. There were definitely a good few

Romany families who were in the area. The word is the deid girl was one of theirs and that's why no one ever came forward.'

'And what do you think of that?'

'Could be,' Kenny conceded. 'Folk say how she was a Romany princess who had been determined to marry her lover, except that he wasn't a gypsy and so her father killed her.'

'Definitely,' Dazza nodded enthusiastically. 'I was talking to a bloke in here who was adamant that she was a gypsy girl. He said it was some other gyppo guy that had killed her – the one her family wanted her to marry. Certain of it, so he was.'

Kenny shrugged, seemingly unconvinced. 'Paedophiles. That's what I heard. She was a runaway, living rough and the bastards killed her.'

'Poor girl,' Narey lamented. 'It must have been horrific.'

'Aye. Months before she was found,' Dazza agreed, half an eye on the barman standing just a few feet away. 'Horrible.'

'A bag of bones inside a red anorak,' Kenny added coldly. 'All broken up and left there to rot.'

Suddenly all three jumped as the sound of breaking glass rang through the pub. The pint tumbler that was being dried had slipped from the barman's grasp and shattered on the floor, sending shards flying to all corners.

The two drinkers on either side of Narey grinned at each other as mocking jeers rose from the pub's other customers.

'That will be coming out of your wages, Bobby,' Dazza laughed at him.

Bobby Heneghan scowled back at his tormentors as he

bent over the smashed tumbler, his hands shaking as he swept the glass splinters onto a plastic brush pan.

'Get stuffed,' he told them, an obvious tremor in his voice.

A plump blonde in a pair of tight denims and a grey sweat-shirt came round the side of the bar and squatted down beside Heneghan, slipping an arm round his shoulder.

'It's okay, Bobby, I'll clean this up. You're due for a break anyway. Go and get a seat and I'll get Moira to bring you a cup of tea.'

Heneghan nodded silently and got to his feet, slipping away without a backward glance and turning a deaf ear to the sniggers from the men beside Narey. The blonde stood too and glared at Kenny and Dazza.

'Leave him alone,' she hissed at them. 'I've told you two a hundred times. This time I mean it: any more of that crap and you're barred. Both of you.'

The men had the good grace to look shamefaced but Narey doubted they meant it. She glanced over to see Heneghan sitting in a chair in the corner, his arms crossed across his chest. Kenny and Dazza saw her looking and let their faces lapse into spiteful grins again.

'Don't worry about old Bobby,' Dazza sneered. 'You'd think he'd be over finding a body after all this time.'

'Aye, silly old sod,' Kenny agreed. 'How about we get you a proper drink and tell you more about the murder?'

Narey smiled sweetly at the pair of them and let a single word slip quietly from her lips: 'Arseholes.'

Bobby Heneghan looked up to see Narey standing at his side, his eyes immediately falling back to the table and the cup of tea that had appeared in front of him.

'I'm really sorry,' she told him. 'I don't know those guys and I didn't realise they were winding you up. I'd never have . . .'

'I know. It's okay.'

'No, really. I feel terrible about being part of that. They just started on about it and I . . . well, I didn't know. Was it you that . . . found her?'

Heneghan nodded without looking up, reached for the tea and edged the cup to his lips.

'Do you mind if I sit down? I really feel like I owe you an apology.'

'Forget it. It's okay.'

Shit, he was a stubborn old bugger. She needed to get him to open up.

'It's Bobby, isn't it?' she asked softly. 'My name's Rachel. Look, this isn't any of my business but it is what I do for a living.'

Finally, he looked up at her, a questioning look on his face.

'I talk to people who have been through traumatic events to help them make sense of what happened and get to the truth.'

'Like a counsellor?'

She nodded.

'I've seen similar reactions many times, even years after the event that causes it. Have you ever been diagnosed, Bobby? Because I'd be sure you are suffering from post-traumatic stress disorder.'

Heneghan's mouth trembled as if he were going to speak but he didn't find the words. Instead, he gave the merest shake of his head. Narey put her hand over his and squeezed it gently, bringing a sad smile to the man's face. His eyes were tired and lined, nervously darting from place to place.

'I know I'm just being a bit stupid,' he said quietly.

She squeezed his hand again. 'Of course you're not, Bobby. You have been through a psychological ordeal. It's not about being strong or "being a man". It's about getting help to deal with it.'

Heneghan sighed.

'Those . . . those buggers at the bar are always taking the piss out of me about it and maybe they're right. Maybe I should be over it by now. It's not funny though. They should try finding a young girl like that – see how they like it.'

Narey's head flash filled with thoughts of Tony, camera in hand, and the peculiar pleasure he would take in stumbling across such a scenario. He *would* like it and that still bothered her.

'I'm sure they wouldn't,' she told Heneghan. 'But how did it happen?'

Heneghan sighed and lowered his voice further, his eyes slowly closing over.

'It was late March and me and old Tam Conway, the bloke I worked with, were going to Inchmahome. The island is shut to visitors from October to April so before it opened up again we would go over and cut the grass, do weeding, repair work, whatever was needed. I remember it was cold because Tam was moaning all morning. That was old Tam though – he never stopped complaining.

'Anyhow, we got the boat over to the island, just the two of us. I always liked the old place. Full of history: Mary Queen of Scots stayed there for three weeks back in fifteen forty something; Robert the Bruce before that as well. And there was the wildlife and all – ospreys and merlins and swans and geese. Brilliant so it was.

'So this day, me and Tam get to Inchmahome. It was raining but not very hard. We got the gear out of the old boathouse by the jetty and split up the way we always did. He'd start at the chapter house and I'd begin at the priory. Suited me fine – meant I didnae have to listen to his moaning. There wasnae much in the way of growth because of the winter having been so harsh, like. The island had been under snow for most of it. So we figured we wouldnae need to be there too long. We could spin it out for a few hours but that would include at least three fag breaks.

'It was that quiet. No like working in here. When Tam was away working on the other side it was like you could be back in Mary's days, ye ken? Just you and the priory and the ghosts. The most peaceful place you could imagine – till I heard Tam shouting, roaring in fact. So I went running to see what was up with him. He'd been working when something had caught his eye, something that shouldnae have been there. It's because it was red, ye see. Everything else was all browns and greens and stone so this red thing stuck out like a sore thumb.

'So Tam goes over and he told me that the closer he got, the stranger it looked. It was half-hidden by the wall and the undergrowth and he reckoned he would only have seen it from the angle where he was standing. Then he could smell it. Says he'd never smelled anything like it in his life. He went right over to it and moved the grass back till he saw the thing properly. I think he nearly died on the spot himself when he saw what it was. That's when he shouted on me.

'Christ, what a mess the lassie was in. I've never seen anything like it – not even on the telly. She'd obviously been there for months and the animals had got at her. Tam threw up and I wasn't far behind him, I don't mind telling you. They'd eaten her face and her eyes and her skin. Black the skin was, this terrible black colour. She had less than half a face and what there was wasn't much like human. Her body was hardly there either, all shrivelled away inside the red waterproof jacket she had on. You got the feeling it was only the jacket that was keeping her bones together.'

Narey shuddered but, unlike at the bar when her reaction was for the benefit of Kenny and Dazza, this time it was genuine. The horror of the girl lying there, broken and eaten, revolted her.

'She had these wee pink gloves on that poked out the end of the jacket sleeves,' Heneghan continued. 'It was only the gloves and her long hair that let you know she was a lassie. Her hair had been blonde but it was all dirty with being on the ground for so long.'

Heneghan drew breath to take a long sip of his tea and Narey could see that it was more than just the exhilaration of telling his story. The man was seeing the girl again in his mind's eye and it was affecting him all over again.

'But for all that, it was the head that was the worst,' he continued. 'I couldnae stop looking at it. It was like a magnet. It was all smashed in above her right eye. There was this big gaping hole and you knew right away it hadn't been done by any animal. Well, not one with four legs. Some bastard had clubbed her head till it was caved in. She was just . . . broken into bits.'

Heneghan's voice trailed off but Narey wasn't for giving him much time to get over the image that plagued him. She wanted to share it, to see it. Tony's taste for the ghoulish had infected her, it seemed.

'And there was nothing there that looked like a murder weapon?' she asked the barman. 'No log or stick or piece of metal?'

Heneghan's eyes suddenly narrowed and he looked at her warily.

'You a reporter?' he asked sharply.

'Christ, no,' she retorted. 'I prefer to be able to sleep at nights and look at myself in the mirror. It's my job, Bobby. I'm a good listener and I know how much it can help people to share their problems. Go on, please.'

The man weighed it up before going on with his tale.

'No, no weapon. Nothing that looked like it might have been used to batter her. We searched right enough and so did the police later but there was no sign of anything. And no one had been on the island since October. Excepting when the lake was frozen, of course.'

'So you called the police right away?'

'Well, we had to get the boat back to the mainland and we called from the hotel. We didnae have mobile phones back then. I said I'd take the boat if Tam waited with the body but he told me to get to fu—. He said no, he wasn staying there himself. Said the body wasn going anywhere so it was okay for us both to go back. The cops were there about an hour and a half later. Took us two trips on the boat to get them all over. Madness it was.'

'So what did they think had happened?' she asked him, waiting for the answers she already knew.

'Well,' he closed in conspiratorially. 'That's the weird bit. They reckoned she'd walked across the lake when the big freeze was there and never made it back across. Spooky, eh?'

Narey nodded, encouraging him.

'Were you there when the lake was frozen, Bobby?'

'Not working, no, but I'd gone over to see what it was like. There were thousands of people. It was like the lake was covered in them. I didnt walk over to the island though. I'd been over it on the boat often enough that I knew how much water was under that wee bit of ice. If the girl had walked over to the island, on her own or with someone else, then no one would have noticed. Anyone could have done anything to her.'

'Who do you think did it, Bobby?'

Heneghan glanced back at the bar.

'I don't know.'

'Have you heard people say that the girl was from a gypsy family?'

'Aye, but I think it's a load of rubbish.'

She held her breath for a second, hesitating.

'Did you ever hear of a guy called Laurence Paton?'

He looked at her as if seeing her for the first time, newly suspicious. His answer was firm.

'No.'

'Are you sure?'

'Look, I don't want to be rude but you ask a lot of questions and I need to get back to work. I don't know anything, right? And I don't know if I'll ever stop seeing that poor girl's face.'

Narey was about to press him further but stopped as she

saw Heneghan's eyes were fixed over her shoulder. She turned her head, following the man's gaze and saw Dick Johnson standing inside the door of The Waverley. The old gardener was shaking a dusting of snow from his shoulders and staring angrily ahead – at her.

CHAPTER 9

'I remembered who your father was after you left,' Johnson snapped at her. 'I don't think you were being completely honest with me, young lady.'

Heneghan looked from one of them to the other, clearly confused.

'Dick? What's going on? I don't understand.'

'What's she been asking you, Bobby? About finding the girl's body?'

Heneghan's confusion turned to anger. 'Aye. Aye, she has.'

'I thought so. She was noseying around the hotel doing the same. Making out she doesn't know anything about it. But she does. Her father was the policeman in charge of the investigation.'

Heneghan's mouth fell open and his lip trembled again. Narey knew arguing was a waste of time now.

'I'm sorry, Mr Johnson. I didn't mean to mislead you but I'm keen to find out anything I can about what happened.'

'You lied to me,' the old man complained.

'Not entirely,' she excused herself. 'I just didn't tell you the whole truth.'

'Well, you certainly lied to me,' Heneghan burst in

indignantly and loudly, his eyes anxiously jumping from one to the other. 'You told me you were a counsellor.'

'No, I didn't,' she said gently. 'You assumed that's what I meant. I said that I talked to people who had been through traumatic events.'

'What is that supposed to . . .'

'How did you know I'd be here, Mr Johnson?' she interrupted.

The old gardener glared at her, his simmering anger obvious in his voice.

'When I remembered who your father was, I knew you'd been stringing me along. I had a feeling you might come out here to talk to Bobby. Didn't expect to see you when I walked in here, right enough. Thought I might get here before you – to warn him.'

'Why would he need to be warned?' Narey asked, becoming acutely aware that the raised voices were drawing a crowd, including the two Neanderthal farmers who had stood either side of her at the bar.

'Bobby's a good friend of mine,' Johnson told her. 'But he's . . . well, sorry Bob, but you're a nervous sort these days – not that I blame him. Never been quite right since he found that poor girl, you see. It's been nineteen years but I don't think that day's ever left him. I knew how he'd react if he knew someone was poking around, asking questions after all this time.'

'I'm only trying to find out what happened, Dick.'

'Why?' The old man was shouting now. 'Why after all this time?'

She ignored his question and asked one of her own.

'What about you, Dick? Where were you when it happened?'

'Home in front of the fire because . . . Wait a minute. How dare you ask me that? What are you suggesting?'

'Nothing. I just need . . .'

Kenny and Dazza were suddenly standing over Narey, glowering down at her.

'What's going on here?' Dazza shouted. 'Why are you asking all these questions, upsetting folk?'

The man's ruddy face was red with anger now, having no doubt eventually managed to work out that she had been lying to him too. He was leaning in aggressively towards her, his burly frame just inches from her much slighter figure.

'Yeah, who are you?' Kenny joined in, his beery breath in her face. 'Making out you didn't know about the murder. Were you taking the piss out of us?'

Narey took a step back, trying to put a bit of distance between herself and the belligerent, half-drunk pair. Suddenly, the space between her and them was filled with another body – Tony.

'Back up,' he ordered Kenny and Dazza, his hands up in front of them. 'What's going on here?'

'Get out of the road before I move you,' Dazza snarled at him.

'Try it,' Tony growled back, his eyes blazing. 'You go near her and I'll kill you – both of you.'

Kenny and Dazza hesitated, looking at Tony and sizing him up. He was about the same height as Kenny but half as wide and nowhere near the size of Dazza. They were probably wondering whether, since he was prepared to square up to both of them, he had more about him than was obvious.

'There's no need for this,' old Dick Johnson was saying. 'Everybody calm down.'

'No chance,' Kenny spat at them. 'This bitch has been lying. She made arses out of us.'

'I'm sure you managed that just fine yoursels,' Tony snapped back, moving forward so that he was toe to toe with both men, his eyes wide and unblinking. 'Now piss off afore I have to make you.'

Kenny and Dazza looked at each other and scowled back at Tony. Dazza pushed a meaty paw into Tony's chest but he responded immediately by thrusting his own hand hard into Dazza. Narey pushed herself into the tiny gap between them, her bag held up seemingly for protection. Dazza's arm, aiming to knock Tony's to the side, caught Narey instead and knocked her bag from her hand, sending it tumbling to the floor.

The men glared furiously at each other as they stepped back slightly, the few contents of the handbag between them on the floor. Chief among them was her police warrant card, sticking out like a sore thumb among a lipstick, car keys, a hair band and a packet of chewing gum. Dick Johnson stepped between them and picked the identity card from the floor, continuing to hold it as he put the rest of Narey's things back into the bag. He handed her the bag and finally the card, making sure that both Kenny and Dazza had noticed it.

'Like father, like daughter, eh?'

'Something like that,' she agreed.

Kenny and Dazza were backing off, maintaining a staring session with Tony but retreating quickly to the safety of the bar. Dick Johnson stood, shaking slightly but with a comforting hand on the shoulder of his friend Heneghan, who looked distraught.

'I think you should go too, don't you, Miss . . . Narey?' Johnson suggested.

She nodded, grabbed Tony's elbow and guided him to the door.

'You do know that those big lumps would have snapped you in two?' Rachel mocked gently when they were driving out of Callander on the road back to Port of Menteith.

'Of course I do. But the important thing was they didn't know it.'

'True,' she laughed. 'And was that also why you did that thing with your accent?'

'What thing?'

'Oh, come on, you know fine well. When you squared up to them, you sounded more "Glesga" than I've ever heard you.'

He grinned. 'Works every time.'

'Thanks. Seriously. It was getting a bit hairy before you stepped in. My hero.'

'Don't take the piss,' he smiled. 'You made sure they spilled your bag deliberately, didn't you? To save me from getting a doing.'

'Well . . .' she shrugged apologetically. 'Tony, you're a lover, not a fighter. Maybe you could prove that later . . .'

He smiled again. 'I could and I will but I thought there was maybe something else we could do after dinner?'

'What's that then?'

'Hm. Came to me while I was watching the game. Rangers were winning so I had nothing better to do than think. Have you seen the rowing boat that's tied up in front of the conservatory? I saw it at breakfast this morning.'

She had seen it: a little white boat that bobbed on the lake beyond the frosted green expanse of lawn.

'What about it?'

'Well, how about, once it's dark and the bar is empty, we go for a little sail? To the island.'

She smiled and nodded again. Her hero.

CHAPTER 10

The further the hotel slipped into the distance, becoming one with the trees and the church and the night, the worse an idea it seemed. The lake was inky black beneath them, the mist an icy chill rising from the surface and eating into their bones. Tony paddled them quietly towards the island while Rachel tried to stop her teeth from chattering.

They'd stolen through their bedroom window and across the lawn where Tony freed the rowing boat from the wooden stake that it was attached to. He let Rachel sit down in the back of the little boat before carefully joining her. There were no oars but he had liberated a kayak-style paddle from the darkened dining room and used it to push them silently from the shore and onto the lake. As he did so, it struck him that the boat was placed there more for decoration than practical use and it might not be entirely sound. He swallowed his reservations down, letting them settle on top of the three glasses of whisky that were stopping him from worrying and reasoned they would find out soon enough.

Tony's camera bag lay on the floor of the boat and he was much more worried for its safety than theirs. They could always swim for it if the worst happened but the bag wasn't going to save his cameras from the murky depths of the lake. It also contained a torch and flash guns that they were going to need when – if – they got to Inchmahome. Rachel looked at the lake. Maybe for the first time, she understood his *sgriob*, her sense of anticipation was tingling just as much as his.

Something flew just over their heads but neither of them could see what it was; they just felt the rush of air and saw the silent shadow slip into the gloom. They were over halfway now and there was no turning back. As Tony propelled them forward, Inchmahome rose out of the mist and darkness and emerged menacingly before them. More by memory than sight, he headed for the right-hand side of the island, knowing that was where the small jetty was with the boathouse behind it. Rachel turned as they got nearer, causing the boat to wobble, as she desperately sought a closer look at the place that had filled her thoughts for so long.

Finally, Tony lifted the paddle onto his knees and let the boat glide soundlessly for the remaining yards to the jetty. When they drew parallel to the little wooden platform, he reached for the camera bag and hauled it safely onto the jetty first before scrambling out of the boat and helping Rachel to do the same. He kept the torch switched off until they were past the boathouse and shielded by it and the trees. Even then, he used it only intermittently – just enough for Rachel to be able to lead the way to the crime scene.

She'd never been there before but had seen enough aerial shots and online maps to know where to take them. The ground was hard with frost beneath their feet and it crunched as they walked, frozen leaves crackling and brittle twigs snapping, the noise echoing off the remains of the priory walls and sounding big in the still night. No one could possibly hear them from the shore, even if anyone was still awake, but they moved without speaking, the enormity of the place suffocating them.

They wound their way through the ancient arches, taking a haunting tourist trail past the south wall of the priory church, then the cloister with the remnants of its warming house and kitchen. Whatever ghosts still lingered there were whispering at them from the shadows and following them past the chapter house and towards the darkest corner of the island.

Rachel slowed to a halt and waited till Tony was by her side. She stretched out her arm and he followed her point with the beam of the torch.

'There,' she whispered.

It was an unremarkable spot compared to the dramatic ruins they had just passed through, an ordinary junction of low wall and frozen ground. They both stood and contemplated it in silence, the intervening nineteen years slipping away before their eyes. Slowly, Rachel knelt and traced the air with her hands, drawing shapes of where the girl's body had been discovered years before.

'She was on her back here,' she said, both her father's words and Bobby Heneghan's coming back to her. 'They said there were weeds up to this height. Heneghan and Conway had to part them with their hands to see what was lying here.'

Tony took his camera bag from his shoulder and took out his Canon EOS-1D, fixing on a flash as he listened to Rachel.

'Her legs were here . . . and here, this one tucked under the other . . .'

Winter was photographing nothing except memories and dirt but his mind's eye was well practised in capturing death's final throes even long after life had been extinguished. The lack of a body and the gap of nearly twenty years didn't stop his imagination from running riot.

He saw the weathered red jacket, faded from its original candy red the same way Lily's blood had lost its vital colour after leaking from her battered skull. He saw her dark blonde hair flecked with blood and dirt as she lay back on a pillow of snow, her head battered, one eye gone and the other shrinking in fright, her mouth wide open, screaming for help that never came, pleading for mercy that wasn't offered.

She was so young, forever young, laid out on a snowy altar with the monks of Inchmahome standing over her weeping. He saw her skin and flesh, a winter feast for the island's wildlife, its surfaces pulled back to expose everything below, her body shrivelling day by day as it lay lonely and abandoned.

Tony fired off shot after shot, his finger hammering at the shutter release even though the girl, her jacket, her blood and her battered skull fragments had long since gone. Rachel looked up at him, seeing him lost in his moment and knowing what he was seeing through his lens. She had seen the collection of gory photographs that filled a wall of his flat in Charing Cross and wondered if this image of what-had-been would find a place among them. His fascination being what it was, she knew it could fit in his collection even if the substance of it existed only in his mind. She realised it already had a place in hers.

'You feel it?' she asked.

Her words broke the trance Winter had drifted into,

causing the murdered girl to fade from his sight, her beseeching mouth and pleading eye the last things to disappear as the flame from his final flash shot petered out.

'Yes, I feel it.'

His camera arm fell to his side, his job done. Rachel took his free hand and gently led him away from the murder scene and back towards the jetty, every step guarded by Inchmahome's mournful monks as they saw their uninvited guests safely off the island again.

CHAPTER 11

Monday 19 November

He looked smaller but she knew he couldn't be. It had been only a week since she'd last seen him but it was the first time since he'd moved into this bloody place. Could a man really shrink in a week? Rachel took advantage of being able to watch him, knowing that he didn't yet realise she was there. They'd told her it would be better if she left it a bit before she went to see him, give him time to settle in without being embarrassed about her seeing him there. So she'd waited, much as it hurt. Christ, he looked sad. People around him chatted away but it seemed as if he'd rather be anywhere else. He appeared older too. There was no getting away from it. Maybe he had done for a while and she just hadn't seen it but now the bloody home was showing it up.

Someone was saying something to him and he looked up, confused, as if he hadn't heard them properly. She hoped that's all it was. He was shrugging at the man who'd been speaking to him and turned away. She'd seen that faraway look sometimes when he was still at home with her mum – seen it but not noticed it.

Deep breath. Now go speak to him.

'Hi, Dad,' she managed as brightly as she could.

There it was: the half-second deliberation as he looked up and didn't immediately recognise who she was. That part of a second could range from almost instant to drawn out, every extra tenth of it meaning so much and so little.

He knew her now though and the smile lit up his face and warmed her heart. He got up and held his arms wide for her like he always did. She knew this time the smile hid awkwardness but she ignored it. She needed the hug at least as much as he did – more.

Now that she was closer, she could see there were a couple of bits of stubbly grey on his chin that he'd missed while shaving and a button undone about halfway up his blue checked shirt. Not much maybe but her dad was always a stickler for being neat and tidy. It worried her to see him letting his standards slip.

'How are you, love?' he was saying. 'How was the traffic?'

'Oh, not too bad at all,' she replied, even though it had been awful. 'How are *you* more to the point? Settling in?'

He lied too. She could see it in his eyes, clear as day.

'Och, yes. You know me. I can make myself at home anywhere. This place is fine. The people are nice enough.'

'How's the food?' she whispered conspiratorially.

'Bloody terrible,' he whispered back. 'Not a patch on your mother's.'

'What have they given you today?'

The moment the words were out her mouth she regretted them. The look of loss in his eyes cut right through her.

'Who can tell?' he laughed eventually. 'It all tastes and looks the same anyway.'

Typical Dad. He would always do anything he could to save her from hurt of any kind. If only she could do the same for him.

'Seriously, Dad,' she persevered. 'What's it like in here?'

'It's okay. It probably sounds silly but I can't take the fact they all know my name but I can't remember theirs. They've all been here forever so when I come in they've only got one name to learn while I've got to try to remember all of theirs. And I'm not doing very well.'

She let the pain of his comment show on her face.

'Hey, don't worry,' he laughed lightly. 'I was never that good with names anyway.'

She knew that was anything but true. She used to badger her dad to tell her about his old cases and he would sit her on his knee and reel off incidents, dates and names without ever having to pause to remember details. He'd had a mind like a vice.

'You shouldn't be in here, Dad. It's not right.'

'I'm afraid it is, love,' he replied with a sad smile. 'I'm just a burden to your mum and it's not fair on her.'

'Mum? Dad . . . Mum wouldn't want you in here.'

Her mum had died five years earlier from breast cancer. Dad had been heartbroken but he'd taken the burden for both of them, as brave and strong as always. It had been the single most devastating event in his life and yet, for now, he seemed to have forgotten it.

'I know she never complained,' he continued. 'But that's your mum for you: she's not the complaining type. But that doesn't mean she deserves to have to wet nurse someone who can't remember if he's eaten or when he last changed his . . . um . . . his socks. See? I can't even finish a bloody sentence sometimes.'

She knew better than to challenge him; getting upset only made him worse.

'I can pop over more often and see how you're doing. I should be doing that anyway.'

'Rachel, you've got your own life to lead. Anyway, this bloody thing means I can go haywire at any time. I wandered out for a walk last week and didn't even tell your mum I was going out.'

'Lots of people do that, Dad.'

'It was raining. Raining and cold and I didn't even think to take a jacket. I was soaked to the skin by the time your mum found me. It's not fair on her.'

Narey could feel a tear rising to her eyes but fought it, the same way she choked back the lump in her throat. It was the last thing he'd want to see and she wasn't going to make him endure it.

'It's not fair on you either, Dad.'

'Ach, well, you get what you deserve in life.'

'Not that again. You've got to stop feeling guilty, Dad. It was nearly twenty years ago. You can't keep beating yourself up about it.'

'Can't I? Well, why do I keep waking up and thinking about it then? Ironic, isn't it? I can't remember a bloody thing half the time but the one thing I'd rather forget . . .'

71

'Let it go, Dad. It's for the best.'

'I can't. I just can't. I keep dreaming about that island. That poor girl.'

A single tear ran down his cheek and dropped with a soft splash onto the collar of his shirt. Another followed. Rachel realised she'd never in her life seen her dad cry – not at a movie, a funeral or a wedding. He'd been the strong one, always there and always tough enough to look after everyone else – until now.

'I'll sort it, Dad. Don't worry. I'll make it right. I promise.'

'Thanks, love. But some things can't be sorted.'

'Of course they can.'

'Hm? Yes, okay. Okay. Anyway, Helen, you take care and I'll see you next week.'

'You count on it. Love you.'

Rachel turned to leave, the tears finally falling. Helen was her mum's name.

CHAPTER 12

Winter was safely back in his office in the bowels of Strathclyde Police HQ in Pitt Street, down in one of the dark places where daylight is a memory and a moment of cheerfulness is a prisoner. It suited him perfectly.

He was thumbing through photographs of near nothingness that he'd taken under the midnight moon on Inchmahome, looking for the soul of a girl long departed amidst the frozen ground and ancient priory. She wasn't there but that didn't mean he couldn't see her. He'd been seeing her, truth be told, almost every night when sleep finally came.

The sound of the office phone disturbed his reverie and he was grateful for it. Not only did it bring the promise of work, it also took him away from the unfulfilled promise of Rachel's cold case. He knew they were both obsessing on it and something about their mutual fascination with it bothered him. Maybe, as an only child, he'd just never learned how to share.

He picked up the receiver, recognising the call as an internal ring, and tried to stifle a sigh when he heard the voice on the other end of the phone belonged to Campbell 'Two Soups' Baxter, the senior crime scene manager and Winter's nemesis. Two Soups had never had much time for Winter as part of the team, believing that his scenes of crime officers did a perfectly acceptable job of recording evidence without the need for a specialist photographer. Naturally, Winter disagreed.

'Ah, Mr Winter. So good of you actually to be in the building for a change. If you could make yourself available for transportation to the east end, then we would be most grateful. Immediately.'

Even when Baxter was in what seemed to be a good mood, he remained a most irritating bastard.

'Yes, of course, What's the . . .' But Baxter was already gone.

Winter grabbed his camera bag, confident that it was, as always, fully loaded and ready to go. He hustled his way to the car park and saw immediately that whatever it was, it was going to be fun. There were more than enough uniforms, detectives and forensics jumping into cars to put Winter's antennae on full alert. This was no break-in at a newsagent. He found himself in a car with two of the forensics, Caro Sanchez in the back with him and Paul Burke at the wheel.

The details were scant but Sanchez and Burke at least knew more than Baxter had bothered to tell him. There were two casualties, probably as the result of some gang-related incident near Dalmarnock Road. One was dead at the scene and the other was being rushed to the Victoria. A crowd of local neds was already in attendance, witnesses supposedly among them, and the uniforms who were first there were having a hard time keeping them back from the scene. Blood and crowds, Winter thought, his favourite.

They picked up the sound of sirens as they approached Swanston Street, the noise fuelling his adrenalin and triggering the familiar itch that signalled the imminent chance to photograph something juicy. As they pulled into Swanston Street, it was chaos. There were kids running everywhere, some laughing, some shouting, all moving at the speed of blur and shouting at the top of their voices. As Winter got out of the car and made to get his gear from the boot, a bottle smashed a few feet away, sending glass flying in all directions. Cops were roaring at the kids. The situation was very close to becoming completely out of control.

'More o' the bastards,' yelled one voice to his left, seeing the SOCOs get out of the car. It didn't matter that they weren't in police uniform, these kids could spot cops at two hundred yards. As soon as they were all togged out in coveralls, they made their way towards a scrum of neds, who were jumping about with their backs to them, with the intention of pushing their way through. Winter slowed his step long enough to fire off a scene-setting photograph of the crowd, seeing that hoodies, low baseballs caps and football scarves over their mouths were the order of the day. He quickly caught the other two up, getting there just as Burke took a punch on the back as they made their way through the throng. The forensic half-turned, angrily intent on giving as good as he got before Sanchez grabbed his arm and dragged him on.

'The wild beasts in their natural habitat,' scowled Burke, in his best David Attenborough voice. 'Completely feral and exceedingly dangerous to approach.'

Winter was first through the throng and the first to glimpse the scene where the body was being attended to, his heart pounding at the sight of it. A tent was still being hurriedly erected to shield the corpse from the view of the baying mob. The sooner that was managed the better. The smell of blood was in the air and clearly powering the pack mentality. Given how much of it Winter could see trickling towards the gutter, it was hardly surprising. There were two separate pools of it but they were forming a single pond of crimson round the half-hidden body.

He strode straight towards the corpse, his camera in hand, pausing only to get a grab of the figure crouching over the body. He moved on quickly, reaching the cop, and was about to look over his shoulder to see the victim for the first time, ready to let it fill his vision and his viewfinder. He wasn't going to allow himself his usual luxury of revelling in the moment before he saw his subject – the moment that always filled him with equal measures of excitement and fear – but as he saw the body through his lens, he stopped and let it swing away from his view.

'Fucking hell,' he exclaimed.

'Don't see that every day, do you?' said the cop below him, his voice deadpan.

'No. You certainly don't.'

Splayed out before him and neatly cut in two was the body of a dog. It was some sort of bullmastiff breed, the kind that the tabloids liked to call devil dogs. This one was already on its way to doggy heaven or doggy hell, depending on just how much of a devil it had been when it was alive.

The dog's mouth hung open and a thick pink tongue hung pathetically between razor sharp teeth. A broad, bejewelled collar was round its chunky neck, a piece of bling that looked even more stupid on the dog when it was dead than it must have done when it was alive.

Towards its middle, the animal's short white fur was streaked in crimson, flecks of red spreading out from its gory core. The sight of the dog's division was nothing short of spectacular. Winter's camera was a blur of clicks and motors as he flashed shot after shot of the beast's deliverance from evil.

The dog's inner organs were spilled unceremoniously onto the frozen concrete of Swanston Street: heart, lungs, liver, kidneys, pancreas, large intestine, small intestine, gall bladder, spleen. All sitting piled one on top of the other in a stew of the remains of its last meal, making a smorgasbord of dubious delight for all to see.

As if that wasn't unpleasant enough, the dog had inevitably shit itself as it went to meet its maker. The resultant smell was horrific – not a treat for anyone's nostrils.

The cut through the animal was remarkable. It couldn't have been neater if it had been carried out on a vet's surgery table and performed by a laser. Winter wondered if that had been the case and the animal had been moved after a dissection elsewhere. There were already signs of partial lividity though and Winter knew enough about forensics to realise that the tell-tale purple marks meant the dog hadn't been moved.

The blood had rushed through the cut like water through the opening in a dam, making a dark, sticky blanket that would never be enough to keep the dog warm. Winter knew it was the sight of the dog, split asunder and swimming in its own juice, that was startling the watching throng of local neds and making their own blood boil. Winter dropped low to shoot across the body, knowing full well it would let him get the snarling, gawping, roaring, fearful faces in the same frame. Neither element made a pretty sight but together it made the peculiar beauty he sought.

There was still more. He was directed twenty yards away, where he was treated to the sight of a lower arm, cut just below the elbow, the job done as neatly as it had been with the dog, sheared off as if by some precision-mastered machine. The arm was skinny and white, pale even before it had been emptied of the blood that had flowed through it and now lay pooled all around. There was the blotchy stain of a homemade tattoo on the forearm, a declaration of love to Mary, which had been scrubbed over in an afterthought. The nails were dark and chipped and painted with nicotine.

Winter stalked his new prey, photographing from every angle, dropping yellow number markers as he went. On his periphery, he sensed cops and forensics closing in on him, anxious to get to work but having to wait till he had finished his. They circled him like hyenas waiting for a lion to have his fill and silently devising a strategy to drag him away from the kill. With a reluctance that growled deep in the pit of his stomach, he knew he'd have to give it up and let them in.

He dropped his arm to his side, camera in hand, signalling the end of his feasting and immediately bodies rushed past him. They all had their game faces on, suitably serious and intent on getting out of there as soon as possible. It was a routine they had danced far too often, the inevitable consequences of letting bored kids run around with recreational drugs and deadly weapons.

Winter backed off to the edge of the circus, casually firing off shots at the crowd and the cops but knowing he was sated by his photographic feed. A detective sergeant he knew from London Road, Aaron Sutton, was standing nearby, hands rooted in his pockets but his eyes scanning the crowd for likely suspects. Winter sidled over and Sutton greeted him with a despairing nod.

'Never ends, does it?'

'Never,' Winter agreed, failing to mention that a dark corner of his heart hoped it never did. 'So who do the dog and the hand belong to?'

'Ah, the Great British pet-loving public. I expected better of you though, Tony. Mention the dog before the severed arm because it seems the worse of the two?'

Winter laughed, conceding there might be some truth in it.

'Maybe. More likely just that the dog is the more unusual of the two.'

'Aye, maybe. The dog is called Klitschko after the boxers. The forearm belongs to a local ned cum drug dealer who apparently goes by the name of Casper. Named, ironically enough, after the friendly ghost. Real name Jason Hewitt and he's on the way to hospital. After he was separated from his arm, he was running round like a headless chicken screaming for his mammy, spurting blood everywhere, making it a friggin' nightmare for your forensic pals. It was his screaming that drew the crowd but it was the dog that got them angry. If Hewitt doesn't bleed to death, then he won't be scratching his arse with his right hand for the rest of his crappy life.'

'What the fuck cut them in half like that?'

'My guess is a sword – samurai maybe. I'm tempted to say "who cares". But I won't. As much as these stupid little fucks are a waste of space, I'll keep on caring because someone keeps on paying me to care.'

'That's so touching, Suttie. I could almost cry.'

'You do that and while you do I'll smack your face, you cheeky git. How's your pal Addison getting on?'

Winter's best friend, Detective Inspector Derek Addison, had been confined to desk duties for the previous six months after being seriously injured while on duty. Pushing pens had done nothing to improve his infamously volatile temper.

'He's helping old ladies across the road, sending birthday cards to Rangers supporters and generally being indistinguishable from a ray of sunshine.'

'A crabbit bastard as usual then?'

'Oh, aye.'

'Well, tell him I'm asking for him. And while you're at it, ask him if he knows of any toerags that are handy with samurais. I'd just as rather catch the bastard that did this before he fancies trying it on anyone else. He still like a Guinness?'

'Of course. He was shot in the head not the throat.'

'Tell him I'll see him in The Station Bar some time soon then. Anyway, nice as it is to chat, I have some rampaging hordes to put in line. Watch yourself, Tony.'

Winter saw the DS sigh and move back into the fray, wondering how they all managed to keep doing it time after time after bloody time. Then he peered into the Canon's digital display and saw the butchered halves of Klitschko and the bit of Jason Hewitt that had been left behind. Okay, maybe he didn't know how or why the rest of them managed to keep doing it, but he knew why he did.

CHAPTER 13

Monday 26 November

It was eight days since Winter and Narey had been to the Lake of Menteith Hotel and Rachel wasn't happy at all. Despite the bombs she'd casually dropped at the hotel and in Callander, and regardless of the ad she'd placed in the Sunday papers, she hadn't managed to kick up the shit storm she'd hoped for. The email address and PO box she'd provided had received no more than a few crank messages and chancers looking for a reward. She'd told Tony it was time to up the stakes.

She should have been investigating an attempted murder of a drug dealer in Garnetbank. Or else a suspicious fatal fire in Cowcaddens that needed a further round of witness interviews. Or a gang-related beating that had been clogging her in-tray for weeks. It wasn't a workload any heavier than any other DS in Strathclyde but Narey was having to keep her plates spinning alongside one of her own. If any of them fell because of that extra plate, then her arse would be on the line. That afternoon, as far as anyone else was concerned, particularly DI Addison, she was in Springburn chasing a lead about a missing grandfather. But she wasn't.

Laurence Paton lived in the Riverside area of Stirling; just ten minutes' walk from the city centre yet quite removed from it, a middle-class area of handsome stone terraces built around the turn of the last century. Narey indicated left just before the railway station and crossed the bridge into the residential peninsula that was looped by the River Forth.

The Ochil Hills cast a stunning backdrop as the road fell before them then rose again, a long if relatively low range of summits that separated Stirling and the Hillfoot villages from the Kingdom of Fife. To their left, the Wallace Monument rose high above the Abbey Craig in stark contrast to the snow-covered hills behind it. The monument, all 220 feet of Gothic sandstone perched on the hilltop, was a magnet for tourists and fans of Mel Gibson's bastardised biopic *Braveheart*.

'Left here,' Tony told her, a set of printed directions in his hand. 'Then right.'

Rachel took them onto Millar Place, then quickly onto Sutherland Avenue before taking another left into Wallace Place, a narrow street dotted with cars and neatly tended gardens, a series of semi-detached villas, most a monotonous pebble-dashed grey fronted by low hedges and fragile fences. A stone, high on the marled wall they were looking for, declared it had been built in 1920.

'You have arrived at your destination,' Tony intoned.

Rachel reversed the Megane easily into a space in front of

Paton's house, turning off the engine and pulling hard on the handbrake until it made a decisive series of clicks and stopped dead.

'Now what?'

'Now we wait,' Rachel replied.

The prospect didn't fill Winter with joy. He'd be there for her but he'd rather have been on the business end of his camera, seeing whatever darkness Glasgow had to offer.

'Wait until what?' he replied.

'Until we're noticed.'

A thin path of slabs ran from the solid low wooden gate that ran from the street to the door, dissecting a pink-chipped front garden. Climbing the walls of the house was some hardy-looking shrub while a drive by the side of the building was paved in the same mix of pink chips and dreary grey concrete. The front door was recessed within a porch, two windows on either side of it. White venetian blinds left the windows guarded but enough light shone through that Tony and Rachel could see there was no light switched on in either of the rooms that faced the street.

'What if there's no one home?' Winter asked her.

'Then we wait until there is.'

Rachel's patience lasted all of half an hour. Tony was content to close his eyes and let his skull sink back into the Megane's headrest, while she was the one who proved more impatient. She gave up staring at the windows, willing someone to look back at her through them, and instead got out of the car.

'Where are you going?'

'Just you sit there. I'm pushing things along.'

She positioned herself, half perched on the bonnet, half standing on the kerb, facing Paton's house. Not looking remotely suspicious, Winter thought. Her white coat was buttoned up to the neck but still she held the collar closed in a vain attempt to keep the chill at bay.

Suddenly, Tony saw a figure behind the venetian blinds on the furthest left of the four windows, a shadow looking out at the street and at Rachel. The shape lingered there before slipping out of view again. Rachel had seen him too; of course she had, for her eyes had never left the house.

Then, from the other side of the road, a door opened and a fair-haired woman in her early sixties stepped onto a gravel path. She was pulling on a coat as she walked, a look of consternation on her face, and making a direct line for Rachel.

'Hello, can I help you?'

The woman's tone of voice was more demanding than attempting to be helpful.

Rachel turned slowly, casually swivelling her head to face the neighbour.

'Help me? No thanks,' she smiled.

The woman looked confused and none too pleased.

'Are you lost? Perhaps I can help you with directions.'

Narey smiled again.

'Nope. Not lost at all.'

'Well, I . . . I was just wondering what you were doing here.'

'So I see.'

The woman hesitated, clearly expecting Rachel to explain herself. Instead, all she got was a calm smile and her stare returned.

'I . . . well . . . I'll be watching.'

'You do that.'

The neighbour's mouth dropped slightly before she turned on her heels and sped back into her house, doubtless ready to tell a long-suffering husband about the rude and highly suspicious stranger in the street.

Narey turned back to Paton's house and saw that the shadow had returned behind the blinds. He – she was sure it was a he – looked back out at her. She could make out fair or perhaps greying hair.

Inside the car, Winter's gaze tore back and forth between the window and Rachel. The shape in the blinds was bulky and tall, clearly staring at Narey but not flinching – neither of them was. Winter realised he was tense, braced to jump out of the car if Paton, assuming that's who it was, left the house to confront her. Rachel probably wouldn't thank him for it, and was perfectly capable of looking after herself, but he doubted he'd be able to stop himself.

The figure left his position at the window, moving off to his left, but Rachel didn't budge. She continued to lean against the car, her arms calmly crossed. In a matter of seconds, he'd returned and was staring at her again. Then he moved, an arm raised towards his head – no, not to his head, not quite yet anyway. He was holding something about chest high, gripping it in front of him as if to let her see it. It was a phone.

Rachel realised what it was and the message he was sending to her. She simply smiled at him and shrugged. The man didn't move for an age, as if trying to decide what he should do, then he brought the phone and his other hand together, punching in numbers. He lifted the phone to his shadowy head and held it there. Winter looked at one, then the other, waiting to see who would blink first.

It wouldn't be Rachel. He knew it. Rather than back off, she pushed herself away from the car and walked deliberately to the left of the brown gate that split the low hedge bordering Paton's castle. She stood right against the hedge, directly in front of the window where he stood. The arm holding the phone fell slowly to his side. The phone call, if he'd actually made one, was over. Then he moved quickly, a decision seemingly made, reached out an arm and the venetian blinds closed, hiding him completely. In quick succession, the blinds on windows two, three and four were also closed, leaving Narey staring at four white shields.

She stood there for a few moments longer before turning slowly and walking back to the car, noticing with some satisfaction that the nosy neighbour from across the street was still watching through her own window.

'Who do you think he was phoning?' Winter asked as Rachel slid back behind the wheel.

'Don't know; don't care. I'm just happy he was spooked enough to have phoned someone.'

'Maybe you should care. If he was phoning the cops, then you're in the shit. You do know that, Rachel, right?'

'He might just have been bluffing,' she pondered, paying him no attention. 'Either way, I think we can safely say he'll remember that we were here.'

'Fine, Rach. Ignore me if you want but you're walking the line here. Now is there any chance we can get back to civilisation? This country living is starting to wear me down.'

'Sure, let's go. I think I've stirred up enough shit for one week. I'm not finished though.'

'I was afraid you were going to say that.'

CHAPTER 14

'Yes, she's gone . . . Of course I'm sure. I saw her drive away.'

'And you've no idea who she was?'

'I told you. None.'

'What did she look like?'

'About five foot four, dark brown hair tied back. Pretty. Wearing a white coat.'

'And you'd never seen her before? What about the guy in the car?'

'I'd never seen either of them in my life.'

'Okay.'

'Okay? It's not okay.'

'Look, just keep calm.'

'That's easy for you to say. It wasn't your house she was standing outside. It wasn't your window she was staring into.'

'It could be nothing. Just a coincidence.'

'Don't tell me it's a coincidence. I know it's not a bloody coincidence. Not this weekend.'

'You have to stay calm. It's vitally important you don't lose focus. Not now.'

'I just can't take this any more. I've lived with it for far too long.'

'Exactly. You've come this far. You've gone through too much to crumble now.'

'Who the hell is she though? What does she want?'

'It doesn't matter. She doesn't know anything. That's all that's important.'

'You can't be sure of that. You don't know.'

'Hold it together. Stay strong.'

'I don't think I can. I just . . . it's too much . . . I've got to go.'

'Laurence . . . Laurence. Hello?'

CHAPTER 15

Thursday 29 November

'You do know that both Paton and the neighbour across the road probably took your registration number?'

Tony and Rachel were in her flat in Highburgh Road, she in a dressing gown and he with his shoes kicked off, lying back on the bed. Rachel was sitting at the computer and working her way through a search engine. It had been three days since they'd returned from their visit to Wallace Place but it was still dominating their conversation.

'I'm counting on it,' she called back over her shoulder.

'What?'

'Look, if Paton has nothing to hide . . .' She let her reply fade.

'Then the first thing he would do is get on to the police and tell them about the crazy woman outside his house the other day,' Winter finished for her.

'Right. Or maybe the second thing. The first would have been to open his door and ask what the hell we wanted. So if we don't hear from Central Scotland cops, then that tells me I'm on the right track. In this case, no news is definitely good news.'

Winter fell quiet, not as convinced by Rachel's argument as she was. The truth was, he wasn't convinced by any of it. He was fascinated by the horror of what had happened in Inchmahome, there was no denying that, but he doubted the good that could come of trying to investigate it after all these years. He could see the strain her dad's condition was placing on Rachel and he was worried where it would lead – not that he voiced any of his reservations. He knew her much better than to think that was a good idea.

'So what do you think you're going to find on the internet?'

Rachel shrugged without looking back at him.

'My dad's files are still held by Central Scotland Police because the case is still open, officially at least. I know most of what's in them. I've spent enough time talking to him about it. So . . . I'm searching everything I can find on here in case it offers something new.'

'Think it will?'

'Probably not but you never know. There is just so *much* of this stuff,' she waved her hand at the screen. 'And it's as full of as many rumours as old Dick Johnson or the public bar in The Waverley.'

'Gypsies?' he asked her.

'Yeah. Romany princesses and honour killings. There's plenty of that. Witchcraft, kidnap gangs and links to every known nutter in the country.'

'The internet's great but there's so much shite masquerading as fact that you can't trust any of it. Anything useful?'

'Maybe, although not directly about what happened. I've been reading about a forensic anthropologist at Dundee University who has done some great work in facial reconstructions from skeletal remains. I was thinking she could help us out.'

Winter let the 'us' pass without comment.

'Recreate an image of the girl's face, you mean?'

'Yes,' she spun to look at him. 'Professor Kirsten Fairweather. It was her team that reconstructed the medieval knight that was found under the floorboards at Stirling Castle. You remember it? They produced a computer-generated image of him. And that guy had been dead for nearly 700 years, so a twenty-year-old body should be a piece of cake.'

'Well, obviously, if you found out who the girl was, then it would make it a hell of a lot easier to find out who killed her,' he conceded. 'Think they'll go for it?'

'That's a slight problem. They'd need a skeleton to work on. The hard bit is going to be to persuade Central to give the go-ahead to dig her up.'

Winter looked at Rachel doubtfully. He had that familiar feeling of knowing full well he shouldn't say something but was going to do it anyway. It was like some form of Tourette's.

'Look, I don't want to be negative here but . . .'

'Course you don't,' she interrupted, immediately irritable.

'It's just that if you want Central Scotland Police on side to exhume this girl, then your case isn't exactly going to be helped by being reported for harassing a one-time suspect.'

Rachel shook her head wearily.

'He's still a suspect as far as I'm concerned. Anyway, that's just a chance I'll have to take. The reconstruction is probably a bit down the line. I need something to work with first. But thanks for your encouragement.'

'For fucksake, Rachel, I'm only pointing it out. You're going out on a limb here and that's not like you. You're normally by the book, sensible and level-headed – the ice queen investigator.'

She glared back at him, indignant at his response, as if he'd been disloyal.

'I've got to do this off the books because *I'm the one* who has to do it,' she argued. 'Don't you understand, it's got to be *me* who sorts it for him.'

Winter returned her stare, wishing he'd never opened his mouth. A silence fell between them, which was rudely broken by the ringing of the telephone. Narey ignored it, continuing to hold his gaze but finally giving in and picking up the receiver.

'Yes?' she demanded angrily, her tone quickly softening when she recognised the voice on the other end of the phone. Whoever it was didn't bother much with pleasantries and went straight into whatever they had to say.

'Yes, sir,' Rachel said finally. 'I was. I was there on Monday. I was only outside his house though. I . . .'

She had been interrupted and was listening intently, lines creasing her forehead.

'I was just passing through and wanted to see where . . .'

The caller had cut in on her again and Winter could tell that Rachel clearly wasn't enjoying what was being said. Then her face fell dramatically and her eyes shot across the room to Winter.

'Yes, sir. First thing. Of course. I can assure you . . .'

The phone had gone dead.

She put the receiver back in its holder and looked at the floor for a moment before lifting her head and looking directly at Tony. He waited for her to speak.

'That was Detective Superintendent Shirley,' she began, an obvious note of shock in her voice.

'Wanting to know if you'd been to Laurence Paton's house.'

She hesitated.

'Yes. He's dead, Tony. Laurence Paton was found dead this morning.'

CHAPTER 16

Friday 30 November

'What the fuck did you think you were doing there?'

DI Derek Addison had never been famed for his good nature or even temper and being forced to become a desk jockey while on the invalid list hadn't changed anything for the better. Being ordered to give Narey a bollocking on the instructions of Central Scotland Police wasn't helping much either.

'I was just . . .' Narey didn't get far with her reply.

'Shut up. When I want you to say something, I'll ask you. Do you know how much I like having to listen to those country bumpkins telling me how to do my job? Do you? Don't answer. I don't like it one fucking bit. Chief Inspector Farmer Hayseed phoned me from Stirling – a place that I didn't even know had telephones – and told me how to tell you off. Can you bloody believe that?'

Narey said nothing.

'I asked you a bloody question, Sergeant,' Addison roared at her.

95

'No, I don't suppose you can believe it, sir.'

'Too right I fucking can't. Lucky for you I'm more mad at them than I am at you. Although unluckily for you it just makes me even madder. Now what the fuck were you doing at this Laurence Paton's house?'

Narey hesitated to see if a reply was expected this time and quickly sensed that it was.

'I was just interested in an old case and I wanted to see where this guy lived.'

Addison stared at her.

'That's a pile of shite, Rachel, and you know I know it is.'

Addison had always been a man who called a spade a fucking shovel. Except that he was as likely to throw another few swear words in there as well.

'It's basically true, sir. I probably stayed slightly longer than I should have done and was maybe a wee bit conspicuous standing at his gate but I didn't question him, threaten him or do anything to put him in a state of fear or alarm.'

Addison shook his head wearily.

'If by conspicuous you meant confrontational, then you're probably right. You know perfectly well that the Scottish Police Service code of ethical practice demands that you "perform your duties in an open and transparent manner" – even if it is a load of old bollocks. Fucksake, Sergeant, do you not think it looks a bit of a coincidence that you were arsing about there three days before Paton fell off a ladder and cracked his skull open? Lucky for you there was a witness who could see that what happened to Paton was just an accident.'

'And a bit lucky I didn't have anything to do with it,'

Rachel fired back angrily. 'And I suppose a bit lucky I had an alibi, being 30 miles away and on bloody duty.'

'Aye, okay, keep your knickers on,' Addison conceded. 'I know you didn't have anything to do with it.'

'Of course I bloody didn't. And I could have you done for that knickers remark.'

'Oh, fuck off and sit down. It's bad enough those teuchters in Stirling giving me a hard time without you starting. You going to tell me what this is all about?'

Addison let his lanky frame collapse into a comfy looking armchair and, after standing indignantly for a few moments, Narey did the same but into a far less comfortable desk chair, her hackles still up.

'You first,' she told him. 'Give me chapter and verse on what happened to Paton?'

The DI sighed and picked up the sheet of paper again.

'Laurence Paton, school teacher,' he began. 'Deputy Head of English at the High School of Stirling. Forty-three years of age. Married to Isobel; no children. Lived in Wallace Place in Riverside, Stirling. He was up a ladder trying to unblock his guttering when the ladder slipped and he fell onto the driveway. He fractured his skull, broke his neck and suffered severe brain damage. He was unconscious when neighbours reached him and pronounced dead by the paramedics on arrival.'

Narey looked back at the DI, expressionless.

'Where was his wife?' she asked.

'Out.'

'Convenient.'

'Not really. He died.'

'Yeah, like I said. Who's the witness?'

'Hm?'

'You said I was lucky there was a witness who could see it was just an accident.'

'Oh, that. Yeah. You've already met her,' Addison glanced at a sheet of paper to check the name. 'A Mrs Helen Haskell. She was the concerned neighbour who was doing her civic duty by asking you what you were doing there.'

Narey rolled her eyes.

'That nosy old bag? Not surprising, right enough. A proper curtain twitcher, that one. What did she see?'

'She was at her front window and saw Paton fall. She ran over to him and saw the driveway caked with the poor sod's claret. She started screaming the place down and another neighbour came running. It was him who dialled 999.'

Narey didn't respond.

'The local cops took the relevant statements and it all seemed tragic and sad but no big deal really until Mrs Haskell mentioned the aggressive and suspicious woman who had been standing outside Paton's house three days before. Mrs Haskell had the woman's car number and like good little polis they ran the numbers as a matter of course. Imagine their surprise and displeasure when it turns out to belong to one of Strathclyde's finest. Imagine too how happy Detective Superintendent Shirley was when they called him.'

Narey closed her eyes and shook her head.

'Your turn,' Addison reminded her.

'Laurence Paton,' she began, mimicking Addison's tired monotone. 'Suspect in the Lady in the Lake murder in 1993. My father investigated the case but the body was never identified and the killer never caught. So there's some personal interest there.'

She paused but it was Addison's turn to say nothing and he let her continue.

'I'd been thinking about the case recently. It's the anniversary of when the murder was thought to have happened. I just wanted to see what Paton looked like and . . .'

'And?'

'And to see if I could spook him.'

'Spook him into what? A confession or falling off a ladder and killing himself?'

Narey raised her eyes to the ceiling and exhaled sharply.

'Okay, don't bother answering that,' Addison continued. 'I know why you'd want to take a look at him. I understand, Rachel. But the thing is: Paton isn't and wasn't a suspect. Not according to Chief Inspector Hayseed and the rest of Central Scotland Police.'

'My dad was a good copper, Addy,' she told him, all formality gone. 'He had a good nose and he was sure Paton was involved. And, come on, it's a bit too much of a coincidence, don't you think? Him dying around the anniversary of the murder?'

'No more than you turning up on the guy's doorstep five minutes before he pegs it,' Addison reminded her.

'Yeah but . . .'

'Yeah but nothing. Who was the mystery guy in the passenger seat when you went to Paton's?'

Narey hesitated and was furious to see it spark a faint smirk on Addison's face.

'That was just a friend who happened to be in the car.'

'Right . . .'

Narey's relationship with Winter was a secret but they both wondered if Addison suspected something. It was hard to tell because he was the sort who always gave the impression of knowing more than he let on. This time, he let Narey squirm uncomfortably before bringing the meeting to a close.

'Look, Central say it's a coincidence, so it's a coincidence. You stay out of their patch and get on with your own job. You hear me?'

Narey opened her mouth to speak, then closed it again.

'You hear me, Sergeant?'

'I hear you.'

'I mean it, Rachel. They're gunning for your ass as it is. Don't give them an excuse to do anything about it.'

CHAPTER 17

Sunday 2 December

It was only six o'clock when Winter strode off Highburgh Road and began to climb the stairs to the flat but it had already been dark for two hours. There was a clean pint glass sitting at his usual place on the pine kitchen table and it caught his eye the moment he entered the flat. There was a strange smell too, something unusual. A tour through his memory bank told him it was food.

'You're cooking?' he called out.

'Don't sound so surprised,' Rachel's voice came back at him from somewhere out of sight.

'You don't cook. You never cook.'

'That's not true.'

She had reappeared from behind the fridge door with a can of Guinness in her hand, a welcoming hissing sound escaping as she tore back the ring-pull.

'It is true,' Tony persisted. 'Reheating ready meals isn't cooking. Putting something in the microwave isn't cooking. Toast isn't cooking. You don't cook.'

Rachel stopped in front of the table as if ready to argue but instead forced a smile and slowly poured the Guinness into the pint glass.

'Well, tonight I'm cooking. There's a steak and ale pie in the oven and roast potatoes in there too. That okay with you?'

'Um, sure. Lovely.'

Tony fell into his chair, lifting the glass to his lips and his eyebrows to the ceiling. He watched her produce another pint glass and place it on the table opposite him. Winter wiped a foamy moustache from his lips and sat back, wondering what the hell was going on.

Suddenly, the intercom buzzer barked into the room. Winter jumped at the noise but Rachel didn't seem surprised. She picked up the wall telephone and listened for a second before replying.

'Hi. Come on up.'

Tony supped on his stout again, waiting for an explanation that wasn't forthcoming. Instead Rachel went to the fridge and brought out a can of lager, immediately opening and pouring it. Shortly after, there was a brisk knock at the door and Rachel opened it to let the slightly out of breath and burly figure of Danny Neilson inside. Winter's uncle grinned at him, enjoying the look of surprise on the younger man's face.

'All right, son?' Danny asked him.

Tony shrugged.

'Um, yeah. I'm not sure.'

'Dinner will be about ten minutes, Danny,' Rachel told their visitor.

'Fine, love. No rush.'

Love? No one called Rachel 'love' without getting his ear chewed off. Winter was even more confused.

Danny slipped into the chair opposite, raised the glass towards Tony and said cheers.

'So how's tricks, son?' Danny asked him after a long sup on his beer, dragging a hand through his greying but annoyingly full head of hair. 'You photographed any good deid bodies recently?'

'No, it's actually been pretty quiet on the corpse front recently.'

'Ach, never fear, it's Glasgow. I'm sure there will be another one along any minute. A nice shotgun wound to the head maybe. Or a machete attack. Maybe even a wee double murder.'

'Aye, Uncle Danny, very good. Now look, what the fu—'

Tony never got to finish his question, as Rachel reappeared and sat down at the table, a glass of white wine in her hand.

'So, Danny,' she began, 'how are things with you? Still working the rank at night?'

Tony's uncle was a former policeman, thirty years on the force and most of those spent as a detective sergeant. He wasn't a man for sitting on his backside during retirement though and had taken a job marshalling late-night revellers at a busy taxi rank. Keeping drunks in line in all weathers was no position for a man in his sixties but Danny could more than handle himself and he blankly refused all suggestions that he should give it up.

'I am, love,' he told Rachel. 'The work of the taxi rank superintendent is never done. There were some right bampots out last night. I'm guessing they were full of the drink after watching the match on the telly. Did you see it, Tony?'

The normality of the conversation was doing Winter's head in. Uncle Danny, for all that he had been virtually a father to Tony after the death of his parents, was the first person ever to visit Rachel's flat while Winter was there. Their relationship remained a secret to all except Danny and he knew only because Winter had desperately needed his help a year before. Rachel had been threatened by a vigilante sniper and rogue cop, and it was Danny Tony had turned to when he needed help to protect her. It was Danny who'd known what to do. Despite all that and knowing about Tony and Rachel, Danny had never been invited to Chez Narey. Yet, out of the blue, here he was, large as life, at the dining table. Cosy.

'What the hell is going on?' Tony finally asked them.

Danny shrugged, seemingly amused at Winter's confusion, while Rachel shook her head at him in exasperation. Finally she blew out her cheeks and arched her eyebrows in surrender.

'Okay, okay. I'll explain but let's eat dinner first. If you knew how tough it was for me to cook this bloody stuff, then you'd know I don't want it to be wasted. Another drink?'

They ate with little more than polite, strained conversation, each appetite ruined by the anticipation or dread of what was to be said.

'First of all, Danny,' Rachel began at last, 'I want to tell you about my dad. He was a cop, just like me, just like you were. He's ages with you so maybe you even knew him. His name was Alan Narey and he was a chief inspector in Central Scotland. No?'

Danny shook his head.

'He was from Glasgow, born and bred, but he preferred not to work over the shop. So he worked out of Stirling, drove in every day. He figured, given the nature of the job, it would be better for me and my mum if he didn't have too many enemies who knew where we lived. That's the way he always was – put us ahead of anything else. He could have made at least superintendent if he'd sacrificed a bit more but it wasn't in his nature. Not that he wasn't dedicated to the job; he was. He cared about people and about the right thing being done. He was my hero. He still is.'

Rachel stopped and took another swig of wine. When she spoke again, her voice was stronger.

'Anyway, you'll remember the Lady in the Lake case, the winter of 1993 and '94.'

Danny's eyes furrowed.

'Lake of Menteith?' he answered. 'Young woman found battered to death on the island in the middle? I remember it. It made headlines for weeks, months.'

'Inchmahome,' she confirmed. 'My dad worked the case. Worked it for months, maybe the only time in his whole career he lived and breathed a case twenty-four hours a day and me and Mum never saw him. The victim wasn't that much older than me and I always wondered if that was part of it, why it got to him so much. But I think it was just because he cared, wanted justice for her. You know how it is, Danny.'

Neilson nodded slowly and gravely. He knew how it was all right. He'd worked on a series of high-profile killings back in the early seventies: four young women who were murdered after nights out in Glasgow. They'd never caught the killer and there weren't many days that went by that Danny didn't think about it and feel guilty about not having done his job.

'Yeah, I know, love. It eats away at you and it doesn't stop.'

'Yes, it does,' she agreed, her voice wavering again. 'My dad's not well, Danny. He's been diagnosed with Alzheimer's.'

Rachel let the sentence hang there and Tony flirted with the notion that she was playing this for sympathy. He immediately reproached himself for thinking it.

'I'm sorry to hear that, Rachel,' Danny comforted her. 'It must be hard'

She nodded, her eyes on the table.

'It's hardest for him. He's a proud man, used to looking after us and now he's struggling to look after himself. He can't always tell you what day it is and he forgets people's names. He puts the oven on and leaves food to burn; he misses appointments and forgets birthdays. It might not sound much but it's . . . it's like you said, it's eating away at him. I can see my dad slipping away bit by bit.'

Tony got out of his chair to go to comfort Rachel but she waved him back down.

'His biggest regret is that girl who was found on Inchmahome – his last major case and the one that stays with him. He frets about it, Danny, and I know he wakes up in the middle of the night haunted by it.'

Neilson sat with his chin on his hands, looking at Rachel, taking in every word she said but giving nothing away.

'I can't do much for him,' she continued. 'I can't give him some magic pill to make it all better. I can't pay for some Harley Street doctor to cure him because there is no cure. I can't even look after him because he's in a home. There's only one thing I know how to do and that's my job.'

Danny slowly took one of his hands away from beneath his chin and held it up in front of him, his palm facing Rachel in a 'stop' gesture.

'I don't want to interrupt you, Rachel, but I can see how much this is hurting you. I know you are going to tell me what you want from me when you're good and ready. Whatever it is, if I can do it, then I will. Okay?'

Rachel smiled sadly and nodded.

'I know you wouldn't be asking unless you felt you really needed to,' Danny continued. 'Just tell me what you want.'

It hurt Winter to see Rachel upset and that was bad enough but it also stung that he was being held at arm's length. She was the one who had to help her dad, he knew that, and it made it difficult for her to let him in. There had always been this invisible police tape between them when it came to her work and he could feel it again now, putting him in his place.

'Why did neither of you tell me about what was happening tonight? Okay, I get that you might need Danny's help with whatever you're planning, Rachel, but you could have told me.'

She looked at him, a faint smile playing across her lips.

'Boys and their egos,' she teased and she rolled her eyes. 'It's not Danny I need, you idiot. It's you.'

Tony brightened briefly before confusion set in again.

'I need help from someone I can trust,' she explained. 'I can't do this by the book and I can't ask anyone from the job. And you . . . bizarrely, you have a knack for this. When the sniper was taking out the drug lords, you saw things we missed and you instinctively knew what to do. You knew how to join the dots. I need that now.'

Tony nodded, appeased but still uncertain.

'It's just that I'm not sure you're capable of doing everything that's needed on your own, so we need Danny to help you out,' she continued. 'He's been round the block and you always say he's the smartest man you've ever known. Every cop I know in Strathclyde who knew Danny says he was top drawer. We need him. I need both of you.'

Both men just looked at her, waiting for the punchline.

'Danny, my dad had a suspect for the killing. It was never anything firm but his nose told him this guy was involved – a student teacher named Laurence Paton. He hung about the scene when they did a reconstruction a year later and admitted he'd been in the area at the time of the killing. He was nervous, evasive. My dad liked him for the murder but never had any evidence to link him, so nothing was ever done. He had Paton in a couple of times under the pretence of interviewing potential witnesses but nothing.'

Danny listened intently, saying nothing.

'On the anniversary of the killing, we went to the Lake of Menteith and made a few waves, asked a few questions, unsettled some dust. Then we went to Paton's house. I made sure Paton knew I was there even though he couldn't have known who I was. Three days later, Paton falls off a ladder while doing DIY outside his house and dies on the spot. What does your copper's nose tell you about that, Danny?'

The older man took a long draw on his beer and let it swill around his mouth, savouring the taste and buying himself time to think. He drew the back of his hand across his mouth and looked at Rachel.

'It stinks,' he told her. 'I was never one for coincidences.'

'Nor me,' she agreed.

Danny chewed on his bottom lip as he considered the options and tried to second-guess what her plan was. Whatever it was, he knew he would agree to it. His blood was already racing and he hadn't felt that in a while. It felt danger-ous and good. It felt alive.

'So what is Central saying?' he asked her.

'Not much. They are insistent it was an accident. Say they have a witness that corroborates it. They say there's nothing to prove Paton had anything to do with the lake killing and I need to keep my nose out of it.'

'Then you'd better do that,' Danny mused. 'We, on the other hand . . .'

She smiled, grateful that he understood.

'I'm going to ask this for the last time,' Tony grumbled. 'What do you want me and Danny to do?'

'If Laurence Paton killed this girl, then I want to find something to prove it. I want *you* to find something. As I said, I need you to do this for me.'

'And how am I going to do that?'

'I want you and Danny to break into Paton's house. I want you to search his home, hack his computer – whatever it takes. I want you to find me proof that my dad was right and Paton killed the Lady in the Lake.'

CHAPTER 18

Tuesday 4 December. 1.00 a.m.

Winter and Neilson parked quietly on Sutherland Avenue, a good few hundred yards away from the corner where it adjoined Wallace Place. Danny had instructed Tony to try to get halfway between the street lights to make best use of such darkness as there was. They quietly got out of the car, shivering as the cold bit into them, and started out on foot.

A glance behind them saw the splendour of Stirling Castle, lit up in its festive finery and sitting proudly on the rock overlooking the town that thought it was a city. Ahead were the snow-covered Ochil Hills, framing the horizon but disappearing softly into a frozen haze.

Danny had driven through to Stirling the night before and checked out the situation. He'd gone so far as to wander into Laurence Paton's back garden unchallenged. He said there was no sign of a burglar alarm and breaking into the place would be a piece of cake. He'd admitted a career that included many hours mopping up after house break-ins was a great apprenticeship for doing it yourself. He'd also gone back that afternoon and knocked on Paton's door, getting no answer, then tried a neighbour, saying he was a friend hoping to pay his condolences. The neighbour had told him that Irene, Paton's wife, had gone to stay with family and wouldn't be back till the next day. It gave them a one-night window of opportunity.

What if someone had actually answered Paton's door, Tony had asked him. Danny had sighed and retorted that he wasn't so stupid as to have left it to chance and had phoned the house twice before making his move to be sure that the place was empty.

But what if there was a burglar alarm, Winter persisted – a unit hidden out of sight maybe? Danny had exhaled again and explained that a burglar alarm couldn't stop anyone from breaking into a house and it wasn't designed to do so. It was a deterrent and there wasn't much point in an alarm that couldn't be seen.

The pair walked silently down Sutherland Avenue, breath freezing before them, lost in their own thoughts about what lay ahead and what had already been. Winter had considered telling Danny about the dreams he'd been having, the ones he couldn't tell Rachel about. In the end, he decided to keep them to himself but couldn't help but wonder if the other two were dreaming the same dreams he was.

They had started the night after he and Rachel had been to the island and he'd 'seen' Lily lying on the frozen ground, abandoned and alone. She'd lain there for four months and part of her was still there, waiting to go home. He'd tried to photograph that part of her, that thing that might be soul or plasma or memory.

The house where Paton had lived was half of the first semi at the end of the street and only a thigh-high fence and a neighbour's garden separated them from the dead man's back door. The gardens on Paton's side of the street were maybe thirty yards long and backed on to more gardens coming the other way, separated by a six-foot-high wall. Bedroom lights still flamed in a few of the homes on the other side of the wall but those neighbouring Paton's house were, reassuringly, shrouded in darkness.

As they approached, Danny reached into the pockets of his jacket and produced two balaclavas. When the headgear was wordlessly shared and pulled on, it was Tony's turn to dig into his pockets and come out with two pairs of nitrile gloves and two pairs of elasticated shoe covers, all liberated from the office stores. They stopped briefly before the rust-coloured fence and slipped the protective coverings over their feet and hands, ready for the task ahead.

With an easy stride that belied his age and increasing girth, Neilson stepped over the fence first, followed by Winter. The photographer was the taller of the two by an inch or so but his uncle Danny was easily the bigger man. Sometimes he looked as broad as he was tall, burly and thickset, and not someone to be messed with despite being in his sixties. The pair of them padded across the mani-cured lawn, their covered footsteps leaving a crunchy wake in the frosted grass, then stepped across a narrow area laid out with stone chips so as to avoid unnecessary noise. No fence separated the neighbour's house from Paton's and they simply walked across the grass to the English teacher's back door.

The houses in Wallace Place dated back to just after the First World War and that, according to Danny, was good news for them and any other would-be housebreakers.

'Old house, old locks,' he'd told Winter.

As they stood outside the back door, their breath clouding the air in front of them, Tony moved from foot to foot in a vain attempt to stop the frost from invading his feet until a glare from Danny brought him grudgingly to a standstill. Neilson reached inside his jacket and brought out a selection of thin pieces of card, the moonlight reflecting off their plastic surfaces. As he approached the door, Winter turned his back, looking around edgily in case their arrival had been noticed and fearful that the time it would take to open the door would put them at risk.

Tony had barely begun to scope the lights in the houses beyond the garden wall, wondering if anyone was watching them through barely closed curtains and reaching for a telephone to call the police, when he heard a hissing sound behind him. He turned and Danny was standing inside Paton's house, gesturing for Winter to join him inside.

Taking a deep breath, Winter crossed over the threshold into criminal activity and stepped into Paton's kitchen, Neilson quickly and quietly closing the door behind him. Both of the men had torches, Danny having been insistent that they couldn't take the chance of turning on the house lights. With no sign of a computer in the kitchen, Neilson led them into a hallway, their plastic-covered feet making no more than quiet sliding sounds as they moved slowly across the carpets.

In the first of two reception rooms facing the street, they saw photographs on the mantelpiece and both men paused to look. A man in his mid-forties looked back at them, his arm around a woman of similar age: Mr and Mrs Paton, they presumed – Laurence and Irene. He had fair hair that was greying at the temples, a tight smile that seemed to be forced onto his lips and a blush to the cheeks of his otherwise fair skin. She wore dark-rimmed glasses the colour of her hair and grinned at the camera in an altogether more carefree way than her husband could manage. Winter knew that he now had a face to put to his mental images of Paton lying fatally fractured and bleeding on the path outside. His internal camera snapped an image that would sustain his need. All the photographs above the fire were of the Patons, either together or individually, but with no evidence of any extensions to the family.

Neilson tugged at Winter's sleeve and led him out of the room, back into the hallway and into the next room. In the light afforded by the streetlamp, they could make out walls lined with books, a low table covered in magazines and then in the corner they saw it: a wooden desk and a computer.

Tony crossed the floor, looking to see the model and age of the PC, running his gloved fingers lightly over it as he appraised it like a safecracker.

Danny raised his eyebrows at him, asking if he could do it. Winter nodded and reached into the pocket of his trousers; it was his turn to bring out a small piece of rectangular plastic and metal.

'What's that?' Neilson asked in a low voice.

'It's a bootable USB stick,' Winter whispered back at him.

'You can buy one for fifty quid but I thought it better that no one knew what we were going to do so I made this one myself. It should do the job. Thankfully his PC is just a few years old so we can bypass the hard drive and use this little beauty to boot it up instead.'

Winter inserted the stick into one of the computer's USB ports and within a minute it had grumbled into life, the noise worrying both of them, and he had access to the computer's files. He swiftly copied everything he could see onto the stick, gobbling up every bit of information.

'Damn,' he muttered.

'What is it?' Danny asked. 'Even I can see the files transferring across.'

'Yeah, and that's fine as far as it goes. We can take the stick and look at everything on here in our own time. But I can't get into his emails this way. He's using Web-based mail rather than something like Outlook Express or Evolution.'

'So we're stuck?'

Winter shook his head and produced another stick from his pocket.

'Plan B. It's not ideal because if someone takes the time to check the log files, then they'll know we've logged in. The other way would have left no trace but the saving grace is they won't know who we are.'

Neilson breathed heavier as he deliberated.

'Okay. Do it.'

Winter switched the PC off again, then put the second stick into a USB port.

'So what's different about this stick then?' Neilson asked as quietly as he could.

'This is a bootable stick as well but I've downloaded the ophcrack ISO on to it. It's a self-contained operating system that includes a password-cracking utility.'

'Am I supposed to understand any of this?'

'Not really. If you did, then everyone would do it. I've downloaded and installed rainbow tables for ophcrack onto the stick. They're precomputed tables for reverse encryption.'

'English, please, son.'

Tony switched the computer on again.

'It's going to tell us all his passwords.'

As the PC hummed back into life, Winter keyed into setup and amended the boot sequence so it would do a one-time boot from the USB stick rather than its hard disk. He then exited setup and let the boot continue, seeing it automatically launch ophcrack and the rainbow tables scanning the user accounts.

'It's brute-forcing the passwords,' Winter explained. 'And now . . . we'll see them displayed in GUI.'

Neilson groaned softly. 'Okay, I'll bite. Gooey?'

'Graphical User Interface. And . . . there we go . . .'

Words flashed up on the screen. Not words really, Winter thought: alphanumerics with numbers substituted for letters in the middle of words.

W4ll4ce
R4ng3rs1873
P4tons16
LP4ton71

'Looks like separate passwords for Laurence and his missus,' Tony mused. 'Probably didn't have access to each other's email accounts. Did our boy have something to hide, by any chance?'

'We've all got things to hide,' Danny muttered. 'What now?'

'Now I write these down . . . remove this magic stick . . . and reboot the PC the normal way. When it comes up again, I'll log in with whichever of these passwords does the trick.'

Within a minute, Winter had Paton's email account laid bare in front of him. It struck him that reading someone else's emails might have left him feeling a bit dirty at the best of times but it was definitely grubby when the person was dead and barely cold in the ground. So be it.

There were twenty-odd unopened pieces of mail in Paton's inbox, the first of them arriving late in the afternoon of the day he'd died. Winter was wary of opening any of them, as that would leave a big, muddy forensic footprint saying they had been there. But from the subject lines, he could see there was the usual share of spam mail offering chances to claim lottery wins and legacies in foreign countries, a larger penis and pills to help keep it interested. There were also a couple of emails from a teaching organisation regarding renewed membership and two notifications from Facebook on his last day on earth. None of that was worth the risk of opening them.

He started going back through the opened mail, working his way through personal messages and hoping he was invading the privacy of someone who had done something wrong. It was the only thing that would justify what he was doing. There was an invitation to a nephew's birthday party Paton would never attend; an update on a fundraising committee raising cash for a cancer charity; a long letter from what seemed to be an aged aunt in Canada; on and on, an endless stream of undeleted banality.

Then he found something much more interesting. The sender was named as a Kyle Irving and the subject line was straight to the point: 'Re: Help'. Winter opened it and found a few paragraphs of what seemed to be advice to Paton. The letter was all couched in jargon that screamed psychology.

Dear Laurence,
I am most concerned with your current psychological state and I fear there is a grave risk of you decompensating back into psychosis. If that happens, then much of our good work may be undone.

You know that your depression is the product of antecedent conflict. While you cannot change those original events, you can control how you react to them now. We need to return to a position of self-efficacy. Once you regain the confidence to know that you can master everything you set out to accomplish, then I'm sure you will see that what currently seem to be insurmountable psychological issues are merely V codes. They are problems of living rather than a disorder.

I urge you to continue to practise levels of processing as we have discussed previously. Your memories are your friend, not your enemy. They are the way to control your guilty feelings.

You must stay strong, Laurence. I am always just a mouse click away if you need me.
Kyle Irving APC, Bsc.
Approved online psychology counselling

Below was Paton's original email Irving was replying to.

Kyle,

I'm really struggling to cope with this right now. I keep thinking about her and I can't sleep at nights. I just keep seeing the look on her face as we walked across that ice. Every time I close my eyes she is looking back at me, asking me why. Wanting to know why I left her there, all cold and alone on that island.

I keep dreaming about the skater spinning, spinning, spinning, turning round and round in my head. Sometimes I think I can feel her pink gloves tickling my bare hands. I wake up and she's gone again.

I don't know how much longer I can go on like this. I need your help. Please.

Laurence

Winter's heart slammed into his chest and he realised his breathing was quick and hard. He felt his skin tingle the way it did when he had a camera in his hand and a broken body to photograph. The email might as well have been drenched in blood given the effect it had on him. He pulled the compact camera from where it nestled in his back pocket and photographed the screen in front of him, making sure he'd be able to show Rachel just what he'd found.

'Okay, paydirt,' Danny was saying behind him. 'Get your photos taken, then let's get out of here. The longer we stay, the greater the risk.'

'No, hang on. There's more.'

Tony's eyes had fallen on another email subject line and

his pulse quickened as the adrenalin shot round his body once again. It read simply 'November 1993' and it was dated just a couple of days before Paton fell to his death. Winter quickly clicked on it, anxious to see what was inside. His eyes darted from the header to the content, taking it all in at once, knowing that he'd hit the jackpot even if he didn't know what to make of it.

It had been sent by someone with the email address justice1993@hotmail.com and the dynamite was in the message.

You seem to think I'm kidding so I will have to prove to you that I'm deadly serious. The choice is yours. Make it quick.

'Oh, fucking great,' Winter could hear Danny sighing behind him.

The email was unsigned beyond the anonymous 'justice1993' tag and it didn't take a detective to work out what that represented. Rachel's dad had been right all along, Winter was sure of it. It had been Paton who'd killed the girl in the lake. What else could this email mean? But who had sent it and how the hell did he or she know what Paton had done? And did Paton's death mean he'd ignored the threat that was implicit in the email?

Winter photographed the email, then exited it to scroll further down the inbox, quickly seeing another email from the same sender, then another further down. He went to the one that was sent first, noting the date on it and realising it was sent on the Monday after he and Rachel had spent the weekend nosing around the Lake of Menteith. That was a coincidence too far for his liking. It seemed certain that

Rachel's intentions to stir things up had had an immediate effect after all.

He opened the first email and felt the rush again as he was hit by another bombshell. This one had been sent not just to Paton but to three other addresses. None of the other recipients was named as such and were only identified by e-addresses that seemed to be a mixture of nicknames and numbers.

dixie1970@btconnect.co.uk;
paddy38@hotmail.co.uk; adamski01@sky.com
November 1993. Lake of Menteith. I don't imagine that any of you have forgotten it. But I bet you were hoping everyone else had. No such luck.
Justice

There was an attachment in the email and when Tony clicked on it, a .jpg opened immediately and his heart missed several beats as he saw it was a scanned copy of the advert that Rachel had placed in the Sunday papers.

Winter managed to find his camera in his hand and focused his attentions on taking a screen grab to ensure they had a note of all the email addresses. Behind him, Danny was swearing and growling under his breath.

Suddenly a noise that came through the wall made both men stop stock-still and they could hear their heart pounding. The initial noise – maybe a floorboard creaking, maybe someone on the move next door – was repeated. Neilson motioned to Winter to stand still. After what seemed like an age, they heard a toilet flush from the next house and they both began to breathe again. Neilson gestured at his watch, indicating that they should hurry and get the hell out of there. Winter shook his head and pointed at the computer screen.

He clicked into the sent folder but it was completely empty, as was the delete one. Paton was either a very organised man, keen to conserve his mailbox limit, or else he was pretty good at covering his tracks. Winter went back into the inbox, wondering how many other emails from the man calling himself Justice had been killed off, and opened the remaining email from Paton's persecutor.

> You must pay for what you have done. There are two ways for that to happen: money or cold justice.

Attached below was Paton's reply to the original email.

> Who is this? What the hell do you want? Leave me alone.

CHAPTER 19

Wednesday 5 December. 11.30 a.m.

Kyle Irving's 'office' turned out to be a house on the south side, just off Shields Road. The leafy drive and the year-old Saab that sat on it suggested the man did rather well out of his pseudo counselling advice. Narey parked up next to Irving's car and rang the doorbell.

She thought she saw a curtain twitch in her peripheral vision, somewhere on the first floor, and it took a while before she heard footsteps approach the door. It swung open to reveal a man in his early fifties with sandy brown hair and a pair of silver spectacles low on the bridge of his freckled nose. A heavy cardigan was buttoned tightly over an open-necked shirt and a pair of slippers peeped out beneath faded denims. The man looked at Narey with curiosity.

'Mr Irving?'

'Dr Irving. Yes?'

'I'm Detective Sergeant Rachel Narey of Strathclyde Police. May I come in?'

Irving's eyes narrowed cautiously and Narey could see his brain working overtime.

'May I ask what this is in connection with?' His voice was the gravelly product of many cigarettes.

'I'd rather explain inside, Dr Irving. It's a delicate matter.'

The answer didn't seem to appease Irving much but he pulled the door wide, reluctantly allowing her inside. Narey quickly stepped through the door and into a hallway that smelled vaguely damp underneath the pervasive odour of stale tobacco smoke. The hall was cluttered with books, bags and umbrellas and looked as if it could stand a lick of fresh paint.

Without glancing back, Irving turned right into a room, clearly expecting Narey to follow him. She'd already decided she didn't like the man and any chances of her going easy on him were disappearing fast. He had led her into a room that seemed to double as a study and a sitting room. Two large bookshelves stood against one wall, the contents apparently split between large textbooks in one and paperback novels in the other. There was a television in one corner and a tired-looking sofa separated it from a dining table that supported a computer and printer. Despite there being radiators on two of the walls, the room was freezing.

'Please, take a seat,' Irving invited her, his tone more welcoming than before. A case of prudence being the mother of politeness, Narey assumed. The man had obviously thought better of his brusque approach.

Narey thanked him and eased herself into the lone armchair, feeling a spring groan inhospitably beneath her as she sat down. Irving's furniture had seen better days. Interesting.

'Dr Irving, I am here in connection with a client of yours. I believe . . .'

'Let me stop you there, Sergeant Narey,' Irving interrupted. 'You must realise I am unable to discuss my clients with you. It's a clearly established matter of patient confidentiality that cannot be breached.'

Narey sighed internally.

'I realise you won't discuss the precise nature of your dialogue with your client but that doesn't preclude you from confirming someone is a client.'

Irving looked at her stonily for a few seconds before giving a curt nod.

'Okay.'

'Thank you. The client in question is Laurence Paton.'

There was the merest flicker in Irving's eyes and a tiny contraction of his temples. Narey got the distinct feeling the man had already made the decision not to register any emotion whatever name was presented to him – or perhaps to the name he was expecting. Irving was deliberating before having to give the simplest of answers.

'Yes, I was helping Laurence.'

Narey nodded. However, she wanted much more.

'It would be very helpful if you could tell me about the nature of the help you were providing Mr Paton.'

Irving bristled and a look of undisguised frustration hung heavily on his worn features.

'Sergeant, I told you . . .'

'And while I do understand the convention of client–patient confidentiality,' she continued, ignoring his protest, 'I also know that in this particular case there is cause to believe you had a duty to warn with regard to Mr Paton's state of mind.'

Irving's mouth abruptly opened and closed again and he looked both furious and troubled.

It was a bluff on her part but 'duty to warn' was the one thing Narey knew overrode the psychologist–client confidentiality contract, and there was enough in Paton's email exchange to make it worth her playing that card.

'Now really, Sergeant,' Irving blustered. 'If you are accusing me of falling below professional standards, then I must protest. I can assure you . . .'

Narey cut across him again.

'Dr Irving, I have reason to believe you had a duty to warn that Laurence Paton represented a danger either to himself or to others. In such a circumstance, you must inform a third party or the authorities, am I correct?'

Irving stared back at her, again seemingly desperate to betray no emotion.

'That is correct but what evidence do you have to suggest Laurence posed such a threat, Sergeant?'

'Mr Paton is dead, Dr Irving.'

There it was again. The same waver in the man's eyes, the same twitch at his forehead. Knowledge or shock or something else in disguise? It had been five days since Paton had died and it was quite possible, if their only contact had been by email, that Irving wouldn't know what had happened to him.

'That's . . . I didn't know. I didn't know that.'

The man was flustered and Narey went for the throat.

'Mr Paton's death clearly gives substantial weight to our belief that you had reason to think he might harm himself. That is something we are obliged to take very seriously.'

Irving blinked at her.

'But he . . . how did he die? And how on earth did you have access to any information that might have made you think that . . . I don't understand.'

'I'm not at liberty to divulge either of those things to you at the moment, Dr Irving,' she lied.

Irving glared at her, his attempts to keep his emotions hidden from her proving an increasing struggle. Instead he settled for another lengthy pause.

'What do you want to know?'

'Everything.'

'That's a rather wide scope, Sergeant. Could you be more specific?'

'Did you ever meet Mr Paton face to face?'

'No. Never.'

'So all your conversations were by email?'

'And occasionally by telephone.'

'So I assume that you will have copies of the emails he sent to you for your records.'

Irving shook his head.

'No. That would be quite unprofessional and would breach the Data Protection Act. I deleted each email once I'd responded to it. I believe Laurence did the same.'

Narey had a strong urge to slap Irving's face but resisted it.

'What was troubling Mr Paton?'

Irving made a great play of sighing and letting his head fall to his chest before replying. He was clearly going to be as difficult as possible and make it obvious he was acting under duress.

'Laurence was suffering from depression as a result of antecedent conflict.'

It was Narey's turn to sigh. Psychobabble, here we come, Narey thought.

'The concept of antecedent conflict is that it is categorised as resulting from a trauma suffered in childhood,' she argued. 'Are you saying that was what happened in Mr Paton's case?'

Irving's eyes grew wide but he kept his mouth firmly closed.

'Which university did you graduate from, Dr Irving?'

'Sorry?'

'Which university did you get your doctorate from?'

'I don't really see what that has to do with anything.'

'I was just curious.'

'Grantchester University.'

Narey feigned puzzlement.

'I must admit I'm not familiar with that particular establishment, Dr Irving. Is that one of the colleges that got upgraded to university status?'

The man squirmed uncomfortably but held his chin high.

'No. It's actually an American university. It's rather highly regarded.'

'Really? That must have been quite an experience, studying in the US. Which city were you in?'

Irving shook his head in exasperation and Narey could see his anger growing.

'I wasn't actually there,' he conceded irritably. 'It was a correspondence-based curriculum but nevertheless . . .'

'Ah, I see,' she let her words linger in the air for effect. 'As I was saying, are you telling me that Mr Paton's problems stemmed from an incident in his childhood? Or was it perhaps something later in his life? Which was it, Mr Irving?'

The man bridled at the lack of title and Narey relished his indignant fury.

'Doctor Irving,' he corrected her, his attempts at hiding his emotions crashing on the rocks of his ego. 'It's Doctor Irving.'

'My apologies, *Doctor*. Did you acquire that title from the same university as your degree?'

'Sergeant, I . . .'

Narey didn't want to hear his bleatings.

'When did this supposedly traumatic incident take place?'

'Later.'

'In his twenties?'

'Yes.'

'At the Lake of Menteith?'

Irving's eyes widened again. 'Yes, I think so. Yes.'

'Tell me what you know.'

Irving ran his hand anxiously through his thinning hair and his eyes scrunched closed.

'Laurence suffered from chronic sleep deprivation as a manifestation of trying to avoid particular recurring dreams. This had a damaging consequence on his health and his ability to function properly within a work environment. Criticism from school management was increasing his issues with self-esteem and also provoking unmanageable levels of stress, as he feared losing his job. I was helping him deal with these concerns.'

'What were the dreams?'

Irving looked into a corner of the ceiling as if seeking an escape route.

'Laurence told me he would constantly dream about walking on water. This is typically a dream indicating the subject has complete control of his or her emotions yet this was clearly not the case with Laurence. He . . .'

'Cut the bullshit, Doctor. We both know the water was frozen over.'

'Yes. He said that in his dream he was walking on a frozen lake. There was a girl by his side and they walked together to an island. They were surrounded by other people at first, who gradually left until there was just the two of them. He wouldn't dream about what happened on the island but the next thing he knew he would be walking back on his own and every footstep he took the ice would melt completely behind him and he would always be only inches away from falling into the lake.'

Narey was aware of the hairs standing up on the back of her neck.

'Was it your belief this dream was based on something that did actually occur?'

Irving's eyes fell to the floor.

'Did Paton ever tell you that he killed the girl on Inchmahome Island?'

'No.'

Narey stared hard at the therapist, forcing him to return her gaze.

'Did he ever tell you he *didn't* kill the girl?'

'No.'

'Did you ever ask either of those questions?'

'No.'

'Why the fuck not?'

'Because that wasn't my job. My brief wasn't to investigate the legal or moral questions of what may or may not have happened but rather to deal with the psychological consequences.'

'Yeah? Well, you should have fucking asked him anyway.'

Narey was still standing on the doorstep, her eyes boring into Irving's, when the man slammed the door in her face. She was left with her nose inches from a white door that was in dire need of a paint job.

'We'll talk again, *Mister* Irving,' she announced loudly, a grim but satisfied smile on her face. 'You can count on it.'

CHAPTER 20

'Irving is a fraud. A snake oil salesman with a pretend degree from a pretend online university and a doctorate you can bet he bought in hard cash. The man's no more a therapist than I am.'

They were sitting round Rachel's dining table again, their three-strong council of war reconvening after her meeting with Irving and Tony and Danny's return from investigations of their own.

'You didn't like him much then, Rach?'

'I wouldn't piss on him if he was on fire.'

'Very ladylike.'

'Oh sod off, Tony. The guy's a creep and I've not had the best of days.'

Winter could hear the tension in her voice. He was well used to dealing with the fallout from the stress Rachel worked under on a daily basis but this was different.

'So apart from really disliking the guy, what did you get from him?'

'He says Paton never admitted to killing Lily but I'm not sure I believe him. In fact, I don't think I believe a single word that came out of his mouth. What did you get on him, Danny?'

Neilson had spent the previous two days chasing paper trails all over town and talking to people who knew people who would know things about the likes of Irving.

'Okay . . .' Danny cleared his throat theatrically. 'Presenting Mr Kyle Irving.'

Rachel and Tony sat back in their chairs, their body language letting Neilson know he had the floor and their complete attention.

'He's fifty-five years old. Divorced, with one daughter he doesn't see very often. Before he decided he was a psychologist, he used to work in sales, moving around between a couple of insurance companies and a medical supplies business. He was born and bred in Glasgow and, except for a short spell in London in the nineties, he hasn't wandered very far from home.

'As Rachel learned when she visited him, Irving's degree and his title aren't exactly what they seem. In fact, they are a pile of shite. Not worth the paper they're written on, which is a few quid and nothing more. There's nothing illegal about what he's doing but it's pretty dodgy all the same. It's the poor saps he's scamming money from that you have to feel sorry for.'

'So how many people is he "counselling"?' asked Tony.

'I was just coming to that, Anthony,' Danny growled at him. 'I suppose the answer is too many or not enough, depending on your point of view. I couldn't get a handle on how many clients he has because he is a one-man bandit. I spoke to an old contact in the psychobabble business and she reckoned he could easily be stringing along dozens, probably hundreds, maybe more. The way the whole

Internet thing works, he could be conning mugs from here to China.'

'I think I need to pay Mr Irving another visit,' Rachel sighed. 'See if my first call has got him rattled enough to tell me the truth.'

They all fell quiet again. The more they found out, the more they knew they still had to learn. A fresh round of beer and tea was set on the table and consumed in silence until Rachel broke it again.

'Okay, Tony,' she turned to him. 'Your turn. What have you got?'

Winter sighed theatrically.

'Okay, well, first of all I took a chance with Paton's email account.' Rachel and Danny looked at him curiously.

'I still had his login details and his password, and I figured I could use them. Someone was blackmailing Paton but that didn't mean the blackmailer knew he was dead. Or if the other three names on the email did. So I sent a message to all of them. From Paton.'

Danny was smiling and Rachel's eyebrows were arched in surprise and dubious approval.

'I got one reply but I don't think it takes us anywhere.'

'Which one?' Rachel asked.

'Adamski. It was sent directly to Paton and not copied to any of the others. It simply said, "Leave me alone". No signature; nothing else. The others might still reply but, so far, that's it.'

'That big build-up for nothing,' Danny sighed. 'I guess it was worth a try. So do you have good news to go with your bad?'

'Well, I also got the crappy lead to look into, of course. This bollocks about Lily being the daughter of gypsies, killed because she wanted to run away with some *gajo*.'

'*Gajo*?' Rachel asked.

Tony grinned.

'I've been doing my research. *Gajo* is the Romany word for a non-gypsy. Like Muggles in Harry Potter, I suppose. Anyway, I've been online to see what I could find out.'

'And?'

'And it's quite interesting actually. There are reckoned to be up to twenty-three thousand travellers in Scotland, all in. But they're broken down into different groups. First up there's your gypsy travellers, far and away the biggest group. They are gypsies by birth or, very rarely, by marriage. They have their own cultural identity and there's a big emphasis on extended families and clan links. They're the ones that have your big fat gypsy weddings and put a curse on you if you don't buy clothes pegs from them. That's a load of old-fashioned bollocks, of course, but you can't beat a good stereotype.

'There are New Age travellers, your anti-war hippy types. There aren't too many of those and they and your traditional traveller families don't really see eye to eye. Then there are fairground travellers, show people. When they're not on the road, they mostly live here in Glasgow, even though most people don't know it. There's a tonne of them in Dalmarnock around Swanston Street, Shore Street and Cotton Street. One article I read reckoned a third of the local population there was show folk.'

'So which group are we looking at?' Danny asked him.

'Gypsy travellers, if the rumourmongers in Callander are right. But even then there's lots of different ethnic groups within that group. Ready? There are Irish Travellers, Romany Chals, Border Gypsies and Welsh Kale Romanies. You can learn a shitload of stuff on the Internet.'

'I don't doubt it,' Danny grumbled. 'But you said it was quite interesting. So how about getting to the interesting part?'

Winter blew out hard.

'Tough crowd. Okay. Most of them are regularly on the move, usually staying in one place for less than a year, sometimes only for five minutes. But the local authorities provide them with official sites so they can settle for a few months and get the kids into schools. I had a hunt round the Port of Menteith area and there are a few official sites for travelling people not too far away but one in particular caught my eye.'

Winter paused as he looked at the other two to make sure they were listening.

'You waiting for a drum roll, son? Spit it out.'

'Aye, okay. There is an official site for travellers in Stirling – in Riverside.'

Narey and Neilson stared at him, seeing the smile slowly appear on Winter's face.

'It's on a bit of land set back from Abbey Road. Less than two hundred yards from Laurence Paton's house.'

Tony leaned back in his chair, a self-satisfied look on his face.

'Probably a complete coincidence,' Rachel countered.

'Almost certainly,' agreed Danny.

Tony's expression lapsed into crestfallen and stayed that

way until Rachel and Danny couldn't contain themselves any longer and sniggered.

'Never trust anything that looks like a coincidence, you know that,' Danny told him. 'How about you and me take a wee drive back out to Stirling?'

Tony grinned.

CHAPTER 21

Thursday 6 December

Winter and Neilson turned left over the bridge before Stirling railway station and drove carefully down the hill into Riverside. The Ochils loomed in front of them, caked in white like giant iced cakes, a pink haze rising over them, suggesting yet more snow could be on its way. The streets hadn't been clear of the white stuff in nearly a week now; it lay piled up and frozen within a few feet of the kerbs on both sides of the road. Driving was a nightmare on the roads that remained open and there had already been several lives lost because of it. Worse still, there was no sign of the freeze beginning to ease.

It had been a week since the pair of them had last been in Stirling, paying an unauthorised late-night visit to Laurence Paton's house. This time it was mid-afternoon but the light was already fading fast and it would probably be dark within an hour. Daylight in Scotland in deep midwinter lasted less than a third of a day and even that was assuming the rare appearance of the sun.

They both cast a glance left towards where Wallace Place lay behind the Edwardian terrace that ran the length of the left-hand side of Abbey Road. On the right was a cycle shop and Danny parked opposite it, leaving a hundred yards or so to go to the opening that would take them into the recessed parcel of land that formed the travellers' site. Neilson and Winter emerged somewhat reluctantly from the relative warmth of the car and zipped up their jackets, Danny pulling a woollen hat over his head as they carefully negotiated the icy pavements.

The entrance to the site, wide enough to take mobile homes, chalets and caravans, was guarded on both sides by a seven-foot-high wall. As Winter and Neilson passed through the opening, they saw a large piece of land with a number of static mobile homes plus caravans of all sizes, trailers, a couple of pieces of what seemed to be fairground equipment and half a dozen cars. Not surprisingly perhaps, given the weather, there was no one to be seen and the two men looked at each other as if deciding which door they should try first. Danny hesitated, then nodded towards the biggest of the caravans, a grubby once-white vehicle on their right that had clearly seen better days. Winter shrugged as if to say 'why not' but before they were halfway there they were stopped in their tracks by a voice from behind them.

'What do you want?'

The pair spun round to see a stocky fair-haired man in his mid-thirties advancing on them. He had clearly stepped out from one of the vehicles to their left. The freezing temperatures didn't seem to bother him as he walked directly over to Winter and Neilson wearing just jeans and a checked shirt.

He didn't stop until he was within a couple of feet of them.

'I said, "What do you want?"'

The man's tone was hostile and Winter could see Danny bristling at his manner. Danny was getting on a bit but that wouldn't stop him from having a go at this guy, no matter that he looked like he could be trouble. There was a scar running under the stranger's left eye and his muscular frame complemented his threatening demeanour; it was more than enough to make Winter think twice about tackling him.

'We're just looking for some information,' Danny told the man without taking a backward step, his voice controlled and non-confrontational but firm.

'You all right, Jered? What's going on?'

Someone else had stepped out of a caravan: a tall, young guy with short dark hair and a sullen expression. This has gone well, Winter thought. Inside the site two minutes and already they were being faced down.

'I'm all right, Peter,' the first man told him. 'Asked these gentlemen a reasonable question but I don't have a proper answer yet.'

'Is that right? Well maybe they should just leave before I make them leave.'

Danny turned to the younger man, an amused smile on his face.

'Now why would you want to make us leave, son? That's hardly hospitable, is it?'

The slim teenager squared up to Danny but was met with a scornful grin that stopped just short of laughing in his face. Before Peter realised it had happened, Danny had reached out a hand and gently tapped the young guy's cheek with his open hand.

'Hey, cut that out,' Peter yelped, stepping back and looking at Danny warily. Neilson simply looked at him and turned back to the man he had called Jered.

'You're right,' he told him. 'You're entitled to a proper answer. We're looking for information about a missing girl.'

'What makes you think she's here?' the aggressive tone was still evident in Jered's voice. If anything, it had hardened.

'We don't. We know she's not here but we hoped you could give us some help finding her. She disappeared a long time ago.'

Jered stared Danny down as he weighed up what he was being told.

'How long ago?'

'Nineteen years?'

Jered's face screwed up in surprise.

'Nineteen years ago? Are you fucking kidding me?'

'Nope.'

'So who is this girl?'

'That's what we're hoping you'll tell us. We think she might have been a traveller.'

Jered looked from Neilson to Winter and back again, chewing on the corner of his mouth. He finally nodded, as much to himself as to the two strangers on his site.

'You'd better come see Uncle then. He's the only one here who might be able to help you. You mind your manners though.'

'I always do,' Danny told him.

Winter and Neilson fell into line behind Jered as he led

them to the large, grimy caravan that had been their first choice. Peter, the angry teenager, watched them balefully, his angst increased by another smirk in his direction from Danny. Jered stopped on the steps to the vehicle and turned.

'Wait there.'

He stepped inside the caravan, closing the door behind him. Neilson and Winter exchanged glances, both wondering what the hell was going to happen next. The difference between them was that Danny seemed to be enjoying himself. Winter settled for moving from foot to foot in an attempt to stop the cold of the snow creeping in through his shoes.

The door opened again and Jered's stern face poked out, gesturing them inside. Winter and Neilson climbed the short steps. The caravan was surprisingly warm, thanks no doubt to the paraffin they could smell as soon as they entered. It was also dark and it took a few seconds for their eyes to adjust after the bright snow-light of outside. When they did, they saw an old man with long grey hair sitting in a battered brown leather armchair by the heater, a blanket wrapped around his shoulders and a steaming mug in his hands. With his dark eyes, sallow skin and long hair, he immediately reminded Winter of a Native American stuck on a white man's reservation.

'This is Tommy Baillie,' Jered explained, taking up a place at the man's shoulder.

'I'm Danny Neilson. This is Tony Winter.'

'Polis?' the old fellow asked them pleasantly.

'No.'

'Sit down, sit down. Can I offer you some tea?'

Both men declined as Danny took a soft, green chair facing the man across the heater while Winter made do with perching on a stack of boxes that wobbled slightly as he sat down. Baillie eyed them slowly as he cradled the mug in his hands, peering at them over its rim.

'Young Jered tells me you're looking for a lost girl,' he said softly.

'Not so much lost as unidentified,' Danny replied. 'Her body was found nineteen years ago.'

Baillie sipped some more of his tea, his eyes closing momentarily as he swallowed.

'Long time ago,' he told them.

'Not that long,' Danny countered. 'Not when you get to our age.'

'Ha,' Baillie cackled. 'Our age? You're just a boy, Danny boy. Cannae be much over sixty while I'll no see seventy again. So who was this girl?'

'She was found at Inchmahome on the Lake of Menteith. It was all over the news at the time.'

'I've not got a television set and I never buy a newspaper,' Baillie replied. 'I've got a radio right enough but that's for the music, not for the news.'

That seemed to be all the old boy had to say on the matter and his attentions had returned to the contents of his mug, alternately blowing and taking wary sips. Then he abruptly stopped mid-sip and looked up at them.

'Where are you gentlemen from?' Baillie asked them. 'Are those Glasgow accents I hear?'

'Yes, they are.'

'Glasgow. Interesting. Interesting.'

Tommy resumed his pedestrian swallowing of the tea, seemingly lost in thought.

'This girl of yours. She was murdered?'

'Aye, she was.'

'A terrible thing. And ye think she was a traveller, this *chavi*, this girl?'

'We think she might have been, yes.'

'Interesting. Interesting. Do you have children of your own, gentlemen?'

'I do,' Neilson told him. 'A daughter. Tony is burden-free.'

'A burden?' Baillie repeated. 'Well, maybe they are at times, right enough. A joy one day and a burden the next but a responsibility till the end of time. Is that not right? Children are very important in the travelling community, Mr Neilson. We are an honourable, proud people and it is my job to protect and preserve the traveller way of life. We live as a culture. It would be a terrible, terrible thing indeed if a young *chavi* was killed like you say. That would be an eternal curse on every one of us.'

'That would be the case in every community, Mr Baillie,' Neilson told him. 'I'm sure we would all want justice if that happened.'

Baillie either didn't hear Danny or, more likely, just ignored him.

'My duty is to protect our children from damaging outside influences. Do you understand? There's a family member, a young cousin of Jered here, who has got himself into serious trouble. Or so we hear anyway. The boy – Sam Dunbar – isn't in touch with the family. But that doesn't mean we don't care. Our problem is that if we go in there to try to sort it . . .'

'All sorts of things could kick off.' Neilson finished the

sentence for him. 'What sort of trouble is it that you think the boy is in?'

The old fellow tilted his head to one side and puffed out his cheeks.

'Narky stuff. Very bad.'

'We're hearing that he's got himself in with some heavy criminals,' Jered grudgingly explained from behind Baillie. 'Sam was always handy with his fists when he was growing up but, if what we're told is right, then he's using more than his fists now. The family in Glasgow say that he's being paid to hurt people. We don't even know where he's living now but we know that he's not with his own.'

'So how have you heard this?' Winter asked, curious despite himself.

'Sam's cousin Noah met him in a pub in Possilpark,' Jered continued. 'Said that Sam had a cut on his neck, a recent one that looked bad. He asked about it and Sam had joked that "it came with the territory". Course Noah asked him what he meant but he wasn't for saying. But Noah said Sam had a pile of cash on him and was flashing it about. Noah did some asking around and was told that Sam was paid to make sure people coughed up or cut them if they'd got out of line.'

'What pub were they in?'

'A place called The Brothers on Saracen Street. You know it?'

'Aye. Lovely place,' Danny answered with more than a hint of irony. 'So I'm guessing there's a reason you're telling us all this, Mr Baillie.'

The old man smiled sweetly.

'I can see why you used to be a polisman, Mr Neilson.'

'I didn't say I was a policeman. I only said I wasn't one now.'

'Oh, I know,' Baillie smiled again. 'But if you live as long as I have, you tend to have a nose for these things.'

The old guy was sharp, that was for sure.

'Fair enough,' Danny nodded. 'So, the reason you're telling us this . . .'

'Like I said, it's my job to protect the family and the traveller way of life. Young Sam's not a bad lad, just a bit . . . headstrong. If he keeps doing what we hear he's doing, then he'll get himself killed. And he'll also bring *lashav* on us: shame. The traveller reputation is bad enough already with all the lies people tell. Thing is, I can't go to the polis even if I thought they'd be interested. There's not what you'd call a mutual trust there and I'm trying to keep Sam out of the jail as well as out of the grave. I also need to stop Jered here and the others from going into Glasgow and making things worse. What I need is someone else: someone who knows Glasgow and would know how to find things out. A person like that would be useful and I'd certainly owe them a debt.'

Winter and Neilson looked at each other.

'So you would be able to offer something in return, Mr Baillie?' Danny asked.

'It would be the honourable thing to do, Mr Neilson. Our clan is many and wide. I think there may be something in what you say about a young girl who disappeared. I'd be prepared to find out more and tell you what you need to hear.'

Winter snapped at the man.

'If you know something, maybe you should just tell us now. The girl was murdered, for fucksake!'

146

Jered pushed himself in front of Baillie, squaring up to Winter until they were standing nose to nose.

'I told you to mind your manners,' he growled.

'No. You told *him* to mind his manners,' Winter corrected him.

'Now, now Jered,' Tommy Baillie soothed. 'Come away from the young man. I'm sure Mr Neilson realises the way these things work. Young folk, eh, Mr Neilson? All that hot blood isn't good for them at all.'

'Right enough, Mr Baillie. You're right enough. Here's what we'll do for you: we'll make some discreet enquiries about your boy Sam. I can't make any promises about what happens to him though. If he's as full of that hot blood as you say, then he'll have to make that decision himself.'

Baillie nodded sagely.

'So very true, Mr Neilson. We can show the young the paths they should take but only they can walk them. You are a gentleman. And I will make . . . how did you put it now, "discreet enquiries" about the young lady.'

Danny put an arm between Tony and Jered, separating them and forcing both to take a step backward.

'Okay. We'll be on our way, Mr Baillie, but we'll be back. One last thing: do you know anything about a man who lived near here by the name of Laurence Paton?'

'No. Never heard of him. How about you, Jered?'

Jered shook his head, still scowling at Winter.

'No. Like Uncle says, never heard of him.'

Winter and Neilson emerged into the travellers' site, the cold immediately attacking them after the warmth of the caravan. As they negotiated the icy steps into the yard, they saw Peter and two other young men standing watching them. The three of them took a few steps towards their visitors but stopped in their tracks when Neilson gave them a cheery wave. Instead, they settled for glaring at the incomers and making a show of seeing them off the premises.

As they were about to exit the site, Winter looked back over his shoulder and nudged Neilson.

'Old Tommy said he didn't own a television set, right? So how come there's a TV aerial stuck on the top of his caravan?'

'I know, son. I saw it on the way in. The lying old bugger was pulling our chain from the moment we walked in there. He either knows a whole lot more or a whole lot less than he's telling us.'

CHAPTER 22

Friday 7 December

The road to Dundee took Narey past Stirling. As the motorway cruised above the ancient capital, the castle resplendent high on the rock but still below her, she couldn't help but think of Laurence Paton. Her dad had been right about him all along. His nose had told him Paton was involved. No one had been able to prove it back then but she was determined she would now. She would also deal with anything else that crawled out from under the same stone Paton had been hiding under.

The drive north wasn't one she took often but this point in the road, towering above the Highland fault line, with the sweep of the Ochils to her right, Stirling Castle and the Wallace Monument ahead of her and the mountains of Ben Lomond, Ben Vorlich and Ben Ledi beyond, was her favourite. That day, with seemingly every inch of the Bens covered in snow against an icy blue backdrop and frozen fields below, it looked even more spectacular than usual. They used to call

Stirling the gateway to the Highlands and high on the M80 you could see why. Narey hoped it would prove to be a gateway of sorts for her too.

Professor Kirsten Fairweather had sounded friendly enough on the phone and certainly seemed intrigued by the little Narey had told her. She'd been unwilling to commit herself to getting involved until she'd heard the whole story so Narey was on her way north to convince her face to face. The whole sorry mess and all its implications were too much to attempt over a telephone.

It wasn't the easiest of drives with snow by the side of the motorway and so much buzzing through her head; she tried to clear the latter by turning the car's CD player up to full blast. Even the contrasting efforts of Kings of Leon, Take That and Plan B couldn't dismiss thoughts of Paton and his blackmailer or the wretched remains of Lily of the Lake – or her dad. The guilt of him being in the home was eating away at her. Narey also felt for Tony, remorseful about dragging him and Danny into this and knowing she should never have persuaded them to break into Paton's house. What the hell had she been thinking? There was just too much bloody guilt flying around and little of it seemed to be attached to those who deserved it.

Somehow, she managed to negotiate the M80 and the M9 safely and a little less than an hour and a half after she'd left Glasgow behind, Dundee loomed into view. She'd never really been one for going along with the usual Glaswegian habit of ridiculing Dundee, making gags about unmarried mothers and it being stuck in the eighties.

Her mum and dad had often taken her to Broughty Ferry

for summer holidays as a child; long days on the beach with fish suppers at Murray's chippy on Gray Street and ice cream from Vissochi's, which was further along on the other side of the road. It was at Vissochi's that she'd lost a wobbly tooth while munching her way through the biggest knickerbocker glory she'd ever seen and had hidden it in case her mum made her stop eating. Holidays in the Ferry had meant regular trips into Dundee and she'd liked the place. Glasgow it wasn't but not so bad for all that.

For years now it had understandably campaigned to get rid of its old tag as the city of 'jute, jam and journalism' and had rebranded itself the City of Discovery, owing to the fact that it had Scott of the Antarctic's old boat as a tourist attraction. Narey couldn't help but wonder what discoveries the city had in store.

CAHiD stood for the Centre for Anatomy and Human Identification and was based in the College of Life Sciences, not far from the main University of Dundee building. A fearsome-looking middle-aged receptionist regarded Narey with some suspicion when she claimed she had an appointment to see Professor Fairweather. The woman directed Narey into a chair and said she would see if the professor was expecting anyone. Narey conceded to herself that her telephone chat with the prof might well have bypassed the front desk but she still wondered if everyone was subjected to this guard dog treatment.

The question was registered redundant a few minutes later when the receptionist was beaten back to the desk by a smiling blonde woman in jeans and a T-shirt, her hand outstretched in greeting. The frosty guard dog was trotting

151

menacingly at her heels, clearly not happy at anyone else being welcomed into the house.

'Sergeant Narey? I'm Kirsty. Come on through.'

'Call me Rachel, please. Thanks for taking the time to see me.'

'No probs. What you told me on the phone sounds very interesting, if mysterious. Annabelle, if anyone's looking for me for the next . . .' she looked at Narey questioningly, 'hour? Yes, the next hour, then tell them I've flown to Baghdad.'

The receptionist nodded truculently and Narey took the opportunity to smile broadly and ironically at Annabelle as she passed on her way into the professor's office. The old bag did her best to smile back grudgingly but failed miserably.

'Sorry about Annabelle,' Kirsty Fairweather said breezily as the door closed. 'I inherited her from my predecessor and she's a pain in the arse. Very efficient and all that but not exactly friendly. She thinks I should still be in school rather than running a university department.'

Narey wasn't sure what she'd expected but Kirsty wasn't it. Still, Fairweather's reputation preceded her and Narey had read enough to know that the prof had been there, done it and bought the T-shirt. She'd worked in Iraq and Afghanistan on behalf of the United Nations, identifying bodies of victims as a prelude to war crimes tribunals, as well as featuring in some heavy duty murder trials in the UK – clearly not just a pretty face.

It struck Narey that it was a wonder the press hadn't cottoned on to Fairweather's youth and good looks and plastered her across the tabloids. She must have been fighting the bastards off with a stick, Narey thought.

'Right, so tell me about your girl. I did a bit of Googling about her before you got here but it was all from donkey's years ago so I thought I'd better wait and get the lowdown from you. They call her Lily, don't they?'

'The press did, yes. As in Lily of the Lake. It stuck. There was huge publicity, initially all over the UK, *Crimewatch* and the like, but after a while only in Scotland. Despite all that, she was never identified.'

'Which is why you're here?'

'Basically, yes.'

'And what about the non-basic?'

Narey didn't much like being on the receiving end of an interrogation.

'I have a personal interest in the case. I'd rather not go into it. All you need to know is that I am determined to find out who Lily was. And who killed her. She was brutally murdered and the person who killed her has never been caught.'

Fairweather held up a sheet of paper in front of her.

'I know. I took the liberty of pulling copies of some of her file. Hope you don't mind.'

Narey did mind. She had been hoping to keep this all under the radar as far as Central Scotland cops were concerned. The professor seemed to read her thoughts.

'I've got a few contacts on CID over there and one or two of them owe me favours,' Fairweather told her. 'I asked a DI if he'd get me these with no questions asked and he agreed. You might know him – Marty Croy?'

Narey shook her head brusquely and Fairweather read the gesture for what it was.

'He won't say anything, Rachel. Not until you want him to.'

Narey gave a curt nod. She didn't have much option but to accept it.

'Have you seen these?' the professor asked, holding the sheet up again. 'It's pretty nasty stuff.'

Narey didn't say anything but held out her hand, trying to suppress the small surge of excitement in her stomach and thinking about how Tony felt in the same circumstances. Perhaps the only difference was she at least had the decency to feel guilty about it.

Fairweather passed the A4 sheet of paper over along with a handful of others. As she turned them, Narey saw that they were all high-quality prints of the original police photographs, all images of the batterered, bludgeoned head and decaying figure of the girl known as Lily.

'Jesus,' she gasped involuntarily, immediately annoyed at herself. She'd seen plenty of dead bodies.

'Not nice, is it?' Fairweather sympathised. 'I've seen plenty and I'm sure you have too but there's something particularly nasty about that being done to a girl half our age.'

Narey couldn't disagree with the professor's sentiments. She was faced with a picture of horror and its constituent parts leapt at her from the page: blackened, receding skin; broken bone; one blind eye; dirt-streaked blonde hair; bite marks.

Something lurched deep inside Narey, something far deeper than the guilty adrenalin rush at seeing these photographs. It was a memory and a knowledge and a determination all rolled into one instant. Danny Neilson had been right with something he'd said to her: in her desperation to help her dad and prove he'd been right about Paton, she was in danger of forgetting the girl at the heart of it. Her intention was right but her motive had been all wrong.

'Pictures of Lily,' Narey murmured.

'Sorry?'

'It's an old song. By The Who, I think. Sorry, I don't know what made me think of that.'

'Before my time,' Fairweather grinned, her smile slowly disappearing, morphing into a frown. She looked at Narey.

'Rachel, if you want my help to find out who she was and who did this to her, then I'm in.'

Narey's eyes closed as she bobbed her head in agreement.

'I do. I wanted to do all this myself but I'm not sure that's possible. I do want your help.'

Another lengthy pause hung between them as Fairweather weighed up whether to ask the question Narey's response begged of her. She decided against it.

'Okay. It will take a bit of time and we'll need Central's permission to get the body exhumed. Marty Croy can help with that and it's probably best if you meet him. From what I can see from the photographs, it should be a piece of cake.'

'You'll be able to put a face to her?'

'I'm sure of it. There will be an amount of guesswork but it will be fairly accurate. The frustrating thing is that it could have been done back then with the right knowhow. It was what it was back in the nineties. We could and would have done so much more with her today. But, all being well, we still can.'

155

'How long will it take?'

Fairweather smiled. 'When it comes to this kind of thing, the old cliché is right: the difficult we can do right away, the impossible takes a little longer. Assuming we are able to exhume her and the skeleton is in good condition, I'll be able to give you a sketch by the next day. A 3D model will take a while longer. To be honest, and I'm not sure I care how terrible this sounds, I can't wait to dig her up and begin to put her together again.'

The professor's chilling enthusiasm reminded Narey of someone else and she made a mental note to keep the two of them apart. Fairweather was young, blonde, pretty and with a ghoulish interest in death. There was no way she was introducing Professor Kirsty to Tony.

'Kirsty, given that you'd already gone to the trouble to find out so much about the case, why did you ask me to tell you all about her?'

Fairweather grinned.

'I wanted to know the stuff that isn't in here.' She indicated the files. 'You know better than I do that case notes only tell you so much.'

'Like my reasons for being involved?'

'Yes. I like cold cases, Rachel. They tickle my bones. Partly it's because I like the idea that the victims aren't forgotten. The very fact that we get involved shows me that someone cares enough to dig them up. I'm always fascinated by the reason why.'

'It's my job,' Narey replied flatly. 'That's reason enough.'

Fairweather smiled and they both knew it was more than that.

'Okay, fair enough,' the professor nodded. 'Let's get to work. I'll set up a meeting for you with Marty Croy and hopefully that will be the first step to bringing your Lily back. "Pictures of Lily" – that's what you said, right? I'll get those for you.'

CHAPTER 23

It took only two rings before Tony picked up. Rachel was sitting in her Megane on the top floor of the multi-storey car park in Bell Street, shivering while snowflakes were swatted away from her windscreen by groaning wipers.

'Hi. It's me.'

'I know. Display, remember. How did you get on with your professor?'

'She's going to do it.'

He could hear the excitement in her voice and was pleased for her. Although he was also increasingly worried she was investing too much of herself in this and he hated to think how she'd be if it didn't pan out as she hoped. Still, they both needed her to know that he was on her side about it.

'Great. That's brilliant news, Rach. How long does she reckon she will need to do it?'

'It all depends on how long it will take for her to convince Central to get their arses into gear. After that it hopefully won't be more than a matter of days.'

'What was she like?'

Rachel hesitated.

'She was fine. Nice. It's snowing a bloody blizzard up here. What's the weather like back in civilisation?'

'Freezing but not snowing at the moment.'

'Good. Have you managed to find the other emails between Paton and Irving?'

'Give me a chance! I'm not sure where the hell to start but it's do-able in theory. The emails still exist somewhere out there in cyberspace. We just need to find out where.'

'Find them for me? Please?'

'I'll try. When are you coming back down the road?'

'Right now. What are you up to?'

'Just sitting in my office waiting for a call so I can get away from this bloody filing. I'm bored off my tits.'

She laughed at him down the end of the phone.

'Sitting there praying for a nice car crash or a stabbing?'

'No,' he answered defensively. 'Well, yes. A bit.'

'Sick fucker,' she laughed again and then she was gone.

She was right though. If there was a choice between admin or photographing the fallout from Glasgow's endless affection for violence, then it was a no-brainer. The truth was that he'd have chosen it over most things. As if on cue, the office door burst open and Paul Burke stuck his head round the door.

'All right? Shift your arse. We've got a job.'

'Something interesting?'

'Suicide.'

Winter groaned. Suicides were far and away his least favourite subject matter. The fact that they intended their own demise took all the fun out of it for him.

'Well, if you don't want it, fair enough,' Burke told him.

'Two Soups will be more than happy to have me doing the photos and we all know how much you hate that.'

Campbell Baxter never wanted Winter on any job but that wasn't what Burke was getting at – there was something else here. The grin playing round the edges of Burke's mouth told Winter that he was at it. And there was also a glint in the man's eye that suggested he was excited about this job, whatever it was. Burke was probably the only one on the forensic team whose appetite for gore came anywhere near to matching Winter's.

'So what aren't you telling me, Burkey?'

Burke grinned even wider.

'It's a belter.'

The hairs on the back of Winter's neck instantly stood up.

'Better than the samurai guy?'

'Way better.'

'What is it?'

'Someone stepped out in front of an express train at Cambuslang station. Body parts spread to the winds. Interested now?'

Winter was out of his chair and pulling on his coat in one swift movement. He was halfway to the door and past Burke before the forensic even had time to laugh.

'I'll take that as a "yes" then, shall I?'

'Take it as anything you want,' Winter shouted back at him over his shoulder. 'But get a move on.'

Burke filled him in on what had happened as they drove to Cambuslang. The station had gained a reputation for jumpers over the years and a lot of drivers hated going through it. The express would belt through the platform at top speed and if someone were crazy enough to step in front of a train, then they'd be wiped out immediately.

It was the certainty of death that attracted them to it. A thousand tonnes of metal hitting twelve stones of flesh, tissue and brittle bone at nearly a hundred miles an hour wasn't much of a contest. Sometimes the train would do such a number on the body that forensic teams were called in just to prove it had actually happened. Traumatised drivers would tell of someone stepping in front of their train but there would be no physical sign of it having taken place. The body could instantly be vaporised on the windscreen, leaving nothing but trace elements that could be washed away by a shower of rain.

That was all assuming that the jumper got it right.

Death didn't become such a certainty if you stepped in front of the wrong train. If it was a slow train, then that could mean broken bones, paraplegia, brain injuries; any number of things that stopped short of death, worse than death. So, it became apparent the would-be jumpers did their home-work first, stalking out station platforms, getting to know which trains stopped and which didn't, memorising the express timetables and also the goods diesels that thundered through without even blinking at the platform. They prom-ised the sweet certainty of an instantaneous demise.

There could be halfway houses though. If the jumper stepped out a fraction too soon, then they fell under the wheels and ended up cut in two – or three. But the real kicker was when they stepped out a fraction too late, perhaps held back by fear or a last-second change of heart. Then the train might catch them a glancing blow, albeit a thousand tonne–hundred miles an hour glance that could be very messy indeed. Then people standing on station platforms had been known to have been showered in blood, bone and entrails as the jumper was ripped to bits.

Stations like Linlithgow on the Glasgow–Edinburgh line had seen their share of jumpers over the years. It was a busy platform, with commuter crowds to provide camouflage for the desperate, yet at the same time express trains battered through without a care in the world. Cambuslang, in the east end of the city, fitted the profile on the West Coast Main Line. Not the way out of Central Station towards London though, as you couldn't be sure that the express had built up a proper head of steam; instead you would wait on the west-bound platform for it to make its return journey, ready to catch it before it puts its brakes on ahead of Dalmarnock. You're not in a hurry if you've got nowhere to go.

Winter and Burke didn't say much on the drive over from Pitt Street. Once Burke had filled him in on what had happened, they both lapsed into a brooding silence, their minds full of possibilities. Although they both had an appetite for what lay ahead, Burke's was professional while Winter's was obsessional. Burke would enjoy the unusual, visceral nature of the case; Winter would positively feast upon it.

As soon as they got on to Main Street in Cambuslang, the quiet organised chaos of the newly formed crime scene loomed large before them and they could see officers direct-ing traffic and a few white-suited worker bees already busying themselves with the business of death.

Winter's itch flared and he found himself hoping the carnage was every bit as bad as Burke had promised. The forensic pulled into the first available space, not having to worry about the double yellows because of the badge displayed on his windscreen. The pair tumbled out of the car and Winter hurriedly grabbed his camera bag from the boot.

As they ducked under the tape, Winter looked to his left and saw a woman standing, ashen-faced, a shopping bag in her hand, fifty yards or so away. She seemed to be rooted still in shock and the hairs on Winter's neck tingled as he looked at her and wondered what she'd seen. He wanted to stand and stare at her but Burke called him on and in seconds they were running down the stairs to the station concourse, landing on the grim brick reality of Cambuslang station, all blackened stone and dreary concrete – a depressing sight at the best of times.

An anxious huddle of people, maybe a dozen of them, were standing against a wall, corralled there by two uniformed police officers, one of them taking notes at the front of the line. Winter could see the emotions on the would-be commuters' faces ranged from disbelief to nervous excitement. A burly figure in a white coverall was waving his arms around theatrically, gesturing angrily at those near him to get a move on. Campbell Baxter's actions were those of a man under pressure. He turned at the sound of Winter and Burke coming down the stairs, a glare immediately attaching itself to his face.

'About time,' he snapped at them. 'Get yourselves covered up. Winter, do what you have to do but get it done quickly. There's work to be done so I can get these people out of here.'

As ever, Two Soups had little regard for Winter's photography skills and, as ever, Winter would pay him no heed and take as much time as he felt necessary. It was an arrangement only one of them was happy with.

'Where's the train?' Winter asked him, regretting the stupidity of the question as soon as it was out of his mouth.

'Glasgow Central,' Baxter told him condescendingly. 'It was halfway there before anyone knew anything about it. It can't stop on a sixpence, you know. It will be examined, and photographed, there.'

Baxter caught the look of annoyance that crossed Winter's face.

'Oh, don't worry, Mr Winter,' Two Soups replied tersely. 'There's more than enough here to be keeping you busy. We haven't found all of him yet. Speak to the sergeant. He'll point you in the right direction. Well . . . directions.'

Sergeant Willie Scott was old school, the kind of copper who had been round the block twice and hadn't been surprised by any of it the first time round. He nodded his head at Winter as he saw him approach, giving off nothing more than an air of mild bemusement at what was going on around him.

'Awrite, son? I hope you've got plenty of film in that camera of yours. This poor bastard is in more bits than ten jigsaw sets.'

'We don't use film,' Winter started to tell him. 'It's all digi—'

'I know, son,' Scott wearily interrupted him. 'I'm not completely fucking stupid. Right, here's the script. The guy was thought to be in his forties, stepped in front of the big choo choo train and was smashed to smithereens. We think his torso was blown away but there's a hand way down the far end of the platform and something that might be a bit of shoulder near it. There's pieces of him up on the main street too. We haven't got a head and maybe we won't get one. That do you?'

Winter nodded, trying not to give away the surge of adrenalin that was coursing through him. The general view of him among the cops was probably strange enough without making it worse. He turned and headed for the end of the platform where the suicide guy's hand was.

The platform end was unguarded and Winter could hear the echo of his own feet as he approached, their beat marching in time to the pounding of his heart. There it was, right enough, a hand cut clean off just above the wrist. Whatever shirt or jacket had been worn by the arm it was attached to had gone. The hand was already deadly pale. The colour, or lack of it, reminded Winter of the woman outside the railway station and he craved to see what she had seen.

The fingers of the severed hand were pointing to the sky, its pallid flesh torn where it had skidded along the rough concrete, seeping tears of candy apple red. Winter zoomed right on it, capturing every pore, seeing it was a left hand and noting the soft skin and absence of any calluses. The owner, whatever he did, wasn't used to hard labour.

The hand was tense, as if beginning to form a claw, perhaps a last-minute change of heart or simply the natural instinct for survival, fighting against the desire for death. The crash of nerve endings, tissue, bone and tendons that were exposed above the wrist didn't display a clean break but a messy one; the victim of the bludgeon rather than the guillotine. Winter popped a yellow photographic marker down beside the hand and moved on in search of more.

It didn't take him long to find the bloodied piece of fresh meat that was indeed a shoulder, stripped bare and broken off as easily as a piece of bread being torn into chunks. The remaining flesh carried no identifying marks, no moles or tattoos, and being devoid of visible expression it didn't interest Winter much beyond the macabre nature of its demise. He picked over the rest of the platform, seeing and photographing shards of bone and slithers of skin, leaving markers at each of them.

As he walked back down the platform towards the shocked huddle of passengers, he held his camera at waist height and fired off shot after shot at the waiting crowd, looking the other way and vainly trying to cover the shutter noise with a cough. The allure for him had always been as much the witnesses as the victim, relishing the voyeurism among the rubberneckers and taking some consolation that they shared his grubby fascination for the ghoulish.

Winter's hero was the great Mexican tabloid photographer Enrique Metinides and it was from him that he'd learned the value of crowd shots, holding them up as a mirror to the scene of death, a counterpoint to the central image in which a being had crossed from one world to the next. Their fear and enthralment, their tears and affectations – all whistling in the dark. Metinides was the king of car crashes, murders and suicides, taking irresistible photographs that also brilliantly captured those who were there to gawp.

Winter climbed the steps back up to Main Street, instinctively photographing the crowds peeking in wonder at the events behind the police tape. He didn't spend much time on them though because he had only one person in mind whom he wanted to find. She was still there, frozen with her mouth open. As he got nearer he could see that she was in her mid-fifties, a neatly dressed woman with her hair tied back, an intended shopping mission now forgotten. She was wringing her hands and nibbling on her own lips as if it could some-how erase whatever it was that she'd seen.

Winter knew she hadn't noticed his approach, her mind consumed, and he stopped and put her firmly in the frame of his Nikon FM2, rattling off a few shots before she or anyone else wondered what the hell he was doing. She was a picture of post-trauma and he had no doubt she would lead him to where he wanted to be.

The woman only looked up when he was a few feet away, his footsteps finally awakening her from her dwam of distraction.

'Where is it?' he asked her as gently as he could.

The woman's eyes widened and she chewed on her lip again before weakly raising an arm and pointing behind her.

'I'm sorry,' she mumbled at him. 'Sorry.'

Winter didn't stop to explain that she had no reason to apologise, to tell her he understood that all she'd been guilty of was being unable to pass on the horror of what she had stumbled across further down the street. Instead he hurried towards it.

The head was sitting in the shade of a wall, at rest against a set of railings that kept it from the road, undisturbed and unnoticed, as everyone's attention had been on the police activity nearer the station. The dark, thick hair that greeted Winter had also perhaps protected it from obvious scrutiny; the last thing a passer-by might imagine he or she was looking at was what it actually was. Winter stepped on by until he was able to turn and see the face of the man who had been unwise enough to step in front of a train.

Winter dropped onto his backside and immediately framed the bloodied head in his Nikon, seeing a man in his mid-forties, his eyes screwed shut and his mouth wide open. The bloodless skin was scraped at the cheek and temple, doubtless from where it had landed, but otherwise the face was surprisingly unmarked. The back of the head had taken a heavy blow and the matted hair had collapsed in like a sunken mine shaft. The head itself had been snapped clean off the neck, probably the only thing that had saved it from being obliterated by the force of the train. The seeping point of separation licked crimson onto the ground.

Winter's lens also picked out pinched red marks across the bridge of the man's nose and above his ears, clear signs of a pair of spectacles that hadn't made the flight through the air with him. He saw a rosy blush on the man's cheeks that could have suggested a fondness for alcohol. The teeth bared by the open mouth were well looked after, white and even, unstained by tobacco. His skin was smooth and freshly shaved. Middle aged, middle class and his head in the middle of the pavement.

What would drive a man to be so desperate as to take his chances with an express train, Winter wondered. He couldn't help but think of the old joke about there finally being light at the end of the tunnel but that it was a train coming the other way. Whatever light this guy had been hoping to see, it had been swapped for a stare into the abyss. Winter would never be able to stop wondering what it was they saw there. But no matter how dark the thoughts that inhabited Winter's mind, he couldn't imagine how bad things would have to be before he did something like take his own life, particularly in such a violent, chaotic manner. A noise behind him made him jump and broke the trance he realised he'd been in. There were four people standing around him, all with their mouths open, unconsciously mimicking the head that lay on the concrete before them. Two of them were young boys in school uniform and the horror in their eyes was mixed with a joy in what they would soon be able to tell their pals. It was a conflict of emotions Winter knew all too well but he couldn't let them see this.

'Piss off,' he told the group but the kids in particular. 'Go on, get out of here.'

The gawpers backed off reluctantly, unable to take their eyes off the head but moving back about twenty yards so they could still see what was going on. Winter got to his feet, standing between them and the severed head, waving towards the police barrier at the station. A constable had already seen them, his attention grabbed by the knot of people, and was now hurrying towards them. Winter threw a number marker on the ground beside the photo scale that already lay there, kneeling again to shoot a final few frames of the head and mentally wishing its former owner farewell.

The clatter of heavy boots signalled the arrival of the uniformed constable, a young guy Winter didn't know. He arrived as a picture of urgency and efficiency and became a bog-eyed tourist as soon as he saw what lay at Winter's feet.

'Jeezus.'

'I know. Just keep that lot there back from it and radio for reinforcements and forensics. Don't worry, it won't bite.'

The constable raised his eyes from the head just long enough to throw an embarrassed glare at Winter, then turned back nervously to the severed head. Winter left him to it, content he had an image that would take its place on the wall of photographs adorning his Charing Cross flat. As ever though, he wanted more; ten paces on from the head he swivelled and captured the cop and the crowd and the bloodied prize between them.

As he neared the station steps again, Winter passed Burke rushing the other way, clearly having been called by the young cop.

'You've missed out big time.' Burke grinned at him. 'They found a foot. Fucking thing was still wearing a sock and shoe. Seeing as you weren't around, I had to photograph it. A belter, so it was.'

'I think you'll find it was you that missed out, mate,' Winter told him. 'I couldn't give a flying fuck about your foot. Hurry along and you'll get my sloppy seconds. You won't be needing your camera.'

Two hours later, Winter stood in front of what he called his wall of excellence. Narey and Addison, the only two other people ever to have seen it, called it his wall of death. It was a label it was hard to argue with.

It was in the second bedroom in his flat in Berkeley Street in Charing Cross but, as he rarely had visitors, it served as an office and a chilling testimony to his love affair with the city's dark side. There were twenty photographs in five rows of four, all carefully mounted and positioned, framed in black ash and hung for posterity. Each represented a moment of finality, death captured in stark monotones and bloody reds.

Winter had this thing about the colour of blood, how it wasn't red at all but a myriad of shades depending on how long the vital stuff had been spilled for. He had seen and photographed so much of it that he had a keen eye for exactly where it sat on the palate that existed behind his eyes. It was a standing joke among the scenes of crime officers that Winter could give an accurate time of death long before it was rubber stamped by a pathologist. From crimson or candy apple, all the way through to sangria or rufous by way of falu, alizarin, carmine or firebrick, he knew every hue.

It took a lot for him to alter the photographs on his wall. A new print had to be pretty special to push out one of the twenty that were there. He had taken thousands of images of thousands of incidents and the wall represented the best – and worst – of them. A car crash, a street fight fatality, a frozen corpse, shootings, stabbings, even a crucifixion – all life and death was there, captured in the moment it crossed from one to the other. It had been months, nearly a year in fact, since he had last made a change but the severed head from Cambuslang railway station demanded to be included. A decapitation was a first even for him.

He hated having to choose which photograph to take down. It wasn't as if he'd ever throw any of them out but his own unwritten rule was that once they were off the wall, then they were off for good. Instead they'd be filed away to be viewed on rainy days and dark moments when he simply felt the need, which meant they'd be looked at often.

Winter scanned the rows of photographs, studying them

even though he was intimate with every pool of blood, every rip and every scream. Avril Duncanson, his first job: a young woman who had vaulted head first through her car windscreen. Salim Abbas, the innocent schoolboy victim of a gang attack; all broken, bruised and bloodied, his body a roadmap of vicious intent. Marie Wylde, the middle-class victim of a drunken middle-class husband, her face lacerated with a thousand cuts. Graeme Forrest, a uniformed cop, an inspector who'd paid the ultimate price for being on the wrong side of the law and been nailed to a door with a pool of blood and fear at his feet. Jimmy Adamson and Andrew Haddow, underworld minions who'd died by the sword they'd chosen to live by, laid out in puddles of rosso corsa, taken out by bullets of vengeance.

Those were the bare descriptions, the things other people might have seen if they were given the chance to see them. Winter saw more. He saw the unmarked loveliness of Avril Duncanson's face: not remarkably pretty but with flawless skin that was all the more astonishing for having somehow survived the windscreen shower. In the dark brown eyes of the boy whose only crime had been to have the wrong colour skin, he saw not only fear but also pity for assailants who were scarred by hate. He saw splendid retribution in the luscious blood pools of the career criminals. He saw beauty where others simply saw death. Choosing which photograph to take down was like deciding which of his children had to leave the bosom of the family home.

With regret verging on guilt, he finally opted to remove his photograph of the body of Bridgeton Elvis. The old man had frozen to death at the foot of a tree near the People's Palace on Glasgow Green one bitterly cold January morning three years before. He'd been a harmless jaikie, fond of the Bucky or whatever other booze was going cheap, and always used to greet the east end cops with a tuneless rendition of 'Jailhouse Rock' every time he saw them. Winter's photograph showed Elvis in the middle of his longest sleep with powder blue cheeks and icicled beard. Winter loved the shot of the old guy but he loved the others more. It had to go.

In its place he hung the Cambuslang commuter. With his eyes screwed shut, the suicide victim stared back at Winter with mouth wide and hope extinguished. Winter had managed to get low enough on the pavement so that he was level with the head and had constructed an angle that gave the impression of a portrait. It would, however, have fulfilled few of the criteria demanded of a passport photograph: it was taken against concrete rather than a light grey or plain cream background; the mouth was open and the eyes were not; the expression was not neutral and the rest of the body was missing.

The shoe that had been attached to the severed foot forensics had found was relatively new, dressy and well polished. It didn't exactly scream poverty. The man's face had been recently shaved and didn't suggest any lack of care. His full head of dark hair might have hinted at someone whose life wasn't full of worry or just a set of generous genes that precluded male pattern baldness. Winter knew that psychological problems ran much deeper than money or material possessions though, and he could only guess at the demons that had made this guy step in front of an oncoming train. Not that the motives mattered – not to Winter – all that counted was the end result.

Winter had never quite got round to confirming the legal, let alone the moral, position regarding the photographs he had hanging in his spare room. It had suited him not to ask the question given that there was an answer he didn't want to hear. He thought of them as his own intellectual property but it was admittedly a possibility that the Procurator Fiscal could have taken a differing view. Some were taken on the department-issued Nikon FM2; others were taken on his own Canon EOS-1D. A couple, like the blood-soaked body of druglord Cairns Caldwell, were even taken on his mobile phone because he'd had nothing else to hand. All, however, were taken while on the clock and that was what gave the cops or the Scottish Police Services Authority a legal claim over them, if only they'd known they were there. The moral claim to have them on his wall was a different matter altogether and Winter couldn't afford to spend too much time debating that with himself.

He turned away from the wall, suddenly feeling the need to see the outside world. His Berkeley Street flat looked out on to the pale sandstone walls of the Mitchell Library on the other side of the street and he drew in the view in a single gulp. He had to press himself close to the glass to see pink sky above the library and found condensation licking against his nose as he did so. It would probably have helped if he'd turned the heating up in the flat, seeing it was a degree or two below freezing outside, but he hated being too warm. Rachel's flat was always like an oven and yet she'd be wearing heavy jumpers or a fleece while he'd be in a T-shirt.

It wasn't the only difference between their flats. Her place was over a hundred years old with rooms you could fly a kite in, the ceilings were so high, antique fireplaces in every one and no parking space within a country mile. His end of Berkeley Street was modern and clinical, devoid of cat-swinging room but with trellised balconies you almost had room to step onto. The style would probably be classed as minimalist but for the clutter. Hers suited her and his suited him.

The Mitchell used to be one of his favourite buildings in the city – until he'd moved in opposite it. It was the largest public reference library in Europe and the font of all Glasgow and global knowledge. He used to love its late Victorian splendour and the sheer physical statement it was designed to make about the importance of knowledge. The building was always lit up at night and undoubtedly a spectacular sight when you zoomed past on the M8 but it was a pain in the arse when you had a giant Christmas tree permanently positioned outside your window. Winter had always been a man more in favour of the dark than the light.

He watched a small group of people hurry along the street, all waddling as quickly as three layers of clothing would allow. There wasn't more than a dusting of snow on the pavement but all the forecasts said there was plenty more to come.

His mind drifted back a couple of weeks and two decades and thought of Lily lying in her snowy grave on Inchmahome. An uncharacteristic shiver ran through him as he closed his eyes and tried to picture her face. Did she have green eyes or blue, was her face lightly freckled to go with her blonde hair? Was she pretty or plain?

Winter opened the cupboards where he kept some of his older prints and the plethora of camera paraphernalia he had amassed, much of it never used as it hadn't proved as handy as the trade magazines had promised. There were a few extra black ash frames in there too, each exactly the same as the ones that held his collection. He took one out, along with a bracket and a couple of panel pins.

He picked a spot on the wall opposite the five rows of four and carefully knocked the pins and bracket into position. Conscious that he was doing so with unnecessary ceremony, Winter placed the empty frame onto the wall and stood back to consider it.

The blank frame blinked back at him, the plain white mounting taunting him with promises of an image unknown. He closed his eyes again and made a silent promise to the girl whose face he couldn't see – his fellow orphan.

'Abandoned and alone,' he said out loud. 'But not for long.'

CHAPTER 24

Saturday 8 December

The R2S system was one of Winter's favourite bits of computer geekery. Normally he didn't approve of anything that took away from the simple beauty of a photograph. He barely tolerated the addition of a frame beyond its practical uses and always shunned any suggestion of digitally enhancing a photograph. It was what it was, warts and all, and would only lose some sense of its identity if you tried to fanny around with it in Photoshop or anything similar.

The difference with R2S was that the guys who invented it had been in the job and thankfully knew just what cops, forensics and photographers needed from it. One of the pair who had come up with it had actually been a photographer with Grampian Police and that probably explained why it ticked so many boxes for Winter. The system allowed him to drop photographs, 360-shots, information, 999 audio calls, whatever, onto the big picture and the whole lot was a joined-up signature that was accessible not only to Strathclyde cops, but all of the Scottish police forces and beyond.

It made Winter's job a lot easier in the court room too. Instead of having to stand there like a spanner holding a glossy A3-sized photograph or handing it round the jury, the whole business was much slicker. The images could be displayed on a screen, enlarged or viewed in sections, turned upside down or back to front. They could be viewed from any other point in the crime scene, giving jurors the chance to see how it would actually have looked from wherever a witness was standing.

There were instances when his work was just too much for some juries to handle. Ironically, the more he liked a crime scene, the less other people seemed to want to look at it. So, in some instances, the R2S team would create a 3D virtual replica of a scene, or perhaps of a body, so it would be more palatable to the sensitive souls on the jury than the real thing. He was pretty sure that would happen in the unlikely event the suicide had to go before a jury, though a fatal accident inquiry was far more likely.

During an investigation, whenever any fresh bit of info became available – whether a new photo or witness statement, a name or place or a blood type – it flashed up to all users of the system. They were even alerted by text message to say that something new had been added. It was an obvious but long-awaited piece of common-sense thinking that meant all parties in an enquiry could communicate with each other.

The R2S for the Cambuslang suicide was split into two distinct parts: the platform from which the guy had stepped in front of the express, thereby leaving various bits of himself behind, and the street where the head was found. In both, Winter had first photographed the scene with the spherical camera, which produced the 360-degree image that every other bit of audio and visual evidence could be dropped onto. It meant he was now able to sit in the cold comfort of his Pitt Street office and pan round both scenes, taking in witnesses, tarmac and platform, disembodied head, severed hand and shoulder bone. He grudgingly admired Paul Burke's picture of the foot that was still wearing a shoe and a sock despite being rudely separated from the rest of the leg.

It had only been a day since the suicide and they still didn't have a name for the victim. He was tagged up as 'Unidentified Male' while the cops waited for someone to realise they had lost a husband or father or son. The portrait photo Winter had taken wasn't exactly the kind of thing they could show on the six o'clock news.

His reverential study of the Cambuslang pics was rudely interrupted by his mobile phone ringing. It was Addison.

'Awrite, wee man? How's things in the boiler room of police investigations? I'm bored off my tits being stuck in here all day. You fancy a pint later?'

There were no medium-sized people in Glasgow; everyone was either 'wee man' or 'big man'. Winter stood six feet tall but Addison's extra four inches in height meant he was duly obliged to label his mate 'wee man'. The two of them were best pals, something that didn't please everyone in the Strathclyde cops but neither of them gave a monkey's. They had shared many a night propping up the bar together or sitting beside each other at Celtic Park. Their shared but differing knowledge of police operations worked for both of them. They knew enough to be able to talk about each other's work but they also knew when to shut up – at least Winter did. Sometimes Addison never knew when to stop and that had only got worse since he'd been off active duty.

However, Winter knew that having a drink with a grouchy Addison would be as nothing compared to how bad tempered he'd be the next time if he didn't. The only way to keep the DI relatively happy these days was to go along with whatever he wanted. Anything for a quiet life, Winter thought.

'Aye, sure. I'm just about finished up in here anyway.'

'Music to my ears, wee man. Why don't you haul your lazy arse over to the TSB and I'll see you in there. Say, in an hour?'

The Station Bar in Cowcaddens was their favourite drinking haunt but it always rankled with Winter that it was round the corner from Addison's station in Stewart Street and nowhere near as handy for him, as he was usually stuck in Pitt Street. Still, he'd long since stopped trying to win that argument as well. Anyway, they kept a good drop of Guinness and that overcame all objections.

When Winter got to Port Dundas Road and pushed his way through the main door of The Station Bar, he saw that Addison had unsurprisingly beaten him to it and was standing at the bar, pint in hand and half of it already gone. He saw Winter coming and tapped his glass, signalling to the barman to pull another two pints.

'Let's grab a seat,' Addison said with a nod of his head to the tables in the rear lounge. 'With all the time I'm spending parked on my arse, I'm losing the ability to stand for more than two minutes at a time.'

Addison slid his lanky frame behind a table in the corner, puffing out his cheeks and exhaling bitterly. Winter immediately sensed a rant coming on and tried to cut his pal off at the pass.

'Have you seen the forecast for tonight? They're saying we're going to get heavy snow.'

'Aye? Brilliant. Just what I bloody need: another reason for me to be cooped up inside. That probably means the game won't be on tomorrow either. Fucking great. It's not bad enough that I can't do any proper police work but now I'm going to have to do without the football as well. This shit is really ripping my knitting, I'm telling you.'

So much for stopping him from going off on one, Winter thought.

'I tell you, wee man, I don't know how much longer I can put up with this,' Addison continued. 'Every other fucker is out there doing the fun stuff and I'm playing at strategy planning with jumped up admin assistants and wet nursing cops who couldn't lace my boots when it comes to proper police work.'

Addison's rant was interrupted by the beaming face of a grey-haired lady, who thrust both it and a rattling can between the two men. She looked at Addison without a response so she shook the can once more.

'For a Christmas party for disadvantaged children,' she announced cheerily.

Addison's face didn't crack. 'Let me see your ID.'

The woman's smile fell as she reached, embarrassed, into her bag and produced a laminated card that proved she was indeed genuine.

'Okay,' Addison nodded, still not putting his hand in his

pocket. 'I didn't say I was going to give anything, I just wanted to check you weren't at it.'

'Here.' Winter dropped a couple of pound coins in the woman's tin and smiled apologetically for his friend.

'I hate bloody Christmas,' Addison muttered.

'So you've said a thousand times.'

'Aye, and here's another thing. You know that Rudolph the Red-nosed Reindeer? See how the other reindeer laugh and call him names, right? And then when he leads Santa's sleigh, they all want to be his pal? Well, if I was Rudolph, I'd have told them to fuck right off.'

Winter knew it was going to be a long session. He began to switch off and let the tirade flow over him, becoming engrossed not for the first time with the ugly yet beautiful scar visible under Addison's hairline: the sniper's bullet had nearly torn his head off his shoulders; it had left a thick, jagged and permanent reminder.

'Will you stop looking at my scar, you sick fucker?' Addison demanded.

'Sorry.'

'Don't be sorry, just don't do it. I'm not an exhibit on your freaky Wall of Death. I'm the one with the scar but you're the one who needs your head examined, wee man. You have serious problems between those ears.'

'Aye, okay. I said I was sorry. It's just a bit . . . magnetic.'

'Only for a sicko like you,' Addison blustered. 'And the chicks, of course. They love it. Actually, talking of the ladies . . . Narey's up to something as well. I don't know what it is yet but I've got a bad feeling the silly cow is getting herself into bother over something.'

Winter tried not to seem too interested. If anyone suspected he and Rachel were an item, it was Addy. It would be just like him to be fishing in the hope that Winter would bite.

'Yeah?' he replied as casually as he could. 'What makes you think that?'

'I probably shouldn't say but she was out in Stirling – Stirling of all places! Poking her nose into some old case that was none of her business. Now she's taking random days off for no apparent reason. There's something going on but she's not telling me what. You and her are pretty pally . . . you any idea what she's up to?'

Winter shook his head.

'Nope. No idea. I'll keep an eye on her though.'

'Yeah, I bet you will,' Addison teased. 'No hardship in that, eh?'

The DI held Winter's gaze, the ghost of a smirk on his lips, defying his mate to challenge him. Tony couldn't get a read on what Addison did and didn't know. The sod liked playing games and Winter was going to do his damnedest not to get dragged into this one. Salvation from Addison's silent interrogation was at hand in the shape of Winter's mobile beeping in his back pocket. He knew right away it was work because of the alert tone and might not have bothered to check it there and then if it didn't offer an easy escape from Addison's stare. He hauled the phone out of his pocket, ignoring Addison's look of disgust.

Winter saw it was a text signalling to him that the R2S had been updated on the Cambuslang case. Addison's games could wait and so could his pint. There was no way he was going to be able to resist a quick look at what had been added on the headless guy. He tapped his way through to the system and brought up the highlighted area where the new information had been placed. As he read it, his eyes widened and he felt a familiar sinking feeling in the pit of his stomach. He instinctively brought his pint to his lips and drew down a large mouthful of the Guinness as he reread what was in front of him. Drawing his hand across his lips, he pushed himself to his feet.

'Addy, I need to go outside. I'll be back in a minute.'

'I take it it's a woman,' Addison jeered behind him. 'One text from her and you jump. You've got to let her know who's boss, wee man. Treat 'em mean and keep 'em keen. It's the way they like it.'

Winter wasn't at all sure that the call he was about to make was the way Rachel *would* like it. She answered on the third ring as he stood outside the pub, his mind racing and his feet shuffling in a vain attempt to keep warm.

'Hi. It's me.'

'So I see,' Narey laughed at him. 'You do know that your name comes up on the screen on these newfangled mobile phone things, right? I seem to remember someone making fun of me for saying the same thing.'

'Aye, very funny. Listen, there's something you need to know. It might be nothing but . . .'

She sensed the tension in his voice.

'What is it?'

'I told you about that suicide I photographed yesterday, the one at Cambuslang station? Well, they've just ID'd him. His name's flashed up on the R2S. He's a guy named Adam Mosson.'

'And?'

'It's his occupation. Rachel, the guy was a school teacher.'

A loud silence came back at Winter from the other end of the phone.

'Two school teachers. Dying in suspicious circumstances,' he continued. 'Maybe I'm being . . .'

'No, you're not,' she interrupted. 'And of course it's his name too. Tony, one of the other three names the black-mailer emailed along with Laurence Paton was . . .'

'I know. Adamski something or other.'

'Yes. Jesus. Adamski was Adam Mosson.'

CHAPTER 25

Monday 10 December

The easy thing, of course, would have been to ask Tony to go to Derek Addison and use the old pals act to get her on the case, explain to him what had being going on and convince him of the truth behind the apparent suicide. The easy way wasn't an option, however, and it was, of course, her fault for keeping their relationship secret. Naturally, Tony hadn't been exactly slow in pointing that out.

It would also have been a hell of a lot easier if she understood just what was going on. Ever since Tony had called on Saturday night, she'd known it was too much to think that Adam Mosson's death was the suicide it seemed. If he'd walked in front of that train, then Narey was sure someone, probably the blackmailer, had driven him to do it. If so, how bad had things been for Mosson that he saw it as the only way out? Of course, the other possibility was that it wasn't suicide at all. The little that had been gathered in the way of witness statements said it was but she could see they didn't carry much weight.

The platform had been busy with commuter traffic waiting for their train into Central and no one claimed to have
seen Mosson actually step in front of the express. A couple of
them had turned in time to see the impact, including a traumatised middle-aged woman who had thrown up not long
after. There was a whole lot of screaming and general chaos,
pushing both towards and away from the point where the
train had struck Mosson. No one there could have been sure
who had done what to whom – far less why – which made it
harder for her to persuade Addison it was worthy of her time.

She knocked on the door of his office and was immediately greeted with a gruff roar that didn't bode well for her
chances. She took a deep breath and opened the door.

The DI was sitting with his feet up on the desk, determinedly lobbing scrunched up bits of paper into a bin in the
corner. Narey stood bemused and watched as he successfully
landed three in a row right in the wastebasket.

'Paperwork,' Addison said without taking his eyes off the
bin. 'This is the only kind that doesn't send me completely
fucking mental.'

The next effort hit the edge of the bin and joined a collection of others on the floor.

'Fucksake. Now see what you've done. What the hell do
you want anyway?'

'A few minutes of your valuable time would be good, sir.'

'Less of the fucking sarcasm. I'm not cooped up in here
through choice. Right, talk.'

Addison swung his long legs off the desk and reluctantly
assumed some vaguely professional position in his chair. It
was blindingly obvious he wasn't in the best of moods and

Narey considered making her excuses and trying her luck another time. However, she knew it might be a warm day in Whiteinch before he was actually in a good mood so she decided to take her chances.

'You'll have heard about the suicide at Cambuslang railway station,' she began.

'No. Next.'

'A commuter supposedly stepped out in front of an express,' she persisted. 'Body parts thrown to the wind.'

'Okay. So?'

'So, I have reason to believe it wasn't a suicide.'

Narey saw a light go on in Addison's eyes and, even though he tried to cover it with a bored expression, she knew he was curious. The bad-tempered bastard was going stir-crazy, and she was suddenly confident he would bite at the lure of an interesting case. She just had to make him think it was all his idea.

'Okay, I'm listening. Tell me more.'

'No one actually saw this guy, Adam Mosson, step in front of the train. I believe he was either pushed or someone forced him into doing it.'

'And you're basing that on what exactly?'

Narey took another deep breath. 'I think Mosson is linked to another case and another death.'

Addison's eyes narrowed and a scowl formed on his lips. 'Okay, why do I get the feeling I'm not going to like this?'

Narey's gaze fell to the floor as she developed a sudden interest in Addison's office carpet. He wasn't going to be diverted though.

'Rachel, what is this other fucking death?'

'Laurence Paton.'

'Oh, for fucksake. You have got to be bloody kidding me. Get out. Get out my fucking office now. As if I've not got enough shit to put up with without you making it worse. Go on, beat it, before I put you back in uniform and have you cleaning up tramps' puke.'

'Hear me out. Please?'

Addison's head fell into his hands as he melodramatically let out a muffled scream. As he sat back up he blew out an exaggerated puff of air and glanced at his watch.

'It's only ten o'clock and I'm already wondering when I can get a drink. That's not a good sign so this better be bloody good. I told you to forget this Paton shit.'

'Yes, sir. I know. And I had,' she lied. 'Then this Mosson thing came up and . . .'

'What makes you think they're linked?' he asked wearily.

'Two deaths: one seemingly an accident; the other seemingly a suicide. I don't think either were what they seemed. Paton and Mosson were both teachers . . .'

'That's it? They were both teachers? Jesus Christ, we'd better get a warning out to Professor Dumbledore. Tell him he might be in danger. Teachers? Is that all you've got?'

Narey realised how thin it sounded but couldn't tell Addison about the other link. They only knew about the adamski email address because Tony and Danny had broken into Paton's house and hacked into his computer. Addison wasn't going to thank her for telling him that.

'Fucksake, Rachel,' Addison continued to rant. 'Mosson was from Glasgow, I take it. Your man Paton was a teacher in bloody Stirling.'

'Yes, but Paton is originally from Glasgow and he studied here.'

'God help me,' Addison muttered before lapsing into a dour silence, his feet back up on the desk again.

'Where?' he asked at last.

'Where what?'

'Where did he study? Jordanhill?'

'I assume so, yes,' Narey told him.

'Don't assume anything. If you do, you make an ass out of you. Not me. Go to Jordanhill and check out the student records. Come back to me with something that actually links Paton and Mosson and we'll see. Until then, drop the fucking conspiracy theories and do some proper work. You hear me?'

'Yes, sir.'

'And don't "yes, sir" me because it only makes me think you're up to something.'

'Yes . . .'

Narey closed the door behind her, nothing more than a faint smile on her lips, leaving Addison to resume his challenge with his paperwork and the wastebasket. It was probably for his own good she hadn't told him she'd already phoned the college and been told that Paton and Mosson had indeed enrolled at Jordanhill in the same year. Now she was going to find out who else had been there with them.

CHAPTER 26

Finding someone in Glasgow who is 'hurting people' is not so much like looking for a needle in a haystack; it's more like looking for hay in a haystack, knowing the haystack might head-butt you at any minute. Rachel had left the search to Winter and Danny, making it pretty clear she thought the whole gypsy thing was probably a wild-goose chase. Between Paton and her regular caseload, she told them, she didn't have time to run down the Sam Dunbar lead as well.

She had also warned Winter off going to get help from Addison. She was taking too many risks as it was and didn't want Addison getting a sniff of what she was doing. He would inevitably ask Winter why the hell he'd been out to Stirling talking to the travellers in the first place. In fact, the very mention of Stirling would have Addison launching into a suspicion-fuelled rant.

Worse still, they knew it might all be a complete waste of time. There was a very good chance that Tommy Baillie was playing them for his own ends but he still represented the only apparent lead they had if the gypsy connection were to stand up.

That was why Winter and Danny were slowly working

their way through an assorted selection of cops, criminals and contacts in an attempt to get a handle on Sam Dunbar. They were all people who could be asked questions without them feeling the need to ask why. Instead, they exchanged scraps of information in return for a few quid, a few pints or a favour owed. Inevitably, there was no end of 'people hurting' reported back to them but none of it added up to much of any use. Instead, the usual suspects had been hurting the usual bampots by the usual methods. Baseball bats, stabbings and heavy bruises were the order of the day from Possil to Partick.

The name Sam Dunbar meant nothing to any of them until they sat down in the Whistlin Kirk at Glasgow Green with a mechanic named Shug Brennan. The guy was a contact of Danny's from way back, a cut and shut expert of some renown whose talents were still in demand from those who couldn't get all the services they required at Kwik Fit. Shug was the sort of happy drinker who got told all sorts of things and was happy to share them with Danny as long as his glass got topped up and his back pocket bulged with spending money.

Winter hadn't met the guy before but as soon as they walked into the Whistlin Kirk, he recognised Shug from Danny's description. The shock of unruly hair was unmissable and its colour seemed to defy nature by existing outwith the confines of a cartoon. It was hair so ginger Winter thought it must have come out of a tin of paint. Shug was known as Irn-Bru Brennan because his hair was the precise colour of the fizzy brew that claimed to be Scotland's other national drink. It wasn't Irn-Bru that was in front of Shug though, it was lager, and Danny went straight to the bar and bought him a fresh one along with a couple of Guinness for himself and Winter.

The Whistlin Kirk was a Celtic pub, which suited Winter and Danny just fine. The green leather seating was matched with whitewashed walls lined with retro Guinness signs above the oak panelling. It was the kind of pub where the only two things on offer were booze and chat. Shug was positioned in a corner under a sign declaring 'Guinness gives you strength', far enough away from anyone else that they could talk without being overheard. Even if the punters smelled cop, his age would have made them think their senses needed retuning. They slid in beside Shug, Danny introducing Winter with a brief nod and just two words, 'Tony. Shug.'

From the point Winter was offered a grudging nod from the Irn-Bru Man, he became part of the furniture as Danny and Shug talked turkey. It was just the way Winter liked it: he was always happier as an observer, sitting back comfortably and watching the play unfold. As the other two men talked, Winter took in Shug's rosy cheeks and reddened nose, which could have been put down to the weather outside but probably wasn't, his nicotine-stained fingers, muscled arms and pot belly. He was no hard man, not by Glasgow standards, but he'd be able to look after himself and, given the nature of his trade, he'd probably have to. The remainder of his first pint disappeared at a rate of knots and a large gulp of the second followed suit after a cursory wipe of his mouth with the back of his hand. Shug spoke quietly, probably the only person in the pub who was doing so, his gravelly cigarette tones disappearing within a few feet of their table.

'Dunbar? Aye, I've heard the name.'

'Tell me about him.'

'I don't know much. Except that the guy who dropped his name suggested Dunbar wasn't the sort ye'd want to bump into.'

'In what way?'

Shug shrugged.

'Bad bastard is the vibe I got.'

'Hardly anything new in that,' Danny replied. 'The place is full of them. Why'd he mention this guy?'

'Like I said, he didn't say much. Got the impression this guy was a new face and my man was wary of him.'

Danny nodded and supped on his Guinness, a foamy moustache forming on his grizzled features. He let Shug's words settle on him, mulling them over.

'Is your guy the sort that normally worries about new faces?'

Shug gave a short laugh. 'No, he's no. And just as well he's no here if you're going to be slagging him off for being scared.'

'So why's he worried about Dunbar?'

'I didn't say he was – not quite. Look, all he said was that there were some people running scared of this Sam Dunbar character. He didn't say that *he* was. Said this Dunbar was making a bit of a rep for himself. I asked him what the guy had done but he just shook his head like I didn't really want to know. "Mental" was all he'd say.'

'So who is this guy who told you about him?'

'Away ye go – like I'm going to tell ye that.'

'Come on, Shug. I need to know who this guy is.'

Shug stared gravely into his pint, looking like a man who'd found a penny but lost a pint of blood.

'Believe me, ye don't need to, Mr Neilson. He's not the sort that's going to take too kindly to being asked that kind of question.'

'Look, Shug. You tell me who he is and I'll take my own chances talking to him. He'll never know it came from you.'

Shug gave a despairing shake of his head and downed a huge mouthful of lager.

'If this comes back to me, I'll no be a happy man. I'm more likely to be a deid man.'

'It won't.'

'Fucksake,' Shug's gruff voice got even lower. 'It's Glenn Paxton. He's a debt collector for Terry Gilmartin. Ye know him?'

'I know the name. Where will I find him?'

'Christ, ye don't ask much, do ye?'

'Shug, you know you're going to tell me and I'll make it worth your while so just spit it out.'

'He drinks in the Roadhouse on Gartloch Road.'

'Aye, right, Shug. How fucking stupid do you think I am? The Roadhouse? I'd be as well going in with a uniform on and a target painted on my forehead.'

The Roadhouse was a windowless brick bungalow sitting back off the road behind Glasgow Fort with only a neighbouring Ladbrokes for company. It was strictly locals only and any strangers would have been seen coming from a mile away.

'Where else does he drink?'

Shug sighed.

'Wednesday nights you'll get him in The Springcroft in Baillieston. It's curry night. And he better never find out it was me that telt ye.'

'Springcroft? That a Brewer's Fayre?'

'Used to be. Some other chain's got it noo. I mean it, Mr Neilson. He cannae know it was me that telt ye.'

'And I told you – he won't.'

'Well, ye better take someone with ye.' Shug gave a withering sideways look at Winter. 'Someone who can handle hisself.'

Danny laughed as Winter took offence. Okay, so he was a lover not a fighter but he was hardly useless either. Being reasonably tall in Glasgow, as he was, meant he'd lived his life having to fend off a succession of wee hard nuts who'd wanted to prove they could fight despite their stunted growth.

'I'm sure we'll be just fine, Shug. Tony isn't as hopeless as he looks.'

Thanks, Uncle Danny, Winter thought. He saw Danny's left hand slip casually under the table and Shug's right hand do the same, neither men taking their eyes off their drinks. No one else in the room would have noticed a thing.

'So what's happening in the motor trade, Shug? Business good?'

'No bad, Mr Neilson. No bad. It never changes whether there's a recession on or no. People always need a motor and if they've got less money to spend, then all the more reason they don't buy one aff the forecourt. Know what I mean? And wherever they buy them from, things always go wrong. Keeps me in beer money, you know?'

'Oh, I know. A bit of cut and shut, remove the VIN number, scratch out engine and chassis numbers, give the engine a bit more va-va-voom and turn back the clock like there's no tomorrow. All in an honest day's work for a dodgy mechanic, eh, Shug?'

Shug's pint had been halfway to his mouth but he carefully put it back on the ring-marked table with a look of righteous indignation on his face.

'Now, haud your horses right there, Mr Neilson. While not acknowledging any of the actions you mentioned, I have to tell you that I take great exception to the phrase "dodgy mechanic". Okay, you may well be using the word in the sense of it meaning illegal. And I'd grant you there may be a small element of truth in that. However . . . dodgy, in the motor business, also suggests incompetence – a cowboy, if ye will. And I'm no having that. I know my stuff. I prefer the term "black market mechanic", if ye don't mind.'

Danny laughed.

'Well, Mr Shug, I apologise if I have offended your professional sensibilities. Heaven fucking forefend if anyone were to think I was suggesting you were in any way unskilled. Fucksake, Shug, half of Glasgow knows that if you weren't a lazy wee shite and as bent as a six-pound coin, you could have been sorting cars for a Formula 1 team. A great loss to the world of Grand Prix racing but a gain for backstreet garages across Glesga.'

Shug puffed himself up, preening at the compliment, and dragged a hand through his extraordinary ginger locks.

'Thank you, Mr Neilson. It's always gratifying when a fellow professional such as yersel recognises the merits of one's work.'

Danny smiled back and began to get up from the table, nodding to Winter that it was time to make a move. However, as he did so, Shug Brennan put a hand on Danny's arm, leaned in towards him and whispered hoarsely.

'Mr Neilson, you be careful with Paxton. The guy's a sort of pal of mine but he cannae half be a fucking bad bastard when he's got a drink in him. Terrible temper the man's got. Call me sentimental but I wouldnae like to see ye get hurt.'

Danny roared with laughter.

'Man of my age, you mean? Ha. I'm touched, Shug. Didn't know you cared. Don't you worry; I'll be fine. I've got Tony here to look after me.'

Danny and Shug both laughed like a couple of fishwives. Winter wanted to smack their fucking heads together.

CHAPTER 27

Jordanhill College of Education had turned out most of the teachers, primary and secondary, in west and central Scotland for nearly a hundred years until it became part of the University of Strathclyde in the early nineties. Among the former students were the two that Narey was particularly interested in. She was on campus with an appointment to see one of the senior members of staff.

A receptionist directed her up one floor and along a corridor until she found the room she was looking for. The nameplate on the door read Dr Hilary Henderson, Vice Dean. Narey knocked and almost immediately a woman's voice called out, urging her to enter.

A short, blonde woman in her late fifties was already bounding towards the door by the time Narey had opened it and stepped through. Casually dressed in jeans and a sweatshirt, and with a pair of glasses perched on the end of her nose, she had her hand out in greeting.

'Sergeant Narey? I'm Hilary. I see you managed to find your way here okay. How can I help you?'

'Thanks for taking the time to see me. It's a bit of a strange one, actually. I'm trying to track down a group of students who were here nearly twenty years ago.'

The woman took a step back in mock surprise, then scratched her head.

'Really? Well, you've come to the right person. I'm the Vice Dean of Education and that basically means I get a posh title because I've been here longer than anyone else. It also means I might be able to assist you with your enquiries, Sergeant.'

The professor laughed at her own joke, then shrugged to show she knew it wasn't really very funny. Narey liked her immediately.

'Please, sit down. So, tell me, who is it you're looking for?'

Narey eased herself into an armchair and took a sneaky look around the impressively messy office, which was over-stuffed with books, folders and half-drunk mugs of coffee.

'I wondered if you might remember two students called Laurence Paton and Adam Mosson?'

Professor Henderson slipped her glasses off and rubbed her eyes.

'You're really testing me now. There've been thousands of students through here in that time. I must admit neither name immediately rings a bell. Tell me more. Oh, and I'd offer you a coffee but I'm afraid I've run out of mugs.'

'That's okay, thanks anyway. They were both here in 1993 . . .'

'The year we merged with the University to create the Faculty of Education,' interjected Henderson. 'I remember that year well so there's more chance I'll be able to recollect the boys. Well, not that they'll be boys any more.'

Far from it, Narey thought. Far from it.

'Laurence went on to teach English in Stirling while Adam taught history at Shawlands Academy,' she told the woman. 'I'm afraid I can't tell you much more at this stage.'

Henderson shook her head, clearly frustrated with herself. She puffed out her cheeks and deliberated. 'Nope, nothing. Let's go and find their matriculation photographs. They might help jog my memory.'

The Vice Dean led Narey back out of the office, down another flight of stairs and into a basement.

'My memory's like a sieve these days. Time was I could have told you the name of every student who'd been here and what they liked on their toast in the morning – not that I ever saw any of them in the morning, I hasten to add. If they'd been training to be primary school teachers, then there's much more of a chance I'd remember them. For every ten primary students going through here, only one is male. It's a bit different at secondary though – three women for every two men. Which still sounds like a pretty good deal for them, don't you think?'

Narey smiled. 'Men always get the better deal.'

'Don't they just. Should I ask why you want to know about Laurence and Adam or is it best that I don't?'

Narey didn't slow her stride or change her tone.

'They both died recently. One seems to have been an accident and the other a suicide.'

'Fucking hell.'

The expletive surprised Narey and she nearly laughed but thankfully managed to restrain herself.

'That's terrible. Well, obviously, anything I can do to help then I will. You said that they "seemed" to be an accident and a suicide . . .'

Narey smiled at her apologetically, making it clear she wasn't going to say any more on the matter.

'Right, right. Understood. Sorry,' Henderson flustered. 'Okay, the old records are in here. They should be easy enough to find.'

After just a few minutes of raking around and some low muttering, which seemed to include more swearing, the Vice Dean let out a whoop of triumph and hauled out two folders. From each she produced a single sheet with a photograph attached. She pushed her glasses firmly up on the bridge of her nose and studied first one, then the other.

'Goodness me. I do remember him. Laurence, that is. I'm afraid I don't remember Adam at all.'

She held out the first sheet of paper, which was headlined with the name Laurence Brian Paton. The photograph showed a young, fair-haired man smiling sheepishly at the camera. He looked tanned and fit, full of the joys of youth. His hair was shoulder length and swept down over his forehead till it fell nearly in his eyes.

'Laurence Paton. Of course,' Henderson reminisced. 'Funny how seeing someone as they were then takes you right back. He was a bright kid, very outdoorsy and sporty. I seem to remember that he was laid back, quite a happy chappy. Oh my God, I can't believe he's dead.'

'Do you remember if Laurence had any particular friends he hung around with at college?'

Henderson held the photograph of Adam Mosson up again and had a second look.

'I really don't . . . Maybe. He's vaguely familiar but my mind could just be convincing me of that. Let me think. So many students under the bridge since then. I'll dig out the complete register from Laurence's year. I'm guessing you'll want that?'

'And maybe the years either side for good measure.'

'No problem.'

'Do you remember anyone called either Dixie or Paddy?' Narey persisted.

Henderson looked perplexed again.

'Let me . . . No. Sorry. Are those nicknames, do you think? I wouldn't necessarily know them by their nicknames. It was very much a register, proper name kind of arrangement. I'm sorry I'm not being much help.'

'Don't worry. The register of names should be a big help.'

'I'll get you copies of them. And of these photographs as well.'

Half an hour later, Narey was sitting at a wooden corner table in Café Gandolfi on Albion Street. The chinking of glasses and the splutter of the cappuccino machine – Gandolfi famously had the first one in Glasgow – failed to dent her concentration as she pored over the list in front of her, desperate for answers to the riddle of Paton and Mosson's email accomplices. Of course, it was possible that the names behind the nicknames weren't to be found in the college register at all. But her gut told her otherwise.

There was no Dixie, no Dixon, no Dickson, no Dickerson, no Dickinson or any of the other variations she had hoped might be there. No one called Richard and, unsurprisingly, no Dixie Chicks. For Paddy, there was better news and yet little extra light. There was a Patrick and two Patricias; there was a Padfield and a Padgett. There were also eight surnames that could have been classified as Irish: Kelly, O'Neill, Gallagher (two of them), Nolan, Moran, Mulvey, Byrne and McCarthy.

In all, there were just over three hundred students on the course, just over a hundred of those men but, of course, there was no certainty that their missing links were male. It was a bloody big haystack but at least she had some possible needles. As soon as she got back to Stewart Street she would commandeer DC Julia Corrieri and get her to work her way through all the possible Paddys.

Narey had first worked with Julia the year before and had initially been driven to distraction by the task of playing big sister to the tall, gangling DC with the awkward, uncoordinated air. Corrieri was smart and determined but by God she was hard work, taking everything Narey said as literally as she did seriously. She had learned quickly though, just as Narey had learned to like her. Sometimes Julia was still so endearingly, fastidiously studious that Narey wanted to slap her but, more often, she wanted to take her home and keep her as a pet. Not that Corrieri was a soft touch: she was an expert in a martial art called Kuk Sool Won and Narey had seen her bring guys twice her size to their knees. Searching under every possible rock for paddy38 was just the kind of thing Julia loved doing and no stone, far less a needle, would be left unturned.

Narey sighed, the enormity of the task barely softened by the tiny dent she'd made in it. The names stared up at her from the list. The faces too: Laurence Paton with his near-blond locks, fresh face and tanned skin; Adam Mosson with his mop of thick, dark hair and brown eyes, studious and serious in his thick-rimmed specs. All of their life in front of them then; now all of it behind them. Narey laid the list of names on the table and stared at it, seeing nothing but convinced that it contained either a killer or a future victim – maybe both.

CHAPTER 28

Wednesday 12 December

The Springcroft was six miles from the city centre, sitting just a few minutes from the M8, which thundered past on its way from Glasgow to Edinburgh. Despite having no shortage of thirsty would-be punters in the surrounding areas, pubs were pretty scarce on that side of the city. Nearby Easterhouse had been famously dry when the scheme was built in the late fifties and stayed that way for years. Baillieston wasn't much better off for boozers and maybe that wasn't such a bad thing.

'So what do you want me to do?' Winter asked as they pulled into the car park, seeing snow piled up at the sides and several parking bays out of commission because of it.

'Just follow my lead and try to look hard. You manage that?'

'Fuck off, Uncle Danny.'

He grinned. 'That's my boy.'

It had been years since Winter had been inside The

Springcroft and right away he saw that it had had a make-
over. Glossy wooden flooring, pastel colours and partitions
gave it a warm, welcoming look, which couldn't be said for
all pubs in the area. It billed itself as a family establishment
but, as the saying goes, you can choose your friends but you
can't choose your family. As soon as they were through the
door, they recognised Glenn Paxton from Shug Brennan's
description.

The debt collector wore a blue New York Yankees baseball cap pulled low over his forehead and was heavily
bearded. Even though he was sitting down, the man gave
the impression of being as wide as he was tall and his broad
forearms came straight out of a Popeye cartoon. The seat
opposite him was empty but the wooden table still looked
as if it had been laid out with enough food for a family of
four. Winter spied two slabs of naan bread, a large bowl of
rice, four separate curry dishes and a jug of lager. Paxton
clearly had a healthy appetite.

From the other side of the room, Winter and Danny saw
Paxton tear into the bread as if his fat life depended on it,
then scoop up heaped forkfuls of curry and stuff them into
his mouth. The man was a massive, bad-mannered eating
machine with streaks of sauce on his cheeks and chin. He
was attacking the meal but it was hard to say if he was
enjoying it. His brooding demeanour didn't exactly encourage approach and Winter instinctively let Danny lead the
way to the guy's table.

Paxton must have been aware of Danny's imposing frame
looming over him as he ate but he didn't acknowledge that
he had an audience.

'Glenn Paxton?' Danny asked.

The man didn't look up from his plate.

'Fuck off.'

Danny persisted. 'Glenn Paxton?'

'Who wants to know?'

'I do.'

'Fuck off.'

Danny pulled back the chair opposite Paxton and sat down, propping his elbows on the table and clasping his hands. At last he seemed to have Paxton's attention and the peak of the baseball cap rose slowly until dark brown eyes glared at Danny.

'I told ye tae fuck off.'

'Yeah, I heard you. But I'd still like to ask you a couple of questions.'

The man's eyes narrowed and the skin tightened across his face in an angry grimace. When he spoke, it was in a low, guttural growl.

'I don't answer questions. You better go away.'

Danny sat back in the chair, his arms crossed over his chest, an air of mock surprise on his face. He held Paxton's gaze and smiled at the man, an action designed simply to irritate and it succeeded.

'I fucking telt you tae fu—'

Paxton's sentence went unfinished as Danny uncrossed his arms and swept the back of his right arm across the table, clearing away bread, rice, curry, plates, jug and pint glass in one motion, sending food, china and glass onto Paxton's lap and the floor. The noise of the shattering plates reverberated round the pub and every head in the place turned towards

208

them, although only for as long as it took to recognise the stature of the men at the table involved. Winter saw every man in the place turn quickly back to his own table. It was the acknowledged order of such things: heads down, eyes averted, doors located and exit points established. Wives and kids were told not to look; whatever it was, it wasn't any of their business.

Paxton's mouth hung open, disbelief all over his fat face and curry all over his T-shirt. He was a volcano about to erupt and his mouth began to stretch into the beginning of a manic shriek. Before he could speak or shout, Danny spoke quietly.

'You're right enough, Glenn. We should probably just go.'

Danny eased the chair back and stood up, seeing the inferno raging in Paxton's eyes as the big man wiped furiously at his curry-splattered chest. His massive hands were going faster and faster as his temper rocketed to boiling point. It was tipped over the edge by the smirk on Danny's face as he said goodbye and nodded at Winter to follow him out of the pub.

As Paxton, struggling to manoeuvre himself out from under the table, roared at them demanding to know where they thought they were fucking going, Danny offered an apology and cash to an anxious waitress. Winter, struggling to know whether to laugh or worry, followed close behind, copying Danny's leisurely stroll out of the pub. He could hear the table and chair scraping behind him, the angry puff of the debt collector as he got to his feet. They were at the front door though, and Danny pushed it wide behind him so Winter could follow him through just before it closed.

Danny walked straight over to the biggest vehicle in the icy car park, a black Ford Galaxy with blacked-out windows that had gangster written all over it. He reached the car just as the enraged Paxton, his breath heavy in the frozen air, came through the pub door with his fists balled and charged towards them. Winter tactfully took a step back and let Paxton continue his rush towards Danny.

'What are you doing beside my car? Yer a dead man, y'old bastard,' he screamed as he swung back his meaty right arm to launch a punch at Danny. The blow never landed, as Danny quickly stepped in towards Paxton and grabbed his left arm, pulling it towards him and twisting as he crashed the man into the car. In an instant, Paxton's arm was behind his back and his face was pressed hard against the metal. Paxton was a big man though and he struggled against Danny's grip, stretching his other hand round to grab hold of his attacker's clothes. Danny raised his eyebrows at Winter, wondering if he was just going to stand there or do something.

In response, Winter stamped down hard on the back of Paxton's calf, causing his leg to collapse at the knee, bringing the big man to the ground with a belligerent groan. Danny smiled approvingly before knocking Paxton's baseball cap off his head and grabbing a handful of his hair. He pulled the debt collector's head back and slammed it towards the car, stopping just inches short of the metal.

'This was all so unnecessary, Glenn. Don't you think? All I wanted to do was ask you a couple of questions. You ready to answer them now?'

'Fuck off.'

'Is that all you can say, big man? I don't think it is.'

Danny nodded towards Winter, who again put his foot to Paxton's calf, this time pressing down steadily until the man yelped. Danny simultaneously knocked Paxton's head against the side of the car.

'What the fuck d'you want, granddad?'

'That's better. One simple question: who is Sam Dunbar?'

No answer came so Danny pulled Paxton's head back from the car, tightening his grip on the hair and making it clear he was ready to crash it against the car again.

'Wait!'

Danny steadied his hand.

'Dunbar works for Terry.'

'Terry Gilmartin?'

'Naw, Terry's Chocolate Orange. Of course, Gilmartin. Now get the fuck off me. If ye'd telt me it was that mental bastard ye wanted to talk about I'd have telt ye.'

'Of course you would have. So tell me about him.'

Paxton spat on the ground and sighed heavily.

'He's new. And I don't like him much. Cocky young cunt, aff his heid. He sorted out two of Terry's boys and Terry liked what he heard, gave him a few jobs to do. I think Terry's got something on him though, keeps him working.'

'What kind of jobs?'

'Frighteners – and worse. Couple of times Terry's wanted people hurt to send out a message. So he sent this mental fucker to do it. Couple of wee chancers were selling on Terry's turf so he got this Dunbar to cut them a bit. Stuff like that.'

'Why do you keep saying he's mental?'

'I think Terry must be paying him in nose candy because the guy always seems to be wired tae the moon. But I don't know if it's the coke or he's just a psycho but the guy enjoys it too much. Ye can always tell the bad nutters when they take a real pleasure in their work. He was sent after some poor bastard to pull him back into line and ended up killing the guy's fucking dug. A dug, can you believe that?'

A bell rang in Winter's mind: Swanston Street. The ned named Jason Hewitt and his dead bullmastiff.

'He killed a dog?' he repeated to Paxton. 'And did he cut the guy's arm off as well?'

'Well, aye. He did that anaw but that was just business. He had nae right to go killing the poor fucking dug.'

Danny looked questioningly at Winter but he just shook his head and mouthed the word 'later' at him.

'So where do we find Dunbar?'

'It's on the east coast, doon the road from Edinburgh. Fuck off.'

'Funny man, Glenn. Where do I find him?'

'Gilmartin will kill me if he thinks I've put ye onto Dunbar. He's got a soft spot for him, sees him as a pet psycho.'

'So we make sure that doesn't happen. Tell me somewhere we can find him, somewhere away from Gilmartin. That will suit both of us.'

'Munn's Vaults on Maryhill Road. He drinks in there. That's aw know and aw you're getting.'

'That's all I need. Okay, Glenn, thanks for your help. You better get back inside before your chicken jalfrezi gets cold. And think of a nice wee story to tell if someone asks why you had to step outside for a while. Maybe tell them some wee lassie's granddad wanted a word 'cos you were cheating on her. How about that?'

Paxton just grunted, his arm still held in place by Danny's strong grip.

'And don't even think of coming after us, Glenn,' Danny continued. 'For starters, I'll finish off this job on your arm and, secondly, I'll be forced to tell mad, mental Sam Dunbar and his boss where I got my information from. Capisce?'

'Aye, okay, okay.'

'Good. I thought you'd see sense but just in case . . .' Danny fished in the man's pockets till he emerged with a set of car keys. 'I'll drop these into the snow at the top of the car park. You can get them there.'

'Fucksake.'

'Ah, come on, Glenn. You know it makes sense. The exercise will do you good.'

CHAPTER 29

Wednesday 12 December. 9.23 p.m.

'DI Sutton, please.'

'Speaking.'

'Aaron, hi. It's Tony Winter. You okay for a quick chat?'

'Tony, how you doing? Yeah, sure. Free as a bird. Apart from a caseload that could sink the *Titanic* and an ex-wife who's making my life a misery by phoning me every five minutes. What can I do you for?'

'I wanted to talk to you about that job we were both on in Swanston Street. The dog that was cut in half and the guy that had part of his arm chopped off?'

'How could I forget? What about it?'

'I was just wondering if you had any more on it. I've been finishing off my filing and noseying through the R2S to see what was doing.'

There was a long silence on the other end of the line before Sutton answered.

'Well, there's not much on the R2S because we don't have

much to put on it. Witness statements gave us fuck all, as per usual. Victims were saying fuck all, as per usual. I don't have a name for it or I'd have pulled someone in. But to be honest, Tony, this is way down my priority list. I've got at least a dozen cases that need attention before this one.'

'Right. So no one's been suggested as the guy behind this?'

There was another lengthy silence.

'I said so. You doing house calls these days as well, Tony?'

'Eh? No. I'm just . . . It was the dog being cut in half, you know. I took an interest in it.'

'Didn't take you for an animal lover.'

'No, I'm not really. But it made a great picture.'

'A great picture? Addison always said you were weird. C'mon, Tony, spill. Why are you so interested in this?'

Winter hesitated.

'It's like you said: I'm weird. The dog being sliced in two and the guy having his arm chopped off just got me inter-ested. It's not the kind of thing you forget in a hurry.'

'Bollocks. If you know something about this, you should tell me. Fuck knows when I'll get the chance to do anything about it but you should still tell me.'

'Aaron, I can't. For a start, what I know might not be right. It could be way off the mark. And . . . I just can't. Not yet, anyway.'

'So why the hell are you phoning me?'

'Looking for info. You heard of any other cases with a similar MO?'

Sutton laughed.

'I just love it when civilians start quoting jargon at me that they've heard on *CSI: Miami*. Okay, so what do you reckon his MO is?'

'Well, the samurai sword, of course. Cutting off arms. And for the record, I don't watch *CSI: Miami*. The guy who plays Horatio Caine is terrible. I'm more of a *CSI: New York* man.'

Sutton sighed heavily.

'Okay. Here's what I'll do: if I get a minute, I'll look through the computer and see if there's anything else like this on the go. If there is, I'll tell you. And if I do, then you tell me what you know. And don't piss me about. Okay?'

'Okay.'

'And Tony . . .'

'What?'

'You're wrong about Horatio Caine. The guy who plays him is supposed to be as cheesy as that.'

'You think?'

'Yeah. Mind you, that thing with the sunglasses gets right on my tits.'

CHAPTER 30

Wednesday 12 December. 11.45 p.m.

'How's your dad?'

'Not good. The home say he seems to be getting a bit worse each week. They're seeing him more than I am and I think they're right. I just can't stand the thought of him slipping away. I feel like I'm losing him.'

They were in bed together, Rachel lying facing the window, staring at the slate-coloured sky, and Tony tucked in behind, his arms around her. He was naked; she was in pyjamas and still cold despite the heating being on twenty-four hours a day since the cold snap began. According to the telly, the temperature would drop to minus fifteen that night and she was feeling every degree of it. It was just after midnight and they were both on in the morning but, despite being tired, neither was ready for sleep.

'I want to tell you that everything will be all right but I can't.'

'I know. He won't get better. But maybe . . . maybe he won't get worse. That's the best I can hope for.'

'But you're doing all you can do for him. You're pushing yourself to the edge as it is.'

'Hm.'

'It's all you can do, Rach.'

'Do you not think I fucking know that?'

Tony didn't react. He knew she didn't mean it. He'd never known her hurt the way she had been the past couple of weeks and he was beginning to feel the hurt pushing him aside. He settled for pulling her closer and letting her blow herself out.

'Shit. I'm sorry,' she breathed, her hands rubbing at her temples. 'Sorry. Didn't mean that. This is doing my bloody head in.'

'It's okay. I understand. Just remember that I'm on your side.'

'I said I was sorry.'

'Just making sure.'

She dug her elbow into him a bit. 'Sod.'

'So where do we go next?'

'We find Dixie and Paddy. God knows where they are or who they are but if we find them, then we start to get to the bottom of this. At least one of them knows what happened. At least one of them knows who's blackmailing them. We'll find them.'

'And Lily?'

'Don't start on me with the forgetting about Lily stuff. I've never forgotten about her, despite what you and Danny might think. I'm sure your sick mind is full of images of her lying on the island but, just because mine isn't, that doesn't mean I don't care about finding who did that to her.'

He said nothing, feeling guilty for something he couldn't control, knowing she had him nailed and not feeling any better for that. His head was his own place – or so he thought. He didn't like the idea of it being an open book, even to Rachel. His dreams should be his own grubby little secrets.

'It's okay,' she told him. 'I think I understand. As much as I understand anything about you, sicko.'

'Ha ha. You should give up policing and become a comedian.'

He began to kiss her neck and move his body against hers, hoping for a reaction but not the one he got.

'Forget it,' she slapped a hand against his leg. 'Not tonight.'

'Jeezus, the sooner we find out who the fuck killed these bastards the better.'

Despite everything, she giggled. 'So that you can get your end away?'

They both laughed and she turned and they kissed before she hugged back into him again, leaving him to his thoughts. He knew she was right – of course she was. When night closed in, his mind was full of Lily.

He did wonder, in his more reasoned moments, why he obsessed about her quite so much. It wasn't because he had photographed her, her shattered skull displayed on his wall with the other trophies of his labours. No, eventually he realised it was because he *hadn't* photographed her. She was a stray soul like him yet she had eluded his lens and his inner itch ached to put that right.

It wasn't that he dreamt about her, more that he couldn't stop thinking about her. In truth he probably couldn't tell where his thoughts stopped and his dreams began; it was just the way his head worked. The image of her filled his mind, her face becoming formed ever more clearly as each day passed. Behind his eyes he could see her pale skin and the light freckles on her nose. There was a cheeky grin in defiance of all they knew had happened to her. Lily was a pretty girl and probably looked even younger than she was – a face that was never going to grow old.

Sometimes he'd think about her like that, fully formed, even though he knew his imagination was taking a leap. Mostly, though, he thought of her as half-finished, the way Fairweather was describing her, the picture becoming fuller and clearer with every passing telephone call or email.

But other times . . . other times he thought of her as she was found: blackened, battered, bloodied and broken. That wasn't how he wanted to picture her but there was no way he could stop himself. That image was buried away in a dark corner of his mind he couldn't help but visit. Fighting it was always going to be a losing battle.

In his waking hours, he could realise the moment when the insects came was a sure sign that he had passed over from imagination to dreams. But there and then, in the depths of the dark night, the line was blurred and his mind recoiled at the illusory sight of ants, blowflies and dermestid beetles gorging on Lily. He had to watch in fascinated horror as flies, maggots and beetle larvae feasted on her flesh. He could hear too: the buzz and the crawl and the chomp. It was his own perfected method of self-torture.

This night, however, the insects hadn't yet come to take their fill of Lily and so he was fairly sure he was still awake and therefore simply tormenting himself. Lily and Paton and Mosson had formed an unlikely chorus line of characters, flitting through his mind in various stages of distress, each leaving a bloody footprint on his fading consciousness. It was somewhere in the midst of this dark meandering that his eureka moment came.

His eyes flashed open and he let the thought run through his head once more for confirmation that it made some kind of sense. Sure enough that it did, he reached for the bedside lamp and switched it on, getting out of bed in the same movement.

'What the fuck?' Rachel grouched, immediately awake and staring at the sight of Tony groping around, naked, among the papers on the desktop. He didn't reply but kept searching until he picked up a sheet of A4 and held it up to the light.

'What the hell are you doing?' she asked again.

Tony looked up at her, then back down at the paper.

'Dixie,' he told her.

'Dixie? As in dixie1970? The other name on Paton's email?'

'Yes. This probably sounds nuts but it occurred to me that . . . well, Dixie is a nickname for footballers. Or it used to be.'

'Right . . .'

'There was a guy called Dixie Dean who played for Everton between the wars. Scored sixty goals in one season. And there was a Celtic player in the seventies, John Deans. He was known as Dixie as well – wee barrel of a guy. I was sure I'd seen the name Deans on the Jordanhill list but I had to check.'

Winter held the papers up in front of him.

'And?' Rachel demanded.

'And I've checked his age against the record as well. This guy was born in 1970. Dixie 1970. His name is Gregory Deans.'

CHAPTER 31

Thursday 13 December. 6.15 p.m.

'Tony?'

'Yeah?'

'It's Aaron Sutton. You might want to get yourself over to Mansionhouse Drive in Springboig. Right away.'

'Sure. What is it?'

'Let's just say that the key words are samurai sword.'

'Leaving right now.'

He drove as fast as he could get away with towards the east end in the evening traffic. As he ran to his car, he tried Danny's mobile but didn't get an answer and left a message saying where he was going. Danny would see the connection right away. Springboig was just five minutes from Terry Gilmartin's home turf in Easterhouse.

There were lots of streets in Glasgow where Winter would have a fair idea what to expect as soon as he heard their name. Mansionhouse Drive didn't fall into that category. It was one of the strangest streets in the city, the product of two very different building eras. If you came from the western end of Hallhill Road, you could see how it got its name: maybe not mansions exactly but big, expensive homes at the end of leafy drives, behind high manicured hedges on a tree-lined street – until you came to the junction of Croftspar Place. The street abruptly changed, from mansion house to Eastern European prison cells: ugly grey mono blocks that were barely worthy of the word house never mind mansion. Croftspar Place marked the point in the road where house prices fell by over a hundred grand and life expectancy by ten years.

Surprise, surprise. When Winter came off Springboig Road onto Hallhill Road, there were no signs of flashing lights and the echoes of sirens were still in the distance. It was only when he was halfway along the more salubrious section of Mansionhouse, the road rutted with ice and snow, that he saw the circus ahead. Sure enough, the cars and cops were en masse a hundred yards past the turn into Croftspar Place. Winter parked as near as he could, battled his way through a fuck-muttering crowd, and flashed his identification at the first constable who tried to block his path. It was the look on the cop's face that gave him the first clue all was not well on Mansionhouse Drive.

He'd seen it before – many times. The guy was young and nervous, aggressive in his uniform because he was trying to cover the fact that he was shitting himself. Other people might have been riled at his attitude or thought he should 'man up' and get on with it; not Winter. He just wanted to know what was so bad behind the lines that it made the cop look so utterly lost. The second Winter saw the guy's eyes, shifting left and right in near panic, he had a hard-on for whatever was waiting to be photographed.

As soon as he got behind the tape, he sought out Aaron Sutton and spotted him waving his arms around furiously and yelling at his cops to get the gathering crowd of locals further back. Winter looked round but could see nothing that merited the level of chaos that was ensuing. There were definite shades of the crowd in Swanston Street when the dog had been sliced in two: loonies baying at the cold moon and a powder keg of resentment that just needed an excuse to blow. There was no sign of blood but there was the smell of it in the air and that was always guaranteed to get crowds going loopy. As Winter scanned the scene from inside the line, he got a real sense of people pushing in and on edge. With a sinking feeling, he wondered if that was all that was responsible for the young cop wetting himself. Then he saw Aaron Sutton and the look on his face.

It was way different from the constable's – Sutton was far too long in the tooth to suffer those kind of nerves – but his weary and worried look was all the more telling for that. Winter felt the potential for terrible things tickling his adrenalin.

He hurried over to Sutton; the DI saw his approach and studied Winter with something that looked a whole lot like he was seriously pissed off. Winter didn't have any doubt that the enraged look in Sutton's eyes was aimed directly at him.

'So what have we got?' Winter asked him, trying to pre-empt the questions that seemed certain to come from Sutton.

The DI stared back at him and Winter instinctively knew that Sutton was struggling between giving him a hard time and having to get on with the job at hand.

'Two hands. Sliced clean off and left lying in the snow.'

'Where are they? And where's the guy they were cut from?'

'One over there,' Sutton pointed. 'And one over there. And it's "guys". Plural.'

'How do you know it's not just one victim?'

'Well, it's possible. But only if he had two right hands.'

'What?'

'Keep up. We have a right hand over there and another right hand over there. This ring any bells with you, Tony?'

Winter ignored the loaded question as best he could and asked one of his own, more in the hope of deflection than anything else.

'So what have we got? A Sharia law vigilante ninja? Someone cutting the hands off thieves?'

Sutton's head tilted to the side and he raised his eyebrows in a show of scepticism. It was a look straight out of the Addison school. Winter gabbled a response to the unasked query.

'I will tell you as soon as I can, Aaron. I promise you that. How about I take some photographs?'

Sutton grimaced.

'Forensics were here ahead of you. Give me one reason why I need you to take photographs of this scene.'

'Look through my camera,' he suggested to Sutton, turning the viewfinder towards the cop.

'Are you kidding me? I've got two bastards running around somewhere with their hands cut off plus a mob ready to go Tonto at any minute. And you want me to say cheese?'

'Just do it. It'll show you why you need me to do this job.'

Sutton muttered something but did it anyway.

'Okay. So what the fuck am I supposed to be looking at? I can't see a thing.'

'Exactly. That's what you'll get if the forensics do pics of the scene in the dark. They will be okay with close-up stuff, not exactly technically brilliant but usable, I guess. But if you want a shot of this scene, then they'll be as much use as a chocolate teapot.'

Sutton looked sceptical.

'So what do you suggest?'

'You need a timed exposure. I can do that; they can't.'

Sutton swore under his breath.

'Okay but this better be good. And you better tell me what you can when you can. I don't need any of this crap. I've got enough on my plate as it is.'

Winter knew the secrets of night-time photography, particularly the first rule, which was that it was as tricky as hell. Basically, all photographs rely on light reflecting back to the camera; when you don't have light, that's a problem. In US crime dramas they'll most likely bring in large floodlights or generators and illuminate the scene. The problem with reality is that American television has a bigger budget than Strathclyde cops. A good camera flash does the job for evidence you can get within a few feet of but if you want something more, then the photographer has to get tricky too.

'I want all the cop cars to turn off their lights,' Winter told Sutton.

'You're joking me, right?'

'Nope. They'll mess up what I'm going to try to do. They need to go. I'll set up, then tell you when I want the lights off. It will take . . .' Winter looked at the sky. 'Four minutes.'

He walked over to where Sutton had pointed previously and saw the first of the two hands, ivory pale but peppered with blood and severed neatly just above the wrist. A blood trail ran off across the snow and ice in the direction of Croftspar Place and there were already yellow numbered markers dotting the direction in which the victim had disappeared. Winter managed to resist the urge to photograph it there and then, knowing the entire scene shot wasn't going to keep for much longer. He checked out the second hand and, sure enough, it too had the thumb on the left as it faced down into the snow, blotchy patches of firebrick red staining the white pillow it lay on.

He pulled himself away from the hands and went to his car, battling his way through the angry crowd of onlookers, and dragged a tripod back to the scene. Given the length of time his shot was going to take, there was no way he could take the chance of any movement that would ruin it. He switched his camera to the 'bulb' setting and fixed it to the tripod, making sure his lens was taking in both spots where the hands were.

'Right,' he told Sutton. 'Ready.'

'Make this as quick as you can.'

Sutton turned to signal to the cops and in an instant the lights of five police cars and two ambulances were switched off, causing an anxious buzz to break out from the gathered mob.

'Hey, whit the fuck's going on?'

'What are they bastards up tae?'

Winter shut out the crowd as best as he could and opened the shutter. Normally, the shutter speed is like the blink of an eye, open for no more a thirtieth of a second – plenty of time for light to flood in. To open it enough to light up this scene was going to take a whole lot longer and, although he could have programmed a setting on the camera, he preferred to do it by hand, judgement and feel. There was no getting away from the fact that he liked the sense of power it gave.

The hordes roared round him and he longed to photograph them too but knew that his flash wouldn't do them justice. Nor could he move the camera now that the process of opening the shutter had begun. All he could hope was that some of the faces behind the line, inquisitive, angry and vengeful, would be captured above the focus of the scene itself.

'They're up tae something!'

'Why've they switched the lights aff oan the motors?' 'Let's riot these cunts.'

Winter held firm, the shutter lead steady in his hand, loving it. Some of the cops didn't look like they were enjoying it quite so much. They were anxious, fretfully looking round the crowd and urging the darkness to end. They stared at Winter too, as if they could force him to end the exposure simply through the power of thought.

'Get the lights on.'

'Get the pigs.'

'Get oot of here, ya bastards.'

From the corner of his eye, Winter saw something move from the right. He whirled his head round but whatever it was had already gone by him, landing with a crash of breaking glass on the road. One of the local eejits had thrown a bottle, causing a huge cheer to go up and the crowd to swell forward.

'Winter! Get this over with,' Sutton shouted at him. 'McKie, Collins, find whoever threw that bottle and drag him out of the crowd.'

'How do we know who it was, sir?' PC Collins shouted back over the rising din.

'It doesn't fucking matter,' Sutton blasted. 'They're all guilty of it. Just grab someone.'

There was still more than a minute left on the time Winter had estimated it was going to need to get a decent exposure and he was determined to give it every second. The time was being stretched to breaking point by the nonsense going on around them and the cops on the front line were getting more antsy with each passing second. Glares were being fired at him as he stood by the camera, seemingly doing nothing. His head raced with thoughts of Sam Dunbar and Tommy Baillie, of how he was going to square things with both the leader of the Stirling travellers and Aaron Sutton.

Thirty seconds left and he saw two bodies being plucked out of the mob by McKie and Collins and being tossed into the back of a van. All it did was enflame the situation and make the crowd surge and yell. Twenty seconds and Sutton was standing right beside him now. He was talking but all Winter could hear was the roaring pack, the rush of blood in his ears, the pounding of his heart. The more pressure he was under to finish the shot, the more his adrenalin coursed through his veins. Ten seconds. A hooded figure broke the ranks and charged towards a copper. Five seconds. They could wait. Four. Three. Two. One. Done.

Winter ended the exposure and the moment. Chaos ensued all around but he had his photograph. Dipping his head to the display, he saw immediately that he had indeed turned night into day, seeing detail, contour and evidence where there had previously been just darkness.

He nodded at Sutton and the DI cursed softly before turning to wave at his drivers and the vehicle lights were immediately switched on, flooding the area and inevitably causing fresh consternation among the crowd.

'You're a prick,' Sutton muttered, with a resigned shake of his head. 'You going to make all this hassle worth my while?'

'I'll do my best.'

'You'd better. I'm not having some nutter running around chopping hands off people. It's bad for business.'

Winter watched with a pang of jealousy as the crime scene guys moved in on the two severed hands, removing them and taking them back to the lab for the easiest bit of fingerprint analysis they'd ever do. The chances of the victims being on record were high and they'd know their identities within the hour. Getting them to talk would be a different matter but Winter was sure he knew who the swordsman was. The big question was what the hell was he going to do with the information.

Nearly two hours later a newly printed image was hot in his hands, the result of the timed exposure. He was pleased with the effort; the scene was nicely and spookily lit up. The two bloodied hands could easily be seen, as could the crowd behind the police barriers. Winter was fascinated by the contorted faces of the mob, all twisted rage and vented spleen, rough-hewn figures straight out of a Peter Howson painting, caricature products of their environment. Because of the exposure time, most of them had moved and wore blurred expressions of fury that only seemed to exaggerate their sense of being beyond reason. Only one figure was almost completely in focus and must have remained still despite the chaos around him.

Tall and broad, he had thick dark hair and wore a full-length black leather coat. He was serious and surly rather than angry like those around him. Above all, he stood out from the rest because he was calm. He seemed to be staring not quite directly at the camera but close enough, perhaps at DI Sutton or the other cops nearby. Winter had only been given the vaguest of descriptions of him before but there was little doubt in his mind that he was looking at Sam Dunbar.

CHAPTER 32

Friday 14 December

All it had taken was a single phone call to the General Teaching Council for Scotland and one returned to where Narey sat impatiently in Stewart Street. Within minutes, identity confirmed, she was given the home address of Gregory Alexander Deans. He was head of the maths department at Cleveden Secondary and lived just three miles away in Vancouver Road, Scotstoun.

It was a long frustrating day waiting for a time when she could be confident that Deans would be home. Narey had been tempted to pay him a visit at school but decided against it in the end. Storming into a classroom, a staffroom or even the head teacher's office had its appeal but she knew it could ultimately work against her. She didn't have that much she could use as leverage against the man and knew he would be well within his rights to demand that she leave the school.

If Deans was a blackmail victim, then there were a couple of things she could deduce from that. First of all, he had something to hide; innocent people don't get blackmailed. Secondly, he hadn't been to the cops to tell them; innocent people don't do that either. If he was afraid, then she wanted him to be more afraid; she didn't want him in a place where he felt secure and protected. No, she decided she would wait until he was home and in the bosom of his family. She was pretty sure they wouldn't be in on whatever dirty little secret he was trying to keep quiet.

She couldn't stay away completely though and drove out to Vancouver Road just before noon to check the place out. It was a leafy, middle-class street but the set-up was slightly odd, with housing on one side and expansive rear gardens on the other, trees peering down onto the road. The Deans residence was a whitewashed mock Tudor house, which neatly matched the snowy lawn that sat behind a low railing. There was something comfortable and welcoming about it, Narey decided as she sat in her car with the engine running and the heat at full blast. It would clearly cost a right few quid but it had no air or graces – a house far too Scottish to do anything as brash as boast about what it was worth. There were few clues as to the kind of people who lived there though; all she could see through the windows was the dark promise of something unknown.

Narey knew she couldn't sit too long on the quiet street, her car billowing exhaust fumes into the frozen air, without someone calling the police. She imagined it was the sort of place where everyone knew everyone else and strangers and their cars stuck out like sore thumbs. She wasn't going to gain anything by having Deans tipped off about her arrival.

Instead she put the car into gear and moved off, turning

onto Earlbank Avenue and heading for Milngavie. She hadn't been to see her dad in five days and the sudden realisation filled her with guilt. She had been so busy thinking about putting the lake killing right she'd forgotten about the person she was doing it for in the first place.

As she drove along Victoria Park Drive North, heading for Balshagray Avenue, she got stopped behind a bus that had pulled in to pick up passengers. She turned her head to see a bunch of kids and adults playing in the park and was at once taken back to snowy days with her dad when she was young. He always seemed to be there, no matter how much work she now knew he must have been doing. He'd take her and her pals sledging, build snowmen and happily be pelted with snowballs until they tumbled home cold and wet to Mum, who would always greet them with a despairing shake of the head that she didn't mean. A car horn blared impatiently behind her, dragging her back to the present, and she stuck an apologetic arm up at the other driver as she moved off.

Twenty-five minutes later she took a deep breath and closed the car door, the nursing home in front of her. She pulled her coat tightly to her, hugging it as much for comfort as for protection against the snow flurry, and made her way down the path into Clober Nursing Home. She hadn't phoned ahead and had no idea if it was visiting time or not but she was going to see him anyway. Good luck to anyone who tried to stop her.

As it turned out, she hadn't even finished stamping the snow from her feet when a concerned-looking young woman came up to her and opened the inner door to allow her inside. Something about her rush to help made Narey uneasy.

'Miss Narey, isn't it? Come on in. It's terrible out there. You have to wonder how long this weather can keep up. The snow is nice at first but I'll be glad to see the back of it.'

The heat hit Narey immediately. Even for someone who hated the cold as much as she did, this was excessive. She tugged her coat off, eager to escape the stifling temperature.

'I know. It's hot, isn't it?' the woman sympathised. 'We have to have the heating up at full blast for the residents. We can't take any chances with them and it's freezing out there.'

A resident. Was that what her father had become? She thought of him as many things: a protector, a provider, a parent, a rock, but not a resident. Never that. She followed the staff member through the corridors of the home till they came to the day room where she knew her dad was usually to be found. They kept going though, past a bunch of old dears who sat together, some chatting, some looking out the window at the falling snow. Narey was about to ask why he wasn't there when it occurred to her that she perhaps didn't want to hear the answer.

They continued until they reached her dad's room and, after the most cursory of knocks, the carer opened the door and stuck her head round it.

'Mr Narey? How are you, Mr Narey? Your daughter's here to see you . . . No, no, your daughter.'

Narey eased her way past the woman and stepped into the room, recoiling instantly as she saw him propped up in bed with his head bandaged. Even worse, he just looked at her blankly, clearly trying to work out who she was.

She hurried over to his side, sat on the edge of the bed and hugged him. He let her do it, neither hugging her back nor trying to stop her. After a bit, he put his arms on her shoulders and eased her away from him so he could take a look at her.

He sat like that for what seemed like an age until she saw a flicker of recognition in his eyes and he smiled a smile that warmed her world.

'Rachel? How are you, love?'

'Fine, Dad. Fine. How are you though?'

'I'm all right; maybe not quite myself this morning. Not sure what's wrong with me.'

She traced a finger gently across the side of his head.

'Looks like you've had a bit of a bump. I think maybe that's the reason.'

Her dad's eyes opened wider in confusion and his own hand reached for his head, following where her finger had been.

'Oh. I don't . . . I don't know how that happened.'

Narey fought back the anger that choked in her throat and just smiled at him.

'It's okay. It doesn't look too bad. Listen, I'm just going to have a word with the nurse. It's so warm in here. I think I'll need to get them to turn the heating down. I'll be back in a minute.'

She kissed him on the cheek, comforted again by the smile he rewarded her with. But as she turned, her own smile vanished and she went looking for the carer who had brought her in. She didn't have far to look: the woman was still standing outside her dad's room. Narey took hold of her elbow and led her further down the corridor to make sure he didn't hear.

'What the hell happened to him?'

'He fell, Miss Narey. Sorry, I thought you knew and that was why you were here.'

'No, I bloody well didn't know. How did he manage to fall? Was no one looking after him?'

'Yes, of course, but we can't be with them all the time. Your father's been getting a bit more unsteady on his feet and he tripped over a plant pot and he . . . he hit his head against the wall.'

'You can't be with him all the time? Then what the hell are we paying you people for? How would you like it if I hit your head against the wall?'

The moment the words were out of her mouth Rachel regretted them. She saw the fright in the woman's eyes and knew she had the wrong target.

'Where's the person in charge? I'm not happy about this. Not happy at all.'

'Mrs McBriar. She's probably in her office.'

'You go find her. Tell her that I'll want to see her after I've spoken to my dad. And make sure she knows I'm not a happy bunny.'

The nurse backed away, obviously happy to be getting away from the crazy daughter. Narey watched her go, mentally kicking herself for losing her temper the way she had. She wasn't finished on that front, not by a long way, but she'd keep it together.

'Hi there,' she said to her dad as she slipped back into the room. 'You miss me?'

For the second time in as many minutes, she regretted the words that fell from her lips. Clearly he couldn't have missed her; he'd forgotten she'd ever been there.

'Rachel! What a wonderful surprise. You didn't say you were coming.'

'No. Sorry, Dad. I thought I'd just drop by.'

'Sorry? Don't be daft. You never have to be sorry for coming to visit your old dad.'

'You're not old.'

'Ha. Who are you kidding? Come over here.'

She sat on the bed again and let him hug her. Funny, it felt so much better than when she had to hug him. He kissed her on her forehead. He could sense her sadness and was making her feel better, the way he always did.

'We need to get you out of here, Dad.'

'No we don't. We've been through this. This is the best place for me. I'm a silly old bugger. I fell yesterday and cracked my head. Silly old bugger.'

'You're my silly old bugger,' she told him as she nuzzled into him.

Her dad laughed but it was an empty sound that coughed and died on the soft skin of her neck. She hugged him tighter and they both let their tears flow. She made a mental note to make sure those were the last tears she would shed that day; instead they would fuel her anger when she went to see the woman in charge.

Mrs McBriar was waiting for her, of course. She sat tense and upright behind her desk, quickly getting to her feet as Narey strode into her office. A handshake was offered and grudgingly accepted before Narey sat opposite the nursing home's owner and stared her down.

'Well?'

'Miss Narey, your father is, I'm sorry to say, rather unwell.

239

His condition is deteriorating quicker than we might have expected.'

The answer wasn't, in any sense, the one Narey wanted to hear but it took some of the wind, or at least the heat, out of her sails.

'Mrs McBriar, how often do residents here fall and injure themselves in this way?'

'It happens. Rarely. By the very nature of old people, they can be frail and unsteady on their feet.'

'My father is neither old nor frail.'

'Relatively speaking, no, he isn't,' McBriar agreed. 'However, his Alzheimer's changes that. It affects his spatial awareness and his ability to judge distances. You have already witnessed his memory loss but he also suffers from poor judgement. His cognitive and behavioural patterns are not what they were.'

'All the more reason to look after him.'

'I agree, Miss Narey. We monitor all our residents round the clock but unfortunately these things can still happen.'

'I want to take my father out of here. I will look after him myself.'

The care home owner looked out of the window for a few moments before turning back to face her.

'I understand that you are a police officer, Miss Narey. Long hours, I'd imagine. Shifts too.'

'I can change that.'

'Can you? I know that your father was in the force for thirty years. He didn't change it and I'm not sure you would find it easy to do so either.'

'Don't presume to know me.'

'I don't but I do know how exacting it is to look after elderly people, particularly those with degenerative conditions.'

'Look after him properly then,' she retorted.

The woman looked back at her quietly and Narey cursed herself for losing her temper. It was bad enough they had let her dad hurt himself but even worse was that this woman was right. She couldn't look after him, not the way things were right now. At least three things needed to be sorted before she could even think about it: she had to find out who Lily was, who had killed her and who had killed her killer. And then there was Tony . . .

'Look after him properly,' she repeated as she got to her feet. 'I don't have time for you right now but I do have time for him. I'll be back soon and we'll talk again. Don't tell me I can't look after him.'

She regretted slamming the office door behind her almost as soon as she had done it. It felt good but even as she fleetingly enjoyed the sound of it banging shut, she knew it wasn't McBriar she was angry at but herself.

CHAPTER 33

They'd driven round Victoria Park several times, giving them plenty of opportunities to see people coming and going from the white house with the snowy garden. Winter was in the passenger seat. They'd timed it right, and had seen a man going down the path muffled up in coat, hat and scarf and letting himself in with a key. After another circuit, they saw that a car had appeared and parked directly in front of the house when there was plenty of space on either side of it. They looked at each other and Narey nodded. It was time.

They pulled in in front of the red Ford, Narey reversing until the bumper of her Megane was all but touching the car behind. They pushed the car doors open against the force of the wind and hurried down the path towards the front door. Narey stopped long enough to pull out her identity card and held it by her side as she knocked briskly on the door. She could hear voices inside and said a silent prayer that it was the husband who lost the argument and had to see who was disturbing their peace.

As the door was pulled back, she saw that her prayer had been answered. Better still, as she raised her ID card, she saw the look that crossed Deans' face and knew immediately they had come to the right house. No one was ever too happy to see police officers on their doorstep but for those with nothing to hide the overriding reaction was surprise. The principal look she'd seen on the face of Greg Deans was fear. Oh, he pulled it back pretty quickly but she'd seen it and he knew she had.

Winter had seen it too. A widening of the eyes and a fleeting dropping of the jaw, muscles tightening, the merest suggestion of a backward step. Winter stood six inches taller than Rachel and watched over her head as Deans' eyes flashed from the card to her and then finally to him. The man had regained his composure by the time he got round to Winter, his gaze level and his mouth relaxed. But he was rattled and they all knew it.

'Yes?'

'Mr Deans? I am Detective Sergeant Narey and this is Anthony Winter of the SPSA. May we talk to you please, sir?'

'Well, yes. Of course. But may I ask what it is in connection with?'

'I think we all know the answer to that, Mr Deans. May we come in? It's rather cold out here on the doorstep.'

'You can come in, Sergeant, but I have to say that I don't know what you're talking about.'

Narey smiled widely and Winter mimicked her gesture, knowing it was designed to keep the man off guard. They stamped their feet on the doormat, leaving as much of the snow behind as they could before entering the house.

'Through here.' It was as much an order as an invitation and the reason became clear as he led them into the sitting room and promptly left them, saying he was going to speak to his wife.

As soon as he left, Winter was back on his feet, camera in hand. Rachel smiled as he stalked the room, quickly and quietly capturing the images of Deans' family life. It was a comfortable room, one for living in rather than adorning the pages of some interiors magazine. The two sofas, a three-seater and a two, looked well used compared to the single armchair, which sat in splendid isolation to the side. A hooded sweatshirt hung casually over the back of the two-seater and a pair of slippers peeped out from under it. A maze of framed photographs was dotted along a mantelpiece and Winter swooped on them, snapping the snaps and stealing the Deans' history. There were what he assumed to be grand-parents and nephews and nieces in various group shots – Christmases, graduations, birthdays and the like – but in the main there were the three of them: Greg Deans, his attrac-tive blonde wife and a flame-haired daughter in her late teens. Winter focused, literally, on what he took to be the most recent photograph of them together.

They were at a wedding, squeezed together in a happy grouping, Deans in the middle. He was in a light grey suit with striped pink tie, his arms around the women in his life. Mrs Deans wore a red pillar box hat above her heavily styled hair and a beaming smile below it. The daughter had a feath-ery fascinator in her red hair and a heart-shaped rhinestone necklace that reflected the sunshine. They were clearly at ease in each other's company, not even a sulky teen embarrassed by being with her parents.

Footsteps signalled Deans' return and Winter stepped away from the sideboard towards the window, making a show of studying the snow-laden garden. As he closed the door behind him, Deans eyed Winter suspiciously, letting his stare linger long enough to let him know he was on to him. Narey caught the play within the play and revelled in it, relishing anything that kept Deans guessing. She wanted him off balance and would cheerfully kick one leg away if that was what it took to achieve it.

Deans had a full head of light red hair and pale, freckled skin. He stood about five foot ten with a stocky build and looked slightly younger than his forty-two years. He was also obviously nervous, his hands popping in and out of his pockets and tugging at his sleeve as he threw edgy glances towards the door, presumably keeping a wary eye out in case his wife came through it.

He clearly wanted Narey to speak first but she wasn't willing to indulge him. Instead, she just sat and looked at him, letting a heavy silence settle in the room, waiting for it to smother Deans' nerve. He pulled at his sleeve some more, wrenched his eyes from hers and looked impatiently out of the window at the falling snow.

'Well?' he asked her at last.

She smiled. It was her way of telling him she'd won the first round.

'It can't be easy to keep an old house like this warm in such weather.'

'What?'

'Places as old as this tend to leak heat like a sieve. You must need to have your heating on day and night.'

'What is it that you think I can help you with, Sergeant?'

'Well, I wouldn't say no to it being a bit warmer to be honest. I'm not exactly keen on the cold.'

'You said we all knew what this was about. Well, I don't.' Deans held his arms wide to emphasise his claim.

She laughed.

'Come on,' she mocked.

'Sergeant,' he snapped, then lowered his voice. 'What is it that you want?'

She smiled again. Round two to her as well.

'Laurence Paton. Adam Mosson.'

He didn't respond but that was more of a giveaway than if he had. He knew the names were coming; he must have done.

'Sorry?'

'Are you?'

'I mean . . . What is this? I'm not playing your games. You either tell me what it is you are talking about or you leave my home. Now.'

'Okay,' she nodded, conceding the point. 'You know both Laurence Paton and Adam Mosson. Is that correct?'

'I went to Jordanhill with them, yes. Long time ago.'

'Uh huh. What was it they called you back then? Dixie, wasn't it?'

There was more of a reaction this time. She saw in his eyes he hadn't expected her to know that. His leg was teetering before her and she was ready to boot him over.

'Yeah, that's it,' she said. 'Dixie Deans, Laurence Paton and Adam Mosson. Oh, and Paddy. We can't forget Paddy.'

Deans looked back at her stony-faced. He had regained control and registered nothing at the mention of the fourth name.

'You know they're dead, don't you?' she asked.

He gasped but something in the opening and closing of his mouth didn't ring true.

'I heard about Adam,' he told her. 'It was terrible. Poor guy.'

'But not Laurence?'

'No.'

'Fell off a ladder. Cracked his skull open.'

'That's . . . It's been a long time since we knew each other. But that's very sad.'

'When did you last see him?'

'Laurence? Not since we were at Jordanhill.'

'And Adam Mosson?'

'I've bumped into him a few times over the years. Our schools aren't that far apart. But I haven't seen him in a year or two.'

'Hm. And what about Paddy?'

'I'm not sure who you mean. I don't think I remember a Paddy.'

'No? Maybe I should ask your wife if she remembers him. Maybe she can help jog your memory.'

Deans' face tightened and she saw anger chase panic across his features.

'I don't think there's any need for that.'

'Not if you can remember on your own, no. Can you?'

'No.'

Narey got up from her chair and began to make for the door.

'No problem. In that case, I'll just have a quick word with Mrs Deans.'

'No. Stop.'

She turned, barely bothering to hide the smirk on her face.

'Well?'

Deans hesitated, his eyes burning angrily into Narey's.

'Well, it could have been Peter Bradley, I suppose.'

'You suppose?'

'It was probably him, yes. He was called Paddy because he was such a big Celtic fan. There weren't many of them on campus. He even called himself it after a while.'

Narey took her seat again, perching on the edge of it so she was nearer to the man.

'Tell me about Mr Bradley.'

Deans drew his hand across his face, wearily rubbing at his eyes.

'There's not much to tell. We were at college together. I haven't seen him since we left. He was from . . . East Kilbride, I think. Somewhere like that.'

'Okay. And do you know where he teaches?'

'No. I don't even know if he still does.'

Narey turned to look at Winter, shrugging at him.

'Do you think he knows?' she asked him.

'I think he probably does.'

'Yeah, me too,' she replied before turning back to Deans. 'We think you do.'

The man's face reddened, not with embarrassment but with the flush of anger.

'Don't come into my house and call me a liar. I haven't seen Laurence or Paddy in nearly twenty years and I haven't seen Adam in ages. I can't help you and I'm going to have to ask you to leave.'

Narey didn't budge.

'What did you tell your wife when she asked why the police were here?'

'Not that it's any of your business but I told her the little I knew: you wanted to speak to me but hadn't told me why. She knows I wouldn't be involved in anything . . . untoward.'

'No?

'No.'

'Well, in that case, maybe you have reason to be worried.'

She received a hard stare from him.

'Is that a threat?'

'Not from me, no. But two of your friends have met with very unfortunate accidents. They do say that things happen in threes.'

'It certainly sounds like a threat.'

'It's a warning, Mr Deans, an entirely different thing.'

Deans got up out of his chair, put his hands in and then took them out of his pockets before crossing his arms defensively in front of him.

'I've already asked you to leave, Sergeant. Now I'm ordering you to go right now.'

Narey nodded. 'Maybe I could have a word with your wife before I go, though.'

'Absolutely not. She's upstairs sleeping. I will not have her disturbed.'

'Maybe next time. Because I will be back, Mr Deans. We both know that.'

Deans walked to the door and held it open until Narey and Winter followed him through it, leading them down the hall to the front door. A blast of icy wind greeted them as he pulled the door wide and ushered them onto the front step.

'If you *are* coming back, Sergeant, then I'd suggest you

bring a warrant with you. Otherwise there's no way I'm letting you in to upset my family.'

'Thanks for the advice. I'll do that. Very protective of your family, aren't you?'

'I'd do anything to protect them.'

'Anything?'

He didn't answer but began to close the door.

'Mr Deans?' she interrupted his movement with the question in her voice.

'What?'

'You didn't ask me why I was asking you about Paton, Mosson and Paddy. Have you received any interesting emails lately?'

The door was slammed in her face.

'You leaving it at that?' Winter asked her as they walked away, neither of them turning back.

'Course not. It might be fucking freezing but I can still make him sweat. The man's a bloody liar. He's in this up to his neck and the only question right now is if he's going to be a victim or tell us what the hell is going on.'

CHAPTER 34

Monday 17 December

The Bank turned out not to be a bank at all. It was a restaurant in Upper Craigs in Stirling, a two-storey sandstone Georgian mansion with a Doric porch of pillars and fanlights at the top of a flight of stairs leading up from the road. It was an impressive building from the outside and Narey cynically wondered if Detective Inspector Marty Croy's ambitions extended beyond lunch.

Inside, it was surprisingly modern, with mood lighting and glass partitions a world away from the building's façade. Croy was already seated when she was shown to a booth of plush leather seats and he got to his feet to introduce himself.

'We could have done this at Randolphfield,' he told her, inviting her to sit. 'But from what I gathered from Kirsten, I thought you'd prefer to keep it away from HQ – for now at least.'

'Yes, thanks. I'm grateful for that. We'll need to go official when push comes to shove but I'd rather keep it between us for now, sir.'

'No problem. Glad to help if I can. And call me Marty.'

Croy was around forty and in very good shape, Narey noticed without a hint of guilt. He had thick, dark curly hair and a roguish glint to his blue eyes. He was a good-looking guy and she reckoned it was at least some small compensation for the generally shitty turn of recent events.

'This is a nice place,' she said, looking around at the restaurant, taking in the sky-high ceilings and the marble columns offset by the modern tones of wood and subdued lighting. It all added up to a luxurious feel. 'Expenses must be better in Central than they are in Strathclyde.'

Croy grinned. 'I wish. Expenses are virtually a distant memory. But I like it here and try to come when I can. It's been all sorts of things, this building. It started out as a private mansion built in the early 1800s before it became a private school for girls. It was a Masonic hall for a while and when I was growing up it was a nightclub named Le Clique, then a fast food joint called Fat Sams and finally the Bank of Scotland took it over before it became this place.'

'So how come you know so much about it?'

Croy had the good grace to look embarrassed.

'Bit of a local history nut.'

'You'll know all about Lily of the Lake, then.'

'Ah, straight to business,' he smiled. 'Fair enough. Yes, of course. I'd have been about twenty, I guess. I was at university in Edinburgh and the fact that it happened so near to home made it seem worse somehow. Everyone was talking about it. It wasn't just that the murder was so brutal, it was this idea of someone going over to the island with her and not leaving a trace. I guess it spooked a lot of people.'

'How long after that did you join the force?'

'Four years. I suppose I'm a bit of a home bird. I came back to Stirling because I like it here. Family and friends are around and that works for me. It was tempting to try for a move to Glasgow or Edinburgh but I've somehow never gone for it.'

'Maybe when you go for a chief inspector's post.'

He laughed, his eyes creasing at the side.

'Maybe, but there's a CI post here I've got my eye on. Maybe when I go for superintendent.'

Narey realised Croy was only half joking and his obvious ambition made her realise how her own aims didn't extend far beyond catching criminals and seeing what happened from there. She was like her dad: take care of the job and leave the ladder climbing to others.

'So, did you ever work on the Lake case?' she asked him. 'Reconstructions, anniversaries and the like?'

'A little. I was involved on the fringes of it when we did an appeal for information on the tenth anniversary of her death in 2003. We went back to the lake, a superintendent did a short piece to camera for *Crimewatch*, we stuck up some posters and did a round of interviews with the locals. It was all superficial stuff really though. Anyway, what's your interest in the case? Kirsten didn't say.'

'That's because she didn't ask.'

'I guess we cops tend to ask different questions than professors of life sciences. But I'm asking.'

There was no getting away from it. In fact, there was every chance Croy already knew about her link to the case. Whether he did or not, the time for covering it up had gone.

'My dad worked the case. So I guess I've got a personal interest.'

'Chief Inspector Alan Narey,' he nodded. 'I remember seeing his name in the case files. I never knew him but some of the guys who came through the ranks with me did. They said he was a very good cop. Don't think I ever heard anyone say a bad word about him.'

The compliment slapped her on both cheeks, warming and saddening her. She wanted to ask more about what the cops had said but wasn't sure she could cope with the answers. Instead she forced out a single word reply.

'Thanks.'

'So why now?' he asked her, with an edge to his questioning that hadn't been there before.

She sized Croy up, wondering who was supposed to be getting information from whom.

'Detetective Inspector Croy, why do I get the feeling you already know the answers to the questions you're asking me?'

Croy sipped the mineral water in front of him and looked at her over the glass as he did so.

'Okay. So your name came up in Randolphfield after the woman in Wallace Place complained about you. It wouldn't have registered a jot if it weren't for the fact that you were a Glasgow copper. It put a lot of noses out of joint over here, I can tell you. If anything, it just made the people who matter all the more certain that, whatever you had to say, it was wrong. You know how territorial cops get and provincial forces are the worst of the lot.'

Narey said nothing. She knew it had been a risk. But she needed the support now.

'Your dad was lead local investigator on the case and Laurence Paton was his chief – his only – suspect,' Croy continued. 'Paton dies and now you turn up wanting a cosy chat about facial reconstruction. Just how fucking noddy do you think we are over here?'

'Not that noddy, I guess,' she grimaced.

'Correct.'

'Okay, that's me told off. So now can we stop buggering around and talk straight?'

'Sounds good to me,' he said, raising his glass of water in a mock toast. 'So what's the deal with Laurence Paton? You really think he was murdered?

'Yes.'

'Hm. That would be interesting. We don't get anywhere enough murders round here. Would look good on the CV.'

She smiled ruefully at him, trying not to look impressed by his approach. He was cocky enough to flaunt the naked ambition routine and the cheeky sparkle in his eyes allowed him to get away with it.

'So can we swing it?' she asked, a hand carelessly toying with her hair. 'I wouldn't, of course, want to stand on any toes at Central Scotland Police but I do want permission to exhume Lily's body.'

'Of course you don't and of course you do. I'd need to get permission from the Procurator Fiscal here but she's generally receptive to sensible requests. Getting the okay from my guvnor might be a bit harder though. He'd want to make sure there was something in this for us otherwise he'd just propose we do the whole thing ourselves.'

Narey knew he was only testing her as part of a prelude to

a bargaining process but the suggestion of taking it away from her still caused her stomach to knot.

'I'm sure there's no need to inflict an even greater work-load on your force than I'm sure it's under already.'

'We like hard work,' Croy smiled. 'We can always find the time to do more.'

'Perhaps a venture of cooperation is the way forward,' she relented. 'After all, Laurence Paton, however he died, died on your patch.'

'So, if we give the go-ahead for Lily to be exhumed, then you'll give us what you have on Paton's death and any possible murder inquiry?'

'Of course,' she lied without a glimmer of guilt.

'In that case, we 'd be grateful for Strathclyde's input into the identification of the girl on Inchmahome.'

'Thank you,' Narey said, extending her hand.

'You sure you don't want a glass of wine with your lunch?' Croy asked, shaking her hand for a heartbeat longer than was necessary. 'You could have one.'

'As a police officer, you should be aware that one shouldn't drink any alcohol at all if intending to drive. But okay, a glass of white – just one.'

'Perfect. In that case, I'd recommend the Petit Chablis to go with the seared scallops with Stornoway black pudding. It's superb.'

'Hm. Black pudding? Not for me,' she replied. 'I don't really have a taste for blood.'

CHAPTER 35

Tuesday 18 December

Julia Corrieri had bounded into Narey's office space with such enthusiasm that the DS had to stifle a giggle at the sight of her. With her mop of dark hair and ungainly stride, a pile of folders under her arm, the tall and gangly DC could have walked straight out of double maths and be on her way to PE. She wore a bashful grin Narey now knew to mean she was pleased with herself.

With a pang of guilt, Narey realised she hadn't spoken to Corrieri since she'd charged her with working her way through the potential paddy38s she'd identified from the Jordanhill records. It was only seeing her approach with what would inevitably be a comprehensive history of everyone on the list, probably down to what they had for breakfast, that Narey realised she had neglected to tell Corrieri it had been none of them. Now she would have to burst the poor girl's balloon.

'Julia . . .'

'I'm sorry this has taken so long, Sarge. There was just so much to cover but I wanted . . .'

'That's okay, Julia, but . . .'

'It's been worth it, Sarge. I have quite a bit on everyone on your list and . . .'

'Julia, will you just stop and listen for a minute,' Narey interrupted her, sharper than she meant to. 'Please.'

'Sorry, Sarge. Sorry.'

Narey felt like she'd told a puppy off for bringing a stick back when she was the one who had told it to go and get it in the first place. The look of hurt in the puppy's eyes pained her.

'That's okay. Look, I'm sorry but I'm not sure the guy we're looking for is on the list you have.'

'Oh.'

'Yeah. I've got some new information and a new name. It looks like we'll have to start all over again. Well, you'll have to start all over again. Sorry.'

'Oh, that's okay. I'll start on it straight away. But there's nothing in here you'll need?'

'Sorry, no. It's another student at Jordanhill altogether. A guy called Bradley. He's . . .'

'Peter Bradley?'

Narey stared at her DC in surprise.

'Um, yes, how did you know?'

Corrieri visibly brightened and delved into one of the folders clutched under her arm. As she did so, she dropped the bottom folder, blushing in embarrassment as it plopped onto Narey's desk. She tried to pick it up at the same time as looking inside the other folder and had to wedge the lot against her for support. At last, she triumphantly produced a couple of sheets of paper that were stapled together.

'Peter Bradley. Born 22 September 1970 in East Kilbride. Attended Halfmerke Primary School from 1975 to 1982 and Hunter High School from 1982 to 1988. He then went to . . .'

'Why have you got all this information on Bradley? Have you got me details on *every* student that ever went to Jordanhill?'

Corrieri smiled shyly.

'No, Sarge. I looked at the list of names you gave me as being potentially the paddy38 you were looking for. I did all of those but it occurred to me that list wasn't . . . no offence, Sarge, but it wasn't necessarily as comprehensive as it might have been.'

'Is that right?'

'Er . . . well, um. Anyway, I also looked at two Smiths, a Connor, a Grady, one with the first name Ryan, one called Maureen . . . and Peter Bradley. I hope that's okay.'

Narey laughed.

'Yes, Julia. It's definitely okay. What have you got?'

Corrieri lit up.

'Well . . .'

Narey patiently sat through Corrieri listing Bradley's CV in minute detail, thinking the least she deserved was the right to share her findings. Narey knew the schools he'd worked in and positions he had held there were unlikely to be of much use to them but they would be itemised nonetheless.

'He moved to Hillpark Secondary in 1988 but only stayed there for one year, which is fairly unusual, though there was nothing on his record to suggest there was any problem. He then taught at King's Park Secondary from 1989, becoming Deputy Head of History in 1995. He held that position until 1998.'

'And then?'

'Then nothing.'

'Nothing?' Her interest was piqued.

'Nothing at all, Sarge. He resigned from the deputy head's position and then we don't know where he went next. His national insurance contributions stopped, income tax stopped, no record of social security benefits, no telephone line or bills. Nothing.'

'Did he die?' Her mind was turning over the possibilities.

'No registry of death, Sarge.'

'So where the hell did he go?'

Corrieri shrugged apologetically. 'I don't know, Sarge. Sorry. If I'd known it was him specifically that you were looking for, then I'd have delved deeper. I can . . .'

'Christ, there's no need to apologise, Julia. You've done well, although we can't leave it there. Go and see what else you can turn up. If he isn't dead, then there must be some bloody trace of him.'

'Yes, Sarge.'

Corrieri hesitated and Narey realised there was more she wanted to say.

'What is it, Julia?'

'Well . . . there was something that I thought maybe you should know.'

'What's that?'

Corrieri looked more awkward than ever and Narey had a bad feeling.

'This may not be right, Sarge, but I heard the information

you wanted on the students might be related to an old case – the Lady in the Lake killing.'

Narey levelled her with a hard stare, all considerations of not upsetting the puppy vanishing completely from her head. Corrieri shifted uncomfortably from side to side under the searching gaze of her boss.

'And where exactly did you hear that, DC Corrieri?'

'Um, canteen gossip, Sarge,' Corrieri admitted with more than a hint of a blush. Narey knew Julia was struggling a bit to cope with the macho nonsense that passed for banter round the station. She wouldn't be the type for gossiping but was trying to fit in and would probably get involved in conversations she shouldn't.

'Who's talking about this and what are they saying?'

'Well, I . . . A few people in CID. I'd rather not name names, Sarge. The word is you're looking into the Lake killing and you're putting yourself out on a limb. That you're . . . well, maybe getting involved in something you shouldn't.'

'And what do you think?'

'Um. I think you'll be doing what you think is the right thing, Sarge. I told the rest of them that too.'

'Yeah, and I'm sure they laughed in your face.' She looked at Julia and knew she was right. 'So why are you telling me this?'

'I thought you should know that people know. And if you want any help, then I'm here. In fact, um, I've actually already started.'

'You've done *what*?'

Corrieri fidgeted with embarrassment again.

'Well, I was going through all the databases for the names

261

you gave me so I thought I'd maybe just take a little look back at the Lake of Menteith case and see if I could find anything that might help. I searched for a record of every missing girl to see if anyone fitted but didn't come up with much initially. I've sent out requests to every force in the UK to ask them to search their case files for anything still open, even if it was a year or two before the body was found. I'm also in touch with the National Policing Improvement Agency's Missing Persons Bureau, the Samaritans, the Salvation Army and Reunite. I, um, hope that was okay.'

Narey shook her head despairingly at Corrieri but a reluctant smile etched itself on her face. She marvelled that the girl could be apologetic about what were clearly natural investigative skills.

'Yes, it's more than okay. What have you got?'

'More questions than answers,' Julia admitted. 'I've already had a lot of cases sent through to me and I'm just trying to wade my way through them, ruling out those that don't fit because of time, height, weight, etc. I got a lot of information, too, from the NPIA and it makes depressing reading. According to them, there's around 350,000 people reported missing every year. Of those, nearly two thousand are still missing a year later. Around twenty people are found dead every week after being reported missing.'

'You aren't cheering me up here, Julia.'

'Sorry, Sarge.'

'Don't be. You've done well and I'm grateful for the help. Keep at it. But don't let on to the sweetie wifies in the canteen you're doing so. They're right – I am out on a limb and I don't want you falling off the branch with me.'

CHAPTER 36

Wednesday 19 December

The morning drive into Stewart Street station from Highburgh Road was even more of a nightmare than usual because of the weather and Narey was already fed up with the day. She inched along Byres Road, then did the same on Great Western Road, cursing the snow, the ice, the lack of gritters and the twat in the silver Ford Fiesta who insisted on being inches from her rear bumper. All that stopped her from getting out of the car and telling the driver to back off was that she couldn't trust herself to keep her temper if the eejit argued back.

To make matters worse, some other clown sitting at the front of the traffic lights at Park Road decided to treat other road users to his right-turn indicator only after the lights went to green. Narey was stuck behind him, knowing full well he wouldn't be able to turn until the filter and she wouldn't get through the lights at all. She thumped her horn and the car behind her did the same, as if it were her fault rather than the twonk in front.

Eventually, her temper fraying further by the minute, she was able to get off Great Western Road and the rest of the journey only took another few minutes. As she turned onto Maitland Street and slowed on the approach to the station, a silver Fiesta loomed in her rear view and passed her. Narey was about to turn into the station car park when she saw the Fiesta pause further along Maitland Street and, on instinct, she drove a couple of hundred yards past the entrance, parked and began to walk back.

She heard a car park not far behind her but she didn't turn round, not even when the footsteps began to close on her. She heard the click-clack of quick steps, realising the person was now only just a few feet behind. Suddenly, she stopped completely and whirled, forcing her pursuer on her sooner than expected and unsettling whomever it was. With the navy blue of the station wall on her right, she spun on her left foot and caught the would-be attacker's collar with her left hand, shoving the person into the wall with her right.

The sound of heels had registered but the fact that her hunter was a woman didn't stop Narey from disabling her. She twisted the woman's left arm tightly behind her back and grabbed her hair, using the leverage to force her face hard against the wall. As the woman squealed in pain, Narey was amused to see a face peek through the window above her head – the duty sergeant, obviously wondering what the hell was going on.

'You all right there, Sergeant Narey?' he enquired in bemusement.

'I'm just fine, Bill,' she told him. 'Just fine. Can't say the same for this one though. Who are you?'

The woman only just managed to squeeze the words out of the corner of her mouth as it was wedged against the wall.

'My name is Irene Paton.'

They sat opposite each other in Café Hula at the top of Hope Street, just a few minutes' walk from the station. A black coffee sat undisturbed in front of Irene Paton while Narey sipped slowly on a latte, simmering under Paton's angry glare. The woman seemed content to smoulder rather than speak and that suited Narey fine, as it gave her time to wonder what the hell Laurence Paton's wife wanted with her. For all that, though, she was also impatient to find out what the new widow had to say for herself.

The café bustled around them but neither woman had eyes nor ears for the chatter or the clink of cups. They were both far too engrossed in their own play to be aware of anyone else's. Paton was nervous, that much was obvious, but she also seethed with a resentment that overrode her anxiety. Narey was unusually edgy too; she didn't like being ambushed, particularly on her own doorstep, and she didn't have a handle on the older woman's motives.

Paton's eyes were puffy and reddened. Hardly surprising, Narey supposed, for someone whose husband had died so recently but it had clearly taken its toll on her. Her dark shoulder-length hair had barely had a brush pulled through it and her face, although made-up, was lined and tired. Irene Paton had been through the mill.

'Why were you outside my house?'

The question came abruptly out of the tense silence and caught Narey off guard even though she knew it had to be coming.

'It was part of an ongoing investigation' was the best that she could come up with.

'Not according to Central Scotland Police, it wasn't. And according to my neighbour, you were rude and aggressive.'

Narey said nothing and Irene contemplated her coffee again.

'Were you having an affair with my husband?'

Whatever it was Narey had been expecting, this wasn't it. She wasn't sure whether to be relieved or disappointed so she settled for surprised. Was this ridiculous assertion really what had driven the grieving widow to stalk a police officer? The weary fire that blazed in Irene's eyes suggested she wasn't joking.

'No, Mrs Paton. I wasn't.'

The widow held Narey's gaze, seemingly desperate to find something behind the bold denial. Narey let her stare, all the time wondering what might have made the woman think such a thing.

'I don't believe you,' Paton continued, although her voice had already lost the little confidence it had previously held.

'I can assure you, I wasn't. What makes you think he was having an affair?'

'Laurence had been hiding something from me for years.'

'Why do you say that?'

Mrs Paton glared at her. 'A wife just knows these things. Are you married?'

Narey shook her head.

'Then you wouldn't understand. You live with someone as long as I did with Laurence, then you know things they barely know about themselves. You know when they're up and when they're down. You know when they're lying to you even when you don't know what about. You know when they're giving you everything and when they're not. There was something Laurence wasn't telling me and he hadn't been telling me for a very long time. I'll ask you again: was it you he wasn't telling me about?'

Tears welled up behind Irene Paton's dark-rimmed spectacles as Narey slowly shook her head.

'Are you sure it was another woman?' she asked gently.

Paton began to speak but bit her lip. She looked utterly lost. Narey's heart went out to her, recognising something in her she'd been feeling herself of late.

'Another woman; another man. I don't know. I know he was keeping something from me. And I want to know what you had to do with it.'

'Nothing. I never even met your husband, Mrs Paton.'

Confusion and doubt were painted all over her face. She clearly had no idea whether to believe Narey or not.

'But why . . .' her voice cracked. 'Why were you outside our house? Laurence was upset after you were there. He wouldn't speak to me, or tell me who you were. Nothing. He was on the phone upstairs and on the computer afterwards for ages but wouldn't tell me what it was all about.'

'Who do you think he was on the phone to?'

'I don't know. If it wasn't you . . .'

'It wasn't.'

'Then I don't know. He'd been on the phone with the door closed quite often recently. My husband had a secret.'

Narey hesitated, unsure how far to push it.

'I think you're right, Mrs Paton. Laurence did have a secret.'

The woman's eyes widened.

'And that's why you were at our house?'

'Yes. But I didn't get the chance to talk to your husband so I'm not certain what the circumstances were. Perhaps you could help me.'

Mrs Paton's eyebrows knotted as she sank deeper into a pit of uncertainty.

'I don't see how I can. I'm . . . Well, yes. If I can.'

Something niggled inside Narey and she wondered if Irene Paton really did know things about her husband he didn't know himself, did he have giveaway 'tells' that only a top poker player or a wife would recognise?

'How long have you thought there was something he wasn't telling you?'

More tears. This time they escaped and ran in thick streams down the woman's face.

'Since I met him. I didn't know it at the time, maybe I convinced myself it wasn't true, but it was always there. I loved Laurence so I looked beyond it. But "it", whatever it was, was always there.'

'What do you mean?' Narey coaxed.

'He'd go quiet, disappear off into himself for no apparent reason and then just as suddenly come out of it. He didn't sleep well either. He was always having these terrible dreams. Nightmares, I suppose.'

Narey tensed. 'Did he tell you what the nightmares were about?'

Irene shook her head.

'He never said. He told me he never remembered them.'

'Did you believe him?'

'No. He'd wake in the middle of the night in a cold sweat. Anyway, he would speak while he was sleeping, while he was dreaming. So I knew what he was dreaming about even if he didn't.'

'Will you tell me what it was?' Narey asked her, desperately trying to keep the excitement out of her voice.

Paton nodded sombrely, gathering herself together before answering.

'It was always the same dream. He would shiver in his sleep as if he were cold, rubbing his hands over his arms to warm them. Sometimes he would say how cold he was, or how he was worried about the ice. It was always about ice. Except . . .'

The woman's voice faltered.

'What else did he say?' Narey prompted her.

'Sometimes he'd say, "I can't leave her." I assumed he meant me. That he couldn't leave me for this other person.'

Narey hesitated, reluctant to ask the question she most wanted an answer to in case the answer was no. She took a deep breath and asked it anyway.

'Did your husband ever mention a name when he talked in his sleep?'

Irene's gaze fell to the table.

'Yes.'

Narey's heart thundered against her chest.

'Barbie – like the doll. He would sometimes, no . . . lots of times, he'd mention someone called Barbie.'

'Did he ever use Barbie's surname?'

'No, never. He would say Barbie and then say, "No, no, no." Sometimes he'd say, "I mustn't. I mustn't." I'd lie there

CRAIG ROBERTSON

and watch him, wondering what it was all about. Wondering who Barbie was and if he'd ever tell me.'

'And you never confronted him about it? Asked him who she was?'

Her eyes closed and she swayed slightly from side to side.

'No. Never. I suppose I was afraid to hear the answer. Do you know? Do you know who Barbie was?'

'Perhaps. I think she was someone from your husband's past – from before he met you,' Narey told her, not quite lying but not quite telling the truth.

'Only from his past? Not from his present?' Irene asked her doubtfully but with a glimmer of hope.

'No, very much from his past,' Narey replied. 'I really don't think he was having an affair.'

The woman sat back in her chair and breathed out hard, looking almost set to collapse with relief.

'Thank you, Sergeant. And I'm sorry I thought . . . well, you know. I hope I'm not in trouble for following you.'

'That's okay, Mrs Paton. You've been through a lot. And no, you're not in trouble. Tell me, though, your neighbour, Mrs Haskell, did she actually see your husband fall from the ladder?'

'Well, yes, she told the police she saw him fall.'

'And she was there quickly after he fell?'

'Yes.'

'Mrs Haskell is the kind who likes to know everyone's business, I'm guessing. The first with the gossip, maybe keen to be the centre of attention?'

Irene Paton smiled for the first time and made to get up from the table. 'I think you just described her to a tee, Sergeant.'

270

As she stood, a thought occurred to her and she suddenly stopped.

'Sergeant, there was something else. I heard Laurence on the phone, not long before he died. I think he thought I was in the garden and couldn't hear him but I did. I don't know who he was speaking to but he was saying it was all his fault. It confused me because he said it was his fault but it wasn't him who'd done it. Does that make any sense?'

CHAPTER 37

Wednesday 19 December. 5.37 p.m.

The heating in the SPSA office in Pitt Street wasn't up to the job of keeping the cold at bay and Winter had decamped to the canteen for some heat and crap coffee served in a plastic cup. He'd been cornered at the drinks machine by a couple of uniforms, Jim Boyle and Sandy Murray, and the three of them had inevitably got into an argument about football.

Boyle was a Celtic supporter like Winter but Murray was a Rangers fan and took delight in winding the other two up at any opportunity. Sometimes the arguments came danger-ously close to getting out of hand and they'd make a point of avoiding each other immediately before or after a derby match, all knowing there might be no going back if some-thing was said that crossed the line.

'What a surprise for you lot to get a penalty,' Murray was saying now. 'It's in the rules that you get one at least every second game, isn't it?'

'It was a stonewaller,' Boyle countered. 'But given that the ref was, by definition, a Mason, then I suppose we were still lucky to get it. And you've got a cheek talking about us getting penalties. Your manky mob does more diving than a fleet of submarines.'

'Ah, here we go. The old paranoia again. It's all the Masons' fault, eh?'

'You've been cheating us for a hundred years,' Boyle bit back. 'Sitting around in the Lodge with your goats and your trouser legs rolled up, finding ways to keep the uppity Fenians down. Just because we're better looking than your lot. It's just jealousy.'

'Aye, that's right. We're all out to get you. We arra people.'

'What does that actually mean, anyway?'

Murray's answer was cut off by the Airwave on his lapel rumbling into life. The constable pressed the response button and a voice from the control room boomed into the canteen.

'Murray?

'Yes, Sarge.'

'Get yourself and Boyle over to The Rock on Hyndland Road. And no, before you ask, it's not an invite for a pint. Some halfwit's taken a tumble down the stairs by the side of the pub and you need to get over there before some other eejit does the same. The guy that fell is in intensive care so see if the local punters know him. His name is Deans. Gregory Deans.'

As soon as he heard the name, Winter was halfway out of his chair. Danny had been right as usual: never trust anything that looks like a coincidence.

Greg Deans. There was no way this wasn't to do with the Lake killing. He texted Rachel so that she had the chance to elbow her way onto the case too. Now he was ready to jump over anyone in the SPSA to make sure he got to take the photographs.

Deans had been carted off to hospital immediately. His injuries were life-threatening so there was no question of him being photographed at the scene. The area had been cordoned off, as much to prevent anyone else from falling down the stairs as to protect the scene. As far as the police were concerned, the blame lay with the snow and ice rather than anything untoward. Winter had already made it clear that he would go to The Rock after the Western although he wasn't particularly bothered if anyone else took photographs at the pub – as long as he got to take them as well.

Winter knew The Rock reasonably well; it was just six hundred yards or so up the hill from Rachel's flat at the foot of Highburgh Road. The steps Deans had fallen down led from the car park to the pub. The car park was on the street behind and sat easily higher than the pub's roof, meaning there was a steep, narrow fifty yards of stone steps down to the side entrance into the pub. The steps were badly lit and it had always occurred to Winter that they would be a prime spot either for a mugging or for an unwary drunk to take a tumble. Deans most likely hadn't been drunk though; he'd been on his way *into* the pub.

From memory, Winter knew there was a flight of steps, then a level area before another flight landed at the side door. This was where Deans had been found unconscious, blood leaking from his head and cuts and grazes to his hands. He'd have to have been falling at some rate to have bounced across the level area but, given the amount of snow and ice on the steps, it was possible – especially if he'd been given a helping hand to get on his way. The man was lucky he was going to hospital rather than the morgue.

The Western Infirmary was very much on its last legs; awaiting closure and demolition, it had been allowed to fall even further into scruffy disrepair. It was an ugly building, grown old and tired through overuse, like a wizened grand-mother who had used all her energy and vitality in caring for ungrateful children. It was to be flattened and all the facili-ties transferred from its site on Dumbarton Road to the extended Gartnavel two miles away on Great Western Road. The death throes had been long and painful, seeing it had been thirteen years since the closure was announced and yet last rites had still not been called.

Winter managed to find a parking space on his second circuit of the hospital car park, currently doubling as an ice rink, and snatched his gear from the boot. He skated across to the entrance and took the well-trodden path to A&E. He'd spent too many Friday and Saturday nights in there for his liking, photographing the monotonously predictable after-math of countless Glasgow nights out. Casualty carnage was par for the course at weekends and he didn't know how the staff had the patience for it, particularly as they were likely to get a mouthful of abuse or worse for their trouble. There was a police room specially built into the corner of the waiting area, the reception staff tucked away behind perspex for their own safety.

This night was still young, however, and none of the hand-ful of people waiting in the rows of blue metal seats looked like they were in the mood for trouble. At least a couple of

them seemed to be nursing potentially broken bones cour-
tesy of the icy pavements. There was no sign of Deans or any
cops, which suggested he had been treated straight away.
Winter went up to the first nurse he could find, introduced
himself and was quickly taken through the double doors
marked 'Patients only beyond this point', then into a room
where, behind a curtain, Greg Deans was lying with his eyes
closed and blood streaked down his face. A young, heavy-set
doctor with extravagant sideburns was standing over Deans
and, as he turned, Winter saw the name Meldrum on the tag
on his blue scrubs. The doctor didn't seem impressed at the
interruption and glared at Winter.

'Yes?'

'Dr Meldrum, I'm Tony Winter. I'm with the SPSA and
Strathclyde Police. I'm here to photograph Mr Deans'
injuries.'

The doctor's brows furrowed, not best pleased at the
suggestion.

'Why? This guy has had a fall down a steep set of stairs.
There is no suggestion of anything criminal. I'm sorry, pal,
but I see no reason to allow you to photograph him.'

Winter indicated with a nod of the head that he wished to
speak to the doctor outside the cubicle and, with an irritated
frown, the medic agreed.

'This better be good,' he muttered at Winter, snapping off
his latex gloves.

'Doctor, it's important that I be allowed to photograph
Mr Deans. Any photographs I take of his injuries may be
needed as evidence in court.'

'I doubt that.'

Winter fought back the first response to fly into his mind.

'Dr Meldrum, I'm asking you to let me do my job. I'll be as quick as I can so that you can continue doing yours.'

'The thing is, my job is treating him for a fall in icy conditions. In case you hadn't noticed, it's treacherous out there. We've been treating breaks and dislocations since this time yesterday and I don't see how this is any different. It's not a police matter.'

Winter successfully struggled with his temper and came up with an answer he'd heard Rachel and Addison trot out a hundred times.

'Doctor, we have reason to believe that Mr Deans' injuries were not the result of an accident and are part of an ongoing investigation.'

The doctor raised his eyebrows almost mockingly and a sneer spread itself across his lips.

'You're kidding me, right? What's this "we" stuff. You're not a cop. How would you know something like that?'

Winter was very close to telling the guy to go fuck himself but managed to settle for a patronising smile, at the same time digging deep into his acquired repertoire of stock police responses.

'I'm sorry to say that's not for you to know, sir. All you do need to know is that a detective sergeant is on her way over here and if she finds that I haven't photographed Mr Deans, then both you and I will be in a lot of trouble – a lot.'

Meldrum stuck his tongue into his cheek as he looked in the other direction, clearly unhappy but accepting that he could do nothing about it.

'Right, just get on with it then. I really don't see the point in this at all. He is extremely drowsy and ought not to be exerted. I'll give you five minutes.'

You'll give me as long as I need, Winter thought to himself. And you'll give us even longer once Rachel gets here. He ducked back behind the curtain, leaving the grumbling doctor behind, and saw that Deans still had his eyes closed.

He quickly drew his Nikon from his bag and quietly lined up a full-length shot of the man on the hospital bed. At once, he saw the vivid flashes where the blood stained him at angry grates on his knees and inner thigh. A large discoloured welt had already formed near his shoulder, doubtless soon to turn the purple of a severe bruising. There was also a large piece of fine gauze covering the cut on his head. Winter focused and fired off a few shots, the clack-clack of the camera shutter causing Deans' eyes to flutter open.

'Who are you?' he asked blearily, unable to focus.

'Tony Winter. I was at your house with Detective Sergeant Narey.'

Deans gazed back at him, clearly trying to sort his muddled brain into some kind of order.

'Oh. Right.' He thought some more. 'What are you doing here?'

'I'm photographing your injuries. You do know that you've had a bad fall?'

'Hm? Yes, yes. They told me. But why photograph me?'

'I think you'll need to ask DS Narey that. She'll be here soon.'

Deans looked confused by the suggestion. Doubtless he'd had enough of Rachel haranguing him at his house without having her nip his bruised and battered head some more. The

278

man closed his eyes again and Winter couldn't tell if he was sleeping or merely letting him get on with it. Either way, he wasn't going to wait to be asked. He took a few steps closer, moving to the left side of the bed, instinctively changing the camera lens in preparation for some close-up work.

Winter itched to take off the gauze that covered the wound on the right side of Deans' temples. He wanted to see and to photograph the extent of the abrasion that had occurred when Deans had learned that being between The Rock and a hard place was no fun at all. Still, the gauze was paper thin and his lens could pick out most of the lacerations caused by the stone steps. They'd clearly torn at his skin, leaving it as raw as if it had been shredded with a cheese grater. The result was a streak of blood from temple to jaw that left its mark on the snow-white pillow Deans rested on. The contrast appealed to Winter as it always did.

Deans' eyes flickered as the camera shutter rattled off frames above his head. He looked directly up at Winter and the photographer couldn't help but fire off another exposure, catching the look of wariness on the man's face. He apologised quietly but both of them knew he didn't mean it.

'Can I see your palms, please, Mr Deans?'

The man didn't say a word but slowly raised his arms from the bed and turned his hands over so that the soft, white flesh showed the lurid scrapes where he'd clawed unsuccessfully at concrete on his way down. Winter closed in on the abrasions, the rip of tissue and the bloody patches where skin should have been.

'You finished?' Deans asked him sourly.

'Nearly.'

Winter swapped his Nikon for the Fuji IS Pro, the ultra-violet infrared camera that would be able to pick up bruising invisible to the eye. He snapped both legs, concentrating around the knees, the torso and arms. Sure enough, it picked up a few extra bumps that would otherwise have gone unseen but not quite enough to satisfy someone with Winter's hunger. He could feel the familiar rush of blood in his ears as he contemplated whether a hand somehow reached from Lily to Deans despite a gap of nearly twenty years.

Voices close behind him abruptly broke his reverie. It was the doctor, Meldrum, and he had someone with him.

'He has a fractured left wrist, concussion and severe bruising to his hip, knee and head,' Meldrum was saying. 'His difficulty breathing suggests he may have fractures to his seventh and eighth ribs. All things considered, Sergeant, he's a lucky man.'

'Thank you, doctor. You've been very helpful. If you could leave us now, please. It's imperative that I speak to Mr Deans now – alone.'

'No problem at all. If you need anything else, I'll be just over there. Nice to meet you.'

Meldrum smiled ingratiatingly at Narey and left them to it, although not before firing a disapproving scowl in Winter's direction.

'How are you, Mr Deans?' Narey asked him after the doctor had gone.

'Sore and sleepy.'

'You're a very lucky man. That's what the doctor reckons.'

'Funny. I don't feel too lucky.'

'No, I don't suppose you do. We need to talk, Mr Deans. I need you to tell me exactly what's going on.'

Deans blinked and looked up at her.

'I fell. That's all I know.'

Narey's voice hardened as her patience thinned.

'Mr Deans, I need you to be honest with me and to think carefully. Did you hear or feel anything before you fell?'

Deans sighed and took his time before answering.

'I'd parked my car and started to go down to the steps. I was just at the top when I think there were . . . footsteps. Behind me. I didn't think anything of it – didn't have time to really. Then it all seemed to happen at once. I just knew I was falling. My head was below my feet and I felt my head rattle, then . . . then it was all dark. Next thing I knew I woke up in here.'

'You fell down two flights of steps, Mr Deans. I don't think you could have done that without someone making sure of it.'

Deans looked confused until her meaning dawned on him.

'What? You think I was pushed?'

'Yes. Do you remember that happening?'

Deans opened his mouth as if to speak, then screwed his eyes shut, searching his memory.

'I don't know. The footsteps and me falling happened almost simultaneously. I suppose I could have been. I'm sorry. I just don't know.'

Narey turned to Winter and regarded him as if he were any other hired help.

'Which officers were at the scene of the incident?'

'PCs Murray and Boyle. They were interviewing people at the scene, looking for witness.'

'And did anyone report having seen Mr Deans fall?'

'No, sergeant. Murray told me two people in the pub heard Mr Deans scream as he fell but no one saw it.'

Narey nodded at the cop, then turned back to Deans.

'If the footsteps at the top of the stairs weren't connected to your fall, then I'd like to know why the person didn't stop to help you. Or at least tell someone they'd seen you fall.'

Deans' eyes widened and his mouth fell open.

'Someone pushed me,' he stuttered. 'Tried to kill me?'

'It looks that way, Mr Deans.'

Narey let the suggestion settle for a few moments, hoping it would suitably frighten him.

'Mr Deans, I'm going to have a police officer posted outside this ward until you are able to go home. I will then have an officer assigned to watch your home.'

'What? You really think that's necessary?'

Narey let slip an exasperated sigh.

'Yes, I do, Mr Deans. I think that whoever tried to push you down those steps wants you dead and will try again. There's every chance that he or she will succeed – unless you let us help you, unless you tell us what you know about what happened to Barbie.'

It was as if she had slapped Deans across the face. The mention of the girl's name, and the very fact that Narey knew it, had clearly shocked him. A single tear trickled down Deans' cheek, then his eyes slowly closed as he nodded his head in a gesture of defeat. As he did so, Winter surreptitiously fired off a single shot of his camera, capturing the man in his moment of surrender.

'You'll tell us about what happened at the Lake of Menteith?'

With his eyes still closed, Deans nodded again.

'And you'll tell us about Laurence Paton? And about whoever else was involved?'

Deans continued nodding his blind, compliant submission until at last he opened his wet eyes and looked up at Narey.

'I'll tell you everything. Just help me.'

CHAPTER 38

Seeing Rachel work was something Winter rarely got the chance to do at first hand. She was always at pains to make sure there were reels of police tape to keep him at arm's length or preferably further. When other cops or SPSA staff were around, which was almost always, she'd make sure he wasn't too close. But now, with Greg Deans in her sights, Winter was all but forgotten. She and Deans only had eyes for each other and Winter relished the chance of a front row seat.

He wondered if she felt as he did at that moment: hairs standing up on the back of his neck, heart beating just that little bit faster, pulse racing. He could almost taste what was to come but then he was just an amateur. This was her job and maybe this was routine, all in a day's work. He doubted it.

Deans had his chin on his chest, defeat written all over his face, struggling to come to terms with what had happened to him. Winter saw his reaction for what it was and hid a smile as Rachel opted not to allow him time to compose himself.

'We're listening, Mr Deans,' she told him.

His head came up slowly, the resentment in his eyes

reserved solely for Narey. Whatever it was that he was about to tell them, it was clear he'd much rather keep it to himself.

'Before I tell you, I want some . . . assurances.'

'I may not be in the position to offer those, Mr Deans. What do you want?'

'I can give you information about a high-profile case. In return for that information, all I'm asking is that my wife and daughter be protected from all this. I want them kept out of it.'

'If, by that,' Narey responded, 'you mean we don't tell them of your involvement, then that might not be something I'm able to guarantee. But I'll do my best.'

'I need to know that I can trust you, Sergeant.'

'That goes two ways, Mr Deans. Tell me your story and I'll do what I can. I'm making no promises.'

Deans looked at her for an age, trying to decide if that was good enough for him. In the end, he must have realised it was the best and only deal he was going to get.

'There were four of us,' he began reluctantly. 'Myself, Laurence, Adam Mosson and Peter Bradley. We weren't all best of pals. Laurence and I were pretty close and we got on well with Adam. Paddy was Adam's mate and, to be honest, Laurence and I weren't so keen on him. He was a bit of a loud mouth, a real chancer who was always banging on about how successful he was with the girls. Adam was a good guy, very different from Paddy, so we put up with his pal. Anyway, we went away for a weekend together.

'It was always a bit of a daft idea. Staying in this bothy that Laurence had been to before near the Pass of Leny in the Trossachs. You know the sort of thing, a restored stone building – an old farmworker's cottage I think this one was – that is left unlocked for shared use. It wasn't exactly the season for it but Laurence was keen on all that outdoor stuff and he was insistent that it would be great.

'The idea was just to get away from studying for a while, take a couple of bottles of whisky and some beer and do some hillwalking. We'd all been on teacher placement and it had been really hard going – or it seemed so at the time. What a lot of fuss we made then over nothing! We talked Adam into going and he invited Paddy along. I wasn't too happy with that but Laurence was cool with it; he said the more the merrier. It would have been okay if the bad weather hadn't kicked in. It was bloody freezing and Adam and Paddy were for pulling out. I mean, it got seriously cold. Minus eighteen degrees, so they said. Laurence talked them into it, though; accused them of being afraid of a wee bit of snow. So we went. Adam drove us in this battered old Volvo he'd got from his dad. We loaded it up with booze and headed to the Trossachs. The roads were terrible and it took us ages to get there. Then we had to walk the last half mile or so across six inches of snow to get to the bothy. It really wasn't a great idea.

'We got a good fire going inside but the wind was still blowing a gale under the door. After a few hours we'd just about had enough of the cold and decided to go to a pub so we could get some heat. We walked back to the car and Adam drove to the Lade Inn at Kilmahog. It was just what the doctor ordered: an open fire and large whiskies. And . . . well, that was where we met her.'

Deans let his head dip again, avoiding their eyes. Winter

had the urge to grab Deans by the hair and yank his head back up to face them. But the man went on with his tale, despite continuing to stare at his chest.

'She was in the pub, sitting on her own by the bar, chatting to the old boy behind the bar. She was good looking: long blonde hair tied back and a pretty face. She was only a little thing, barely over five foot, and we thought she was a couple of years younger than us. It was Paddy, of course, who went in first. He went straight up to her and started giving her this load of patter. It seemed to work, though, because next thing she was over at our table and we were all having a great laugh . . .'

Deans' voice faltered, the mention of laughter sitting uneasily with the rest of his story. He lifted his head, staring sullenly at them.

'She said she got called Barbie. We assumed it was a nickname because of her looks and, no, before you ask, she never mentioned a real name. She was English and said she was on a gap year before starting university and was bumming round Scotland. She came out with some hippy nonsense about trying to "find herself". We all liked her; that was obvious. And she seemed to like being the centre of attention. She told us she was nearly skint so we bought her drinks all night.

She'd been going to stay in the pub overnight but Paddy talked her into coming back to share our place. She was all for it and . . . well, so were the rest of us. Adam hadn't had as much to drink as the rest of us but he probably still shouldn't have been driving. He did anyway and we all went back to the bothy. We had some more beers – a lot more. And . . .'

'And?' Narey demanded.

'We had sex.'

'We? You and Barbie?'

'All of us. We all had sex with her.'

Deans let his head fall again but this time Narey wasn't going to let him get away with it.

'Look at me,' she insisted. He did so but shamefaced, embarrassed rather than angry.

'We all had sex with her,' he repeated. 'Paddy started it but then it . . . it just got out of hand. We were all drunk and it just happened. She wanted it. Let me be totally clear about that: she wanted it. If anything, she was the one who was in charge.'

Deans took a deep breath and let it back out in a heavy sigh, rubbing at his eyes and wincing at the resultant pain to the cut on his head.

'In the morning . . . well, the morning wasn't so good,' he continued. 'We were all a bit embarrassed. Not so much Barbie – she was a bit of a free spirit, I suppose – but the guys couldn't really look each other in the eye. Even Paddy seemed uncomfortable. If anyone took it worse, it was Laurence. I think he really liked Barbie. I'd seen it in the pub on the Friday night; he was looking at her like a lost puppy. By the Saturday morning, he couldn't look at her at all. In the afternoon, Paddy was back to his pain-in-the-arse normal self and he and Barbie were joking around like nothing had even happened. Laurence went off on his own, saying he was going into Kilmahog to bring back some food.

'When he came back late in the afternoon, just after it had got dark, he was full of the news from the Lake of Menteith. He said everyone in Kilmahog was talking about how the lake was frozen and they were curling and skating on it. He said people were coming from all over the place to go on the ice. Laurence was up for going over there on the Sunday but the rest of us had already decided to go hiking over to Callander to see the Bracklinn Falls. Barbie, well, she saw how disappointed Laurence was and said that she'd go with him to the lake. I don't think he knew how to react. He was still awkward about what had happened the night before but he couldn't really say no.

'We stayed at the bothy again that night and had plenty to drink but nowhere near as much as the night before. Everyone was edgy. Nothing happened. Well, I don't think so anyway. Paddy and Barbie disappeared at one point, saying they were going to get more beer from the car. They were gone a while and I think the rest of us wondered what they were doing. I certainly saw the look on Laurence's face. He wasn't happy.

'On the Sunday, Adam, me and Paddy headed off on foot and Laurence and Barbie hitched into Port of Menteith. I could see he still wasn't too sure about it but they went anyway. It was the last time any of us saw Barbie. When we got back from Callander, Laurence was at the bothy, alone. He told us he'd had a big argument with Barbie and she'd gone off on her own. She'd had everything with her in her rucksack so she didn't need to come back to the bothy to get anything. That was when Paddy dropped the bomb.'

'What bomb?'

'He said it was probably just as well that she was gone. She'd told him the night before she wasn't on a gap year but that she'd run away from school. She was fifteen.'

Winter felt a sickening sensation somewhere deep in the

pit of his stomach as his eyes flew to Narey, whose stare was fixed hard and angry on Deans. He, in turn, had found a spot on the floor that captured his attention.

'Paddy thought it was funny but the rest of us certainly didn't. Adam went for him and we had to pull him off. We were in deep shit. We were teachers, or training to be, and if it came out that . . . well, we'd never work. She was under age and that made us . . .'

'Rapists?' Narey offered. 'Paedophiles?'

'No!'

'Legally there's no doubt about it,' she confirmed.

'Sergeant, we didn't know. And, yes, it would definitely have made a difference – a huge one. There's no way I'd have . . . not if I'd known. But it put our careers in danger if anyone found out. We'd be finished. And after all that work . . .'

'My heart bleeds for you,' Narey snarled.

Deans clenched his teeth.

'Adam and I demanded no one ever breathe a word about it and the others agreed. We packed up immediately and went back to Glasgow.'

'And?'

'And we never mentioned it again – even to each other. We could barely cope with seeing each other. Then, four months later, a body was found on the island.'

'A body? Her body, you mean. Barbie's body.'

'We didn't know,' he protested weakly. 'Not for sure.'

Narey laughed sarcastically.

'You knew. Of course you fucking knew.'

'No. Laurence had said he'd argued with her but that she was fine. He said she was fine when he left her.'

'Bullshit. You knew it then and you know it now. Why didn't you report it to the police?'

'It wouldn't have changed anything. Except that we would all have faced prosecution.'

'Mr Deans,' Narey shook her head almost as much in disbelief as anger, 'trust me, you haven't escaped prosecution. It is highly likely that you will be charged with attempting to pervert the course of justice. If I can think of anything else with pervert in that I can charge you with, then I will.'

Deans' mouth fell open pitifully and his lower lip trembled.

'So what did you and your pathetic pals do when you heard about the body being found on Inchmahome?'

'We met. Once. For five minutes. We agreed we would never meet again, never talk to each other again.'

'And Paton?

'Nothing was said. Nothing was asked. It was over.'

'Like I said, pathetic – and cowardly. You saw the newspaper reports. You saw the TV appeals. And you never thought to put a family out of their misery? You never thought to help the police? To save hundreds of man-hours, hours that could have been spent investigating other crimes? You never thought to do the right fucking thing?'

'I didn't know what happened – not for sure. Yes, I was sure it had to be Barbie but it could have happened after Laurence had left her. I'd have been hanging him out to dry.'

'And yourself.'

'Yes. Yes, I'm not denying that. I'm not proud of it.'

'Well done.'

Deans flared at her sarcasm and the pair of them locked

eyes, apparently trying to stare each other to death as far as Winter could see. There was something amounting to genuine hatred between them but Winter knew there would only be one winner and it wasn't Deans.

'And you never thought to come forward any time over the years?' she scowled at him. 'God knows there must have been plenty of appeals.'

'I was married, and a father. I couldn't put all that at risk.'

'So tell me about what happened recently. Tell me about the emails.'

'How do you know about them?'

'Mr Deans, let me make something quite clear because you don't seemed to have grasped what is going on here. Even putting aside for a second that a girl was murdered, we have two highly suspicious deaths that seem to be linked to it. Someone is knocking off your old pals and you might be next, which would be a terrible shame. So, here's the deal: I ask the questions and you fucking answer them.'

Deans simply nodded, the fight seemingly gone from him.

'I got an email from someone claiming to know what had happened back then. There was no name as such, just a Hotmail account in the name of Justice 1993. It was sent to me, Laurence, Adam and Paddy. There were a couple of follow-up emails but they seemed to be only to me. If the others were copied into them, their names didn't show.'

'Did he ask for money?'

'Not at first. He just made it clear he knew, or thought he knew, about what had happened. Then he said we had to pay. Said we could pay either in cash or in what he called "cold justice". Obviously I emailed back asking who it was, but I was wasting my time. When he wouldn't tell me, I said I wouldn't deal with someone if I didn't know who they were.'

'And his response to that?'

'That he would have to show me the consequences of saying no. I don't know what I thought was going to happen. I didn't think he would . . . I never thought that. Then I heard about Adam – how he'd committed suicide.'

A single tear ran down Deans' face and it struck Winters that it might have been poignant but for the fact that he was crying for himself, not for Barbie or Adam.

'Did you believe it was suicide?' Narey persisted, clearly unmoved by the display of waterworks.

'Yes. No. I don't know. The papers were clear that it was. But it seemed too much of a coincidence. I was scared. I began to look at getting some money together but then . . . this.'

'Your push down the steps might have been a warning, Mr Deans. It was either a reminder to you to hurry up or maybe the person just didn't care whether you died or not.'

Deans attempted a glare but his heart simply wasn't in it.

'So who do you think your blackmailer is? I assume you've wondered about that.'

'I've not thought about much else, Sergeant. I don't know. I'm sure no one else knew at the time. I suppose maybe the landlord at the pub where we met Barbie did. No one else knew. Laurence and Adam are gone so that leaves Paddy Bradley. Or else one of them spoke about it. I certainly didn't. If anyone had blabbed, it would have been Paddy. He liked the sound of his own voice and he could never resist playing the big man – particularly in front of women. My guess? If anyone talked, it was him.'

'We would like access to your emails, Mr Deans, to see if there is anything else we can get from them. It may help us identify the blackmailer or your attacker.'

'You don't think they are the same person?'

'I'm keeping an open mind about it.'

'Okay. Again, I'd ask if you would do it when there's no one else in the house. Sergeant, my wife will leave me if she finds out about what happened. My daughter . . . she would be so ashamed. Please.'

Rachel laughed bitterly.

'For a schoolteacher, you aren't very bright, Mr Deans. Someone is trying to kill you. That's why I'm going to put a cop on guard at your front door. Did it not occur to you that your wife might just wonder why?'

Deans looked defeated.

'But, okay,' Rachel conceded, 'you let us in and give us computer access and you can tell your wife what you like for now. But this will all have to come out in the end. Did you make contact with any of the others after you received the emails?'

'No.'

'Why not? Was it not the natural thing to do?'

'I didn't want anything to do with it. I guess I was burying my head in the sand.'

'Mr Deans, you are in danger of being buried completely. Do you not realise that?'

'I do now. But I couldn't have contacted them even if I'd wanted to. I don't where they live now – lived. I don't know where they lived.'

'What about Peter Bradley? When did you last hear anything about him?'

'Years ago – maybe twelve, fourteen years ago. I heard he'd dropped out; not just out of teaching but out altogether.'

'What do you mean?'

'I heard he'd gone off the radar and out of mainstream society. The word was he'd married some girl from a gypsy family and was living that lifestyle now. No one knew where he was living.'

CHAPTER 39

Narey and Winter stood in the chill outside the Western, joining a throng of frozen smokers who were hopping from foot to foot in a futile attempt to keep warm while they coughed away the last of their health. A couple of them were in real danger of hypothermia; pyjamas and a dressing gown offered little protection against sub-zero temperatures. One woman in her mid-fifties, her face as grey as slate, was even attached to a portable drip as she puffed away. You had to admire their dedication.

Narey had her mobile to her ear and her other arm wrapped round herself for warmth as she impatiently circled while waiting for her call to be answered. The doctor had eventually ushered them out, saying that Deans needed to rest. Narey hadn't disagreed but had told Deans he could expect to hear from her very soon.

The DI sounded typically grumpy as he barked into the phone – not exactly filling Narey full of confidence but not putting her off either.

'Where the hell are you?' he demanded on recognising her voice.

'The Western. A man named Greg Deans was seriously injured in a fall and I . . .'

'A fall? Why the fuck would you be interested in a fall? And who the hell is Greg Deans?'

'Well, I don't think it was an accident and Deans . . . Deans was a student at Jordanhill with Paton and Mosson. He was . . .'

'Jesus Christ. Not this teacher bollocks again. If you haven't got anything better to do with your time, then I can find you something.'

'No, sir. This is serious. I think we've got two murders on our hands and an attempted murder.'

'We've been through this, Narey. Even if Paton was murdered, he isn't on our books; he's on Central's. And you still haven't told me what the fuck makes you think there's anything going on here at all.'

'Look, if you could just trust me on this for now and get a uniform to watch over Deans, then I'll explain the rest at the station. The link between these guys is concrete. I'm certain about this, boss.'

She knew the silence on the other end of the phone was Addison trying to think of another reason to argue. The longer he went without saying anything, the surer she was she'd persuaded him. He was as argumentative and confrontational as they came, but she was confident he respected her judgement – even if he'd never tell her that.

'You'd better be not just certain but fucking right,' he finally growled. 'Do you know how much those pencil-pushing pricks will bust my balls if I can't justify the man-hours spend of even a single woodentop? If there's anything I can't stand in this world, it's dealing with fucking accountants.

They've got the personality of cheese but they're vindictive bastards.'

'I am right,' she told him. 'Get me a uniform out here and I'll come straight in and tell you the lot.'

'Fucksake. The sooner I get out from behind this desk the better. You lot are doing my head in.'

The line went dead and Narey knew that was going to be as close to agreement as she was going to get. She'd wait until the constable arrived, then go to see Addison. Obviously she wouldn't tell him everything – just the part she felt would be enough. Addy had been round the block often enough to know that information came from all sorts of places you might not want to share with your superior officer.

As she was putting her phone back into her pocket, Narey looked up to see two women rushing to the hospital entrance. They were clearly agitated and the younger of the two was wiping tears from her eyes. As they brushed past, she saw that Winter knew who they were and raised her eyebrows at him questioningly.

'That's Deans' wife and daughter,' he told her. 'I recognise them from the photos in their house.'

'Poor cows,' Narey muttered. 'They're in for a nasty shock about Daddy.'

'So you're going to tell them?'

'Of course I am. It's only a question of when. At the moment it gives me leverage over him so I'll keep that while I need it.'

'You're all heart. What did Addy say?' he asked her.

'Your pal isn't exactly happy but then he never is. He's

sending someone over to keep an eye on Deans. I'll stay here till he arrives. What are you going to do?'

Winter looked up at the grey skies, which had a hint of pink, suggesting yet more snow could be on the way.

'I'm going to go over to The Rock. I want to get some pics from the scene.'

Narey swore under her breath and looked at her watch.

'Shit. You're right. I'll need to go there too. You go ahead. I'll join you as soon as the cavalry arrives.'

'Didn't I hear you telling Addy you'd be going straight to Stewart Street?'

'What are you, his bloody secretary? I'm going to The Rock and Addy can wait. That place is being treated like the scene of an accident but it's a crime scene.'

Winter grinned at her and she knew he'd been winding her up.

'Piss off,' she laughed. Her smile quickly disappeared, however, and was replaced by a serious frown.

'So . . .' she began. 'Our man Bradley may be living as a gypsy traveller.'

'Didn't see that coming. It was all I could do not to let my mouth fall open like a halfwit when Deans said it. What the hell's going on, Rach?'

'No idea. You're the gypsy expert, you tell me.'

'I can ask some of my new friends, I guess. But I already know they aren't exactly keen on sharing things with outsiders. Which reminds me: if what Deans says is right, then the "gypsy bride" rumour is a load of crap. Danny and I have been chasing this Sam Dunbar guy for nothing.'

'Not for nothing,' she disagreed. 'It's too much of a

coincidence. There's some link we're just not seeing. It looks like we'll need the help of your pal Tommy Baillie to find Bradley. That might mean sorting out this Dunbar character. I might need to get Addison to put someone on this.'

Winter shook his head.

'No. The last thing that Baillie wants is the cops involved in this. If we want his help, then we have to keep them out of it.'

Narey exhaled noisily.

'Christ. I'm being asked not to do my job a hell of a lot these days.'

'Well . . .' he hesitated, although perhaps not for as long as he should have done. 'You are not doing your job quite a lot these days.'

'What's that supposed to mean?'

'Rachel, you've been out on a limb for so long you'll be getting splinters in your arse. You've been doing too much stuff that isn't authorised and you need to watch it before you get into trouble.'

She stared hard at him but couldn't muster up any real resentment because she knew he was right.

'You let me worry about that. Right now, we have other things we need to bother about.'

'Like who is Peter Bradley? Our blackmailer, our killer or the next victim?'

She shook her head.

'Yes, but it doesn't matter which he is. Not right now. Whichever of those things he is, we need to find him as quickly as possible.'

*

The Rock was surrounded by residential housing, most of it of the high-ceilinged, corniced, spacious Victorian and Edwardian variety. As such, the low, flat-roofed white pub with its beer garden spilling onto the street was an oddity for that part of the west end. Whether it was a rock, an oasis or a sore thumb rather depended on your point of view. Winter had, inevitably, had a drink in it a few times, on his own and with Addison to watch football, and he quite liked the place.

He knew the short cut to the side entrance from the Dowanhill side, the one Greg Deans had taken down from the car park on Crown Terrace wasn't the kind of route that appealed on a dark night, particularly to women, as it wasn't overlooked and was poorly lit.

Winter parked up above the pub and followed Deans' route to the steps. Blue and white tape had been tied across the top to stop anyone else venturing down but there was no sign of Murray or Boyle. Winter's heart sank as he saw the number of footprints in the snow around the car park and at the area at the top of the steps. The only bonus was the crisp snow, which meant the prints that hadn't been trodden over stood out nice and clear. He laid down a black photo scale and photographed the footprints as best he could, cursing the number that had been crushed down by another boot, leaving patterns that were all but useless.

Photographing the prints from a regulation 90-degree angle, using a macro lens and with a 45-degree flash to avoid washing out the detail, he was still able to pick out a few good tracks. He'd photographed Deans' shoes before leaving the hospital so he would be able to separate those from the others at the scene and it would hopefully give them something to work with. For all that though, he knew it was more in hope than expectation. Who knew how many people had walked over the area either before or after Deans was pushed.

Winter made his way to the top of the steps, seeing just how steep and narrow they were, seemingly tumbling forever into the darkness below. The winter foliage pushed in from left and right, making the descent seem even sharper. He made his way down a couple of steps at a time, stopping only to photograph likely looking prints until he reached the first landing and spied a flattened area where it seemed likely Deans had fallen. The snow was compressed but not trampled and there were a few drops of blood to the right-hand side of the landing and then again a few steps further down. It looked as if Deans had hit the level area, then continued to tumble, probably out cold by that stage and unable to stop his momentum.

The biggest pool of blood was at the bottom, just a few feet from the pub's side door and the place where Deans had come to rest. Blood had soaked into the snow and become frozen there, capturing Winter's attention the way blood always did. He photographed the blood spatter from every angle with his macro lens, marking out the contours of the snow compression to show where Deans had landed.

So why had the attacker not finished Deans off? Maybe he'd thought the fall would have done the trick. You could see the reasoning in that: the guy's head was going to bounce off successive sets of concrete steps. While the blow may been cushioned by a layer of snow, there was hard ice underneath. Also, Winter thought, Deans would have made the trip to the bottom a whole lot quicker than his assailant and there was every chance that the crash of the fall would have alerted someone and brought them out from the pub. Then again, maybe Rachel was right and the push had only been a warning to Deans. Either way, Winter knew there was little he was going to be able to offer forensically to the debate – too many pairs of feet had seen to that.

He turned and looked back up the stairs to see where the attacker would have stood. It was doubtful if they could have seen from there whether Deans was alive or not. He had still been unconscious when he was discovered by customers and staff so presumably he hadn't moved after he hit the bottom. There was every chance he'd simply been left for dead.

The voice that came from behind him seemed, not for the first time, to read his thoughts.

'You seeing dead people again?'

'You shouldn't creep up on people like that, Rach.'

'Course I should,' she laughed drily, glancing up and down the stairway before planting a kiss on his lips. 'It's my job. So what have you got?'

'Not much,' Winter admitted. 'Half of Glasgow seems to have been walking over the area at the top of the stairs. The blood trail suggests he hit that first landing up there and kept rolling till he ended up right here. I've got pics of what I can but I doubt it will do us much good.'

'Pretty much what we expected,' Rachel agreed. 'Still, I do have some good news.'

'Oh yeah?'

'Things are looking up at last. I've just had a call from Marty Croy in Stirling. The Procurator Fiscal has given them the go ahead to exhume Barbie's body. We're going to dig her up in two days.'

CHAPTER 40

Thursday 20 December. 10.00 a.m.

'Dad? Dad, are you still there?'

She hated the phone calls. Hated them for how impractical they were and how she couldn't tell if he'd fallen asleep, switched his mobile off or forgotten how to work it. Above all, though, she hated the impersonal nature of it and the fact that it was so blindingly obvious she hadn't taken the time to go and see him face to face.

'Dad, just say something and let me know you can hear me.'

She always resisted the urge to be impatient with him or to raise her voice. Whatever the reason for the lack of response, it wasn't his fault. None of it was his fault. It was that horrible, hateful disease. She spent what little free time she now had reading up on it and none of it made her any more optimistic about what was to come.

How did they treat a disease when they didn't know how it was contracted in the first place? Nearly half a million people in the UK were affected by Alzheimer's and yet no son or daughter or grandchild could be told for sure how they'd got it. A combination of factors was the best answer that could be offered: lifestyle; unknown environmental factors; and, most scarily, genetic inheritance. The greatest risk of all was growing old and she became irrationally angry at reading that. How the hell was her dad expected to avoid that?

She now knew about 'plaques' and 'tangles' that developed in the structure of the brain, killing off brain cells and leading to the broken pathways and muddled thinking she'd seen manifested so clearly in her dad. She knew of all the medical treatments, both established and in testing. She knew there was no cure. She knew her father might have had the disease for years, with it developing silently all the while. She knew everything except what to do next.

Above all, one word kept reappearing in everything that she read. A word that she had grown to despise: progressive.

'Hello?'

'Hi Dad. It's Rachel.'

The silence again. Was he trying to remember who she was? Was he upset at hearing her voice, even though he'd clearly forgotten speaking to her just a minute before? Or had he gone?

She filled the interminable quiet with guilty thoughts of her absence and dark fears of how bad it might get and how quickly. Once this case was over, she kept telling herself, she would make things right. She would take him out of the home whether he liked it or not and get him to come live with her. It would mean moving and it might mean the end of her and Tony but what was more important than looking after her dad?

'Hello, Rachel.'

It never failed. Words of recognition melted her heart and cheered her no matter how dark and cold the day had been. It was the one advantage of speaking to him by telephone: she had the luxury of letting a happy tear streak down her face without worrying it would upset him.

'Hi Dad. How are you?'

'Oh, I'm fine, love, just fine. How are you, more to the point?'

'I'm all right, Dad. Just a wee bit worried about you.'

'Me? No need to worry about me. I'll be fine. I'm a bit lost just now without your mum but she'll be back soon. Don't you worry, love.'

'Okay, Dad, I won't.'

'Good girl. Now tell me, have you done your homework? You know what your mum's like. She's going to give you a hard time unless it's all up to date.'

It was her turn to be quiet. Not just because she was upset about him not knowing how old she was or that her mum was gone; but because it struck her how much better and simpler it was when all she had to worry about was getting her homework done on time.

'It's done, Dad. I promise.'

'Good. You're a good girl, Rachel. I love you, you know.'

'I know. And I love you too, Dad.'

She wondered if he really did know how much she loved him. She didn't say it enough and never had. Was it now too late for her to say it and be able to hope he'd remember?

'Dad? Dad, are you still there?'

Another silence filled the line. This time it didn't end. Rachel put down the phone.

CHAPTER 41

The snow was flaking gently onto the steeple of the converted church that was Oran Mor when Narey hustled along from Hillhead subway station. Lunchtime groups were filing into the restaurants inside, some obviously dressed up for office Christmas lunches, and she could only wonder at the state the same well-attired people would be in later when Oran Mor's neon halo lit the night sky.

She couldn't see Danny at first but then he stepped out from one of the building's sepulchral shadows and through the throng towards her. There were people buzzing left, right and centre, shopping bags flying like weapons, but they simply bounced off Danny and on to their next victim as he strode forward to greet her with a hug.

'Can you believe all these people?' he asked. 'Have they nothing better to do than shop, eat and drink?'

'I don't think they do. Come on, let's walk down Byres Road.'

Narey slipped her arm through Danny's and they turned back onto the west end's main thoroughfare. Oran Mor meant 'the great melody of life' in Gaelic and it had often occurred to Narey that the phrase applied equally well to Byres Road. It was the heart of the west end and home to some of its best pubs and shops. It was largely void of the global conglomerates that homogenised the city centre and instead let local businesses flourish, producing a quirky mix you didn't get anywhere else. The eclectic mix didn't apply just to the shops; students, arty types, boiler suits, middle-class mums and flat caps all strolled together cheek by jowl down its length.

'I don't know how you can live here, Rachel,' Danny muttered. 'It would do my head in. Having a couple of thousand people constantly living on your doorstep isn't my idea of fun.'

'Don't be such an old grouch,' she laughed. 'You're sounding as bad as Tony. I love it. There's always a buzz along here and you're in the heart of it all. Sometimes I just stand at the window of my flat and watch them all going by. You see some sights.'

'Aye, I bet you do. But if I wanted to see a circus, I'd buy a ticket. It's not even as if these clowns are funny.'

'Some of them are.'

'Aye, okay,' Danny's grumpy expression as he eased her between oncoming bodies suggested he didn't entirely agree. 'So did you get anything from Greg Deans' home computer?'

'Not a lot. Sure enough, the email was there from Justice, identical to the one you found on Paton's PC. The follow-up saying they had to pay was sent to them separately but the messages said much the same thing. There was an email back from Deans asking who was emailing him but strangely enough the blackmailer didn't want to tell him. Deans, gutted that his brilliant plan to uncover the fraudster didn't work, told him to go do one. Unbelievably, that didn't work either.'

'And they let these bloody eejits teach kids? Did you get anything else?'

'Nope. Nothing incriminating at all but we've taken it away and the hunchbacks in forensics are going to go over it to see if he's left any fingerprints deleting anything.'

'Right, well I won't pretend I've any idea what that means except I guess it backs up his story.'

'It does. I'm still going to do him for something before this is finished though – assuming he lives that long. So what is it you've got?'

They were passing Hillhead station and a teenager was sitting on the ground in front of them, a folded newspaper keeping his bum from the snow, playing 'Baker Street' on the saxophone. He was very good but Danny still looked down at him as if he should be at school learning quadratic equations.

'See what I mean,' he told Narey. 'Unfunny clowns.'

'I'm not sure he was trying to be funny, Danny.'

'Anyway, I've put out some feelers about Kyle Irving and got some feedback about the man's finances.'

'I'm not going to ask where you got this.'

'No, you're not. It seems that however many clients Irving has, it's not paying the bills. That big old house in the south side comes with a hefty mortgage and he's way behind on it. Losing the place is a definite possibility.'

They'd stopped at the lights opposite Tennents Bar, where Highburgh Road became University Avenue, officially the biggest pain in the bum set of traffic lights in the city. Narey's flat was opposite Tennents but, despite the fluttering snow, she didn't want to go inside yet.

'Let's keep going,' she told Danny. 'And you keep telling me about Irving. By the time these bloody lights let us cross I should know everything.'

'Well, our man Irving isn't exactly rolling in the ill-gotten gains of his psychobabble. He's behind on his car too and that big Saab might be going back whence it came. If it does, then he'll struggle to get much of a motor right now as his credit rating is shot to hell. From everything I'm being told, Irving is officially skint.'

'No question of any of this being wrong, I take it?'

'None whatsoever. Let's just say that the info is so sound you could take it to the bank.'

'Right . . . It fits with the vibe I got when I went to his house. I definitely got a sense of financial struggles when I was at his place. He barely had any heating on, even though it was below freezing outside.'

The green man had appeared at last and they crossed further down Byres Road, Narey just avoiding a cyclist who was apparently colour blind or just didn't give a toss. There were a few people sitting at a table outside the Blind Pig despite the fact that it was cold enough to make brass monkeys distinctly uncomfortable. No weather seemed to be too cold to stop smokers from freezing their own balls off.

'So any suggestions as to why Irving is broke?' she asked Danny.

He shrugged. 'My guess is the ex-wife has rooked him but I don't know for sure. I also had someone tell me Irving likes a bet, lots of bets. I don't suppose it matters – bottom line is the guy has no money.'

'Having no money makes people desperate.'

'It certainly can do.'

They walked in silence past the Western, Narey still hanging onto Danny's arm. Thoughts of Deans being patched up in A&E after being thrown down the stairs at The Rock flooded through her head but she still couldn't dredge up any sympathy for him no matter how hard she tried.

'So how's your dad doing?'

'He won't get any better, Danny.'

'Let me put it another way. How are you doing?'

'I'll be fine.'

'Rachel, you're a lot better at asking questions than you are at answering them. I asked how you were.'

'I heard you.'

'Christ, you're hard work. No wonder Tony's so bloody miserable all the time.'

'Hey,' she laughed. 'And he's not miserable all the time.'

'No, he's a barrel of laughs, our Tony. Listen, love, I know better than anyone how hard it hit him when his mum and dad died but he should be past that by now. It's not healthy for him to be so bloody morose. He should have been an undertaker rather than a photographer.'

Narey punched him on the arm.

'Leave him alone, Danny. Like you said, you know better than anyone that he's not had things easy. Okay, so he deals with it in his own way but I think it's . . . cute.'

'Cute? Did you think Saddam Hussein was a wee bit cheeky or Fred West was adorable in a homicidal kind of way?'

She arched her eyebrows at him reproachfully. 'Out of order, Danny, even as a joke.'

'I love the boy, Rachel. You know that. He's like a son to me. He can photograph every dead body from here to Timbuktu if he wants – as long as he's happy in his miserableness. And I reckon you make him happy.'

Narey said nothing, just looked at her feet as they kicked through the dirty snow. There weren't as many people down at the far end of the street; fewer shops equalled fewer crowds. She glanced across the road at the University Café and contemplated the benefits of a cup of tea, a plate of homemade lasagne and a chocolate snowball. She tugged on Danny's arm and, seeing no traffic, dragged him across the road.

The University Café was one of her favourite places in the city, virtually unchanged from when it had opened nearly a hundred years before and owned by the same family, the Verrecchias, from day one. As soon as they pushed through the doors, they were assaulted with heat and steam and the smell of food on the go. It was a mostly studenty crowd that was in and Narey smiled to herself at Danny's mock disapproval. There was space in the corner at one of the narrow Formica tables and she sat at one of the flip-down red vinyl seats and patted the one next to her, knowing full well that he'd pretend to be put out.

She opted for the lasagne and Danny ordered a fish supper on her recommendation. The students on the table next to them seemed to think it was still morning – maybe for them it was; fry-ups and breakfast rolls were the order of the day.

'So does he make you happy as well?' Danny asked her as if the previous conversation had never ended.

'Can I ask you something, Danny?' she replied.

'Sure.'

'Our neighbour there,' she nodded towards the student nearest them, 'has a morning roll with a sausage in it, right? So in the west of Scotland vernacular that is obviously a "roll 'n' sausage". My question to you is: does that mean a "roll and sausage", a "roll on sausage" or a "roll in sausage"? I've never been sure.'

Danny shook his head at her.

'That is one of those questions to which there is no definitive answer, like "Is there life on Mars?" or "Why do women talk so much shite?". The sausage is in the roll not on it so it has to be a "roll and sausage". But stop avoiding the question: does Tony make you happy?'

She let her head fall back against the wood-panelled wall, narrowly avoiding one of the tall jars of old-fashioned sweets that were dotted around.

'Yes, I think.'

'Good, I think. And if you don't mind me saying so, I'd suggest you remember that with all this crap that's going on. And before you bite my head off, there's something else you should remember.'

'I do mind but okay. What else should I remember?'

'You.'

She made a face but Danny ploughed on regardless.

'I ask how your dad is and you say he won't get better. I ask how you are and you say you'll be fine, as if you don't matter, as if it's all about your dad. Is that right?'

'Listen, Danny . . .'

'No, *you* listen. I'll answer the question for you: it's not right. It isn't right at all. And I know that because I've got a better idea of how your dad would feel about it than you have. Do you really think he'd agree that you don't matter?'

A waitress slipped a steaming plate in front of each of them. Rachel smiled her thanks and waited for the girl to leave.

'Gimme peace, Danny. And stop trying to psychoanalyse me. I'll deal with my dad in my own way and my own time.'

'And how is that going to affect you and Tony?'

'Pass the salt.'

'Okay, two final things. First, your dad wouldn't thank you for doing anything that would make you unhappy. Secondly, you really need to use less salt. It'll fuck up your arteries.'

Narey sprinkled more salt on her lasagne, paused to stick two fingers up to Danny, then sprinkled on some more.

CHAPTER 42

Thursday 21 December. 4.30 p.m.

This time when Winter and Danny drove back into Bridgend Caravan Park, they knew just where to head. Danny parked outside Tommy Baillie's home, recognising the bashed car that sat beside it. The snow piled on top suggested that neither it nor Baillie had gone anywhere for days.

Their exit from their own car attracted the attention of a yelping dog, a brown and white mongrel that seemed unperturbed by the cold or the snow. The barking brought the wary head of Tommy Baillie to the caravan window and he nodded to his visitors before opening the door to greet them.

'Come away in,' he told the two men. 'Far too cold to be standing *avri* on a doorstep. The chill's going right through my old bones. Not seen weather like this in years.'

They followed Baillie inside, immediately grateful for the warmth of the caravan, and accepted his invitation to take a seat. The old man had a pipe on the go, puffing it contentedly as he waited for his guests to settle themselves.

'So you have some news of young Sam, I hope, gentlemen.'

'We have,' Danny agreed. 'But it's not . . .'

Before Danny could go any further, he was interrupted by a sharp rap at the door and, the stocky figure of Jered Dunbar walked in without waiting for an answer. Closing the door behind him, he stood and glared at the visitors in his usual sullen and threatening fashion.

'Uncle,' he nodded at Baillie.

'Relax, Jered,' Baillie told him. 'Gentlemen have just come to let us know what they learned about cousin Sam and his activities in Glasgow.'

Jered stood grudgingly by the door, accepting the old man's counsel to relax but still obviously on edge.

'And to get some information in return,' Danny reminded Baillie. 'This arrangement was to benefit both parties, Mr Baillie.'

A flicker of a smile crossed the man's mouth as he nodded in agreement.

'Ah, yes, your long-lost girl. A proper sadness that was and all. I think it is only right we help each other after such a terrible thing, Mr Neilson.'

Danny levelled Baillie with a hard stare.

'Yes, except the help you were offering us was a load of old bollocks.'

Jered immediately took a step forward, anger blazing in his dark eyes, but Danny wasn't fazed for a second.

'Cool your jets, son,' he growled dismissively. 'The grown-ups are talking. Listen and you might learn something.'

Jered looked towards Baillie, who nodded quietly, and the younger man fell back against the caravan door, still bristling with resentment.

'I think Jered was a bit perturbed by your rudeness, Mr Neilson. He's not used to guests talking in such a manner. Explain yourself, please.'

'My pleasure. We've gone out of our way to find out what your boy Sam has been up to. And what we've discovered is very interesting indeed.'

Danny saw the looks that flashed between Baillie and Jered.

'And it was our intention to pass this information on to you,' he continued. 'But now we learn you aren't going to be keeping your side of the bargain – because you can't. The girl who died wasn't a runaway gypsy bride and there wasn't any sort of honour killing.'

'I never said there was,' Baillie replied softly.

'No, you didn't, you devious old bugger. But you let us think there might have been.'

Baillie puffed on his pipe and tilted his head to one side as if considering the suggestion.

'Well, I suppose I can see how you might have got that impression, Mr Neilson. But a bargain, in our community, is a bargain.'

'And in ours, a con is a con.'

Danny let the impasse hang between them, sensing the impatient irritation of Jered and the calmer but still expectant air of Tommy Baillie.

'So what are you proposing, Mr Neilson?' Baillie enquired. 'I'm keen to find out what young Sam is up to so that we can help him.'

'I'm proposing another bargain.'

'Oh? And what would that be?'

'You want to find Sam Dunbar. And there's someone we want to find.'

'Not your murdered *chavi*?'

'No.'

'Then who?'

'A former . . . what's that word you used, Tony? . . . *gajo*, that's it. A former *gajo* who married into the traveller community.'

Jered and Baillie looked at each other again across the room but said nothing. Instead, Baillie puffed reflectively on his pipe again, taking an age before replying.

'There's a few of those around but not too many. Does he have a name, this *gajo* of yours?'

'Bradley. Peter Bradley. He was sometimes known as Paddy.'

Baillie smoked his pipe some more and Danny could see full well the old boy was playing him, trying to regain some of his lost advantage.

'I know the name,' Baillie told him at last.

'You know the name,' Danny repeated as if not believing a word Baillie said. 'But do you know him?'

'I may have known him,' Baillie conceded.

'Mr Baillie,' Danny sighed. 'This could take a while and we're both getting far too old to be wasting time, don't you think? I'll ask you again. Do you know Peter Bradley?'

Baillie worked his pipe, a playful look in his eye as he regarded Danny. A large puff of white smoke signalled a decision had been made.

'I met Mr Bradley a couple of times, although it was many years ago. He wedded the daughter of a cousin of a cousin of mine. Caused a bit of a storm at the time but he's settled now, or so I suppose. Bit of a lad, if I remember rightly.'

'And do you know where he is now?'

Baillie pursed his lips as he shook his head.

'I do not. I haven't heard mention of him in a long time. It's the nature of our community, Mr Neilson, that we travel. We don't go sending Christmas cards to the same address every year like your people do.'

'But you could find out where he is.'

'And I could also ask why you want to find him.'

'You could but I wouldn't have to tell you. Not given that you need to know where wee Sam is and what he's been up to.'

'But you, Mr Neilson, need to find wee Paddy Bradley. So I think that makes us even.'

'Mr Baillie,' Danny sighed. 'You have dicked us about once already. I'm not going to be happy if you try to do it a second time. You understand me?'

At that, Jered Dunbar sprang forward, his muscular frame heading straight at Danny until he was right in his face, their noses just inches apart.

'You need to learn some respect! You don't talk to Uncle like that.'

Danny grinned and shoved his face forward so it was right up against Jered's, his eyes challenging the younger man to make a move. He could smell sweat, testosterone and a faint whiff of apprehension.

'And you're going to be the one to teach me some respect, are you? Bigger men than you have tried in the past.'

'Aye, well you're not as young as you used to be, old man,' Jered snarled.

Danny pulled his head back and butted Jered square and hard on the forehead and the bridge of his nose, causing him to crumple immediately and fall to the floor. Blood poured from Jered's nose and he threw a hand up to it to stop the flow. His eyes glared furiously at Danny but he made no attempt to get to his feet.

'Now that,' Danny said genially, 'is a lesson in irony. You accuse me of lacking respect for your elders and then insult me and call me an old man. The irony of that would have been lost on you if I hadn't made my point. So there you go, lesson learned and no hard feelings, eh?'

What seemed like a small laugh escaped from Tommy Baillie but it was quickly covered by a cough. Jered's eyes flew to Baillie and, whatever he saw, it convinced him to stay where he was.

'I think we've all learned something here today, Mr Neilson,' Baillie said quietly. 'When it comes to matters of trust and respect, they have to be earned. I'll find Paddy Bradley for you if you bring Sam Dunbar to me. Now, do we trust each other to do that?'

Danny smiled at the old man. 'I think we have to, don't you?'

Baillie nodded.

'How's your head?' Tony asked Danny as the caravan door closed behind them and they were immediately hit by a freezing gust of wind.

'Ach, it's fine. Nothing in there to damage anyhow.'

'I'm beginning to agree with you,' Winter smiled. 'About your new deal . . . will he do it?'

'I think so. The notion of a bargain means something to him – a matter of honour, if you like. What do you think?'

'I think you're right. But either way, we can't hang about waiting for him to come through with his side of it. We need to sort Dunbar out and quickly.'

'Correct,' Danny agreed. 'Because if we don't get Dunbar off the streets before he kills someone, then we're fucked. He's cut a dog in two and sliced the hands off some drug dealers. That we can work around. But if he murders some fucker with that sword of his, then we can't hand him over to Baillie. He's DI Aaron Sutton's if that happens.'

'And if Sutton gets Dunbar, then we don't get Peter Bradley.'

'Right. And if we don't get Bradley, then your girlfriend is in big trouble. Because this whole thing is going to blow up in her face.'

CHAPTER 43

Friday 21 December. 6.30 a.m.

'Why can't they fucking dig people up in the summer? The ground is rock hard and I'm bastarding freezing.'

'And why the hell are we doing this anyway? I heard it was some bint from Strathclyde was behind this. Why aren't the Weegies through here doing their own dirty work? Too high and mighty to get their hands dirty?'

'Dirty and frozen. This is fucking ridiculous.'

A voice from behind them, low but firm, pulled the two boiler-suited constables back into line.

'Harrison. McLaughlin. Shut your mouths and show a bit of respect. Remember where you are. I know this isn't much fun for anyone but I don't want to hear you two bitching. Understood?'

'Yes, sir.'

'Sir.'

'Now get on with it. The sooner we get this done, the sooner we can get out of here.'

Winter watched the two cops submit to Marty Croy's bollocking, then turn and head silently towards the large white tent that stood in a corner of the otherwise desolate terrain of Brig o' Turk cemetery. It was just minutes after the agreed 6.30 a.m. start and a low mist hung over the old graveyard, thick in the cold grey light of a frozen morning. It was dawn in name only; the night still clung on, reluctant to give up its grip to such an imposter as this poor excuse for daylight.

The ground lay thick with crisp snow and was disturbed only by the rough-hewn upright headstones that poked their way through, all wearing thick caps of white above their grey suits. Bumps in the surface of the snow hinted at the flat slabs of stone that lay beneath, markers to the long-since departed. Winter watched Rachel flinch as an icy wind whipped across the exposed cemetery. The nearest trees, standing petrified and distant, offered precious little protection from the devil's glacial breath. It made every person dotted around the cemetery shiver as if it were their own grave someone was walking over.

The car's dashboard had suggested it was minus twelve degrees and the temperature showed no sign of rising any time soon. The cops who were there to bring Barbie back into the world were bulky under their overalls, suggesting multiple layers of clothing in a vain attempt to keep the chill at bay. Even Winter, as cold-blooded as his name, felt the frost invade his bones and he had to fight to keep his teeth from chattering.

Brig o' Turk was about seven miles from the Lake of Menteith as the crow flies. However, the crow would have to

325

fly across the Menteith Hills and Loch Venacher, so it was about twice that distance by road via Callander. In 1994 it had been decided not to bury Barbie in the little cemetery at Port of Menteith as they were keen not to encourage tourist ghouls. Instead, her body was spirited away to Brig o' Turk and, after a brief ceremony at the local church, was laid to rest in the dead of night. Winter had seen the church in the first light of that morning, spectacularly perched on the edge of Loch Achray, only three frozen and threadbare trees between it and the iced surface of the loch.

Now he watched men emerge from cars and vans, eerie figures in white suits, white masks across their faces, gliding across the white landscape, all armed with picks and shovels they knew were unlikely to be up to the task of breaking the ground that held Barbie's remains. That was why the heavy artillery was also getting wheeled in. Two big cops were hauling a pneumatic drill through the mist, their breath exploding and freezing before them with the effort of crossing the graveyard. Behind them, two uniformed constables, the only ones not in boiler suits, stood guard at the cemetery gate to deter any locals awakened by the noise that was about to disturb them at that ungodly time of the morning.

For the moment, after Croy's censorship of the two moaning cops, all was silent but for the sound of feet crunching on snow and the quiet whirr of a camera shutter. Winter knew that all he was getting were overexposed shots of white on white as mist enveloped grey light but he loved every frame. Sometimes the burly men traipsing in and out of the graveyard would look at him suspiciously, others would glare but mostly they had their heads down and their minds on the grim task ahead.

It was a bizarre scene being played out under the disapproving frown of the rugged cliffs that had glowered over Brig o' Turk since the hamlet first emerged. Also watching, from the other side of a wall, were two bemused but unconcerned deer. It was unlikely that either the cliffs or the deer had ever witnessed anything like this reluctant resurrection.

The gang was all here: Rachel; Croy, the Stirling DI; the local coroner and Procurator Fiscal; a small gaggle of press tipped off, no doubt, by the local cops; and Addison. He stood alone to the side, his face mask hanging loose below his chin to accommodate the cigarette in his mouth. Addison's enforced sabbatical from front-line duty had come with dire warnings from his doctor about not overdoing it, cutting down his alcohol intake and certainly not smoking. Typically perverse, Addison had reacted by taking up fags again for the first time in nine years.

The trail of smoke that was disappearing into the mist above Addison's head was joined by puffs of breath as he muttered away to himself. Addison had insisted on getting out of the office to witness the exhumation but that obviously wasn't stopping him from grouching. The rest of the cast, the two sentry constables apart, were inside the tent and Winter strolled over to join his mate on the periphery of the graveyard.

'Colder than a witch's tit,' Addison grumbled. 'But you'll be loving this, of course, you sick fucker. All this digging up the dead will be right up your street.'

'I'm just an impartial observer. Just doing my job.'

'Ach, don't give me your shit, wee man. I know you.'

Winter didn't bother denying it a second time and the two men stood and looked around them. The tent that covered the would-be graverobbers looked as if it had landed from Mars, absurdly inappropriate against the rural backdrop, serving only to highlight the affront against nature that was about to take place.

'Going in?' Winter asked him. .

'Aye, in a minute. I was just letting the eager beavers in first but there's no show without Punch.'

'So, what? You're just staying out here to piss off the locals because they can't start without you?'

'Something like that, wee man. The yokels need to know who's really in charge here. Okay, let's go.'

Addison squeezed the end of his cigarette and threw it on the ground, pulling the protective mask over his face.

They didn't say another word as they made their way across the snow. All they could hear was their own footsteps and the wind that whistled through the cemetery and froze their ears. Not another sound until they reached the tent and Addison turned to face Winter and winked at him.

'Show time, wee man,' he murmured. 'Show time.'

They pushed their way inside and were met by expectant and impatient faces. If the looks were intended to chastise Addison, then they clearly didn't know him.

'Morning, gentlemen. Let's get on with it, shall we?'

Winter was glad of the mask hiding the grin that had spread across his face. There was little Addison relished more than pissing people off.

'Good idea, Inspector,' Croy responded, clearly irritated.

'We've had a couple of investigatory prods with the shovels while we were waiting for you and they aren't going to do the job. We're going straight in with the jackhammer.'

'Fair enough,' Addison replied, clearly still at the wind-up, 'I agree.'

Winter noticed that Rachel, standing to the side of the group, didn't look impressed by her DI's cheek. Instead, she looked at him wearily as if he were embarrassing her in front of her new friends. Winter wasn't entirely sure he liked that.

Croy nodded at his men and they began to bring the pneumatic drill forward.

'Just a minute,' Winter interrupted. 'I want a shot of the headstone first.'

There were tuts of exasperation all around as the Stirling cops showed their continued annoyance at the Weegie interlopers. The short bespectacled woman whom Winter and Addison knew to be the local Procurator Fiscal looked back at Croy and simply shrugged. Winter hadn't waited for permission anyway. As soon as the words were out of his mouth, he had crouched at the far end of Barbie's grave and framed a full-length shot.

He inched closer, ignoring the scowls that peeped out at him between mask and protective hoods, and filled his viewfinder with Barbie's headstone. It was a simple stone, much newer than the vast majority in the cemetery, solid grey and not yet beaten by wind or rain.

UNKNOWN
Died circa November 1993
I will fear no evil for thou art with me
Rest in Peace

The inscription managed to be poignant in its sparseness and touching in its message of hope beyond rationale. The top line was simply the reason they were there – to try to turn the unknown into the known. The last line was maybe a forlorn hope until then but the labours that were to follow perhaps gave Barbie a chance of peace after all.

Winter circled the stone, taking it from far more angles than was necessary, knowing full well it was increasing the impatience of the boiler suits and he would see the results of their irritation on their faces. Many Strathclyde cops had grown wise to Winter's fixation for trying to include them in scene-setting shots but this lot were suitably naive for his purposes and a few cute tilts of his camera went straight over their heads – metaphorically at least. It rewarded Winter with hard stares and angry glares above Barbie's headstone, fittingly furious by her grave and only he would know they were fuming at him rather than Barbie's killer.

Finally, he stood back and let the cops about their business, having toyed with them long enough for his own purposes. As he did so, he caught a glint in Addison's eyes that managed to express both approval and distaste. He glanced at Rachel and got only half of the look he did from Addison. She didn't seem best pleased.

A brawny cop paced round Barbie's grave, pushing to manoeuvre the gathered throng back, reserving a particularly violent gesture for Winter, in order to clear safe space for the pneumatic drill to begin its work. Once they were far enough back, Croy surveyed the room like a magician ready to perform his greatest trick but waiting until he was satisfied that his audience were suitably in awe of his talents. Croy looked towards the two other senior figures in the tent.

'Ms Cruikshank? DI Addison?'

The Procurator Fiscal and the Glasgow DI nodded back at him, and Croy turned to the constables who held the drill and repeated the gesture. The officers swapped fleeting glances before one of them reached down to flick a switch and a low rumble immediately began to disturb the uneasy silence that swamped the room. Within seconds, it grew and grew until the noise became a clatter that turned into a pneumatic thunder, which must have rattled into Brig o' Turk and halfway to Callander. It was loud enough to wake the dead.

The drill bounced back off the frozen earth at first, barely biting the surface; six feet below seemed a long way off. It was like drilling through concrete and the cop's swear words only went unheard because of the infernal racket of the jack-hammer. It took just a few minutes to confirm what they'd all known: it was going to be a long, hard shift till they got anywhere near the girl's coffin.

Half an hour passed and half a foot of soil had been displaced. The cops had changed shift on the drill; the first two having fallen back cold and hot and glad to be replaced at the helm. It was obvious that the initial rush of anticipation had already worn off and a weary hush had settled over the tent instead. It was hard work over the drill and nearly as hard to stand there and freeze while the others worked. After a while, Addison looked over to Winter and jerked his head in the direction of the tent opening.

'I need to go over the photographs I want you to take,'

he murmured, the words meant more for Croy's ears than Winter's.

Winter followed him out until they were back in the open graveyard and saw that fresh snow was falling softly.

'Fuck this for a game of soldiers,' Addison muttered. 'Let's get in the car.'

'Discuss photographs?' Winter asked incredulously.

'Don't be so bloody stupid. What would I be interested in that for? No, I'm thinking car heater, Adele on the CD player and a wee drop of magic heating mixture,' he said with a hearty tap against his back pocket. 'I came prepared.'

They dodged past the waiting press pack and settled in his car, which was parked round the corner and out of sight. Addison switched the heating up to full blast, turned on the music and produced a hip flask of whisky from his pocket.

'What is it?' Winter enquired.

'Ardbeg.'

'Very nice.'

'Too right it is.'

Addison swigged a mouthful of the cratur and shivered as it disappeared inside him. Winter followed suit, letting it warm his mouth before it slid down and set fire to his throat.

'Better,' Addison sighed.

'Yeah.'

They sat in silence and looked through the windscreen, watching the flakes tumble onto the ground. Adele crooned in time to the drill and the flask was passed between them at regular intervals, only sips now but Addison's share was still bigger as the DI took full advantage of not driving.

'Funny fucking business this,' Addison offered.

'Yeah.'

Adele had stopped rolling in the deep and now she was banging on about rumours.

'So how come you knew about it?'

'What?'

'How did you know about this Lady in the Lake stuff? Our DS Narey been chatting to you?'

'A bit. Said she wanted photographs done and she'd rather keep them in-house than let Central do them.'

'Right.'

Addison rolled the window down an inch or two and lit a cigarette, drawing deep on it and puffing the smoke towards the gap.

'You do know this car constitutes a place of work and therefore you are breaking the law by smoking.'

'I'm a police officer – of course I know.'

Adele was now turning tables.

'What do you make of that prick Marty Croy?' Addison asked.

'Nothing much.'

'He and Rachel seem a bit chummy, don't you think?'

'Never noticed.'

Addison aimed another long gasp of cigarette smoke through the open car window.

'Good-looking bastard, too. I hope he's not mowing Glasgow's lawn.'

'We should head back in and see how they're getting on.'

'Suppose. Cosy in here though.'

'I'm going in for a look.'

'Sit on your arse. It's colder than Thatcher's heart out

there. Being stuck in the office does my head in but at least it's warm.'

'You stay if you want but I'm going back in.'

Winter heard a stifled laugh as he slammed the door closed behind him. Sod him. Back inside the tent, the work continued and he could see they'd made significant progress, although there was still a long way to go. His eyes were drawn to Croy and Rachel, standing side by side and observing the dig. As Winter watched, Croy leaned in close to Rachel, far closer than was necessary and whispered something. Whatever it was, Rachel smiled and dug her elbow playfully into the DI's ribs. Winter's immediate urge was to grab one of the shovels and wrap it round Croy's head. It was also his second urge.

He managed to resist it but sent some serious thought waves over to Rachel, mentally ordering her to look at him instead. Bizarrely, it seemed to work and she stared over at him, confusion quickly giving way to annoyance. She said something else to Croy and headed out the door, a passing glare telling Winter to follow.

'What the hell was that look for?' she hissed at him when they were both outside.

'What was Croy saying to you?'

'Sorry?'

'Croy. He whispered something to you that made you laugh. The two of you seemed pretty pally.'

Her eyes flashed back angrily.

'Are you jealous?' she hissed. 'Unbelievable. What are you, twelve? Stay out of my way, Tony. I'm doing my job here and I can't afford to have it cocked up because of your fragile ego.'

'I'm doing my job too. Or at least I will be as soon as your friend Croy gets his flatfoots to dig a fucking hole. I'll be in the car.'

As Winter slid back into the heat of the car, Addison greeted him with an exaggerated smile.

'Change your mind?'

'Just shut the fuck up, give me some of the whisky and change the bloody record. Put something else on instead of that sentimental pish.'

It was three torturous hours before the cops were far enough down into the frozen grave that they could abandon the jackhammer and begin the even more laborious process of finishing the last painful foot or two by hand in case they hit the coffin and damaged its contents. The clang of shovels echoed round the cemetery as they dug, a jarring cacophony that seemed more in keeping with the surroundings yet more eerie in the morning mist.

The extra toil also forced the cops to haul in large gas heaters to provide more heat inside the tent. Despite the temperature climbing to a balmy minus eight, the officers were complaining it was so cold the sweat was freezing on their backs. By eleven, they were almost out of fit constables, as the digging took its toll, but they knew only the final inches of soil lay between them and their prize. At long last the resounding clang of metal on wood rang around the tent like a shot from a starting pistol.

Every eye turned to the two cops inside the grave. Addison, back inside after his prolonged break, shot a glance at Winter and they both instinctively took a step forward to get a better view. The group had been joined by a young, pretty blonde that Winter took to be Professor Kirsten Fairweather and the Central Scotland pathologist, Dr Angus Comrie, an angular man with tufts of grey hair on either side of a bald pate. He was dressed in a ground-length green apron, the only person in the tent wearing anything other than white, and he assumed control of the final proceedings.

'Gently,' Comrie told them softly. 'Scrape away the last of the soil until the coffin lid is exposed. Do not rush at this stage.'

Ten minutes later, they could see fully exposed oak and Winter rattled off a further series of photographs, documenting the first sight of the coffin in nineteen years. Dr Comrie instructed the officers to fix ropes to the rings on the lid and they were at long last ready to raise Barbie from the grave.

Winter's eyes scanned the tent and he knew, beyond doubt, none of them was feeling what he was. Rachel was probably the closest but even she was consumed by expectancy rather than the more primeval urge that had a grip on Winter. Nothing could drag him from that spot until he saw Barbie emerge. He couldn't help but think that his mother, the woman who had lost her life because of his stupidity, had been only a few years older than Barbie when she died. He knew it wasn't the time to think about it and tried to squeeze the comparison from his mind, forcing himself to remain in the moment.

After such a long and backbreaking effort, it took only seconds for the coffin to be raised fully and laid out on the canvas sheeting that surrounded the hole. Winter's senses were on full alert as Comrie, calm and dignified, had the officers remove the screw that held down the lid. Addison and Croy, as the senior officers present, took a place on either side of the coffin and constables stood at either end, their hands poised to remove the cover. Winter strode forward forcefully, straight in front of a cop he could hear cursing behind him. His shutter finger was itching like a gunfighter's, his nerves jumping and heart thumping.

For a split second, the base of the coffin disappeared from Winter's viewfinder and it took him that moment to realise it had been caused by the lid passing through his sights. And, suddenly, there she was.

Barbie.

Winter's mind and finger were a blur as he raced off shot after shot. She filled his frame – her broken bones, her gaping smile.

'Enough,' Comrie instructed. 'This isn't a red carpet. She isn't some kind of film star.'

Speak for yourself, Winter thought.

CHAPTER 44

Barbie's coffin had been carried from Brig o' Turk cemetery and placed, with as much solemnity as the situation demanded and as much decorum as it allowed, into the back of a waiting hearse. By then, it was nearly noon and a large crowd of curious locals had gathered at the gates, trying to uncover the reason for the rare drama that had visited their sleepy village.

Few, if any, of them had known that Barbie rested there in the first place but soon enough they all knew she had departed. If Professor Fairweather did her job, if Rachel did hers and if Winter and Danny could help with their own brand of amateur assistance, then it was to be hoped that Barbie would never return to Brig o' Turk. Instead, she could be buried properly at a place that suited whatever remained of her family when they were found.

Rachel had followed the hearse, first into Stirling, where Dr Comrie carried out the procedural necessities before signing Barbie over to the pastoral care of Kirsten Fairweather, then on the road to Dundee in the wake of the professor's procession.

In terms of practical use, there was no real point in Narey

being there when Barbie arrived in Dundee but she felt the need. Fairweather was going to do the clever stuff in terms of finding out who Barbie actually was.

When she got to the Centre for Anatomy and Human Identification, Narey had to freeze under the ever-hostile stare of the steel-haired Annabelle. Rather than give Kirsty's formidable receptionist the pleasure of turning her to stone, Narey phoned Julia Corrieri to get an update from Glasgow, safe in the knowledge it would annoy the receptionist.

'Hi Sarge. Good drive?'

'The road is covered in snow and ice, there were constant flurries on the windscreen, making it almost impossible to see, we were following a hearse, which meant we pissed off every nutter who wanted to drive at a hundred miles an hour despite the conditions, and therefore we were treated to gestures of finger abuse every two minutes. So, yes, a great drive. What have you been doing?'

'Um, well this morning I was at Peter Bradley's mother's house in East Kilbride.'

'Any use?'

'Not a whole lot, Sarge. Sorry. Margaret, the mum, was a nice enough woman but she said she hadn't spoken to Bradley in years.'

'Did you believe her?'

'Yes. She seemed really worried at first when I said I was there about her son. I think she thought I was going to tell her he was dead. When I said I was trying to find him, she was so relieved she'd have told me anything I wanted.'

'So when did she last hear from him?'

'She said she used to get a Christmas card from him every

year but they stopped without explanation in 2004. There would be a different postmark on them every year, all over Scotland and down into England.'

'Did you get a note of the postmarks?'

Anyone else, providing they had indeed done their job properly, might have been insulted by the question but not Corrieri. Instead she was quietly pleased to have the chance to show her thoroughness. Narey heard the rustle of paper as Julia opened her ever-present notebook.

'Inverness, December 1999. Dumfries, 2000. Kendall, 2001. Oban, 2002. Aberdeen, 2003. I've already contacted the relevant forces in case Bradley has cropped up on their books but nothing back so far.'

'Okay, good. What did she tell you about Bradley?'

'Well, she's his mum so nothing bad. Said that he'd always been "a lively lad". That was the nearest thing to criticism she wanted to offer. Said he was the life and soul, liked by every-one, no real enemies. I asked her if he had a bit of a temper and she immediately said no. She said it too quickly if you ask me and made me think it wasn't the truth.'

'What about the gypsy traveller link? Had she heard about it?'

'Yes, Sarge. It was all she knew though. She'd heard it the same way others had and nothing more. He hadn't told her he was getting married or moving away with the travellers. All she knew was that the Christmas cards were signed "Peter and Gaby".'

'The gypsy bride?'

'She assumes so. So do I.'

'Any friends who might know where he is?'

'Margaret Bradley said she'd spoken to all the ones she knew and they were as much in the dark as she was. They'd known Peter was seeing someone before he left but none of them had met her and had heard nothing from him since.'

'So where does that leave us?'

Corrieri sounded apologetic. 'No further forward. Sorry.'

'Don't apologise, Julia. You did well. Anyway, we're inches forward even if it's only in things we don't know. At least we now know we don't know them. Okay, I've got to go. We're about to start here.'

The outer door had opened and Kirsten Fairweather emerged, smiling grimly. Her blonde hair was tied back in a ponytail and she had quickly changed into jeans, a hooded sweatshirt and trainers since her drive north with Barbie's body.

'Rachel, I know speed is of the essence for you so I'm not going to stand on ceremony; instead I propose to begin the facial recon right away. Seeing as you're here, you're welcome to sit in on it.'

'I'd like that. It would be good to see how the process works. And, well, to be honest, it just feels like the right thing to do. The first step in bringing her back, hopefully.'

Kirsten smiled, more warmly this time.

'Having seen the skull, I'm confident we will. We'll need to do some mirroring work of the shattered part of the cranium but that won't be a problem.' Kirsten paused thoughtfully. 'We're always told you should disassociate and feel no personal connection to the subjects and I'm sure police officers are told the same. But I think I always do at least as good a job if I do feel a connection. And I feel one here.'

'Me too,' Narey admitted. 'I'm a police officer but I'm a person first. And you'd have to have a heart of concrete not to feel for this girl.'

'Come on,' Kirsten told her, taking her arm. 'I think we should go meet her.'

Fairweather led Narey deeper into the department, opening a white door to reveal Barbie's skeleton laid out on what looked like an operating table. Despite the glimpse when she'd emerged from the frozen earth in Brig o' Turk, it was still a shock to see their girl lying there, her broken skull smiling up at the ceiling.

The professor went to the side of the lab and produced a hand-held device that looked to Narey like the speed scanners traffic cops sometimes used at the roadside. There were two metallic heads, however, rather than one and she advanced on Barbie's prone frame, angling the device towards her.

'It's a laser scanner,' Kirsten explained. 'It's called a FastSCAN Scorpion. There's a single-camera version called a Cobra but the dual camera gives us more detailed scans in fewer sweeps and the cameras view the laser from both sides. It's a great bit of kit: the entire system fits into a briefcase and we can take it anywhere.'

The professor began sweeping the Scorpion across the skeleton, steadily working her way from top to toe.

'It feeds straight into our computer system as a 3D model,' she continued. 'It's digitising her shape and surface contours as we speak. The areas we'll have to reconstruct before we go much further are . . .' Kirsten paused by the skull and gestured with her finger. 'Obviously here . . . and here. The nose is missing, the eye socket badly damaged and parts of the

342

forehead boss and coronal suture are also missing. But we can fix that.'

Narey must have raised an eyebrow at the casualness of the remark because Kirsten hurriedly explained.

'We will mirror the missing area simply by making a copy of the existing side and creating a symmetrical skull. It's a bit misleading, as we are all naturally asymmetrical, but it will be close. If we had part of the nose, then we could do the same thing but as it's entirely missing, we'll fill it in using one from a template of skulls to get one that fits. It can be very accurate. The good news is that the mandible is intact; the jawbone is the most difficult thing to recreate.'

Narey turned to the computer and saw that a 3D image of the girl was already on the screen. It was a million miles away from Inchmahome.

'After we fill in the missing areas, we'll dip into our database of muscles. They are all pre-modelled and we import them individually onto the frame. It's the musculature map that gives us a detailed image of what she really looked like. That will probably be as far as we get today but I'm intending to come back first thing in the morning and continue from there.

'We use sets of tissue depth data depending on where the subject came from. Obviously we know Barbie was a white European but if she was black African or, say, Korean, then we have data from there. When we get to that point, you'll see little pegs over her face representing tissue depth and then we'll put a layer of skin on top of that.

'It's all about using the clues we have. The teeth will tell us about the mouth, for example, and we can create its shape from there. If hair were found, as it was in this case, then we can input its colour and length. If there is clothing, then we can learn about stature. Normally, when we do facial mapping we don't have as much to work on as we do here. We tend not to know skin colour, fat or thin. We're in good shape with her, Rachel.'

'So by tomorrow we'll see her as she was?'

'Yep. If we wanted to go all the way and have a 3D animated model, then that would take another two weeks. It can be a bit frustrating. We get from skull to face in two days; one day for muscles, one for skin; but it takes them a fortnight to add colour and hair. I'm guessing you don't have that long.'

'No, I don't. Strange, isn't it? We wait nineteen years to see her and suddenly we're in a hurry that could literally mean the difference between life and death.'

Kirsten looked at her in confusion.

'Not her life obviously, so whose?'

Rachel knew she'd said too much but instinctively she'd trusted Kirsten from the moment they'd first met.

'Well, that's the thing; I can't be entirely sure. But I know if we can find out who she is, then we'll be a lot closer to finding out who killed her. And if we do that, then we might just stop someone else from ending up the way she did. Put it this way: tomorrow can't come soon enough.'

CHAPTER 45

Friday 21 December. 3.25 p.m.

Munn's Vaults on Maryhill Road wouldn't have been Winter's first choice for a quiet drink and, coming just a few hours after he'd frozen his arse off at Brig o' Turk cemetery, it was just about the last thing he needed. Still, he and Danny weren't out for a social beer so it didn't matter that they'd be surrounded by tracksuits, baseball caps, aggressive stares and the continual rattle of pool balls. Instead they'd sit quietly in the darkened pub and await their prey.

With its long, low frontage, Munn's sat opposite boarded-up shops and scruffy tenements. Its neighbours were bookies, off licenses, To Let signs and abandoned buildings. To be fair, it had cleaned up its act from days gone by and the word was that the new owners didn't stand for any trouble. First sign of bother and the offenders were chucked out and promptly barred from the premises. It still carried a reputation from past regimes that meant some people were wary of crossing its threshold but it was unlikely to put off the kind of person who wielded a samurai sword. Sam Dunbar drank in Munn's so it was to Munn's they were going.

They both ordered pints on the basis that it could be a long shift and sitting without alcohol in front of them would send out all sorts of warning signals to the locals. They would think them to be either cops, customs and excise or Christians, and any of those things would mean not being trusted in Munn's. The pints would be supped slowly, milked for all they were worth, because the last thing that was going to help if they did encounter Dunbar was them being drunk. Everything they knew about him suggested they'd need every ounce of their wits about them.

A hollow-cheeked ned in a blue baseball cap and matching trackies was checking out Winter and Danny from the pool table. He looked like he hadn't eaten for a month beyond a feast of yum yums or jam doughnuts from Greggs and the odd bag of chips. Being held up by his pool cue and scratching the growth on his cheeks and chin, he seemed to have the idea there was some mileage to be gained from the strangers. He mumbled something to his mate at the table and sidled up to Winter.

'Awrite, big man? How's it gaun? Cauld outside, innit?'

'Aye,' Winter responded, neither wanting to engage with the junkie or antagonise him. 'Freezing.'

'Aye, freezing,' the ned repeated. 'Freezing.'

He just stood there, mouth slightly open and eyes somewhere else, waiting for Winter to come back with his contribution to the sparkling conversation. When Winter didn't oblige, the ned carried on regardless.

'Game of pool, big man?'

'Naw, you're all right.'

'Gaun, just one game. Play you for a pint.'

'It's not my game. Try someone else.'

'Just for a pint, eh? I'm wasted, like. You'd probably beat me easy.'

Danny put his head forward so it was almost resting on the bar and tilted it so he could look the ned in the eyes.

'Wee man?' he growled. 'Gonnae just piss off, eh? He's no wanting to play you.'

'Okay, okay. No problemo,' the junkie slurred. 'Not a problem, big man. No worries. What about you then?'

'What?'

'You want a game? Play you for a pint, like.'

Danny chuckled despite himself.

'Naw. Now fuck off.'

'Aye, aye. No problemo, big man. No problemo. *Asta la vista*.'

With that, the junkie threw his weight to one side, spun on one leg and did a neat volte-face until he lurched back towards the pool table, where he held his arms out wide to his mate. 'Naebody wants to play me. It's 'cos ah'm like the Ronnie O'Sullivan of this pool table. Top dog.'

'Aye, you are that, Spanner, no come on. Hit the baws, eh?'

Danny sipped at his beer and shook his head in mild disbelief at the departing junkie. Harmless enough as long as you weigh more than a bag of tatties and didn't try to get between him and a strawberry tart or a score of smack. He was just about to share some tales of junkie-baiting in days of yore when the front door opened and a broad figure walked in.

It was the long, black leather coat that caught Winter's eye first. In an instant, he was back in Mansionhouse Drive, seeing the world through his camera's timed exposure: the crowd behind the two severed hands; the tallish guy, clad in black hide – the same figure that had just walked through the door of Munn's.

Danny saw him too and even if they hadn't both studied Winter's photograph, it was likely they'd have known their quarry for who he was as soon as he came through the door. There was an air of confidence about Dunbar that translated easily into menace. His eyes immediately scanned the bar to see if anyone was going to challenge him but none was forthcoming. Indeed, there was a noticeable scattering of bodies and the two wasters who had been inhabiting the pool table were suddenly gone as if they'd been picked up by a gust of wind. Dunbar pulled up a bar stool and perched on it, his leather coat almost skirting the floor like a vampire's cape.

'Usual?' he was asked from behind the bar.

'Aye.'

The barman held a glass under a vodka optic and deposited a double in it before adding a shot of cola and setting it down in front of Dunbar. He shoved a fiver at the barman and waved away the offer of change.

Winter and Danny had made sure they hadn't looked over at Dunbar. They sipped on their pints and chatted quietly until Danny nudged Winter and nodded his head in the direction of the now vacant pool table. Both men got off their bar stools, made their way to the table and dropped coins in the slot to set up the game. Danny made sure he was noisily enthusiastic about the pots he made and encouraged Winter to do the same. They laughed a lot and jeered each other, successfully managing to sound like a pair of clowns. When Winter won the frame, Danny made a clumsy attempt to hide the fact that he was handing over a tenner, making it very obvious in the process.

They were on their second frame when Dunbar approached them. He stood quietly for a few minutes, weighing up the standard of their play and sipping on his vodka and Coke. Clearly he wasn't too impressed by what he saw because he put coins down on the rim of the table to signal that he wanted to play the winner. Danny, in the process of potting the six ball, glanced up at him but contrived to look indifferent about the prospect of someone else joining their game. Neither he nor Winter looked at Dunbar throughout the rest of the frame, just concentrating on each other and the game until Winter knocked in the black ball to snatch another victory.

As soon as the black dropped, Dunbar stepped forward, slipped his coins into the slot and the pool balls clattered into the tray. Without saying a word or looking at Winter, he arranged the balls in the triangle, placing the 'big balls' and 'wee balls' to suit him. Only when he was satisfied did he stand up straight and look over.

'Play you for twenty quid.'

Winter looked at Danny, who simply shrugged. Now able to look at Dunbar properly without raising suspicion in him, they could both clearly see a glassy look in his dark eyes that had been fuelled by something other than vodka.

'Aye, okay,' Winter agreed. 'Why not?'

Dunbar, still wearing his leather coat, broke off and immediately left Winter with an opening he took advantage of, pocketing three balls before missing. Dunbar grinned at the miss and chalked his cue before knocking in four balls of his own and looked good to win the frame quickly before a ball rattled in the jaws of the pocket and stayed out. Winter stepped back in, potting two more, then snookering Dunbar behind the black.

The younger man didn't look at all impressed and arched his eyebrows disapprovingly at Winter as if he regarded it as unsporting. Winter merely shrugged in return, indicating that he should just suck it up and get on with it, immediately remembering the nature of the man he was winding up and regretting it. Dunbar got low over his shot and tried to come off the side cushion but failed to hit anything, leaving Winter with two shots. He knocked a ball over a pocket before potting it, then another before clipping the black into the middle bag to win the frame.

He stood up from the table and looked over at Dunbar, who wore a scowl but was fishing in his pockets for money. He produced a twenty and dropped it contemptuously on the table for Winter to pick up. 'Another frame,' he demanded.

Winter picked the cash up from the table and pocketed it. 'If you're sure.'

Dunbar's answer was to drop coins in the slot and send the balls crashing back into play. As he busily racked them up on the baize, another punter wandered over to the table to place a coin on the table so he could play the winner. Without looking up from the table, Dunbar reached for the coin and threw it across the room.

'What the fuck are you doing?' the other guy protested.

Dunbar didn't look at him but continued to rearrange the balls in the triangle.

'I said what the fu—'

Dunbar turned, looking up to stare into the eyes of the slightly taller man who confronted him. Maybe the guy recognised Dunbar or maybe he just recognised the look in his eyes because he took a step back immediately. Dunbar followed him with a step of his own and the other guy retreated two yards, then another, albeit with an outstretched arm and mutterings of discontent. Within seconds he was safely back at the other side of the bar, his dignity almost intact.

'Your break,' Dunbar told Winter.

Swallowing hard and wondering just what they were getting themselves into, Winter broke off, scattering the balls across the table. Dunbar, his large voddie freshly restored, moved in to the table and swiftly potted four balls before finally missing. Winter knocked in three of his own before leaving the cue ball tight on the bottom cushion. The safety shot forced Dunbar to let Winter in again and he potted another two balls, an attempt at a third coming back from the knuckles of the middle pocket. When Dunbar moved in again, it was with the merest hint of a stagger and both Winter and Danny thought the vacant look in his eyes had increased. Sure enough, he potted just one ball and Winter stepped in to win the frame.

The twenty-pound note lay crumpled on the table almost as soon as the black hit the back of the pocket. Dunbar stood and stared at Winter, anger and frustration pouring out of him.

'A hundred,' he grunted.

'What?'

'A hundred quid for the next frame.'

351

CRAIG ROBERTSON

Winter again looked over to Danny, who responded with a wary shrug of his shoulders.

'Okay, but it's the last frame,' Winter replied.

'Sure. Let's see the colour of your money first. The big guy here can hold the stakes. He's not going to run anywhere. Sure you're not, big man?'

'Not me, son,' Danny agreed with him. 'I've never run in my life.'

The two men produced one hundred pounds apiece and handed them over for safe-keeping. Danny and Winter sought each other's eyes over Dunbar's head, anxiously seeking the reassurance that they both knew what the other was up to.

The gleam in Dunbar's eyes was wild now, a slippery yet distant self-confidence that knew no wrong. He prowled round the table, clearly enjoying living on the edge.

'Your break,' Winter told him.

'Bollocks. Deciding frame. Toss for break. Call.'

'Tails.'

Dunbar lifted his hand from the coin that sat on the back of his hand. 'Tails fails,' he announced.

Winter powered his cue through the white ball, sending it spinning into the pack and bursting it open. Balls spiralled round the table but none of them dropped into a pocket. Dunbar was straight onto the table, his eyes searching the balls for a likely opening, before he got down low to knock a long six-ball into the far pocket. Another three balls quickly followed without touching the sides and, although he looked to be in difficulty with his next shot, Dunbar cleverly doubled a ball into the middle pocket before tucking the white safely

352

onto a cushion. Winter was forced to take on a long pot into the opposite corner, knowing that if he missed it, then Dunbar was probably going to be left with three relatively simple shots to win the frame and the cash. He glanced up from the table to see Dunbar's eyes on his and he held them for a couple of seconds before going back to the cue ball and striking through it. The 12-ball rocketed towards the far pocket but just caught the jaws and rebounded out again.

Dunbar smirked evilly and stepped in to pot the last of his two balls and then sank the black confidently into the corner. He stood up from the table and turned towards Danny, his hand outstretched.

'Money.'

Danny handed over the two hundred quid and Dunbar quickly trousered it, downing the last of his vodka as he prepared to leave.

'Not so fast,' Winter blurted out. 'You hustled me, you cunt.'

'Dry your eyes,' Dunbar laughed. 'Learn your lesson and get some practice in. You're shite.'

'No way. I want my money back.'

'Fuck off. Seriously, fuck off. I'm leaving and if you don't want to get hurt, then get out of my fucking way.'

Winter stepped back as Dunbar came towards him, letting him past on his way out the door. Behind Dunbar's back, Danny signalled for Winter to wait and give him a head start before going after him. Winter did as he was told and Dunbar was almost out the front door when he shouted after him that he wanted his money. Dunbar didn't turn round but just laughed derisorily.

Winter and Danny started after him, ignoring the hushed warning from the barman to leave it alone. When they got onto Maryhill Road, the snow was falling once more and they saw Dunbar twenty yards ahead, his black leather coat flashing like a diamond.

'You did know you were being hustled, didn't you?' Danny asked Winter quietly.

'Course I did. I'm not completely stupid. Anyway, don't be so sure you know who was hustling who.'

Danny nodded and smiled as Winter called after Dunbar again.

'You. Fucking wait.'

'Fuck off,' Dunbar shouted back over his shoulder. 'You don't know who you're messing with.'

Dunbar walked on unperturbed past the bookies and the derelict structure at the end of the block before turning right up the grassy bank towards the canal. It was exactly where Danny and Winter hoped he was going and they speeded up after him. As they came round the corner and on to the square of scrubland, they saw Dunbar waiting patiently for them.

'I don't have a problem with you two,' he slurred. 'Don't make me have one.'

'We want a word with you, son,' Danny told him.

'No, you don't. Believe me, you don't.' Dunbar's eyes were wild. 'Go away before this goes bad.'

'Sorry, but we can't. You're finished here.'

Dunbar took an uncertain step to the side, his hesitant movement punctuated by a stamp of his left foot to steady himself. As he did so, he reached with his right hand inside his leather coat and emerged with something in his hand that gleamed in the moonlight. Dunbar continued to raise his hand high above his head until they could see he held a samurai sword. Now they knew why Dunbar wore the full-length coat.

'Fucksake,' Winter gasped to Danny. 'I thought you roofied this bastard.'

'I did. He should be out for the count by now.'

Dunbar whirled the sword in an arc above his head, slicing through the falling snowflakes and staring at the two men through bleary eyes. The sword sang through the air, its swish the only sound Winter could hear above the pounding of his heart.

'Any bright ideas?' he asked Danny.

'Like I told the kid, I've never run in my life. Getting a bit late to start now.'

Danny slipped his jacket off and wrapped it round his left arm. Winter followed suit and took a few paces to his right as he watched Danny move to the left, both holding their barely protected arms in front of them in a poor imitation of shields.

Dunbar was clearly struggling under the influence of the liquid Rohypnol Danny had dropped into his vodka as he played pool, reeling slightly from side to side, but he kept a firm grip on his sword and was flashing it before him. Danny and Winter cautiously approached him from either side, inching nearer but wary of the scything blade.

Winter, seeing what Danny was doing, suddenly shouted at Dunbar, grabbing his attention. As he did so, Danny threw a ball of snow into Dunbar's face, momentarily blinding him, and followed it up with a charge towards his sword arm. He got within a yard of his target before Dunbar instinctively lashed out, the arc of his blade catching Danny high on his shoulder and causing a spurt of fire engine red to erupt. Danny cried out and fell back, his right hand clutching at his left shoulder. Winter hurled in from the right, crashing a boot into Dunbar's thigh and sending him sprawling back onto the ground, knocking the wind from him.

Winter rushed to Danny, seeing the blood pouring from the wound and staining the snow. Danny had been relatively lucky: the sword had sliced through his flesh but hadn't bitten deeper than an inch or so. Winter unwrapped the jacket that covered Danny's hand and switched it to his shoulder to stem the flow, watching as the last few drops fell onto the white. From behind him, he heard Dunbar scrambling unsteadily back to his feet, his sword flexing protectively in front of him. He backed away towards the canal towpath, his sword always between him and his attackers.

Winter started to his feet to go after him but Danny caught his arm.

'No. Let him go. Don't be fucking stupid. I'm in no state to tackle him and you can't do it on your own.'

'So much for the plan to spike his drink.'

Danny grimaced, as much at the pain from his arm as Winter's dig at him.

'It worked – to an extent. It's probably the only reason we've still got both our hands but I'm guessing the cocaine is keeping the GHB at bay for now. You still got those twenties you won from him?'

'Yeah.'

'Good, because if we don't get Dunbar tonight, then the tech boys can get DNA from those.'

'*If* we don't get him tonight?'

'We give him a ten-minute head start. There's no way we want to catch him if the GHB hasn't worked; he's far too fucking dangerous for that. On the other hand, if it does the trick, then we'll find him no bother even with that start.'

'Danny, you need to go to hospital.'

'And I will – after this. Jesus, why does it have to be so cold? Here, take my jacket, it's not doing the job.'

Danny took off his shirt, letting the wound temporarily run free again until he'd instructed Winter how to fix a tourniquet to his shoulder with one sleeve and wrap the other round the cut. As Danny stood bare-chested and blood-streaked in the snow, Winter shook his head in disbelief. Uncle Danny was over thirty years older than he was but still tougher and braver than he'd ever be. Mind you, his admiration for his uncle didn't stop him from wishing he'd photographed the gaping sword wound before it had been covered up.

When Danny had his jacket back on, he glanced at his watch and forced himself to pace round the scrubland for a few minutes, keeping warm and marking time until they went after Dunbar. Finally he nodded at Winter and they warily started down the towpath, knowing full well that the samurai could be waiting for them at any point on the unlit path. They edged along, Winter somewhat uncomfortably in front, his eyes straining in the dark for any sign of Dunbar. In the end, they almost fell over him.

They were no more than a yard from his prone body when Winter's leading foot brushed against the blade of the sword, causing it to sing sadly and for Winter nearly to soil himself.

'Jesus,' he gasped, stepping back and forcing Danny to walk straight into him.

Dunbar was out cold, the sword abandoned by his side. The GHB had taken its toll at last and, along with the cocaine and the vodka, was going to give Dunbar a long sleep and a monstrous hangover. Danny reached into his jacket pocket with his good arm and produced plastic bindings.

'Put these on him,'

As Winter tied up Dunbar, Danny managed to fish his mobile out of his trouser pocket. After a few seconds, his call was answered.

'Jered Dunbar? It's Danny Neilson. I've got something for you.'

CHAPTER 46

It took an hour and a half before Jered and two of his fellow travellers from the Stirling site managed to make their way to Maryhill but Sam Dunbar hadn't stirred. Winter and Danny had managed to keep him off the snow so he didn't freeze to death and had marched him back and forth to keep his circulation flowing as well as theirs.

They heard the gypsies coming before they saw them, the three figures finally emerging from the snow and advancing on them. Danny had his jacket zipped to his throat so they couldn't see he was shirtless beneath it, not wanting to give any hint he was injured and he and Winter were at a distinct disadvantage.

'What have you done to him?' Jered demanded when he saw that his cousin was unconscious.

'Saved his life probably,' Danny replied.

Jered looked doubtful.

'How do you reckon that?'

'He was strutting round Glasgow slicing into people with that sword. He wouldn't have lasted more than a year before someone killed him. It was prison or the grave for him – no other choices. You realise that?'

Jered pursed his lips but nodded sullenly.

'Who was he working for?'

'You don't want to go there, Jered. The guy is heavy duty. He'll be pissed enough that Sam has gone missing without you going in there and making it worse. Stay away.'

'Okay, but tell me what you know. Why was he doing it?'

'Money,' Danny answered flatly. 'He was earning big style but he also needed it to pay for his new habit.'

Jered looked confused.

'Cocaine,' Danny explained. 'You'll need to get him off it and it will be painful. I think that stuff was what made him start using the sword. He faced us down with it but he gave us the chance to back off. That's the only reason he's going back with you rather than inside. You understand me?'

'Okay...' The words stuck in Jered Dunbar's throat. 'Thanks. We'll deal with him from here.'

'Not quite so fast, Jered. We have a deal.'

Jered looked to his two companions, both shorter than Winter and Danny but one wiry with flinty eyes and the other broad and muscular. With one and a half sets of arms between them, it was going to be a struggle to take these three on the tight confines of the towpath, particularly as the good pair of arms belonged to Winter. Jered moved in close on Danny, nose to nose like they had been back in the caravan when Danny had head-butted him.

'I don't like you much,' Jered told him, his accomplices now tight to his shoulder. 'No respect. And don't think I've forgotten what you done to me.'

Danny didn't blink, just stared back at Jered, noticing how the bridge of his nose was still swollen and slightly misshapen.

'And this is our business not yours,' Jered continued. 'Uncle shouldn't have got you involved. Sam is family.'

Winter moved forward, standing shoulder to shoulder with Danny, joining in the staring contest as best he could.

'If it was down to me, then we'd be breaking the ice on that canal and you'd be going in it. But Uncle says different.'

'Your uncle is a wise man,' Danny told him. 'Just saved you from a broken neck. Where's Bradley?'

Jered's lip curled back as he inched closer to Danny, his head bobbing slightly as if he were making his mind up whether to butt him.

'We don't know yet. We're looking and we'll find him soon enough. You'll have to trust us on that.'

Danny held his ground, his head against Jered's.

'Not good enough. Where is he?'

'All we're sure of is that he's in Scotland, somewhere in the west. Uncle is a man of his word. When we know, we'll call you.'

'You better.'

Danny looked down at Sam Dunbar, still out cold at their feet.

'Take your rubbish and get going back to Stirling. But Jered? I don't give a damn if you take him to Riverside or Russia. If he comes back to Glasgow, then he goes to jail. No second chances. Understood?'

'Pick him up,' Jered told his mates. 'I'll take this sword if it's his.'

Winter put his boot firmly over the blade of the sword. 'No chance. That's going nowhere. It's done enough damage.'

Jered looked from Danny to Winter and back again before giving up the ghost.

'Hurry up, you two. Let's get out of this place.'

They watched the three travellers go down the towpath until they disappeared into the snow, the sound of their labours soon waning as the night swallowed them up.

Winter looked at the samurai sword at his feet and tried to figure out the best way to pick it up without inflicting further damage on the fingerprints and DNA it held on its surfaces.

'Think that will be enough to keep Aaron Sutton happy?' Winter asked him.

'That and knowing the sword and its user are off the street. Anyway, it will have to be.'

'How's your arm?'

'Nearly falling off.'

'Let's get you to hospital.'

'Aye, whatever. Jered and his bloody uncle better not be buggering us about. Bradley is the key to all this. But something isn't right – all those rumours about Barbie being a gypsy bride and now Bradley living as a traveller. You know how I feel about coincidences. Something's wrong here and I just can't see it.'

CHAPTER 47

Saturday 22 December. 10.20 a.m.

Narey was up before nine and had worked her way through a stodgy fry-up in the hotel restaurant while flicking through the newspapers. She read both a tabloid and a broadsheet but soon discovered she didn't have much of an appetite for either. What passed for news in both of them seemed to pale beside the things that were going on in her own life.

She had been tempted to go straight over to CAHiD to see how Kirsten was getting on but knew it wouldn't do much good for her to be standing over the professor's shoulder while she worked. Hard as it was, she would stay away until she got the call to say that the job was done. It didn't stop her thinking about it, mentally filling in the gaps in Barbie's broken skull just as the computer reconstruction system was doing, seeing the girl become flesh in her mind.

There was still maybe half a day until the model was completed and there was no way she could hang about in her hotel room until then but, equally, she couldn't venture far or do anything worthwhile in case the call came through. It was snowing again but, despite that, she decided to go for a walk – anything to take her mind off what was happening. She found herself wandering down towards the river, the silvery Tay as McGonagall put it, shining under a wet sun and looking icy cold. To her right, the rail bridge snaked out into the river and across to Fife, and across to her left, the road bridge did the same, the ends of both disappearing into misty clouds of snow.

She walked across to Discovery Point, where Captain Scott's Antarctic exploration ship was permanently docked. It was a big tourist attraction for the area and Narey couldn't help but think that being built to cope with winter at the South Pole was pretty handy preparation for a long winter in Dundee. The ship had been built in the city, right enough, so the people who put it together obviously knew a thing or two about surviving in a cold climate.

Her dad had taught her all about Captain Robert Falcon Scott and his Antarctic expeditions on the *Discovery* and the *Terra Nova*. She'd thrilled to his tales of the race to the Pole, of being beaten there by Amundsen and of Captain Oates saying that he was 'going outside and may be some time'. Her dad was her own Captain Scott, her hero.

Narey instinctively reached for her mobile, feeling the need to hear his voice. She listened as it rang and rang, before finally going to voicemail but she hung up without leaving a message. She paced back and forth in front of the *Discovery*, looking up to the heavens to see the snow tumbling towards her, sticking out her tongue and catching flakes the way she had when she was little.

She phoned back and this time it was answered on the fourth ring. The voice on the other end sounded very small and a little afraid.

'Hello?'

'Hi Dad. It's Rachel.'

A long pause. 'Who?'

'It's Rachel, Dad.'

'I don't know a Rachel.'

'Yes you do. I'm your daughter.'

'Daughter? I don't have a daughter. Who are you? Why are you saying this?'

'It's okay, Dad. Don't worry. Look, I'll call you later. Okay?'

'No! Don't call me. Don't. I don't know you.'

He hung up on her.

She stood in front of the ship and let tears run down her face, breathing hard, telling herself she was away from him for a good reason. She was there for him. She just wasn't *there* for him.

She wandered away from the riverside and back towards the city centre, her collar turned up fruitlessly against the snow. People were hustling past her on either side but she'd rarely felt so alone. Tony was only about ninety miles away but it felt as if he were on the other side of the world. How far away would he want to be when she told him about her planned changes for their relationship?

In the end, the call from Kirsten came much earlier than Narey had expected. The professor had been in the lab since before it was light and she phoned to say that if Narey headed over to CAHiD, then the girl would be ready by the time she got there.

The College of Life Sciences was on Dow Street, only a

ten-minute walk away and she hurried straight to it. The white, six-storey building looked impressively anonymous from the street but it held one of the leading centres in its field in the country, if not the world. Narey was shown up to Kirsten's lab, a keen surge of expectation running through her and the adrenalin taking over from the despair she'd been feeling about her dad.

'Wow, you were quick,' Kirsten smiled from behind her computer screen as Narey came through the door. 'Did you run?'

'A bit,' Narey admitted. 'Is she ready?'

'Almost. You caught me out slightly but . . . I'm just refining the skin tone to make sure . . . yes, okay. I'm happy with that. Do you want to see her?'

Narey knew she had no simple, satisfactory answer to a question like that. She was aching to see the girl but she was also scared about where it might lead. Be careful what you wish for, that's what they said. Instead, she settled for a simple unsatisfactory reply.

'Yes.'

Kirsten grinned and beckoned her to the other side of the screen. As Narey walked round the terminal, there she was, looking back at her as if she were real. Lily. Barbie. Fully formed, three-dimensional, not living or breathing, flesh but no blood. It was incredible. In little over a day, she had been transformed from skull to face, turning on the screen in front of them, all but alive from every angle.

'There is some guesswork, of course,' Kirsten warned. 'But we have some very clever software and we can be confident it's accurate. This is how she looked.'

Narey almost unconsciously took the seat in front of the screen and just sat there, staring at the girl. She watched her revolve slowly before her, still wondering who she was but knowing they were now so much closer to finding out.

'Can you give me an image of this that I can send to Strathclyde?'

'Of course. One touch of a button.'

'Great. I want to send this to my DC. She's the one who has been going through all the missing persons data. If anyone is going to be able to put a name to the face quickly, it's her.'

Two minutes later Narey had Julia Corrieri on the other end of the phone and they were waiting for Barbie's face to appear on her computer screen in Stewart Street.

'What's happening down there today, Julia?'

'Pretty quiet at the moment, Sarge. I'd just come in to go through these files one more time before I go over to Vancouver Road to take over guard duties at Greg Deans' house.'

'How is he?'

'Scared. Scared and very annoying. He is always . . . Hold on. It's here.'

There was a tense silence on both ends of the line as the image unfolded before Corrieri.

'I know her, Sarge. She's on my list, I'm sure of it. Her name is . . .' Corrieri paused to make sure she was right. 'Claire Channing. She's from somewhere in the north of England. Wait a mo, let me . . .'

On the other end of the phone, Narey puffed out her

cheeks while Corrieri shuffled through some papers. It wasn't impatience at the DC's actions; it was tension, pure and simple.

'Yes,' Corrieri confirmed jubilantly. 'Claire Channing. Born in May 1976. She was from Whitby in North Yorkshire. Her parents, Edward and Emily Channing, reported her missing in September 1992, the year before. And yet . . . sorry, hang on, Sarge.'

Narey could hear Corrieri softly reading aloud and sounding as if she had repeated it to make sure she had heard herself correctly in the first place.

'Okay, Sarge. I could be wrong. The initial missing person's report from North Yorkshire Police is the one that has the photograph attached but there is a follow-up from 1994 after the body was found on Inchmahome. They went back to the parents just in case but were told that it definitely wasn't her. That was the last they had on it.'

Shit. Why could nothing ever be simple, Narey thought.

'Email me the photograph of the Channing girl, Julia. But what's your take on it looking at her?'

'Well, I mean . . . I'm sure it's her, Sarge. The likeness is very strong. I'd say that unless Claire Channing has a twin, then it's her.'

Within minutes, the image from the North Yorkshire file had been spirited back up the line to Dundee and popped up on the screen before Narey and Fairweather. It was stunning. Narey couldn't help but smile at the look of satisfaction on Kirsten's face. She and her scanner and her software had done a remarkable job.

*

Narey sat in her car and pulled out her mobile, her overnight bag in the boot, ready to make the drive back south to Glasgow. First she called Tony and told him about Claire Channing and what she wanted him to do. Then, taking a deep breath, she hit another number, dreading it but needing to do it before she went any further. It rang.

'Hello?'

'Hi Dad. It's Rachel.'

'Rachel! Hello, love. It's so good to hear your voice.'

'And yours, Dad. It's so good to hear yours.'

CHAPTER 48

Winter was standing before the fax machine in his Pitt Street office, wondering when he'd last used the thing. Whatever the answer, he knew he'd never been remotely as anxious to see anything appear from its black plastic mouth.

He'd been pacing before the fax for the past few minutes, urging it to deliver. The gloom of the poorly lit room swamped him as he waited, feeding his anxiety and quickening his pulse. Would she fit the image that taunted and tempted him in his dreams? Would he know her?

Winter knew it mattered more to him than it should have done but he wouldn't change that even if he could. It went beyond ghoulish interest: he cared. He wanted to see her and he wanted to see her now. Lily. Barbie. It had been ten minutes since Rachel had said she'd fax the image – ten long minutes.

When the beep that signalled the arrival of the fax burst into the quiet of the room, it made Winter jump and sent his heart thudding into his ribcage. For that momentary beat, he suddenly wondered whether he really wanted to see her after all. The thought lasted as much time as it took the noise to fade.

The wait wasn't over, however. He had forgotten how

bloody slow and inefficient fax machines were when you were used to email or text. The paper edged agonisingly from the feeder, testing his patience and his nerves. When she eventually began to emerge, pixel by laboured pixel, it was head first, her blonde hair filling the top of the page.

It took an age for her eyes to appear, peeping out below a flaxen curtain of eyelashes. They looked up at him from the tray, spring sky blue perhaps, lighter than he'd expected, wide set and deep. In his imagination, her eyes were pleading, appealing to him for help. Sometimes they screamed and he'd stare deep into them, trying to see the reflection of the person who had caused them to cry out in such pain. But the eyes that looked back at him now were disappointingly expressionless.

The paper eased on, revealing the bridge of a slim nose peppered with the faintest of freckles that spread engagingly onto high cheekbones. Her face was narrow and her ears stuck out ever so slightly. As her lips emerged, he saw that they were full and symmetrical, turning up into the beginnings of a natural, youthful smile that defied any attempts at making it impassive.

Her chin carried a mark just right of centre; not a natural cleft but probably the result of an accident, maybe falling from a swing or a bicycle, its faintly irregular contour having been raised by the professor's scanner. It didn't scar her looks but offered character and insight into the girl she had been.

When the last of the paper had filtered through the fax machine, Winter hesitated before picking it up, leaving her lying alone and untouched on the tray. Breathe. Deep. He finally picked her up, holding the paper gently, almost reverentially, and looked at her properly for the first time.

371

Her face was lean and the skin taut. She was a pretty girl, not beautiful perhaps but attractive in an outdoorsy, fun-filled kind of way. He liked her. She was friendly and open but there was a suggestion of something more, a hint of rebelliousness maybe. He read mischief and kindness. Winter knew he was seeing all sorts that probably weren't there, things that certainly couldn't be seen by eyes alone. He was able to see those things because he'd seen her before.

She was the girl who visited him in his sleep. His fellow waif and stray. The little sister he'd never had. The photograph he never took. Lily. Barbie. Claire Channing. Who was she really? It scared him at least as much as it excited him to know that he was soon going to find out.

CHAPTER 49

Saturday 21 December. 1.17 p.m.

Twenty minutes after they received the call, Winter and Danny were on their way to Whitby. Rachel had resisted the urge to call Addison or anyone else at Strathclyde, and certainly not anyone at North Yorkshire Police, reasoning to herself that the identification wasn't confirmed and she'd rather be sure before she made it official. She knew, of course, that the truth was far different.

Winter had asked her to phone the SPSA and make up some kind of story to keep his bosses happy. He knew Baxter would go spare about him missing yet another shift and all he could do was hope her plan to come up with some bullshit about vital photographs and identification would be enough for there to be a job for him still when he got back.

Danny was driving, which meant they could probably knock half an hour off the estimated three hours and forty-five minutes the online directions had suggested. Danny had always had a heavy right foot behind the wheel of a car but rejected Winter's notion that it was because Strathclyde's boys in blue had let him off speeding tickets for years. He also had a much simpler idea of directions than Winter's computer.

'South past Carlisle, hit a left at Penrith, left a bit again at Scotch Corner and keep going till we're nearly in the sea. Simple.'

That was more or less it for conversation until they were nearly at Lockerbie, both of them consumed with their own thoughts of what lay at the other end of their journey, letting music on the radio fill the void.

'I still think we should have phoned ahead and told them we were coming,' Winter piped up. 'Christ, if it is their daughter, then this is going to come as a bit of a shock. You not think we should have warned them?'

'No.'

'That's it? No.'

'Aye, that's it. Tony, there's more harm than good to be done by telling them we're coming. I don't want them prepared.'

'What? You think they had something to do with it?'

'I don't know, do I? Okay, it doesn't look like it at the moment but if I've learned anything in thirty years on the job . . .'

'Oh fuck, here we go again . . .'

'If I've learned anything, it's that nothing would surprise you. And I'm not taking the chance they might just be involved. When we knock on their door, assuming it is still their door after all these years, I want to see the look on their faces. I want to be sure it's real.'

'You're a sick bastard, Uncle Danny.'

'And this coming from a man who covers his bedroom wall in photographs of dead people?'

'Piss off.'

They lapsed into regular silence again after that, pierced only by Danny swearing at the radio DJ's choice of music and Winter telling him to leave the bloody channels alone. They were near Barnard Castle when Danny's mobile began ringing. He fished it out of his jacket pocket, took one look at the caller display and threw it over to Winter, who juggled with it before he too saw who was calling: Jered Dunbar.

'Hello.'

'Neilson?'

'No, it's Tony Winter. And anyway, it's *Mr* Neilson to you.'

'A hard man when you're on the other end of the phone, eh? Where's Neilson?'

'Mr Neilson's driving. Talk to me.'

There was a long pause on the other end of the line.

'Okay, monkey, but you make sure you pass it on to the organ grinder. I've got a message for him from Uncle: Peter Bradley is at the travellers' site in Dumbarton at Dennystown Forge.'

'Thanks, Jered.'

'Don't thank me. If it were down to me, I'd have told you nothing. Anyways, word will likely have got to Bradley by now. He'll know you've been asking about him.'

'You make sure of that?'

'He's family.'

The line went dead and Winter placed Danny's mobile on the dashboard, taking his own out of his pocket and finding

Rachel's name in his contact book. Danny looked over at him with raised eyebrows but Winter just lifted a hand to tell him to wait and he'd find out.

'Mr Neilson,' Danny laughed. 'I liked that. You're learning, son.'

Rachel picked up after a few rings and it was immediately obvious that she was driving too.

'Hi, Tony. Go ahead.'

'We've just heard from Jered Dunbar and he's told us where Bradley is.'

'Excellent. Where?'

'He says he's at an official council site in Dumbarton. It's called Dennystown Forge.'

'*Says* he is? You not believe him?'

'I don't know. Probably, yes. It came from Tommy Baillie and I think he'd be straight with us. We've still got info to put Sam Dunbar in jail.'

'Christ, don't remind me. I'll get my jotters for that one if anyone finds out. So what's your problem with what Jered told us?'

'He said Bradley might know we're coming. I don't know if he was just winding me up or what but he hinted that he or someone else let Bradley know.'

'Shit. Let's hope he's winding us up. Okay, I'd better go. You far from Whitby?'

'Less than an hour.'

'Let me know as soon as you've spoken to them, Tony.'

'Yes, Sarge.'

'Ha ha. I'm really grateful for everything, Tony. I promise I'll make it up to you when you get back.'

'Promises, promises. Rachel, we may actually know who Barbie is and where Bradley is. This could all be over soon.'

'Yeah, maybe. But so far we don't have anyone. Let's not count any chickens.'

For the second time in a few minutes, the phone line went dead on him.

CHAPTER 50

Detective Constables Julia Corrieri and Mike McCaughey had been given babysitting duties for Greg Deans. Corrieri, ever Narey's eager beaver, didn't mind in the slightest but McCaughey was more resentful of the task, given that it was mind-numbingly dull. While Corrieri had used the time to pore over her missing persons lists in the hope of seeing something she had missed the first time, McCaughey just watched TV or complained. He'd much rather have been out on the street, doing his action man routine with dealers or gangsters and he wasn't slow to tell anyone who would listen.

Deans had dispatched Janet and Leanne, his wife and daughter, to his sister's house in Aberdeen to get them away from any potential threat – and any further prospect of them knowing what he'd got involved with when he was younger. Narey had agreed to the move readily. While she didn't have much time for Deans' pleas for secrecy, she did want to keep his family out of harm's way.

For the two and a half days that they had been looking after Deans, the detectives had worked twelve-hour shifts: Corrieri was there from noon till midnight and McCaughey took over until she returned the following day. It wasn't so much that it was inappropriate for Corrieri to be there at night; it was more that there would be fewer opportunities for McCaughey to moan at someone. As a result, by the time Corrieri got back, he was bored, frustrated and grouchy.

He knew by the knock at the door it was her but McCaughey still insisted that Deans retreat into the sitting room until he had opened the front door. He eyed her up through the peephole and pulled the door ajar slightly in an overly theatrical manner, his blond hair pushed back on his head.

'Password?'

'Plonker.'

'That'll do. Thank God you're here. I'm bored out of my tree.'

'Nothing happening then?'

'Sadly not,' he grimaced.

'You'd actually prefer it if someone attacked Deans so you'd have something to do?'

'Yeah,' he grinned.

'Boys . . .' she shook her head despairingly. 'All the same. Okay, macho man, you can go fight crime on the mean streets of Gotham. The cavalry's here.'

'Fight crime? I wish. I'm off home to get some kip. Deans is in the front room.'

Corrieri groaned internally. She had been charged with befriending Deans in the hope that he would let slip some nugget of information he'd been keeping from the cops up till then. She chatted to him, listened to his worries about himself and his family, put up with his protestations of innocence about what had happened in the Trossachs and generally tried not to show that Deans made her skin crawl.

It was partly that she knew what he, Paton, Mosson and Bradley had done with the girl all those years ago. She wasn't a prude and it wasn't the sex she had a problem with. If Lily, who they now knew as Barbie, was a willing participant, then that was down to her. It wouldn't have been Corrieri's choice but the girl was young and drunk yet seemingly able to make her own mind up about what would happen. Corrieri was determined not to judge her but she reserved the right not to allow Deans the same luxury. For a start, he was old enough to have known better and, much more than that, he was a coward to have kept the truth to himself for so long when the girl's parents must have been desperate to know what had happened to their daughter.

The only slack she was prepared to cut him was that he did seem genuinely terrified about anything happening to his family. DS Narey was more sceptical and felt Deans was at least as concerned about covering his own backside as he was about protecting his wife and daughter. However, Julia, with her Scots–Italian background, was all about family and gave Deans some credit for his worries. It meant she was alone with him in the big house on Vancouver Road, something she didn't particularly like, but that was her job.

There was something she was getting from Narey as well that was throwing her a bit: the DS was normally as cool as they came but this case seemed to have her on edge. Corrieri didn't know the full background but was aware there had been moves going on before the rest of the squad knew anything about them. Whatever it was, Corrieri trusted Narey completely and knew she'd be doing the right thing. It was a standing joke in Stewart Street station that Corrieri was in awe of the DS and the mickey-taking annoyed Corrieri for one very good reason: it was true. There was less than ten years between them but Corrieri knew Narey was everything she wanted to be in terms of being a cop.

She knocked politely on the door to the sitting room and was beckoned in to see Deans sitting in the armchair, a pile of books by his side and his left hand running fretfully through his reddish hair. He looked up expectantly at her entrance.

'DC Corrieri. Do you have any news?'

'No, I'm sorry. There's nothing happening.'

The man's face fell and he pinched the bridge of his nose and rubbed his eyes.

'I was just hoping . . . Your colleague refuses to tell me anything. But I need to know what's happening with Bradley. Surely you people must be closer to finding him by now.'

'We're doing everything we can, Mr Deans. We'll find Peter Bradley sooner rather than later.'

Deans' fist pounded into the arm of his chair.

'That's not good enough. Two people are dead. I'm . . . I'm scared.'

Three people are dead, Corrieri thought. And perhaps if you hadn't been a coward and an arsehole, then all three deaths could have been avoided, starting with the girl on the lake. However, she knew her opinions didn't matter and they were certainly not what Deans wanted to hear. She had, she reminded herself, at least to appear to be neutral.

'I understand that, Mr Deans. You have round-the-clock protection. Your family has been moved. Peter Bradley is being pursued. We are doing all we can after a . . . late start in trying to find him.'

Deans' mouth opened, then reluctantly closed again.

'I'm sorry. You're right but I'm still worried. I think Paddy Bradley knew my sister lived in Aberdeen. I know it was a long time ago but if he remembers . . .'

'Mr Deans. I know you're anxious but I really don't think Bradley, even if it is him behind this, will think they've gone to Aberdeen.'

'Anxious? I'm absolutely terrified,' he shouted, his composure gone again. 'It's all very well for you to say he won't know they've gone there but they're not your family; they're mine and it is my duty to protect them from all this.'

Corrieri just looked back at Deans, anxious not to agitate him any further. She reached for her usual mantra in situations where she struggled for answers, the one the CID room laughed at her for: What Would Narey Do? Keep him calm, feed him any old baloney – whatever it took to stop him from losing control.

'Mr Deans, if it puts your mind at rest, I will speak to the officers from Grampian and get them to increase their tours past your sister's house. I will also speak to DS Narey and get a progress report on Bradley. Will that help?'

Deans smiled weakly and let his head fall briefly into his hands. 'Yes. Thank you. It's a weight off my mind. I know you and your colleagues don't approve of me but I've only ever done what I thought was right for my family.'

Corrieri nodded at him. 'I'll call my sergeant now.'

She ducked out of the room, wondering whether to go ahead with a call to Narey or not. The DS might not thank her for a call that was pandering to Deans' insecurities. On the other hand, pretending to call her would leave Corrieri a hostage to fortune if something went wrong and she had given Deans false information. She'd make the call.

'Hello?'

The echo on the line and the repetitive rush of passing traffic made it obvious that Narey was driving. Corrieri's guilt at phoning her immediately doubled.

'Oh sorry, Sarge. I didn't realise you were on the road.'

'It's okay; I'm hands free. What do you want?'

'I'm with Deans and he wants to know what's happening with Bradley. Deans is terrified he's going to go after his wife and daughter. I wanted to give him something to put his mind at rest.'

A rumble of passing thunder suggested something large, maybe an articulated lorry, had gone by Narey's car. The line was crammed with the din and it took a few seconds longer before Narey could make herself heard above the noise.

'Well, either he or you must be psychic. We've got something on Bradley at last. He's at a travellers' camp in Dumbarton and we're going to try to pick him up from there. He knows we've been asking about him though, so I'm just hoping to Christ he hasn't gone on the run.'

Another artic rumbled by, causing Narey to pause and repeat herself.

'I'm taking a team over there when I get back to Glasgow. Shouldn't be much more than an hour. Meantime you sit tight on Deans . . . I said, sit tight on Deans . . . Don't give him details; just tell him we are on to Bradley. Any worries, then get McCaughey back out of his bed and tell him I said he has to be there too. And tell him . . . I said, tell him I don't want to hear any of his whining.'

'Yes, Sarge.'

'And Julia? Keep an eye and an ear on that creep Deans. I've got a feeling there are still things he hasn't told us. Let him think you're on his side. Okay?'

'Sarge.'

When Corrieri got back to the living room, she found Deans pacing back and forth in front of the fireplace, obviously anxious to hear the result of her call to Narey.

'Well?'

'There's some good news, Mr Deans. I spoke to DS Narey and she says they have a definite lead on Bradley.'

'Well, that's fantastic. When are they picking him up?'

'Soon, hopefully. But there's no guarantee, Mr Deans. There's a chance Bradley knows we're on to him and he may yet do a runner.'

'What? How can he know? Where is he? Is he anywhere near my family?'

'No, sir. We think he's at a gypsy traveller site at Dumbarton – nowhere near Aberdeen.'

Deans hands flew to his head again and his anxiety was clearly greater than ever. He paced more quickly and scrabbled at his hair.

'That's not good enough. Not good enough. I can't believe you people have let him know you're coming after him. I want officers at my sister's house. Do you hear me? Once every few hours isn't good enough. Phone her back. Phone her back – now!'

'Sit down, sir,' Corrieri ordered him. 'If you sit down and

show me you can be calm, then I'll phone DS Narey again.'

Deans stopped still in his tracks, retreated to his armchair and forced himself into it.

'Please,' he begged her.

Corrieri closed the door behind her and made her way into the other front room, where she drew a deep breath and said a silent prayer that Narey wouldn't think her completely useless for not being able to keep the man under control.

'Yes?' her voice sounded impatient.

'Sorry, Sarge, it's . . .'

'Yes, Julia? What now?'

'It's Deans again, Sarge. I'm sorry but he's insisting that we up the patrols round his sister's house in Aberdeen. He wants you to guarantee it personally.'

'Chrissake. That man has got a bloody cheek.'

'I know, Sarge, but he's bricking it. I think he's becoming paranoid. And you did say I should let him think I was on his side.'

Narey sighed.

'Yes. Yes, I did. Okay, tell him . . .'

'What the hell?'

Narey could hear the sound of breaking glass in the Deans house even from her end of the receiver.

'What was that Julia?'

'I don't know, Sarge. I'll need to go . . .'

Her reply was cut off by a muffled banging, swiftly followed by a scream and a roar of pain that came from a man's voice further inside the house.

'Julia,' Narey shouted down the phone. 'What the hell is happening there? Julia?'

'It's Deans. He's being attacked. I'm going . . .'

The next thing Narey could hear was the noise of a door being kicked open and slamming against a wall. She heard Corrieri call out twice.

'No. No!'

Then Narey was subjected to the sickening sound of something heavy and hard being battered against DC Julia Corrieri.

Then, worse still, she heard nothing.

CHAPTER 51

The line went dead and all Narey could do was pray the connection was the only thing that had done so. She took a quick look in her mirrors and flung the car across two lanes onto the hard shoulder. Horns blared and brakes screeched but she didn't have time to care.

She punched the numbers she needed into the handset and drummed her fingers impatiently, waiting for someone to pick up. Anyone would have done but she was still relieved to hear DI Addison's voice. He began to speak but she shouted over him.

'It's Narey. You need to get as many cars as you can to Deans' house in Vancouver Road – now. And a couple of ambulances as well. Deans has been attacked . . . and so has Julia Corrieri.'

'Jesus Christ. How do you know this?'

'I was on the phone to her when she was hit. Look, it doesn't matter now, Addy. Time for that later. Just get people over there. Please.'

'Where are you?'

'On my way back down the road from Dundee. I'm a bit north of Stirling. Let me know as soon as you know anything.'

'Will do. Get here when you can but keep your car on the road.'

Addison hung up the phone and immediately dialled Control to get the nearest cars on their way to Scotstoun, closely followed by ambulances and as many CID, uniforms and support staff as he could raise. He bolted from his office, stopping just long enough to tell his startled secretary where he was going.

'Get a hold of Detective Superintendent Temple and let him know that an officer has been seriously injured in an incident in Vancouver Road. Tell him the incident is ongoing and I'm on my way there now.'

'But sir,' she protested. 'Your injury. You're not supposed to . . .'

'To hell with that. Just tell him where I've gone.'

Addison was halfway to Deans' house when the first call from the scene came through on his Airwave terminal. The note of tension in the caller's voice put him on edge immediately.

'Sir. It's PC Whitfield. I'm in the premises at Vancouver Road. I was told to call you when . . .'

'Yes. What's happening? How is Corrieri?'

'DC Corrieri is unconscious, sir. She has been beaten over the head and there's a lot of blood. We're still waiting on the ambulance.'

'What about Deans?'

'Sir?'

'The householder. How is he?'

'There's no one else here, sir. There are signs of a break-in in the kitchen, glass all over the floor and footprints round the back door. There's blood there too, sir. And a trail of it leading towards the front door.'

'Shit. What about Deans' car? It's a blue . . .' Addison struggled to remember what Narey had told him. He was rusty after so many bloody hours spent writing damn reports. 'A blue Focus. It should be parked outside.'

'No, sir. There's nothing there except DC Corrieri's pool car. Although . . . there is a clear patch of ground suggesting something has driven off recently.'

'Shit, shit, shit. Okay, I'll be there in a few minutes. Get the paramedics to her as soon as they arrive.'

'Yes, sir.'

Addison switched off the call and booted his foot harder to the floor, his siren demanding a clear path through the mid-afternoon traffic. Being a Saturday in the run-up to Christmas, there was no shortage of people making their way to or from the shops and progress was much slower than he would have liked even once he had bludgeoned his way onto the Clydeside Expressway. What should have been a fifteen-minute drive turned into twenty and he was just hoping the ambulance got there in half that time.

As he turned off Norse Road into Vancouver Road, he allowed himself to breathe again when he saw uniformed cops already blocking off the access points and a fleet of emergency vehicles on the scene. He parked on the first available bit of road, taking care that he didn't obstruct the ambulance's exit, and ran towards the house. He was half-way down the path when he was met by two paramedics in green coveralls coming the other way carrying a stretcher. Corrieri's head was already in a neck brace, an oxygen mask over her mouth and her face streaked with blood. One eye was closed over and the other was covered in a swathe of bandages.

'How is she?' Addison demanded from the first of the two paramedics.

The man shook his head gravely.

'Not good. Severe blunt force trauma. Response signs are poor. We're taking her to Gartnavel now. We've got to go.'

Addison nodded them on their way and hurried down the path, seeing the bulky, white-suited figure of Campbell Baxter, the scenes of crime manager from the SPSA, standing just inside the doorway.

'Suit up,' Baxter demanded, holding out a set of white coveralls, shoes and gloves for Addison to put on.

'Jesus, I don't have time for this shit,' he complained, putting the gear on anyway. 'What have you got?'

'We're not long here,' Baxter told him, clearly irritated by Addison's reaction. 'We managed to get a few positional shots of DC Corrieri before the paramedics removed her. There's no sign of the object used to strike her and we're working on the basis that the assailant took it with him.'

'Did the neighbours see anything?'

'You will need to ask your officers that but I believe the answer is no. The houses opposite are gardens rather than front entrances so any witnesses would need to be from the homes on either side.'

'And Deans?'

'The blood in the kitchen is not DC Corrieri's so we're working on the basis that it's the householder's until we get confirmation. The blood trail that leads to the front door and then along the path you have just contaminated is the same blood as the victim of the kitchen attack.'

'So Deans has been abducted?'

'DI Addison, you know I can't . . .'

'It looks that way, guv, yes.'

DC Mike McCaughey, recalled from his bed, had appeared over Baxter's shoulder.

'I've already given his car registration to Control and they're on the case now. Do you think it's Peter Bradley?'

Addison blew out a puff of irritated air.

'He'd have to be favourite. Get cars over to the travellers' site in Dumbarton and interview every fucker there. Jesus. Okay, show me where this guy broke in and then someone get me Narey on the phone. She's the one who started this mess.'

As soon as Narey had ended the call to Addison, she put her foot on the accelerator, bursting down the hard shoulder and pounding her horn until she had enough speed and room to pull back onto the road. She switched to the outside lane at the first opportunity and flattened it.

Her head was racing, too, with thoughts of Deans, Bradley and, above all, Corrieri. She kept hearing the sickening sound of something heavy being smashed against something frag- ile, followed by the worrying sound of silence before the call was cut off. Corrieri was her DC, they worked well together and liked each other. Corrieri was her responsibility.

Narey looked at the clock and the speedometer and pushed her foot harder against the accelerator in a fruitless attempt at more speed. She bashed her fist against the steering wheel in frustration, unintentionally beeping the horn but glad of the noise and the signal of intent to other drivers. Seeing it was nearly half past the hour, she switched on the radio too, seeking Radio Scotland and some news from Scotstoun.

There was no mention of it, the news being led, as it had been for the past week, by the extreme weather. Road closures, school closures and accidents were the order of the day yet again. There were knee-jerk calls for investment in new machinery to keep the roads clear and opposition politicians demanding the head of the Transport Minister because lorries were being parked up on the M8. There was good news too though, according to the newsreader: the arctic weather had brought an opportunity for skiing to those who could get to the slopes and there was the promise of fun and games on Scotland's only lake.

Narey's heart skipped a beat at the mention of the Lake of Menteith and the confirmation that it had frozen over sufficiently to allow people onto the ice. Apparently the public were descending on the lake from all over central Scotland and impromptu curling matches were already taking place. Narey knew she was breathing heavier and her mind was working overtime.

She jumped at the sound of her phone and veered slightly across the lane, skirting dangerously into the rutted ice and snow that fringed the road before pulling the car back into a straight line.

'Yes?'

'It's Addison. Rachel, Corrieri is in a bad way. She's being taken to hospital now. I'll let you know more when I get it.'

'Shit, shit. What about Deans?'

'He's gone. It looks like he's been taken in his own car.

We're guessing it's Bradley. We've had one sighting of the car heading out of town along Great Western Road.'

There was silence from Narey's end of the phone.

'Rachel? You still there?'

'Yes. I think I know where he's going.'

CHAPTER 52

Narey took the Dunblane junction onto the A820, swerving past a car that was dawdling in the outside lane and pulling straight out in front of another as she crossed the bridge over the motorway towards Callander. The country road was narrow and winding and she prayed she didn't get stuck behind a tractor. She hammered her foot to the floor, only reluctantly slowing as she neared the village of Doune.

She was still doing fifty as she hit the village's constricted streets, alarmed to see schoolkids strolling along the pavement and running across the road. One wee boy dashed out twenty yards in front of her and she hit her horn and her brake together, causing the tyres to squeal and locals to glare at the car. She hit her horn again, continuously this time, as she barged her way at speed through the village's main street with its collection of small shops, forcing pedestrians to pay attention to her and stay the hell out of her way.

A sign forced her to take a right at the village cross and she raced down a narrow one-way street past little whitewashed, turreted houses until the road rose again, a pub to her right and a churchyard on her left. A car was sitting at the give-way sign, waiting patiently to turn left but Narey didn't have time for such a luxury. She went inside the car onto the wrong side of the road and, horn blaring again, barrelled her way into the traffic and onto the road towards Callander, finally able to give in to the pressure that had been screaming from within to accelerate fully again.

Her Airwave burst into life and Addison shouted at her.

'We've picked them up near Drymen using number plate recognition. The camera showed two people in the front seats. We're trying to get road blocks in place but Bradley's got a head start on us and a number of routes he can take.'

Damn it, she thought. Why did Tony and Danny have to be down south? Going to visit the Channings suddenly seemed a wild-goose chase and she'd much rather have had them with her. They were part of this, not Addison and certainly not the rest of Strathclyde. It was their case, their capture, their kill. She reminded herself it was just as much about finding Barbie as it was about catching her killer. The difference was that her killer was on the run while Barbie, sadly, was going nowhere.

Every car that slowed her down or flashed their lights as she performed an overtaking manoeuvre was cursed or occasionally gestured at – frequently both. She hit an open section of road and kicked the car past eighty miles an hour, swinging it round bends, praying there wasn't another maniac coming in the opposite direction or a patch of black ice lying unseen with her name on it.

The road was lined on both sides with frozen trees and the fields were oceans of white. It seemed the further she went, the more desolate and arctic the surroundings became. The frost was thicker, the snow deeper and the temperatures lower as every passing mile took her further into the countryside.

Callander loomed and she was grateful that at least it wasn't summer, when the main street would have been choked with tourists and their cars. It was busy enough though, and she caused chaos as she veered from one side of the road to another, shooting through a red light and forcing other cars to slam on their brakes. As she sped past the Waverley Hotel, she couldn't help but think of Bobby Heneghan pulling pints inside and the battered body he'd found on Inchmahome. Was the body of Greg Deans going to be waiting for her when she got to the Lake of Menteith?

The traffic lights at Cross Street were at red where she needed to turn left and a queue of six cars was in front of her but Narey switched again to the wrong side of the road, obliging oncoming traffic to screech to a halt as she swung round the queue, onto Bridge Street and out of town. As she passed the high school, the road suddenly opened up, stretching straight as far she could see and she floored the Megane, hitting ninety, knowing that the snaking, undulating terrain of the Queen Elizabeth Forest was only minutes away.

Addison burst onto the radio again, demanding to know where she was but she used the excuse of the stuttering line to shout that she couldn't hear him and switched it off before he could say anything else. All she wanted was to get to the lake and Bradley. Nothing else and no one else mattered.

The forest was a bleak, alien landscape, its trees petrified, its surface characteristics rendered featureless by a blanket of snow. Narey hacked her way round its rally course, her right foot lurching from accelerator to brake, warily looking out for deer and ice until she roared out the other side of the park. To her left, a glimpse of the lake unexpectedly appeared between barren trees and moments later she saw the first sign pointing to Port of Menteith. There was more traffic now and she couldn't get past; she sat simmering slowly as she progressed at tourist pace towards the lake.

She saw that cars were lined up along the side of the road and their passengers were out and walking two deep by the verge. As she finally got nearer to the corner that led down into Port of Menteith and the lake, she suddenly saw there were already Central Scotland cop cars on the scene. For a second she thought they had beaten her there in pursuit of Bradley but then she realised they were there to deal with the crowds that had turned out to go on the lake. Christ, there must have been thousands of people there and she cursed every one of them. It was going to make it all the harder to find Bradley and Deans.

Narey got to the corner and flashed her ID at the cop who had stopped her from taking the turn down towards the hotel. The cop refused to budge initially and demanded a closer look, causing Narey's impatience to rise still higher.

'Sorry, Sergeant,' the cop apologised on seeing she was genuine, 'but it's crazy here today. They are all desperate to park as close as they can but there's just not enough room. Some madman's already driven right past me to get down to . . . Sergeant?'

Narey stood on the accelerator, forcing the constable to stand aside, and raced past him with a screech and plunged down the hill towards the hotel, church and lake. The narrow road was lined with people, all wrapped up in their winter finest, and a few of them had to step hurriedly to the side as Narey's Megane hurtled by. She took the sharp right into the car park, causing another gaggle of would-be skaters and curlers to scatter at her approach.

As soon as she turned, she saw the agitated crowd at the far end of the car park. There were maybe a dozen people buzzing around a blue car and she knew immediately that they were excited by far more than the prospect of walking across the ice. She parked as close as she could and jumped out of her Megane.

'Police,' she called out, her ID in her hand. 'Move back, please. Police. Move back.'

A few of the people on the fringes of the crowd heeded her call and, as they turned, she saw their open mouths and ashen faces and knew what they had seen. In slow motion, they moved for her one by one, in increasing states of anxiety, some pointing beyond the car. As they cleared away, she could see there was just one figure in the dark interior of the car, slumped forward in the passenger seat, head bowed. Instinctively, she put her hand on the bonnet and felt it was hot in contrast to the freezing conditions around it. It hadn't sat there long at all.

Narey had to tug at the coats and jackets of the final few rubberneckers to get them to move and saw that they hadn't necessarily stayed looking by choice: they'd been transfixed. As she finally got the last of them out of her way, Narey tugged at the passenger door and opened it to be met by the familiar, sickly smell of blood.

She looked inside and found herself involuntarily taking a step back at the sight that greeted her. No wonder she could smell blood – he was drenched in the stuff. It was spilling down his chest and soaking his shirt and woollen jumper, down to where his wrists were scored red with tie marks. Going against every forensic procedure she'd been taught, Narey caught him by the hair and lifted his head up.

His throat had been cut and the blood that poured from it was still warm and bright red. It struck her that Tony would call it pillar box red, meaning it hadn't been exposed to the air for long. The man's mouth hung open and his eyes were wide with shock. His face looked so different to how she'd seen it before, disfigured in death as opposed to being vibrant in life. All around her, she could hear the clamour of people and muffled screams of shock and murmurings of fear and prurient excitement. She should have moved them on but instead she stood rooted to the spot and looked as much a rubbernecker as any of them.

CHAPTER 53

Tony and Danny had reached Aelfleda Terrace on Whitby's East Cliff, a spectacular spot with views high above the harbour, the marina and the town. They stared down into the ravine, snow-topped houses below them and across the harbour to the busy West Cliff. They were standing on the doorstep of a picture-book house with a wonderful view. And they were about to rip it all apart.

The petite, fair-haired woman who opened the door smiled at them expectantly over a pair of silver-rimmed glasses, tugging a heavy cardigan closer to her as she was met by the frosty air of the outside world.

'Yes? Can I help you?'

Emily Channing's accent wasn't the broad Yorkshire of Barnsley or Leeds; it had more than a hint of Teesside about it and yet something different altogether. A local accent for local people, Winter thought.

'My name is Daniel Neilson and this is Anthony Winter,' Danny told the woman. 'We're investigators working in conjunction with Strathclyde Police.' It was near enough to the truth to pass scrutiny.

'Oh.'

This was clearly not what Mrs Channing had expected to be greeted with on her doorstep.

'I . . . don't understand. Strathclyde? That's Glasgow, isn't it?'

Winter felt the first puff of the icy ill wind that was going to blow through the Channing's cosy cottage.

'Yes, ma'am. This is a rather delicate situation. May we possibly come in? We may have some news about your daughter.'

The woman's mouth dropped open and she reached out to catch hold of the doorframe.

'Claire . . . Have you . . . have you found her?'

'It would be better if we could talk inside, Mrs Channing.'

'Yes, yes. Of course. I'm sorry. Please, do come in. I mean . . . yes, please.'

Before the woman could back away from the doorway sufficiently for the men to pass, her husband appeared, as tall and thin as she was small and plump. He had picked up on the tone in her voice and concern was written all over his lean features.

'Ted. These men are from Scotland. From the police. They have . . . some news.'

'News?'

'News.'

'Is it . . . um? Um. Come in.'

Winter and Danny were ushered into a floral explosion of a front room with a coal-effect gas fire burning away furiously in the centre of the far wall and invited to take a seat. Danny indicated they would rather stand but it might be better if the Channings sat. The words caused a ripple of panic in Mrs Channing but her husband seemed unruffled by the implications of Danny's suggestion.

'Tea?' Ted Channing asked them.

'No, sir. Thank you. It might be better if we just . . .'

'Terrible cold spell, isn't it?' the husband continued to chatter. 'Although it's probably much colder and snowier than this where you gentlemen are from.'

'Ted,' his wife stopped him. 'The gentlemen have come a long way. I dare say it's important.'

'Thank you, Mrs Channing. I'm afraid it is. We've been working on what is often referred to as a cold case.'

Ted looked as if he were going to make some nervous joke about cold being apt but the utter inappropriateness of it dawned on him just in time.

'We have reason to believe the case we're investigating is related to the disappearance of your daughter.'

Ted stroked his chin as if he were confused but behind his eyes the fuse had already been lit. His wife sat with her mouth open and hands trembling.

'Claire didn't disappear,' Ted corrected him. 'She ran away. She said she was going to but we didn't . . . didn't believe her.'

'I'm sorry, Mr Channing. I realise this is very difficult but if I can just explain the circumstances of our visit, then . . .'

As Danny spoke to the parents, Winter's eyes and mind drifted to a solid oak sideboard that stood against one wall and was creaking under the burden of a family history in photographs. He moved nearer to survey them and saw Mr and Mrs Channing in various stages of their lives, from a carefree couple in their twenties through to being young parents, then the parents of a teenager. Then there were more, but considerably fewer, photographs of them in middle age and with considerably fewer smiles.

Among them all was the girl: baby, toddler, child, teenager. Winter watched her grow before his eyes, taller and fuller, freckles appearing and fading, pigtails replaced by flowing locks, braces there and then gone. The constant was the smile; wide and engaging, confident and just a little cheeky. In what he took to be her parents' last photograph of her, she was in her mid to late teens, hair long and summery blonde, her hand shading her pale blue eyes from sunshine and the wide grin spreading across her face. She had on a bright red T-shirt, which showed off the heart-shaped rhinestone necklace that stood out against her suntanned skin. He wondered how long before she left home and fatefully journeyed north it had been taken.

For it was her. There was no doubt that the photograph of Claire Channing was an incredibly close match for Kirsten Fairweather's reconstruction model. Winter had a printed photocopy of the image burning a hole in his jacket pocket and he both longed for and dreaded the moment when he would take it out for them to see. They could, he thought incongruously, be sisters. This lost girl in front of him and the girl found on the island on the lake – the one and the same.

His thoughts were interrupted as Danny's tortuous explanation to the parents flooded back into his hearing.

'Mr and Mrs Channing, I take it you were familiar with the case in Scotland in which the body of a young girl was found murdered on an island in the Lake of Menteith? This would have been around eight months after your daughter left home.'

Danny let the words hang in the room, as much a test of their reaction as it was a gentle unravelling of the unwanted truth.

'I'm not sure,' Ted Channing murmured, seemingly trying to remember. 'That would have been February – no, March – 1994. Is that right?'

Winter heard the growing impatience that underlined Danny's reply.

'Yes, Mr Channing, March 1994. You must remember the case. It received considerable publicity. There were nation-wide appeals to try to discover the victim's identity.'

The word 'victim' sent another shockwave around the room and Winter saw Emily Channing shake.

'I . . . I think I do. Terrible thing,' Ted conceded. 'But what does that have to do with us?'

Tears had begun to run down Emily's face but her husband didn't notice.

'Did it never occur to you or your wife that the girl who was found might have been your daughter?' Danny continued.

'Well, no. Not all,' Channing replied. 'I mean that was in Scotland. Claire wouldn't have been in Scotland. She was never going to Scotland. She said she was going to France or possibly Ireland. She never mentioned Scotland.'

Danny let him bluster on, hoping it would blow itself out. It didn't.

'Why would we think that might have been Claire? Of course we didn't.' He was standing now, getting more anxious. 'Do you think it might have been Claire? Why would you think that?'

Danny turned slowly from the man and held his hand out

towards Winter, who reached inside his jacket and produced the sheet of paper Danny wanted.

'This,' Danny explained, 'is a computer-generated facial reconstruction of the girl who was found murdered.'

He held the image up in front of them and Emily Channing screamed. Her husband's gaze fell to the floor.

'It isn't her,' he mumbled.

His wife screamed again, this time at him.

'Oh Ted.' Hot tears were streaming down Mrs Channing's face. 'Of course it is. We knew,' she shouted at him. 'We both knew. Of course we did.'

Ted turned from his wife and, for no other reason than to avoid her gaze, faced the opposite wall.

'Every time it appeared on the news,' his wife continued. 'Every time it was mentioned on *Crimewatch* or *Newsnight*. Every time, we'd both blank it as if it had absolutely nothing to do with us. Never even so much as an "Oh, that girl must be about Claire's age" or "Oh, I wonder if . . .". Nothing. We shut it out and just refused to . . .'

Emily Channing stopped mid-sentence and hammered the heel of her hands onto her husband's back, thumping them off him but still not achieving the desired effect. He continued to face the far wall, head bowed.

'You're still doing it,' she shrieked at him. 'Face me, Ted. Face the truth. We can't keep hiding from this.'

She thumped her husband again and he slumped to his knees, put there more by the revelation he'd been shunning than the renewed pummelling on his back. Even when he was on the floor, she continued to hit him and he refused to acknowledge a single blow.

'Mrs Channing,' Danny gently chided her.

She turned quickly, as if surprised there was anyone else in the room, and looked back and forth between Danny and her husband until she realised what she'd been doing and instead cradled him, caressing his greying hair.

'We knew and we didn't,' she tried to explain to Danny, her face streaked from crying, her eyes red. 'We shut off. We shut down. The police came to the door and asked if the girl in Scotland might be Claire but we told them it couldn't be, she wasn't there, she didn't own clothes like that girl did. And that was true. It was never, ever mentioned. Not between us. But we both thought it. I did. Ted . . . Ted must have too. If we didn't mention it, then it wasn't true and one day she would walk back through the door . . .'

'No.'

The monosyllable was blurted out from Ted Channing in a single sob, trying to cut off his wife's seeming acceptance of the unacceptable. She pulled his head closer to her but another muffled 'No' could still be heard.

'The argument was about nothing, you see,' Emily continued, her voice wavering and choking back fresh tears. 'Nothing at all – just teen stuff. Claire was always a free spirit. So when she said she was leaving we didn't pay much attention. Then when she did go we just thought she'd come back in her own time. And we thought that and thought that for . . . forever.'

Danny nodded gravely, touched by the couple's grief.

'What is it that you know, Mr . . . Mr . . . ?'

'It's Neilson, Mrs Channing. We have uncovered witnesses from the winter of 1993, when we believe Claire was in the area of the Lake of Menteith. One of them has positively identified a girl matching her description . . .'

Somewhere during the previous conversation, Winter had tuned out. He didn't know the point at which he could no longer hear anything that was being said in the room but he slowly became aware that all he could hear was the faint bell that was ringing in the recesses of his mind. Almost unconsciously, he had turned away from Danny and the Channings and had gone back to the sideboard with its assortment of photographs. He stared at it, absorbing the image and trying to join up pathways, trying to be certain.

Suddenly he knew how he could be sure: his camera. He turned back to where it sat on the arm of the Channings' printed sofa and grabbed it. He flipped furiously through the images on his memory card, desperately trying to find the set of photographs he wanted. He was sure – something inside him was screaming that he was right – but he had to see it. He rattled through the images, going past what he was looking for and back again, past the dog cut in half on Swanston Street, past the severed head in Cambuslang, past Dunbar's severed hands on Mansionhouse Drive, past the photographs at the Western and The Rock then back until he came to the photographs he had taken in Greg Deans' house on Vancouver Road.

There it was. The image he'd taken uninvited from the framed photo on the Deans' mantelpiece: Deans with his wife and daughter at a wedding. The blonde wife in her pillar box hat and the flame-haired daughter with the unmistakable heart-shaped rhinestone necklace.

'Deans,' he said out loud.

CHAPTER 54

Narey had only seen photographs of Peter 'Paddy' Bradley from his student days and she'd never seen him with his throat cut and swathed in blood but there was no doubt whatsoever that he was the man sitting dead in the car in front of her right then.

She closed the car door and turned to look at the stunned faces around her. She decided that the best of a bad bunch on the lakeside was a sensible enough guy in his mid-thirties, broad in his red ski jacket and intimidating enough to make others do what they were told.

'What's your name?' she asked him, showing him her ID.

'Bruce. Bruce Gleeson.'

'Okay, Mr Gleeson. You're in charge. No one other than a police officer opens that door. Can you do that for me?'

'Um, yes. No problem.'

'Good. Thank you. And you . . .' she said to a boy in his late teens. 'I need you to run to the top of the road or else the first police officer you see and get them down here. Tell them what's in the car and get them to inform Strathclyde Police as well as Central. Got that? Strathclyde.'

The kid nodded and ran off in the direction of the road,

panic and determination written all over his face.

'The rest of you get back from the car. It's not a show. Go.'

As the crowd backed away, sure to return, Narey broke into a run and sprinted across the car park to the side of the hotel where it met the lake. Her stay there with Tony seemed so long ago and yet it had been the start of all this. Any thoughts that might have turned to regret were dismissed as soon as she saw the frozen lake. The sight that greeted her pushed all other considerations aside: it was teeming with people.

There were so many of them that even trying to put a figure on it seemed impossible. Three thousand? Six? The ice swarmed with bodies: all shapes, sizes and ages. They crawled over the frozen lake like multi-coloured ants, scurrying this way and that, blurring together and moving apart. They were skating, sliding, walking, curling, running. They were everywhere. And somewhere in the middle of them, seen but unseen, was Greg Deans.

It was obvious now that Deans had abducted Bradley rather than the other way round. Of course it was possible that Deans had overcome his captor and killed him in a struggle but that wouldn't have explained the mark of zip ties round Bradley's wrists. It had been Deans all along. He had played them and he was still playing them. The return trip to the Lake of Menteith was all part of his grand production, which meant the final drama had to be played out on the island. The only thing that he couldn't have accounted for was the number of people there and that, perhaps, had thrown his plans into disarray.

Narey took her mobile from her pocket to check how far

away her back-up was but saw that she had no signal and remembered Tony's constant complaining about not being able to use his phone when they'd been at the hotel.

She could wait or she could go after Deans alone. The deciding factor was her dad: she'd said she would fix this for him and she would. His last case would be closed.

She knew Deans couldn't be far ahead of her and desperately tried to spot him among the thousands on the ice – so many of them taking the chance to walk across to Inchmahome. The difference was that Deans would be on his own; almost everyone else was in couples or groups. Her eyes searched deeper into the lake, over sledges and dogs, teams of curlers, kids playing impromptu ice hockey, nervous couples tiptoeing across the frozen playground. It was hopeless. She'd never see him. Looking around she saw a couple standing on the shore, about twenty yards away, watching the action, and noticed that the man had a pair of binoculars round his neck. She ran over, shouting to them as she went.

The man looked up, startled and confused, but readily agreed to her request when Narey showed him her badge. Armed with the binoculars, she hurriedly began sweeping the arctic panorama, desperate for a sighting of Deans. She flew by anyone milling around the middle of the lake or anyone in a group, looking only for the lone wolf, the single needle in the moving haystack. There a stray skater, there a lone walker heading for shore, there a single figure walking to the island but, just as suddenly, the smaller shape of a child could be seen with them. Back and forth, she trained the binoculars, seeing hats everywhere, brave and foolhardy souls in kilts, ski jackets in twos and threes but no . . . wait. She pulled her glasses back and looked again at the figure she had passed by: a man, on his own, head down under a black ski hat and heading directly towards Inchmahome. He wasn't stopping to take in the view but was moving, relatively slowly, unobtrusively, towards the island. She had no doubt: it was Deans.

Without a word, Narey thrust the binoculars back into the midriff of their owner and took off onto the ice without a second thought. She made a straight line towards Deans and hurried as fast as the surface would let her. On the ice, the noise was so much greater than it had been on the shore. She was buffeted by the sound of people laughing and screaming, cheering and whooping. And the roar. She knew that curling was known as 'the roaring game' but now she suddenly knew why. The rumble of the granite stones being hurled across the hard surface of the ice rose up at her and shouted at her, filling her ears with dire warnings that she ignored. She dashed across one of the makeshift curling lanes, was yelled at by angry players and had to leap over one of the large stones, with its spinning handle, as it sped within inches of her ankles.

She still had a vague sightline on the figure she was sure was Deans, gaining ground on him all the time as he walked and she ran. She was determined to bear straight for him, fearful of losing him if she was forced to change direction. A couple loomed in front of her and she barged apologetically into the shoulder of one of them as she hurtled by. Narey ran on but only another ten yards before her right foot slipped from under her on the ice and she crashed down onto her left knee, pain shooting through it. She got up but it felt as if she were the only one in the world standing still as the rest of the crowd whirled round her. She ran on again but slower now, the ache in her knee signalling some damage. The man in the black ski hat was ahead though and that drove her on.

Abruptly, she saw movement from the corner of her eye and glanced over to see a string of young skaters in their early teens swoop round in a giggling chain. They were arcing across the ice, eight of them hand in outstretched hand, forming a fifteen-yard human barrier. Narey continued to run even though they were only a short distance away from her. She shouted at them to move but the kids were too engrossed in their fun to hear until it was too late and she burst through their chain, sending three of them sprawling onto the ice with angry, high-pitched yelps. It was the combined complaints of their friends that did it though. The noise was enough to make Narey's prey turn on the ice to see what the commotion was.

The reddish hair peeked out from beneath the ski hat and the eyes were wide. Deans stood for a moment, taking in her presence before turning again, this time breaking into a run. Narey took off after him, her injured knee being compensated for by her fewer years and greater fitness. She was still gaining on him.

As she watched, Deans moved off to the side towards a family group of parents and two children. For a moment, he vanished from sight and, although Narey was within ten yards, she worried she'd lost him among the crowd.

Just as suddenly, Deans reappeared, holding something large in his hands. She didn't have time to work out what it was before Deans heaved his arms back then forward, letting the object hurtle across the ice towards her. It was a child's sledge, all wood and metal runners, and it was on her before she knew it. Perhaps if her knee hadn't been hurt in the fall, she might have hurdled it but she'd barely got her feet off the ground when the sledge crashed into her shins and sent her flying face first onto the ice.

Narey managed to get her left hand down to break her fall but ended up wishing she hadn't. She still smacked the side of her head against the rock hard surface but also had an aching pain spreading from the heel of her hand. As she picked herself up again, there was no sign of Deans. The family whose sledge had been taken from them pointed towards Inchmahome but Narey was already sure that was where he'd be heading. She limped towards it, the frosty shores of the island still a hundred yards away across the lake.

The boathouse loomed large in front of her and Narey lifted herself off the ice and onto the snow-covered jetty and the island. Memories came back of her midnight trip there with Tony, their eerie visit in the mist to see the ghosts of nineteen years before. This was different though – very different. One of the ghosts of that winter was here and alive.

There were others on the island too, a handful of couples and groups moving quietly through the newly misty glades and ruins of Inchmahome as if cowed by their surroundings. The only noise that came from them was the sudden breaking of twigs, an unexpected cough or irreverent laughter that echoed off the ancient walls of the priory. They paid Narey no attention and she guessed that they'd been the same when Deans had slipped by them. She'd slowed her pace now, wary of everything and everyone around her and far more concerned by who might step out from behind cloisters, a tree or the remnants of a wall.

Narey tread carefully past the old kitchen and on to the chapter house, the number of shadowy visitors thinning as she went deeper into the far corner of the island. As their numbers decreased so did the noises they caused to jump out of the mist, meaning she could hear her own breathing all the more clearly, heavy and laboured and advancing before her in the chilled air.

There was still a mass of footprints in the crisp snow but she couldn't be sure whom they belonged to. Not that it particularly mattered – she was sure where he'd be and had been convinced of it even as she'd stood between the church and hotel and surveyed the scene on the lake. The murderer returning to the scene of the crime might have been a cliché but it was often no less true for that. Deans was going back to the dark corner where he'd killed the girl who became Lily who became Barbie.

Narey slowed further, aware of the slight limp of her left leg, which dragged through the top of the snow and signalled her arrival. As she passed the corner of the chapter house, she stood and listened, hearing only the merest rustle of the wind through the petrified trees and the distant shouts of skaters who could have come from another world. With no help to be had from the sounds drifting through the air, she breathed deep and turned the corner into the clearing – and saw nothing.

Exhaling slowly, she stood still again, her eyes scanning the scene, every nerve on edge. She saw footprints, possibly fresh ones, stretching all the way to the low wall that had half-hidden the girl's battered body. There was also – was there, she questioned her eyesight – some sort of disturbance to the snow where she knew the body had lain all those years ago.

She instinctively began to move towards what she saw by the wall but had taken only half a step when she felt the taste of blood in her mouth and the perplexing darkness that came from behind her eyes as her head rang and swirled and crashed. The view in front of her dropped dramatically as she pitched forward and the world ran psychedelic and out of focus until her head came thankfully to rest on a cooling pillow of snow.

CHAPTER 55

Cold. Cold and dark. And quiet. The first thoughts licked at her consciousness, nudging her awake inch by inch in dark and dreamy tones. She felt wonderfully relaxed, with a warm and woolly glow that defied the strange chill that nibbled at her outside. The warmth was on the inside, circling her head and muddling it, making her wonder if an empty bottle of wine was responsible for the pall of fuzz and fog. But it wasn't wine; part of her knew that.

She really was cold. Her eyes flickered open but there was no more light than before, just a sea of black. Christ, her head wasn't warm; it hurt. Cold. Snow. Deans. Memories poked their way through the snow and the fog, stirring proper consciousness. She opened her eyes again, still seeing darkness but this time seeing it shimmer.

She was on the island. Inchmahome. It was dark and yet light. As she struggled to lift a heavy arm to paw at the horizon, she heard the soothing sound of snow landing lightly, like the air being let gently out of a balloon. The noise was at first comforting but as her head cleared, it worried her more. Her arm struggled to move, sluggish like her thinking.

It was only when she felt the cold on her face that a real

measure of awareness kicked in. There was dark beyond the immediate light and the wetness of the cold clung to her. Snow. She was under snow. The knowledge had her awake with shock, her arm flailing upwards in panic but held back by the weight of the snow on top of it. She pushed again and felt the snow move, forcing on until her hand was beyond it and in the open air.

She kicked with her legs too, feeling the same initial resistance but then the same movement. As she did so, the ground inches from her head rang with a thud that made it shake. She knew immediately that her hand being seen had triggered the attack and she had to move. She guessed left rather than right and scrambled as quickly as she could to that side, pushing up and rolling away, snow falling past her as she moved. The thud came again, crashing into her right shoulder, the pain dulled by the knowledge that the blow had landed where her head had been.

She continued to roll, desperately trying to move away from the attack that continued to come. A blow caught her on the top of her thigh, pounding into the flesh and sickening her. More swipes missed though, every sound of the weapon against the ground giving her hope as well as saving her from pain. She was on her back now, her hands behind her as she scrambled away, giving her a view of Deans as he stood over her, a golf club in his hand, at least now able to see it coming at her. A glance to her side told her that she'd been lying on the very spot where the girl's body had been found, a large mound of dispersed snow signalling the makeshift grave that he had tried to form for her.

Deans' eyes were wild and staring, almost unrecognisable

from the man she had seen in the Western or his house in Vancouver Road. He swung the club back and then down, erratically slamming it into the ground as she just managed to move her leg to the side in time. She put a hand to the back of her head and found it wet; bringing it up she saw it was coated in thick red. As she looked up, he'd hoisted the club back above his shoulder, ready to strike again.

'Why did you do it?' she stopped him.

'Never you mind.'

The club came down again, catching her a glancing blow on her foot as she failed to move it quickly enough. The club was immediately raised above his head.

'You killed the girl, didn't you? You killed Paton, Mosson, Bradley. They were your friends.'

'They weren't my friends.' Deans strangled the words in a hoarse scream. 'They would have ruined everything.'

'So you killed them. Like you killed Barbie.'

'Fuck you. You know nothing. You were as bad as they were. Would have ruined everything. Would have taken away my family.'

Deans was spitting in his rage, his words burbling out furiously, one tripping over the other. He advanced on Narey, the club high behind his head and gripped tightly in both hands. When he was stood above her, his legs straddling hers, she lashed her feet up and crashed them into his groin with as much force as she could muster. Deans yelped and staggered back, the golf club falling from his grasp and landing a yard away from Narey.

She got unsteadily to her feet, the pounding in her head increasing as she rose. She knew she couldn't stand for long and doubted she would be able to wrestle Deans for the club. Instead she staggered across to where he stood, massaging his aching bollocks and clearly trying not to throw up. She grabbed his hair and lifted his head up, easily arcing out of the way of his flailing arm, and punched him full in the throat.

The effort was enough to send her crumbling back to the ground but, bad as it was for her, she was able to look up and see that it was much worse for Deans. A violent choke of air shot from his lips and he fell back clutching at his throat, all but immobilised. Narey let her head settle back onto the snow as she caught her breath, safe in the knowledge that Deans had none of his own, safer still that she was a lot nearer to the golf club than he was.

She felt the back of her head throb and wondered if the club that had caused it was also what Deans had used on Julia Corrieri. Christ, Julia. What had that bastard done to her? Narey propped herself up on her elbows, her head spinning and other spots of her body crying out in sympathy: knee, hand, shoulder, thigh, all aching in a chorus of pain.

'Why did you kill Barbie?'

Deans answered in a hoarse gargle, 'Fuck you.'

'You know that you've nowhere to go. It's finished.'

'It isn't.'

'Yes. You've lost your family. You do know that, don't you?'

'Shut up'

'You can't sort this.'

There was a long silence from Deans and, when he didn't respond, Narey started to get back to her feet.

'Don't move,' Deans groaned at her.

'Why should I do that?'

'I'll tell you.'

Narey eased back, as glad not to make the effort to get up as she was to hear what he said.

'So tell me.'

Deans panted, struggling to talk. When he did, it came out croaky and weak.

'We all met Barbie in the Lade Inn at Kilmahog. Like I said. And she came back to the bothy with us. Paddy and Adam, they were all over her. They'd made sure she was drunk before we left the pub and when they got back here . . .'

'Who had sex with her?'

'Paddy. Outside while the rest of us were in the bothy. And then, later, after more drink . . . she and Adam went out for a walk.'

'And you and Paton?'

'No.'

'You didn't want to?

'No. Well . . . I didn't do it with her. Okay? Laurence liked her. A lot.'

'And you liked her,' Narey guessed. 'But she didn't like you, didn't fancy you. What was it? Your red hair? Did she not fancy gingers?

'Shut up. Just shut up!'

Narey laughed at him.

'I see it now. Your mates had sex with her. You wanted to have sex with her too but she didn't want you. You were snubbed. Resentful. Angry.'

'I told you to shut up.'

'And Laurence Paton . . . He went with Barbie to the Lake of Menteith. You told the truth about that. Yes. Laurence went with her and you thought he was going to get what Paddy and Adam had got. He probably thought that too.'

'Fuck you.'

'But not fuck Barbie, eh?'

'Shut it. That dirty slut went with them but not me. Then she waltzed off with Laurence. I liked her. I actually liked her but Paddy and Adam, they just wanted to shag her. It was me who liked her.'

'So what did you do?'

Narey heard something that might have been a sob or a gulp coming from Deans before he answered.

'Adam and Paddy were going to Bracklinn Falls and I told them I was going to stay at the bothy. But instead I went to the lake. I knew they were going to walk to the island. I wanted . . . I just wanted to know what they were doing. The place was teeming with people and they probably wouldn't have noticed me anyway but I walked round and onto the island from the other side. They were walking hand in hand like . . . like fucking sweethearts. I was mad at her for treating Laurence like that after what she did with Paddy and Adam.'

'And for not screwing you.'

'They argued,' Deans ignored Narey's jibe. 'They were only on the island a few minutes and they were arguing. Laurence tried it on and she knocked him back. The bitch said no even though she'd been such a slut the night before. I was . . . it just wasn't . . .'

'Fair?'

'I don't really know what happened. Laurence left and the

next thing I knew I was standing over her. I'd hit her. And hit her. Over and over. There was blood everywhere. The snow was soaked in it. I got this tree branch and just . . . hit her. I don't know how many times. She was . . . she was dead.'

'Twenty-two.'

'What?'

'You hit Barbie twenty-two times. Quite the big man.'

A troubled silence fell between them, broken only by the whisper of the wind and the call of a pair of geese overhead. Narey's head throbbed and she wondered how much blood she had lost.

'What did you do with the branch?'

'I threw it as far across the ice on the far side of the island as I could and left it for the lake to melt. Then I went back to the bothy. I got there before Laurence and no one knew I had left.'

'So was the rest of what you told me true? About making a pact not to talk about it because she was under sixteen?'

'Yes.'

'And who told them that she was only fifteen?'

He laughed inanely.

'I did. I told them that Barbie had told me she was fifteen but it wasn't true. Paddy and Adam nearly shit themselves. Laurence too. She was never mentioned again.'

'Until this year.'

'Yes. Until those adverts in the Sunday papers. Then those emails. Everything was fine until then: my wife, my daughter, my job. Everything had been perfect until then. It was all going to be ruined. She'd have left me. I told you that. Couldn't let it happen.'

'So you assumed it was Paton, Mosson or Bradley? The only ones who knew you had all been with the girl. And you decided to take them out.'

'Yes.'

'You made Paton and Mosson look like accidents. You even faked an attack on yourself, you sick bastard.'

Narey suddenly let out a tired, ironic laugh. This one, unlike the others, not done by design to wind Deans up even further. This one she simply couldn't help.

'What's so fucking funny?'

'It's not so much funny as sad, Deans. You see, I don't think it was any of them who were blackmailing you.'

'What? But . . . then who?'

'I'll tell you after I arrest you,' she taunted him. 'Right now all you need to know is that you killed Paton, Mosson and Bradley for no reason. All that trouble and all you did was fuck up your own life as well as theirs.'

Deans sat in sullen silence, chewing on her words.

'What about Bradley?' she asked him.

'Fuck you.'

'The rumour that "Lily" was a gypsy girl. That was no coincidence, was it? You started that rumour because you wanted to find out where Bradley was. You couldn't find him, so you used us to track him down.'

'I started that rumour years ago, the first time I heard that Paddy had married into travelling folk. I wanted to know where all three of them were. I needed to know – just in case. I knew if Paddy was with gypsies, then he'd go off the radar. I wanted a way of being able to bring him back in.'

'Very clever.'

'But not as clever as you, is that right, Sergeant Narey?' he growled. 'Well, it seems there's something you've forgotten.'

Narey heard not just the renewed confidence in Dean's voice but also realised that it was stronger than it had been.

'And what's that?'

'You remember what happened to Paddy Bradley?'

'Of course I do.'

'So you tell me: how do you think I managed to slit his throat with a golf club?'

Narey's heart stopped for a second. As much as she didn't want to, she sat up and looked over at Deans. Like her, he was propped up on his elbows but his right hand held a knife – a large kitchen knife. He'd been telling her the truth about what had happened in order to buy himself time to recover from the punch that she'd delivered to his throat.

Deans got to his feet, the knife held before him. Narey scrambled towards the golf club but he was on her before she could pick it up, slicing at the back of her hand with the blade and drawing a bright red line that bled from her knuckles to three inches above her wrist. Clutching at the cut, she was forced to fall back and he was on top of her, pinning her to the ground.

Deans used his weight to hold Narey in place, making sure she couldn't swing her legs at him this time. To seal the deal, he held the knife to her throat.

'You came to my house,' he snarled. 'My wife was in. I'd spent nearly twenty years trying to do the right thing, to make it all right. Then you came and threatened to ruin everything.'

Deans stuck the point of the knife to Narey's neck and pushed it forward, drawing blood.

'I could still have made it all okay. When your DC Corrieri told me where Bradley was, I went after him. To finish it. I wanted to bring him back to the scene of the crime. Have it look like he killed himself here – out of guilt. But there were so many people. I didn't expect so many. I couldn't . . . We were surrounded by people.'

Narey just stared up at him, refusing to show him the fear that coursed through her. Her heart hammered at her ribcage; every nerve jangled. She wanted to buck him off but her arms were trapped by his knees and he was too heavy. And the knife was so close. He pressed it forward again, an inch or two from the first cut, drawing another sliver of blood from her throat.

'The first cut was for Laurence,' he told her. 'The second was for Adam. And this . . . this is for Paddy Bradley.'

Deans pushed the sharp tip of the knife slightly lower on Narey's neck, forming a perfect bloody triangle and pushed it so that it broke the skin and sent a cold, agonizing tingle through her. The three lines of red trickled down her throat. He drew the knife away slowly, its blade glinting in the moonlight, and held it over her.

She'd decided that she had one last desperate gambit: if he came in close enough and if she could dodge the knife, then she would head-butt him as hard as she could and try to get out from under him. It was a terrible plan and a terrible option but it was all she had.

'Even with all the people here, even then I might have got away,' Deans continued, gibbering now. 'It was Bradley. Everyone thought it was Bradley. I was going to the island to be safe. Then you . . . you turned up.'

She tried to shrink back against the snow-covered ground, seeking every inch of space to allow her to move away and up.

'I've cut you for Laurence; I've cut you for Adam and for Paddy. And this is for the girl.'

Deans drew the knife back, cold madness in his eyes, and she readied herself to move her head to the side, then to thrust it up and into his with every ounce of strength she had left. Damn, the knife was so close . . .

It all seemed to happen at once. The shouting, the momentary hesitation by Deans, the flash of dark chrome, the groan and Deans collapsing on top of her, his weight pinning her to the island.

And the knife. The knife being dropped only inches from her throat and piercing her neck as she moved.

CHAPTER 56

'You'd better not have been there for any length of time listening to what that maniac was saying,' she snapped at Addison.

'Christ, that's the thanks I get for saving your life? And stop moving, will you? How the fuck are they going to stem that bleeding if you keep wriggling about. And no, we only just got here. It's a long bloody walk over that ice.'

'Walk? You better not have bloody walked either.'

Addison gave her a weary shake of his head and puffed out his cheeks.

'You know what, I'm beginning to wish I hadn't bothered. How about we wake Deans up, give him his knife back and I apologise for hitting him over the head with the baton?'

Narey grinned at him, the movement causing her skin to contract and the wounds in her neck to shriek with pain.

'Anyway,' Addison continued, 'it wasn't really me who saved your life. It was Tony Winter.'

'Tony?'

'Hm,' Addison watched her reaction. 'Tony got me on the phone and told me that it was Deans who was behind it all.

Otherwise we might have found Bradley's body and taken that as being the end of it. Tony said that Deans would be heading for Inchmahome.'

'How did he . . . ?'

'Well, that's the funny thing. Tony . . . *photographer* Tony . . . was interviewing the parents of the dead girl, Claire Channing. Any idea how that happened?'

Narey gave an awkward shrug.

'Course you don't. Anyway, Tony saw a photograph of the girl in the parents' house. Seems she was wearing this necklace that Tony had seen before. He checked his photographs and, sure enough, Deans' daughter was wearing the exact same necklace. Seems our man here was sick enough to have kept a souvenir of his big day on the lake and given it to his own daughter. Psycho or what?'

'Jesus.'

'I know. Tony tried to call you but couldn't get a signal because you were out of the range of civilisation. He got hold of me though and told me to get here as quickly as possible. Seems he was really worried about you.'

Narey refused to give Addison the reaction he seemed to be looking for.

'I'm glad he was or I might not be here. Deans had us all fooled. He even faked that attack on himself at The Rock. I should have wondered why he was going for a drink there when it was so far from home. It was because he knew those steps were perfect for "falling" down.'

Addison grinned.

'I know. Tony's ahead of you there too. He must have picked up a few tips from me. He reckons Deans must have cut his head with a knife and then thrown himself down those stairs. What a fucking fruitcake! Tony said we'd probably find a knife thrown into the bushes next to the steps above the pub.'

'Worth a look,' she admitted.

'It already has been. I got a call to say they'd found a knife covered in snow but with blood still on the blade. They're analysing it now but it will odds-on belong to Deans.'

'Tony,' she laughed lightly, causing another pain to shoot through the incision in her neck. 'Who'd have thought it?'

From behind them came the angry convulsing sound of Greg Deans wakening from the baton blow to his head. He was held by two uniformed cops and could do nothing except stare hatefully at Narey.

'I think you're entitled to this one,' Addison told her. 'Charge him.'

He held out a hand and helped Narey to her feet. She began to walk slowly towards Deans, preparing the charge list in her head, when she stopped and turned back to Addison.

'What am I charging him with?'

'What?'

'How is Julia Corrieri?'

'Let's get off this bloody island first. We'll need to get you properly examined. That wound on the back of your head is even worse than the one at your throat.'

Something in the way he spoke wasn't right. Showing concern for her like that wasn't Addison's way of dealing with things.

'Cut the bullshit, Addy. What aren't you telling me?'

Addison swore under his breath and rubbed at his eyes before crouching down so that he was looking Narey in the face.

'Julia didn't make it. She died in the hospital.'

CHAPTER 57

Wednesday 27 March 2013

Spring seemed the wrong time for a funeral somehow. The new life that pushed up through the earth of the vast cemetery in Whitby appeared to be mocking the ceremony that paraded in front of it. Snowdrops, daffodils and primroses triumphantly announced their rebirth with no thought to the feelings of mourners.

It was the second funeral Tony Winter had attended that week and, even for someone with his peculiar interest in death, it was at least one too many. At Daldowie Crematorium in Glasgow, Strathclyde Police had been out in force to grieve for one of their own. Julia Corrieri's family were at the helm, clearly still distraught despite the three months that had elapsed. Winter sensed resentment in their mood and a grudging acceptance of the attending police.

Rachel had been devastated by Julia's death and was wracked with guilt at her own part in it. If she hadn't stirred things up, if she hadn't gone after Deans, if she hadn't been so desperate to find out who Lily/Barbie was: it was the mantra she festered on. If she hadn't done her job and if Julia hadn't done hers, Tony had reminded her. They were both doing what they were paid for and what they had chosen to do. It failed to make her feel any better and just gave her the excuse to be mad at him instead – which was what he wanted.

At Julia's funeral, he'd wanted to go to Rachel, to hold and comfort her. Just to take her hand would have made him feel so much better even if it would only have had a fraction of that effect on her. Instead, he had to stand at the back and watch her hurt.

There were no such issues of perverted protocol in Whitby, however. Tony stood in warm sunshine not far from the pair of Gothic cemetery chapels that were dramatically connected by a pointed archway, its steeple rising to the heavens. Beside him were Rachel, Danny and Rachel's dad – nothing to hide and nothing to explain. They had travelled down together from Glasgow to pay their respects to Claire Channing and her parents.

Winter had been introduced to Rachel's dad and been welcomed warmly by him. Inevitably, Alan had forgotten Tony's name a few times on the long drive to Whitby and seemed confused by his relationship with Rachel at others. He wasn't the only one, Winter thought.

Rachel had sat her dad down in the nursing home and explained to him everything that had gone on. It had taken a while. The enormity of it had distressed him as much as it confused him.

Alan had broken down when she told him how his instincts had been right about Laurence Paton. For all the things that had slipped temporarily and permanently from his memory, her dad vividly recalled the gut feeling he'd had when he spoke to Laurence Paton. Okay, Paton hadn't killed the girl but he was still guilty of a silence that could have spared her parents years of anguish and forlorn hope. Alan Narey's own guilt was that he hadn't been successfully able to pursue the lead he'd been so sure of.

He had rebuked Rachel for even investigating the case and apologised for her having to do so. He was annoyed at her and grateful, saddened and sickened at the consequences of the new investigation. He was pleased, once he finally grasped all that had happened, at the outcome but Rachel had sensed it hadn't been enough to put his mind at ease.

Tony looked at him now, standing on the tree-lined gravel path next to Danny, who was trying to swap police stories with him, Alan chewing uncertainly on his lower lip and his eyes wandering warily to left and right.

'It breaks my heart to see him like this,' Rachel said behind Winter.

'I know. But you've done what you could to help him – with Claire at least.'

'Yeah. Maybe. He isn't settled yet though. I'm hoping that when Deans goes to trial, I can tell him that it's finally over. But that's another two months away.'

'Kyle Irving's trial is before then, isn't it?'

'Yes, next month. Hopefully he won't be practising his fake psychotherapy for a while.'

'How long do you think he'll get?

'Years. We've got blackmail, perverting the course of justice and interfering with a police investigation. The bastard . . .'

she lowered her voice, 'the bastard saw pound signs. He was happy for us to think that Paton was the killer. He reckoned he could make a fortune by writing a book about it: "inside the mind of a murderer" – that sort of thing.'

'How much of it do you think he really knew?'

'Plenty. He knew about the four of them meeting the girl even if he didn't know for sure that one of them had done it. Paton had spilled his guts in therapy and he obviously knew enough to get email addresses for Mosson and Deans and to make up a false one for Bradley to fool the others. Paton was full of guilt about leaving Claire on the island and that bastard Irving took full advantage of it to try to sort his money problems.'

'If he hadn't, then Deans wouldn't have reacted the way he did and we might not have found out what the hell happened.'

Rachel laughed bitterly.

'True, but I'm not about to be thanking him for that,' she told him. 'It's not like you to be seeing silver linings where I'm seeing clouds. Usually it's the other way about.'

'Maybe I'm seeing the light?'

'Yeah, right.'

She drew a finger tenderly down Tony's cheek and left him to rescue her dad from Danny's war stories. Tony turned his back to the path they'd stood on and regarded the marble headstone propped up by single red roses strewn at its base. The flowers had each been dropped there by one of the mourners at the request of Claire's parents.

The principal inscription on her headstone mimicked, word for word, the sentiment carved on Lily's anonymous grey slab in Brig o' Turk.

I will fear no evil for thou art with me

It had been a long time since Tony had had any faith in the protective power of God to deliver anyone from evil and clearly Claire Channing had a very good reason to have feared it. Tony's belief in life after death was on a par with his belief in God but he knew that it was possible to live *with* death. He had done so with his parents and now Claire's parents would do so with her. In a strange sense that at least meant she wouldn't be alone.

'Dad?'

The anxiety in Rachel's voice caused Tony to turn away from the headstone and back to her. He saw Alan Narey yards ahead of her, heading determinedly down the path to where the Channings stood hand in hand by the door to the chapel. Rachel swivelled anxiously to Tony, then back to her father before trying to catch up with him before he reached Claire's parents.

Tony could see that she wanted to run after him but a graveyard was hardly the place for that. Instead, she scurried down the path, gently trying to call him back. Winter passed Danny as he went after her, despite knowing that if she couldn't get to her dad in time, then neither could he. He was at her heels but she was still a few yards from her father, who was now at the shoulder of Ted Channing.

'Excuse me,' Alan Narey began softly. 'Mr . . . excuse me.'

Claire's father turned, red-eyed and slightly bewildered, ready to accept what he must have assumed were more condolences. He obviously didn't recognise Alan Narey but stretched out his hand to take the one that was offered to him. Mr Narey wrapped his other hand over Channing's and held it there.

'I need to apologise to you,' he told the girl's father.

Rachel was at her dad's side now and placed her hand on his arm, trying to lever his hand from Channing's but her dad wasn't for letting go.

'Sorry, I don't understand . . .' Ted Channing was saying.

'Come on, Dad,' she told him. 'Let's not bother Mr Channing. This is a difficult day for him.'

'No,' he told her. 'No, Rachel. I need to speak to Mr . . . Mr . . .'

'Channing,' the father told him. 'Why do you need to talk to me?'

'Please, Dad.'

'Mr Channing, I have to apologise to you – about your daughter.'

'Claire? Why?'

'Claire? I didn't know that was her name. We called her Lily but we knew that wasn't her name. We didn't know her real name.'

Channing looked confused. 'And that's what you're sorry for?'

'No. Yes. That too. But I'm sorry because . . . Mr Channing, I forget things at times but I remember your daughter. But I didn't do the right thing by her. I let her down.'

Channing was fighting to hold back fresh tears, visibly gulping down his emotions.

'How? I don't understand.'

'Dad. Please, let's leave Mr Channing.'

Alan Narey turned to speak to her, his mouth opening

but, after an awkward pause, closing again. He thought about it some more.

'No. You leave me. I need to speak to him.'

She knew he had forgotten her name.

'I was a policeman, Mr . . . Mr Channing. I was supposed to find out who killed your daughter. And I didn't. I'm sorry but I didn't.'

The man looked back at him, a tear forming in the corner of his eye.

'I did my best. I thought I did. I . . . you see, I let her down. I'm a father too, Mr . . . I know what a father would feel. I felt it.'

'But this, this is your daughter?' Channing asked him.

Alan turned and looked at Rachel as if only just realising she was there.

'Yes. Yes, it is.'

'Mr Narey, *your* daughter found the man that killed mine.'

'She did?'

Alan looked at Rachel, confused anew. She nodded at him and was rewarded by a glow of pride.

'I'm . . . I'm still sorry,' he told Ted Channing.

Claire's father tried for an answer but instead opened his arms and the two men hugged, tears tumbling down both their cheeks. They held on to each other for a while until Alan abruptly broke the embrace, looking at Channing with some surprise and turning to his daughter.

'Can we go home now, Rachel? Your mum will be worried about us.'

She didn't have the heart to tell him about her mother but instead took his arm in hers and they began walking back down the path together.

Tony stood aside to let them past, falling into step with Danny and selfishly wondering if either Rachel or her dad had even noticed his presence. It had always been the way he'd liked it, observer rather than combatant, a bystander to tragedy. Now however he was beginning to wonder whether being on the outside of things was where he wanted to stay. Being on the inside brought the risk and reward of hurt and intimacy.

Just as suddenly, Alan Narey stopped again, a look of consternation on his face, and stood still for an age.

'There's a saying, Rachel. It goes . . . no, no, don't help me. I'll remember it. It's about . . . dammit.'

Winter could see that the pain on her dad's face as he struggled with his memory cut Rachel in two.

'Yes . . .' He took a deep breath and nodded with relief. 'You cannot wash blood with blood. Yes, that's it. All you do is make things even worse. That's what that man Deans tried to do though: wash blood with blood.'

Rachel hugged her dad close, burying her head into his shoulder.

'Blood is strong,' she told him. 'It makes people do things, good and bad. Come on, we'll take you back. And I'm going to visit every day. You'll soon be sick of the sight of me.'

Winter stood behind them, jealous of their closeness but also absorbed. He wondered lamely whether it was worse to have lost your parents, as he had, or to lose them regularly as Rachel was now fated to do with her dad.

He thought of the futility of washing blood with blood. And he wondered if he'd ever be able to stop doing it.

Rachel slowed her step, turning to him with a warm smile and waiting till he caught them up. She slipped her right arm through his, her left still entwined with her father's. Danny stepped up to join them on the other side, linking his arm through Alan Narey's and completing an unlikely yet appropriate chorus line.

Together they walked back up the cemetery's main thoroughfare, the twin chapels directly ahead of them, separated and connected by the towering steeple with its theatrical archway leading to the world beyond. Resisting a last glance over his shoulder towards Lily's final resting place, Winter forced himself to look ahead. He couldn't deny that it made quite a picture.

Acknowledgements

I owe gratitude, as ever, to everyone at Simon & Schuster UK; particularly my editor Maxine Hitchcock for her endless supply of ideas, patience and reassurance. Thanks too to Emma Lowth and Florence Partridge for always being there to offer help when needed, which was often.

My head and heart – if not my liver – thanks my agent, Mark "Stan" Stanton for his continuing wise counsel. Less wise but nonetheless welcome advice came from my good friends in The Midnight Plumbers, particularly in this instance to Robert Clubb for his invaluable knowledge of computer geekery.

For equally expert assistance, I am grateful to Professor Caroline Wilkinson of the Centre for Anatomy and Human Identification at the University of Dundee and to Andy Rolph and the staff of R2S Crime in Aberdeen.